The Tegen Cave

Inge-Lise Goss

Published by Olivebranch Press

DEDICATION

To my husband, Peter, for all his support, encouragement, and patience.

CONTENTS

ACKNOWLEDGMENTS

My gratitude and everlasting appreciation goes out to Julian Seymour who gave me numerous suggestions and comments that helped in so many ways to improve my story. I am also grateful to the Borders Writers Group for their critiques of my novel. In addition I want to thank my early readers, Shandra Winters and Nicole Varela, who managed to read every word of my rough draft, and provided me with the reassurance I needed to continue pursuing my dream. I also want to thank my wonderful editors: Lisa Binion and Rebecca Graf at Silver Tongue Press, Sally Michaels, and Nancy Biford. I want to extend a special thanks to Michelle McCarty, author of *The Jewel Box* for all her edits, comments, and writing tips she so freely gave to help polish my novel.

PROLOGUE

As they drove away from town, Candice placed her hand on his thigh and gently squeezed. He turned, his dark blue eyes glowing, and gave her a coy smile. She sensed something was wrong from his distant behavior at the restaurant. She peered out the side window as the city lights vanished behind them and thought, *Does he know about me?*

Towering pine trees and leafy maples lined the road. Thick clouds snuffed out the moonlight. "The hotel was only a couple of blocks away," she said.

"I want to take you some place special."

Her body tingled as she leaned closer and caressed his muscular arm. "Your room was pretty special last night."

"This place you'll never forget."

Candice could no longer spot any house lights through the dense foliage. A ping of uneasiness flew over her since she had only known her date for less than two days. Wanting to make her weapon easily accessible, she snatched her purse from the floor and lowered it onto her lap. "How far away is this place?"

"Right up here." The blue-eyed man steered the car onto a dirt lane almost hidden by the overgrown shrubs and spreading trees. The corner of a stone house appeared, only lit by a sliver of the moon between the passing clouds.

"Whose house?" Candice asked. Then she blinked as the harsh glare from headlights approaching behind struck the side mirror. "I thought we were going to be alone."

"Maybe the driver's lost. Let me check." He stepped onto the ground.

Candice pushed her long, blonde tresses away from her eyes as she turned, looked through the back window, and watched a man climb out of the vehicle as her date walked toward it.

The clanging sound of metal being hit echoed through the car. Candice swung her head around and saw a guy tapping on the car's hood, flanked by two other men. Her light hazel eyes darted between them looking for weapons. None were visible. Wondering what was going on, she stuck her hand into her bag, searched for her pistol, and smiled when she felt the cold steel.

Her car door flew open and she gazed up at her date. "You a cop?"

"Far from it." He leaned down and slid his hand behind her neck.

Something sharp scraped into her flesh. "Ow!" she yelled, tugging on his arm. "What have you got?" He flipped his hand over, revealing his palm. She stared at his fingers, trying to grasp what she was seeing as perspiration drizzled down her face. "What the..?"

"Crimes have consequences."

"Who...what are you?" She attempted to raise her gun, but didn't have the strength to free it from the bottom of her purse.

He dropped a spider on her chest just above her low-cut sweater. She opened her mouth to scream. No sound escaped. "She's ready," he said to the other men.

They lifted her limp body and headed toward the back of the house. Passing the stone structure, her date envisioned the pretty brunette he spotted in the hotel lobby and thought, *She'll be the next one I bring here.*

1

THE PACKAGE

I stared at the brilliant crimson stone in the ring on my finger. He had given it to me when I moved into his home in Houston, Texas. Flashing back to what had been one of the happiest days of my life, my hand shook more than I expected when I slipped it off. I placed the sentimental ring on the shelf next to my cell phone and closed the locker door. I leaned against the wall with quivering lips, feeling I had betrayed him. With everything I had learned, I knew we could never be together again. Still, part of me wanted to leap out the side doors and apologetically run back to him. I couldn't justify it to the voice inside me that screamed to never look back. My heart and mind warred against one another to rationalize my fear, obsession, and sense of justice into one clear guiding sentiment. I was left paralyzed and confused in the crossfire.

Inhaling deeply, I forced myself to put on a pair of large, worn jeans and a plaid shirt with tattered cuffs, the frumpy clothes I had brought in my gym bag. Since I prided myself on stylish fashion, I hoped to avoid any recognition. Then I tucked my long, brown hair under a floppy brimmed hat and hid my eyes behind a pair of oversized sunglasses. Grabbing my previously packed duffle bag, I headed to the fitness center's exit.

The clock on the wall read 7:45 a.m. I had fifteen minutes to get to the bus depot before my imaginary yoga class came to an end. I hurried through the parking lot to the sidewalk and began to jog the rest of the way. I resisted the urge to glance over my shoulder. It felt as though my past was catching up with me already. I started to sprint and held back tears as the wind bit my dry cheeks.

I entered the brightly lit depot with floor-to-ceiling windows on one side. Sunlight shone on rows of seats filled with people, while others milled about. Despite the ban on smoking, stale cigarette smoke lingered in the air. I peered out through the automatic glass doors. No one had followed me. My departure in 20 minutes was bound for Rapid City, South Dakota, but that was not my final destination. With potential danger lurking in any corner, I needed to get away fast, and that bus was the next one scheduled to leave Houston. I had purchased the ticket yesterday at a different location. It was here waiting for me under the name Ethel Martin, the name that appeared on a driver's license I had retrieved from the lost and found at work. I hoped Ethel, whoever she was, wouldn't get in trouble because of me. The picture on the license was hazy. I still held my breath when the ticket agent looked at it since, except for the brown eyes, the description didn't fit me. I was 24, five-foot-eight, and weighed 125 pounds. Ethel was older, taller and heavier.

With my ticket in hand, I went outside and scanned everyone I passed. I sat close to the rear of the bus and stared at the passengers as they boarded. Two broad-shouldered bald men wearing reflective sunglasses, black suits, and ties entered the bus. They began walking toward me. I froze, thinking they were coming for me and it would be over soon. Was that bulge I saw under one arm a holster? They moved along the bus aisle with a wide gait, then sat in a middle row without looking back. I sighed with relief.

A stocky, gray-haired woman made her way down the aisle. "Is this seat taken?" she asked with a warm smile.

"No, not at all." I dipped my chin at the seat to welcome her.

Her body made a tired thud as she sat down next to me.

The engine roared, and the bus pulled out of the depot. I lowered the brim of my hat, leaned against the window and cried as I thought about Conner. I hated leaving him. My heart was broken. He had become part of my life. Now I was alone again.

"Are you okay, my dear?" the gray-haired woman asked.

I tried to come up with an excuse and thought of a lie. "Yes. Lost my job and apartment."

"Oh, you poor thing." She handed me a tissue and patted my arm. "Are you traveling to relatives?"

She seemed like a sweet woman, probably someone's grandmother. "No. Don't know where I'm going. Just need to get away and find a job elsewhere."

"Maybe you should think about Billings, Montana. It's such a nice place with friendly people. That's where I lived until my husband passed away. Now, I travel around helping out the kids, but I miss Billings. My brother moved there and immediately found a job. Hope to go back someday."

4

For half an hour she raved about Billings' nearby lush forests, high-quality schools, and its wonderful climate with the changing seasons.

"I've never lived any place where it snows," I said, and thought maybe I could forget Conner in Montana. I decided to make Billings my destination. Leaning my head against the window again, my eyes watered, and then I sobbed.

During my first six weeks in Billings, I hadn't seen anyone following me or skulking around. I was pleased at how well I had planned my escape and was glad I didn't change my name. In the local phonebook, there were three people named Sara Jones. Thousands more across the country. My parents had chosen that name well; it suited my purpose in a way they never could have anticipated.

Now I had a job and a car. Hopefully with the help of Nancy Stewart from the property management company, I'd find an apartment. Then I could finally move out of the Towne Hotel.

On my way to the elevator I ran into Brett, a 25-year-old petroleum engineer living in the hotel while on a short work assignment. His room was right next to mine. He was good-looking, well-built at six-foot-three with a short-clipped beard and sandy brown hair setting off his deep blue eyes. I'd noticed him in the lobby when I checked in. He caught my glance as he left the hotel with a woman. We had become good friends who occasionally went out together, but not romantically. I passed him often in the hallway after he finished his morning jog.

"Going apartment hunting?" he asked, dabbing his forehead with the towel hanging from his shoulder.

"Yeah."

"How about a movie later?"

"Sounds good."

"Give me a call when you get back. I'll be at work finishing a project and maybe swiping pens—a little white collar crime."

"On Saturday?"

"Unfortunately. You know I'd rather be reading Kafka, perusing world news, or eyeballing pretty chicks in the lobby. Anything, but work. But a man's gotta make money for cool jogging shorts." He lifted his sun shades while raising his eyebrows.

I grinned and turned to leave. "See you later."

He snapped the towel he had worn on his shoulders into the air and made a loud pop as he often did as an extra goodbye salute. As Brett headed toward his room, I waited for the elevator and fantasized about him. He was sharp-witted, charming, and well-read. Maybe he could make me forget Conner.

As I entered the lobby, Ralph, the hotel clerk, raised his arm and motioned to me from behind the check-in counter.

"Good morning, Miss Jones."

"Hello, Ralph." I gave a pleasant head bob to our short, stocky man who greeted everyone with a smile.

He picked up a small package from the counter. "This was dropped off for you a few minutes ago."

A wave of terror crept through my body as I wondered if Conner's family had found me. "Thanks," I said, hesitantly taking the package. My eyes focused on it, searching for the return address. There wasn't one. I noticed the postmark said Billings.

"Are you Sara Jones?" a well-dressed, slender woman in her late thirties said, walking up from behind me.

"You must be Nancy Stewart."

"Yes." She stretched out her hand, and we shook.

"Would you mind waiting here while I run this package to my room?"

She held up a thick folder. "There's a long list of apartments that might interest you. I'd like to narrow our search before we leave. Could we talk about them upstairs where it's quieter?"

"Of course."

When we reached my room, she sat on the sofa and laid out some documents on the coffee table. I stood next to the window looking for mysterious cars and opened the package. Inside was a gray box. I raised the lid and found a silver ring with a large black stone. No note—nothing indicating who sent it. Could it be from Brett? I knew he wanted to be more than just friends. Needless to say, after what I had been through I wasn't ready to get involved in an emotional or romantic relationship. Even though I knew about Conner's family's business, I still missed him and as must as I tried, still could not suppress my constant thoughts of him from filling my head. I put the opened box down on the table next to Nancy's documents.

"Oh, what a beautiful ring," she said. "Is that stone an onyx?"

"I don't know."

"I worked for a jewelry store several years ago. Would you mind if I looked at it?"

"No, go ahead." I wasn't concerned about the stone; I was concerned about who had sent it.

Nancy carefully took the ring out of the container and held it up in the light. "Oh, how brilliant." Rotating it around, "Ow!" she yelped, and dropped it.

"What happened?" Panic hit, sending waves through my body.

"Something bit me."

"What?" I tried to project an air of calm despite my growing fear.

"A bug. I think it was a spider," she said, looking at her hand.

"Are you all right?"

"I can't move my fingers." Her lips quivered. "I don't feel well." Her eyes drooped and her face became shockingly white.

With all I knew about arachnology, I couldn't think of a spider that could cause this quick a reaction. My eyes flitted back and forth over the floor searching for it. I caught a glimpse of a brown spider crawling under the cushioned chair.

"Let's get you to a doctor."

She put her arm on the edge of the sofa and made an attempt to rise. "Can't stand," she sighed, her voice just above a whisper.

I tried to pull her up by her arm.

"Talk...hard...mouth...," she gasped. Her hands trembled; beads of perspiration trickled down her forehead. Then she became completely motionless.

"I'm calling 9-1-1!" I eased my arm around her and laid her down on the sofa. Picking up the phone, I felt my muscles tightening and a clutching sensation in my chest, fearing the Crussetts had found me and Nancy was suffering for it.

"What is your emergency?" a man asked.

"A woman has been bitten by a spider. It's paralyzed her," I said, breathlessly.

"You are calling from the Towne Hotel?"

"Yes. Room 841."

"An ambulance has been dispatched."

"Nancy, the ambulance is on its way," I said in an uneven voice after the call. "Can you talk?"

No response. Her eyes were wide open and hazy, her skin ash white and shining with perspiration. I hurried to the bathroom, moistened a washcloth, and returned to Nancy, placing it on her forehead. Then I held her limp, damp hand and said, "If you can hear me, shut your eyes." Fidgeting with my fingers, I gave her a moment to respond. Her eyes remained fixed, staring straight ahead. "Can you move them at all?"

A knock on the door startled me. I opened it. Two paramedics came in, pushing a gurney. Standing behind them, I continued observing Nancy, hoping she'd show some sign movement was returning to her body.

"What's your name?" a paramedic asked, leaning down next to her.

"Her name is Nancy Stewart," I answered.

"How are you feeling, Ms. Stewart?"

She didn't utter a sound as he checked her pulse while the other paramedic checked her blood pressure.

"When was she bitten?" he asked.

"Ten, fifteen minutes ago. Right before I called 9-1-1."

After they finished taking her vital signs, they lifted her onto the gurney and rolled it to the elevator. I grabbed my purse and followed.

A crowd had gathered in the lobby. I watched along with numerous people as the paramedics put Nancy in the ambulance and drove away. While the crowd dissipated, I went to the front desk.

"What happened?" Ralph's face filled with concern.

My eyes momentarily flashed to the entrance looking for familiar, unwelcome faces. "I'm not sure." I turned back to Ralph. "I think she was bitten by a spider in my room."

"Who?"

"A woman from a property management company."

"Holy Mary, Mother of God." He performed a rapid catholic sign of the cross. "Stay down here while I contact an exterminator."

I headed to the pay phones that lined the far wall, called Nancy's office, and explained what had occurred.

"What hospital?" the receptionist asked.

"I don't know. I assume it would be the one closest to downtown."

"Thanks for the call." She hung up.

I sat on the bench by the check-in desk and worried about Nancy. She came to help me and now she was in the hospital, probably taking my place. But based on everything I knew about spiders, I suspected the paralysis was temporary and she might be fine after she received the medication to counteract the venom.

My mind drifted to the fate of the spider. My parents were arachnologists, and spiders were always sacred to them. They never would have allowed one to be harmed, even if it were poisonous. I was convinced the spider had been planted in that box. It didn't deserve to die because of that. It's just a scared, delicate creature doing all it knows. I hoped I'd have a chance to find it before the exterminator arrived.

Ralph leaned over the counter. "They'll be here within the hour. You shouldn't go back to your room until they're finished."

"But I need to go up and get a few things." I rubbed my arm, trying to keep goosebumps to a minimum.

"Just grab your bare necessities and don't be hanging around long with those nasty bugs."

"Thank you, Ralph." I nodded in appreciation and went to the elevator. In my room, I searched around the windows, the corners, the bathroom, and only found a black spider. I thought Nancy had been bitten by the chestnut brown one I saw on the floor. It looked something like a hobo spider.

After placing the black spider on the outside ledge where it would be safe, I heard a knock and closed the window.

Opening the door, I saw a heavyset man wearing a grey uniform with DB Exterminators woven above his pocket. "Please come in."

He entered with his equipment. "Miss, you'll have to stay out of your room for four hours. Also, you can't sleep in here tonight. I'll let the hotel clerk know."

I picked up my purse and swept my eyes over the room one more time. I hoped I would spot the spider. When I failed, I bit my lower lip and retreated to the hall.

Just then, Brett stepped out of the elevator. "You okay?" he asked, putting his arm around my shoulders. "Ralph told me what happened."

"Yeah. I was searching for the spider. It might help her if they knew the type it was." I didn't want to tell him how I felt about spiders. People always thought it was strange. "But now the exterminator is here."

"The sooner it's gone the better. I don't want an ambulance coming for you."

"You didn't per chance send me a gift?" I felt silly and presumptuous the second my question flew out of my mouth.

"No, but if you'd like a gift from me, I'd be more than happy to oblige." He tilted his head to the side and offered a wink.

"I'm sorry, that's not what I meant. I guess I'm just stressed out."

He caressed my arm. "No, I'm the only who should be sorry. You've had a bad morning. But why did you ask if I had sent you a gift?" Brett raised a brow, showing concern.

"The spider came in a package."

His eyes narrowed. "You thought I sent you a spider?"

"No. No. It was in a small box with a ring. If you had sent it, I wanted to contact the jewelry store and tell them what happened in case there are other spiders."

"The ring must've been sent by another admirer," he said, smirking. "What was the return address?"

"There wasn't one. It was postmarked in Billings."

"Mind if I take a look at the box?"

"Let me see if I can get it." I opened my door, stuck in my head, and asked the exterminator, "Can I get something?"

"Yes, but hurry," he said, spraying a corner.

Only Nancy's documents lay on the table; the box and ring were gone. "Have you seen a small box and a ring with a black stone around here?" I pointed to the coffee table.

"No, ma'am. I haven't started working on that part of the room yet."

I scanned the floor again, returned to the hallway, and shut the door. "Strange. I can't see the ring box anywhere. I told Nancy I'd come to the hospital so I need to get going."

"Would you like me to go with you?"

"If you don't mind." I felt relieved I wouldn't be going alone. Nancy had been bitten in my room so her family might think I was somehow responsible. I wondered if that might be right. If the Crussetts had found me, the wrong person became the victim. I knew whomever they had sent wouldn't leave without getting their target. They'd be hanging around somewhere waiting for an opportunity.

When we stepped out of the elevator, Ralph motioned for me to come to the counter. "Here's your messages, Miss Jones." He handed them over.

"Thanks, Ralph," I said. "Where's the closest hospital?"

"Just a few miles away." He pulled out a map from under the counter. "Let me show you."

"Would you mind giving Brett the directions while I read these?" I asked, holding up the messages.

He nodded and talked to Brett as he highlighted the route on the map.

The first message was from Betty Madsen, the receptionist at Nancy's office. It read: "I haven't been able to locate the hospital where Nancy was taken. Could you give me more information?"

The second one came from Nancy's brother. It read: "Can you tell me where the ambulance took Nancy?"

There were three other similar messages. My eyes darted to the door and I tried to recall the name on the ambulance. Nothing came to me. I turned back to the check-in counter. "Ralph, do you know what ambulance company picked up Nancy Stewart?"

"No. Is there a problem?"

Tapping my fingers on the counter, I replied, "Her co-workers and family can't locate the hospital."

"Did you call 9-1-1?" Brett asked. "Or did Ralph?"

"I called." Again, I tried to sound calm as my adrenaline spiked.

"Let me check with 9-1-1," Ralph said. "They'll know."

Brett and I sat down while Ralph called.

The exterminator walked over to the counter and put his equipment down on the floor. As soon as Ralph hung up, the exterminator said, "I'm finished. No one should go in the room for at least four hours. And no one should sleep there tonight."

"I'll move her to another room." Ralph multitasked by looking at vacancies while dealing with the bug man. "Thank you for coming so quickly."

Brett took my hand. "You can stay in my room."

I brushed away chills his touch brought, and tried to handle his offer with a modicum of diplomacy. "Brett, I'm not really comfortable with staying there overnight. I'm just not ready for another relationship yet."

"I didn't mean to insinuate we would be bed partners. You'd sleep in the bed and I'd take the sofa."

"Let me think about your kind offer, but first I need to find Nancy." I walked beside him to the counter.

"They have no record of your call," Ralph said.

"That can't be. I talked to them," I snapped. Shaking my head, I glared at the phone. "If I didn't, then who requested the ambulance? Let me call them." I picked up the receiver and dialed 9-1-1.

"What is your emergency?" a woman asked.

"Earlier today I called because a woman had been bitten by a spider in my room at the Towne Hotel."

"Miss, I just talked to the hotel clerk about that and checked all our records. No one has called today from the Towne Hotel," she said firmly.

"I talked to a man and he sent an ambulance."

"That is impossible. Our male employees all work the nightshift. This morning you would have talked to a woman."

"I called," I hissed, feeling irritated they couldn't keep better track of their employees.

"I'm sorry. We log all our calls, and there wasn't one from the Towne Hotel."

I slammed down the receiver. "They claim I didn't call."

Brett held my shoulders. "Relax. She'll show up."

After taking several deep breaths, I asked, "Ralph, can I see the yellow pages?"

He handed it over, and I flipped to ambulance companies. Only three were listed. Brett sat down while I made the calls. When I finished, I felt discouraged and gave Ralph back the phone. "None of them sent an ambulance. I watched the paramedics put her in one."

"Even if I didn't get the company name, I saw an ambulance. Here," Ralph said, handing me more messages.

I quickly glanced through them. They were all the same: "Where is Nancy?" An uneasy feeling vibrated through my body as I became more convinced the Crussetts had found me. Conner knew I liked spiders and I wouldn't have hesitated to pick one up. Did someone think Nancy was me? We were about the same size. We both had brown hair. Hers was short and curly, while mine was long and wavy. She was older, but, from a distance, they might not have noticed. If she had been mistaken for me, I knew she'd never be found.

Another large group of people converged into the lobby. Glimpsing out the window, I saw a parked tour bus and sat down next to Brett.

"Anything new in the messages?" he asked.

"No. I better contact the police," I said, reluctantly.

"Do you want to call them from my room?"

My eyes darted back and forth over the crowd milling about as I searched for unwelcome familiar faces. "Yes. It won't be noisy there."

Brett had a corner room with two windows, one on each exterior wall. As soon as we entered, I placed the call and talked to an officer named Lieutenant Barnes. After I filled him in, he asked me to come down to the police station.

"I'll be there soon," I said and then clicked off.

"Let me take you."

Standing quietly, I felt a knot in my stomach and bit my lips, speculating how much the police would want to know. If I mentioned the Crussett family and they weren't involved, I'd be responsible for letting them know where I was.

Brett wrapped his arm around my shoulders. "Is something wrong?"

I gazed at him and saw the concerned expression on his face. He was my only friend in Billings. I needed to confide in someone. "I don't know. I came to Billings to get away from some people, and now I'm wondering if they've found me."

"I suspected you were running from someone. Whenever we go anywhere, your eyes are always scanning the crowd. Even today, I noticed you looking at everyone who entered the hotel."

"I don't know what to do," I said with trembling lips. "Could they have put the spider in the package? How much should I tell the police?"

"You don't have any proof the spider was deliberately sent. If someone wanted to harm you, that was too elaborate of a plan. There wasn't a guarantee the spider would bite you."

"You're right." I rubbed my forehead. "Spiders can't be trained. That's just a conclusion I jumped to since there wasn't a return address and Nancy is missing."

"Before you say anything to the cops about your personal situation, wait and see if someone takes credit for the ring."

"That's what I'll do. I didn't mean to burden you with my problem."

"Sara, I'm glad you did." He tenderly squeezed my hands. "Ready to go?"

"Yes. Let's get this over with before Nancy's family shows up here."

In the lobby, Ralph again handed me more messages. I thumbed through them. They were all about Nancy, except one. It was from Sherman's, a department store in Billings, asking if I received the gift they sent.

I sighed with relief. "The ring came from Sherman's," I told Brett. "Last week, I was their 100,000th customer. They said I'd receive a prize, but I had no idea it would be that nice. Well, except for the deadly spider."

"All that worrying for nothing." He tapped his forefinger across the end of my nose playfully.

I appreciated him wanting to lift my spirit. "Let's just cross fingers I'll be able to find the ring when I have more time to search my room."

Brett pulled into a parking stall in front of City Hall. We headed to the entrance while I admired the building's Art Deco design with its ornaments and motifs. Trying to delay my meeting with Barnes as long as possible, I stopped and read the police memorial. Then Brett took my hand, and we stepped across the threshold. The foyer was a large open space with signs posted next to the hallways. We went to the right, the one marked police department, and headed through another set of doors. We stopped at the information desk.

"May I help you?" a female officer asked.

"Yes. I'm here to see Lieutenant Barnes."

Just then, a robust man with a thick handlebar mustache approached the desk from the other side. "I'm Lieutenant Barnes," he said in authoritative voice as he walked toward us. "You must be Miss Jones."

"Yes," I said, shaking his hand. "This is my friend, Brett Daborel."

After they shook hands, Barnes led us into a conference room. Brett sat patiently at my side as I watched Barnes curling the ends of his mustache while I repeated everything I had already told him over the phone.

13

"Nancy Stewart's family and co-workers have been trying to locate her. They've left me these messages." I held them up.

"I'll take those." Barnes' husky hand reached forward as I handed them over. "We'll locate Ms. Stewart and contact her family along with everyone who left you a message. In case we need any additional information, will you be staying in Billings for a while?"

"Yes. I'm planning on making this my home. Will you let me know when you find her?"

"We'll keep you informed."

I left City Hall feeling relieved professionals would be searching for Nancy. They had the skills and resources needed to locate her.

"That wasn't so bad, was it?" Brett asked.

"No. They didn't ask anything about my personal life."

"I didn't think they would." He opened the car door. "Where do you want to go for lunch?"

"I just want to go back to the hotel."

"You have to eat. There's a new Italian restaurant that just opened. How does that sound?"

Since he had been so supportive, I agreed and said, "Good."

During lunch, he talked about the new movies in town we should see. Finally, after working on me for an hour, he convinced me to go with him to the matinee of *The Other Woman*; probably to get my mind off Nancy.

After the movie, we returned to the hotel; Ralph waved his hand, gesturing us over.

"Lieutenant Barnes and Sergeant Harmon just left. They asked some questions about the 9-1-1 call. According to them, I confirmed everything you had already told them. Then they checked out your room. They just did a walk-through because of the strong smell of pesticide." He picked up a key from the counter. "There weren't any rooms available on your floor so I've put you in room 720 for the night. You should be able to go back to your room tomorrow."

"Thanks." I took the key. As tempting as it was, my senses warned me against accepting Brett's offer of sleeping in his room. I would stay in a separate room.

My room reeked from the chemicals in the poisonous spray. I quickly gathered a few things and headed to room 720.

The sound of a door slamming awoke me. I flipped on the nightstand lamp and glimpsed at the clock: 1:30 a.m. I turned off the light, rolled over on my side, but I couldn't seem to relax enough to drift off. Instead, I thought about Nancy's disappearance. I couldn't shake the feeling the Crussetts were somehow involved even if they hadn't sent the ring. Maybe the spider didn't come in the box. I flicked back on the lamp, climbed out of bed, and checked the deadbolt lock to make sure it was securely in place.

Getting under the covers, I reached for the lamp switch and felt something drop on my hand. I looked and saw a chestnut colored spider, like the one I spotted on my floor after Nancy was bitten. A chill ran through my body as I decided to catch it. Climbing out of bed, I kept my hand rigid. The spider began to crawl up my arm while I walked to the bathroom. I took a tissue, placed it in the spider's path, and let the spider move onto it. Carefully, I picked up the tissue with the spider cradled inside and dumped out the contents of my make-up bag. As my heart raced, I eased it in, zipped up the bag, and then smiled to myself.

Wondering if there were more spiders, I slipped on my robe and searched under the bed, the dresser, the nightstand, and pulled down the bed covers. Nothing. I was content that it was safe to go back to bed. Lying between the sheets, I found it impossible to sleep. I rose again and made a cup of coffee.

I sat down in the cushioned chair and appreciated the peace and quiet as I sipped it. Leaning back, I closed my eyes and wondered about everything that happened the day before. I felt a sting on my foot, looked down, and saw a chestnut brown spider crawl off it. I flinched, and my mouth popped wide open. I knew I needed to stay calm to slow down the spread of the venom in case it was the same kind that had bitten Nancy.

I picked up the phone and punched Brett's number.

"Hello," he answered, sounding groggy.

"I've been bitten."

"Damn! Be right there."

Slowly, I stood, unlocked the door, and left it ajar. I eased back down in the seat and examined my foot.

Brett rushed in. "Have you called 9-1-1?"

"No. I don't have any of Nancy's reactions." I raised my foot and wiggled my toes. "Maybe this was a different species. I caught one. It's in my make-up bag in the bathroom."

He went into the bathroom. I scanned the floor, attempting to find the spider. A minute later, he came back. "There wasn't a spider in the bag. I pulled out the tissue and shook it over the sink."

"Was the stopper closed?"

He nodded. "I closed it. A spider didn't go down the drain."

"I thought I had it well secured," I said, feeling disappointed.

He knelt next to me and ran his hand over my foot. "No bumps. There's a small red dot here," he said, pointing to it.

"It must've been a different type of spider. Nancy became almost immediately paralyzed."

"Maybe she just had an allergic reaction. Come to my room. If you display any symptoms, I'll call 9-1-1. If that should happens, I'm going with you in the ambulance."

I felt uneasy about going to his room. At the same time, I was scared and wanted company. "Okay," I agreed.

He insisted I stay seated while he gathered my things. Holding onto my arm, he led me to his room. I told him I'd sleep on the sofa. He was determined I take the bed.

In the morning I found myself refreshingly not-dead.

"When do you want to go to breakfast?" Brett asked, opening the drapes.

"Just give me half an hour." I left his room to freshen up in mine.

As I stood in the hallway, fumbling through my purse for my room key, a tall handsome man with broad shoulders, deep brown hair, and dark eyes walked past me. He appeared just a little older than I was. He wore a perfectly tailored navy-blue, pinstriped suit and looked too polished to be staying here. This was a nice hotel, but definitely not a four-star.

He stopped at the next room. I noticed him glaring at me through penetrating eyes.

Feeling uneasy, I quickly turned the key, hurried inside, and bolted my door. As I sat on the bed, I sensed there was something familiar about him and wondered if he was connected to the Crussetts. Was he an employee?

The picture of my parents on the nightstand caught my eyes, and then I remembered. It had been four years ago at their funeral. He had glared at me there, too. I didn't have the foggiest idea who he was. I continued thinking about him as I showered and dressed.

Bending down to put on my shoes, I saw the ring with the black stone lying on the floor. Slipping it on my finger, I felt a slight shiver run through my body. Strange. The ring fit perfectly. How did Sherman's know my size?

Lieutenant Barnes and another man were standing by the check-in desk talking to Ralph when Brett and I stepped out of the elevator.

"Miss Jones," Ralph said loudly, raising his arm and waving his fingers. After we reached the counter, he continued, "I've been calling room 720. You didn't answer. Lieutenant Barnes would like to talk to you."

"I only spent part of the night in that room," I explained.

"Good morning, Miss Jones and Mr. Daborel." Barnes' big hand engulfed mine during our polite handshake. "This is Sergeant Harmon. He'll be assisting me with the investigation."

"Hello," Harmon said, and we shook hands.

"Nancy Stewart's body was found around 1 a.m." Barnes ran a finger over his mustache, and then curled the ends of it with his thumb and index finger. "We need your help to identify the paramedics who picked her up. We'd like you to come to the station and look at some mug shots."

I cringed. Mug shots? Even if attempting to murder someone by using a spider seemed completely ridiculous to some people, I knew the Crussetts had killed before in absurd ways. Maybe I was just being paranoid, but this happening after I escaped them—the coincidence was too convenient. My hands trembled; I held them together tightly and asked, "Where was she found?"

"Behind the Alta Bar. Signs indicate her body was moved to that location after she died. She wasn't easy to identify. We only received confirmation an hour ago that it was her."

"Why wasn't she easy to identify?"

"I'd rather not go into the specifics," Barnes answered, still curling his handlebar mustache. "When can you be at the station?"

Brett and I glanced at each other. "After we've had breakfast," I said, wanting to calm my nerves before I went.

"I'll take you," Brett volunteered. He turned away from Barnes, raised his brow, and whispered, "Don't want you to be alone with Mr. Mustache."

I bobbed my head in agreement. Since Nancy's body had been moved to a place where it could be easily found, I suddenly doubted the Crussetts were involved. Anyone who crossed their paths typically ended up in staged accidents, or they were never seen again. Easy discovery was not their MO.

"We'll see you later this morning," Barnes confirmed and left with Harmon.

"I'll be going there this afternoon," Ralph said. "Since the lobby was full of guests, I only caught a glimpse of the paramedics' faces when they wheeled her out. Lieutenant Barnes still wants me to look at mug shots. I gave him the names of the guests I recognized in the lobby. He's planning to contact them."

"I don't think I can identify them either," I said. "I was looking at Nancy, not the paramedics."

"Let's get something to eat." Brett leaned closer to my sweater-clad arm, then his hand gave my elbow a gentle touch as he guided me into the coffee shop.

After the waitress handed us menus, my thoughts drifted back to the Crussetts. Would Nancy's death make the national news? Then they'd know where I was. My mind churned and a foreboding feeling pressed against my chest as I closed the menu. "I'm not hungry after all. I think I'll just have coffee."

"You need to eat something. How about toast or a bagel?" Brett asked.

The waitress returned with coffee and, to please Brett, I ordered a toasted bagel. He ordered a large breakfast that included a side order of pancakes. Obviously, the police investigation wasn't affecting his appetite.

He took my hand. "Don't worry. I'll be with you. The cops just want you to look at mug shots, nothing more. If you don't recognize the guys, that's not a problem." He held up my hand and gazed at it. "Is that the ring you were sent?"

"Yes. I found it on the floor and decided to enjoy my prize."

Brett studied the ring. "Sherman's gave you this for being their 100,000th customer?"

"Yes. Boy, I wonder what they'll give their 1,000,000th customer."

"Maybe a car?"

"Or a boat?"

"Nope, it's got to be a trip around the world. You up to staying in Billings long enough to see if you can win it?"

"Yep. I'll start hanging around their cash register when they reach their 999,950th customer."

"That should work. It'll probably be a trip for two. Want my company?" He gave me a mischievous grin.

"Sure. I'll need someone to carry my luggage."

"That's all I'm good for?"

Before I could answer, our orders arrived.

Brett waited for me to start eating, and then he dug in. Between bites, he asked, "Have you got any plans for this afternoon?"

I still sensed I was in danger and needed to move out of the hotel as quickly as I could. "I have Nancy's list of apartments. I want to check some of them out."

"Would you like me to drive you around?"

His invitation caused the corners of my mouth to curve up. Not wanting to be alone, I had to resist the urge to hug him, before I calmly answered, "I'd like that."

Brett and I were at the police department for almost three hours while I searched through mug shots. Barnes had another officer put together a composite of the men based on what I remembered. None of the computer-generated images looked right. Both paramedics had medium-brown hair and were over six feet tall. Outside that, my memory wasn't very helpful.

Walking to Brett's car, I saw a short, lean man putting a note on Brett's windshield.

Brett recognized him. "What's up, Adam?"

"I've been trying to reach you. Left a couple of messages on your cell," Adam said, retrieving the note.

"Turned it off when I got here. How'd you find me?"

"The hotel clerk."

A stern expression flashed across Brett's face as a tiny furrow of annoyance appeared between his eyes. "What's the problem."

"Baxter's going to be in town tomorrow instead of Tuesday."

"What time?"

"He lands at 8:30 and he's driving straight to the office. Have you got the report done?"

"Almost."

"That's what I thought. Housman wanted me to track you down so you could work on it today in case it wasn't finished."

"Tell Housman I'll have it on his desk at 8 a.m."

"Sorry about ruining your Sunday."

"It's not ruined. See you tomorrow." Brett watched Adam stroll to a waiting sedan.

"You don't need to take me apartment hunting. You can work on your report."

"I want to drive you around. I'll finish the report tonight."

After a disappointing afternoon since we were only able to look inside one apartment, we ate dinner at the hotel and said goodnight.

Back in my room, I thumbed through the list of apartments again, trying to recall those closest to where I worked. I needed a Billings road map to pinpoint the locations. There was one in my glove compartment. I headed outside to get it.

My car was parked in a dimly lit area of the hotel parking lot, next to an alley. Moving in that direction, I heard heavy footsteps on the pavement behind me. My eyes darted right and left hoping to see other people. The parking lot in front of me appeared deserted. The footsteps became louder sending chills through my body.

My heart raced. My lips quivered. I sucked in air, and then I held my breath as I quickened my pace. I didn't dare turn around and knew I was being paranoid. People came and went all the time. Then I saw a couple getting into a car, and my heartbeat slowed down. Breathing easy again, I peeked over my shoulder. No one was behind me. I did see several people walking toward the hotel. Finally I reached my car, unlocked it, and opened the door. I leaned down and took the road map out of the glove compartment.

As I stood up, he was right next to me. His penetrating, dark eyes met mine. My breathing became erratic and I froze.

.

2

TOO MANY

A loud diesel engine started close by and broke my trance. I attempted to speak, but the words refused to come. As the dark-eyed man continued staring at me, I fiddled with the keys clenched in my hand so the end of one protruded between my fingers. If he touched me, I was prepared to defend myself.

"Sara," I heard Brett yell.

I turned around and saw Brett hurrying toward me. When I looked back at the dark-eyed man, he was gone.

"What are you doing out here?" Brett reached out and held onto my arm. "You okay?"

"Yes," I muttered and shut my car door. "A hotel guest just startled me. That's all."

"Were you going somewhere?"

"No. I wanted to plot out the location of the apartments we drove by, and my road map was in my car," I said as we headed back to the hotel. "How did you know I was out here?"

"The window above my desk overlooks the parking lot. I thought I saw you. I called your room, and you didn't answer, so I came out here." A brief smile flickered on his lips. "I assumed you were making a getaway from the cops," he joked.

"No. I don't want the Crussetts and the police looking for me. The police might think I had something to do with Nancy's death if I left town immediately."

"Are the Crussetts the people you're running from?"

I bit my lower lip wondering how I allowed that name to slip out. "No," I lied as my heart pounded in my chest. Changing the subject, I took his hand. "How is your report coming along?"

21

"Almost finished." He lightly squeezed my hand. "Why don't you continue living at the hotel until the cops get whoever's involved with Nancy's death?"

"I'm still trying to sort out what happened. The spider venom paralyzed her. Was it temporary or is that what killed her? Lieutenant Barnes doesn't want to tell me the condition of her body. Had she been mutilated?"

"You're not the blame for whatever happened to Nancy, so try not to worry about it," he said as we reached my room. "The cops will solve the crime." Brett stood next to me while I unlocked the door. "Sleep well."

"I'll try my best. Good night." I went inside and bolted the door. Living in this room wasn't anything I wanted to do any longer than necessary. I laid out the map and began plotting the apartments as I thought about the guy in the parking lot. He hadn't touched me. All he did was stare with those dark eyes. Maybe he recognized me from my parents' funeral. If that was it, he should have said something.

In the morning, I didn't see Brett or the dark-eyed man before I left the hotel. The accounting firm where I worked was a short distance away, so I always walked.

As I turned on my computer, my office phone rang. "Sara Jones. May I help you?" I answered.

"Miss Jones, this is Lieutenant Barnes. A man exhibiting the same symptoms as those you described for Nancy Stewart was taken to the hospital last night."

"Was he bitten?"

"We don't know. Shortly after he arrived, two men dressed like paramedics took him out of the hospital on a gurney."

"Did an ambulance bring him to the hospital?"

"No. His friend, the bartender at the Alta Bar, drove him."

"The same place Nancy Stewart's body was found?"

"Yes."

"Didn't anyone try to stop the paramedics from taking him?"

"A nurse did. They told her the patient had to be transported to another hospital because of his insurance."

"What hospital?"

"He hasn't showed up at another one. The nurse and a few hospital employees were able to give a description of the two men. We'd like you to come in and look at the composites."

"I can be there right after work."

"Thank you, Miss Jones."

At 5:10 p.m., I walked into the police station. Barnes led me into a conference room. We sat down and he laid out two computer generated images.

He rested his elbow on the table and began curling the tips of his mustache. "Do you recognize either of these men?"

I pointed to the guy with the medium brown hair. "He looks familiar, but I can't say positively he was one of them." I placed my finger under the other picture of a man with light tawny-brown hair. "He wasn't one. Both men had medium brown hair."

"Are you certain?"

"Yes," I replied without hesitation, feeling irritated since I had already mentioned that to him the previous day.

"Hair can easily be dyed." Barnes picked up a pencil and scribbled over the man's hair in the composite. "How about now?"

"I still don't recognize him."

He held up the other image. "We'd like you to come back and identify him in a lineup once he's been apprehended."

"I can't say for sure he was one of them."

"Maybe seeing him in person will trigger a memory." Barnes rose to his feet and picked up the composites.

"I'll help any way I can." I stood also, eager to leave. "I need to get going, but call if anything new surfaces."

Entering the hotel lobby, I saw Brett sitting on a couch, thumbing through a magazine. He stood. I knew from his drooping eyes and his worried expression that I should've called and told him I'd be late. All during dinner, he kept telling me I needed a cell phone. When I ran from Conner, I'd left mine. Prior to the police investigation, I didn't have any reason to have a phone. After Brett's pleading, I agreed to get one as soon as I could.

While I tossed and turned in bed, I couldn't stop thinking about Nancy, the spiders, and the Crussetts. The night before, I'd slept in this room. No spiders. No problems. If the Crussetts knew I was here, I wouldn't be sleeping in this bed again. Or anywhere else. Finally, I relaxed and dozed off.

The loud ringing of the hotel phone woke me. I fumbled for the switch on the nightstand lamp and nearly knocked the phone onto the floor. After flipping on the light, I lifted the receiver. "Hello."

No one spoke.

"Hello?" I said again and waited for a response. Then I hung up and attempted to go back to sleep when something moved on my legs, tickling me. Slowly, I pulled back the blanket and looked down. My legs were dotted with chestnut-brown spiders. I panicked. As familiar with them as I was, I made my best effort to stay calm. That was my only hope to keep from being bitten. A few slow, shallow breaths helped. Trying to stop them from moving up my body, I yanked down the bottom of my nightshirt and wrapped it tight around my hips. Recalling what happened to Nancy, I didn't want to be alone. I stretched out my hand, picked up the phone, and called Brett's room.

"Hello," he muttered.

"Spiders," I whispered. "All over my legs."

"Stay as still as you can," he said, sounding anxious. "I'm on my way."

"No. I can't get to the door. See if Ralph will let you in."

"Is your window open?"

"Just a crack."

"I'll get in that way." He disconnected before I could tell him not to do that.

I put down the receiver and looked at my legs, wondering how I could prevent being bitten and gather up the spiders at the same time. I picked up the tissue box from the nightstand, pulled out all the tissues, and laid them on top of the spiders. I heard the creaking sound of the window opening and within a minute Brett was by my side.

"You shouldn't have climbed on the ledge," I admonished while tearing off the top of the tissue box. "It was too dangerous."

"It wasn't a problem," he replied, grabbing the phone.

"What are you doing?"

"Calling 9-1-1."

"No. I can handle this. If they come, they'll kill the spiders."

"But, Sara—"

"Put down the phone," I snapped and glared at him. Then remembered I needed to stay calm.

"Okay," he relented, placing it back in its cradle. His face creased with concern. "If you didn't want my help, why did you call?"

"In case I develop any of Nancy's symptoms."

"Can I call 9-1-1 then?"

"Yes." The tissues on my legs were full of spiders. Making sure they were fully enveloped, I slowly picked up one corner of the box and carefully placed the tissue inside it. "Sorry I got mad. I know you're worried about my safety, but I want to catch them. If they're the same kind that bit Nancy, it might help toward solving the case."

"Catching one would be enough. Let me call room maintenance. They'll have some kind of poison to take care of the rest."

"No. I want to capture all of them." I continued gathering the spider-saturated tissues and putting them in the box.

He stared at my legs, rubbed his chin, and swallowed hard. "Is there anything I can do?"

"See if you can find a container in the bathroom that can hold spiders." I put more spiders wrapped in tissues into the box until it was almost full. Then I saw Brett coming out of the bathroom with an empty shampoo bottle. "How do you think we're going to get them in there?"

He had a sheepish grin on his face. "Hadn't thought about that."

"Can you carefully take this and put it in the bathtub?" I held out the tissue box. "Make sure the bathtub plug is closed. I don't want them going down the drain. Then take a wet washcloth and wipe the sides of the tub. That might prevent them from climbing out. After that, can you see if there are any tissue boxes in the cabinet under the sink?"

"Yeah," he replied, gingerly taking the box. He walked slowly to the bathroom with his arm outstretched and held the spider-filled box as far away from his body as possible.

I felt calmer. If any of the spiders had bitten me, I didn't exhibit any symptoms yet. I was sure they didn't get in my bed by accident. There were too many. They must have been planted. How and by whom? Crussetts? I just couldn't believe they'd go to this much trouble. Why not just shoot me? Unless it was because they wanted something first.

Brett came back carrying one box. "There weren't any more." He placed it on the bed next to me.

Searching for something else that could be used as a container, I scanned the room. "My duffle bag. Can you empty it and bring it over here?"

He nodded and headed toward the dresser as I tore off the top of the other tissue box and emptied it. Putting down the bag, Brett gazed at my legs. "How can you stay so calm with all those spiders crawling on you?"

"My parents were arachnologists, so I'm used to spiders. I think they're beautiful, misunderstood creatures. They are actually very gentle and fragile. People are just afraid of them because they have so many legs. Their webs are a survival mechanism which I've found unique and enthralling since my earliest childhood memory. Spiders are fascinating, and there's nothing else like them on earth. It's weird people can be scared of spiders and not butterflies or ladybugs. Sure, they can bite you, but only if they're scared. More people have been hurt and killed by other people than spiders."

He cocked his head to the side as a look of dismay briefly flashed on his face.

I could tell he didn't share my viewpoint. Hardly anyone did. I continued gathering up the spiders until I couldn't see anymore. Brett carried the box and duffle bag into the bathroom. I raised my legs, moved to the edge of the bed, and stood up. Glancing around, I spotted a few stragglers on the floor. I laid tissues in their paths and collected them.

"It looks like this is all of them." I handed the tissues to Brett, and he put them in the bathtub.

I slipped on my robe and went into the bathroom. I wanted to check and make sure none of the spiders had crawled out of the tub while Brett searched under the bed.

The bottom of the bathtub held the filled tissue boxes and my duffle bag. I couldn't see any spiders climbing up the sides. In fact, looking at the containers, I couldn't see any spiders at all. I picked up a box, held it over the sink, and closed the stopper. Then I pulled out a tissue and shook it. No spiders. I pulled out another one. No spiders. I continued pulling them out until the box was empty. Then I emptied the other one and took several tissues out of the duffle bag. "When you put the containers in the bathtub, did you see any spiders crawling up the sides of the tub?"

"No."

I dumped out the bag, looked around the corners of the bathroom, under the sink, in the drawers, and cabinet.

"The spiders are gone," I said, feeling bewildered. "What could've happened to them?"

Brett came into the bathroom. "They can't all be gone. There were too many." His eyes darted around the room. He looked at the floor and raised his feet cautiously, checking under each foot.

I stared at the empty boxes. "They're gone."

He picked up a few tissues lying in the sink and shook them. He looked at me and shrugged his shoulders. "Where did they go?"

Bending over the tub, I checked the plug. It was securely in place. Then I noticed the overflow drain. "They must have crawled out here." I pointed to it and instantly felt sad. "They probably all drowned."

A blood-curdling scream rang out. I hurried to the hallway door and swung it open. Several guests were peering out their doors.

Down the hall, a blond-haired, stout man wearing only a pair of pajama bottoms emerged from his room. "Help! Spiders are all over our bed. My wife's afraid to move."

I ran toward him followed by Brett and some of the other hotel guests. When we reached his room, his wife's eyes were wide open and perspiration was streaming down her face. She wasn't moving. I didn't see any spiders on the bed.

Brett picked up the hotel phone standing on the desk. "I'm calling 9-1-1."

The stout man shook his wife. "Shelley, talk to me," he pleaded. "Say something."

Brett finished the call and grabbed my hand. "Let's get out of here. We can't do anything for her."

I agreed. I didn't want to be involved in another investigation. We hurried back to my room as a crowd gathered in the hall.

"At least now we know what happened to the spiders," he said, closing the door.

"How do you think they got to their room?"

"I haven't got a clue. Let me see your legs."

I sat down, lifted up my robe, and saw over a dozen red spots below my knees.

He ran his hands over them. "You've been bitten. How do you feel?"

"My legs don't hurt or itch—nothing." I wiggled my ankles and moved my hands over my shins. I felt small bumps. They didn't hurt when I touched them. Then I saw my toenails had turned a reddish-purple color. I looked at my fingernails. They were the same color. I shuddered. "What's wrong with my nails?"

Brett held my hand and stared at my fingernails. His eyes dropped to my toenails. "I don't know."

I ran my fingers over my nails. "They don't hurt. Maybe I'm having some kind of reaction to the spider venom, just not like Nancy's."

He moved his thumb over each nail. "They're smooth. They feel normal." His brows drew together. "Are you feeling okay?"

"Yes."

"You must be immune. Maybe the discoloration of your nails has nothing to do with the spiders. Let's wait and see how they look tomorrow. Now, I think we should both leave this hotel. A friend at work, Rex, is leaving for an assignment in Texas. He's heard about Nancy Stewart's death and said I could stay at his place while he's gone. His house has five bedrooms. Why don't we both stay there?"

I hesitated wondering if it was a good idea to stay there with him. I didn't want him to think our relationship could go beyond friendship.

"Sara, you'd have your own bedroom. We wouldn't share."

"Okay. Just until I find an apartment." I wasn't sure how long I'd remain in Billings, so I no longer planned on looking for an apartment. I didn't want to tell Brett about that.

"Do you want to stay in my room tonight?"

"Yes. In case I develop any of Nancy's symptoms, I wouldn't be able to call you or unlock the door."

As we went toward Brett's room, I saw a gurney being rolled down the hall by two paramedics. The vision hit me. I stopped and stared as my spine stiffened. I should have been the one strapped down and being wheeled out. The spiders had been in my room first. Staying in the Towne Hotel was getting more dangerous. Two victims. Something was definitely going on, but what?

Brett took my arm. "Sara?"

I turned and looked at him. "We can't stay here any longer. We have to get out now."

"It's late. I haven't seen any spiders in my room. I've sprayed around the windows and the baseboards. You'll be safe there for tonight." He wrapped his arm around my shoulder. "I won't let anything happen to you."

Since it was after midnight, I reluctantly agreed, "This time I'll sleep on the sofa."

"No, that's where I'll sleep. You take the bed." Then he grinned. "Unless, of course, I can sleep with you," he said in a joking tone.

I shook my head. "I'll sleep in the bed—alone."

The room was dark when I awoke feeling nauseous. Without turning on any lights, I staggered toward the bathroom and tripped on a shoe. The lights flicked on.

"What's wrong?" Brett asked, moving toward me.

"I don't feel well." I turned on the bathroom light, closed the door and bent over the toilet. After heaving up everything in my stomach, the room swayed as I tried to stand. My legs buckled and I collapsed on the floor.

"Can I get you anything?" Brett said loudly through the door.

"Just let me sleep," I mumbled as I pushed my hands under my head.

"Maybe it's from the spiders. Let me take you to the hospital."

"No...Please...Just give me time."

"I'm coming in." Brett pushed the door open. He took a washcloth, soaked it and wiped my face. "Can I carry you back to bed?"

"I better stay here," I said, softly. Then my stomach churned. Holding onto the toilet, I pulled myself up to a kneeling position and threw up yellow fluid. The retching continued with the liquid flowing into the toilet until I had no more to give. My whole body ached as the vomiting turned into dry heaves.

"What can I do?" Brett asked.

"Nothing." I gasped for air.

He sat on the floor next to me until I released my grip on the toilet bowl and lowered my head to the floor. He stood, soaked the washcloth again, and wiped my face. Then he went into the other room and came back with a pillow. He eased it under my head and laid a towel on top of me.

"Thank you," I whispered, closing my eyes.

When I stirred, my hand touched a cold, hard object. Opening my eyes, I discovered I was lying on the bathroom floor and remembered vomiting last night. I held onto the rim of the bathtub, forced myself up to a sitting position and saw Brett sleeping on the bedroom floor next to the door. Clutching the edge of the sink, I rose and splashed water on my face.

"How are you feeling?" he asked, standing up.

"Oh, so much better. It must have been something I ate."

"You were pretty sick last night. Why don't you go back to bed?"

"No. Whatever it was, it's gone." I picked up the pillow, walked out of the bathroom with it, and looked at the clock on the nightstand. It said 6:35 a.m. "I need to get ready for work."

"Don't you think you should take it easy today?"

"I feel fine."

"Let me see your fingernails." Brett held up my hand. "The discoloration is gone."

Casting my eyes over my nails and down to my toenails, I breathed easier. If the reddish-purple color and being sick were reactions to the spider venom, they had cleared up quickly.

As Brett and I walked out of the elevator, Lieutenant Barnes and Sergeant Harmon stepped in. We politely smiled at each other while the elevator door closed. I felt relieved they didn't mention last night's incident.

"Miss Jones and Mr. Daborel," Ralph said from behind the check-in desk. "I'm afraid I'm going to have to move both of you to other rooms. The exterminators are coming around noon. They'll be working on the top four floors. Did you hear what happened last night?"

"Yes," Brett replied. "We saw the commotion in the hall and asked one of the guests. She said a hotel guest had been bitten by a spider. Do you know her condition?"

"Lieutenant Barnes said the ambulance broke down on the way to the hospital," Ralph began with raised brows, "and she was transferred to another ambulance. Her husband went with her in the other ambulance. It never made it to the hospital. Both of them are missing. We've never had any problems in the hotel before. We did have a guest who died from being mauled by an animal. That didn't happen in the hotel."

"When was that?" I asked.

"A month or two ago."

"I read about an animal attack in the newspaper right after I moved to Billings. A woman who was wanted by the police in Oklahoma."

Ralph nodded. "That was her. We were happy the hotel wasn't mentioned. The reporter just said she was staying in Montana, hiding from the law."

"Did the police ever figure out what type of animal attacked her?" I glanced at Brett who was looking down at the floor. Maybe he felt uncomfortable talking about things like this.

"No," Ralph replied. "None of the tests they performed were conclusive. One lab blamed the other lab for sterilizing all the potential evidence. Based on all the scratches on her body, the police thought it was a mountain lion. Sergeant Harmon said Nancy Stewart's body was covered with scratches. They're speculating that maybe her body was left behind the Alta Bar and the same animal—"

"Ralph," Brett interrupted. "I don't think you should discuss the condition of Nancy Stewart's body with Miss Jones."

"Oh, I'm sorry, Miss Jones."

"Don't be," I said. "I asked you the questions."

"Even if the animal attack didn't take place at the hotel, it was still hard to deal with since she was staying here. We helped make arrangements to ship her body and packed all of her stuff. This is worse. We have a guest and a visitor bitten by spiders in the hotel. We've even made national news."

"Wha—what did you say?" I stuttered as a cold chill washed over me and I felt a lump in my throat.

"With three people missing after spider bites, Billings has made national news. It's on all the stations."

"Miss Jones and I will be moving out," Brett said. "We'll be staying at a friend's place."

"I don't blame you," Ralph remarked.

Brett took my hand as we walked away from the counter. "You look pale. Are you still feeling okay?"

"Yeah, I'm fine. Just hungry."

A television hung high in every corner of the coffee shop. We watched as we ate breakfast and saw Barnes being interviewed. He didn't say anything I didn't already know. Then several pictures of the Towne Hotel and the hospital appeared on the screen. Fear shot through my body when I saw a picture of myself.

"This is Miss Sara Jones leaving the police station," the reporter explained. "She was with the first victim, Nancy Stewart, when she was bitten and reported her disappearance to Lieutenant Barnes."

Trying not to show any emotion, I took a few shallow breaths as a wave of panic swirled up my spine. This was what I feared might happen. Too many were bitten and missing for Billings not to make the national news. I had hoped my name wouldn't be mentioned and worse, my picture. I couldn't stay here any longer even if I hated leaving Brett. I didn't want him involved in my problems. He would be no match for the Crussett family.

"What time do you want to check out and go to Rex's place?" he asked. "I can take off work whenever you're ready."

"There's a report sitting on my desk that needs to be finished, so I have to work for a few hours. I could be ready to leave around 11:30," I lied.

After I left the hotel and walked one block, I turned and went back. From my room, I called the accounting office and told them I had a family emergency and needed to go to California for a few days. I didn't want them to know I wouldn't be back in case the police tried reaching me there. Then I packed and put my cell phone in my purse. I wanted to call Brett later and tell him I was okay; otherwise, he might think something had happened to me.

Getting on the elevator, I wondered if I would ever find a home where I wouldn't fear pursuit. It seemed like I was closing another chapter of my life.

"We'll miss you around here," Ralph said as I handed him my key.

"The office isn't that far away. I'll come by and visit sometime."

"That would be nice." He gave me my final bill. "Will Mr. Daborel be checking out soon?"

"Probably not until around eleven." I took money out of my wallet and placed it on the counter to settle my account.

"Can you leave a forwarding address?"

"I don't know it. Let me give you my office number." I wrote down the number for him.

"Thank you, Miss Jones. Do you want help with your luggage?"

"No, thanks, I can manage. Bye for now, Ralph." I held onto the handle of my suitcase and headed to the exit.

Driving away from Billings, I couldn't quit thinking about Brett. Tears welled in my eyes and trickled down my cheeks. I had made a mistake by letting myself get attached to him. I knew I would miss him and hoped he wouldn't try to find me.

I had no idea where I was going. Wherever I ended up, I'd need money. My parents had left me an appreciable amount. I planned on getting a funds transfer when I reached the next large city. That way if it could be traced, it wouldn't be traced to my final destination. I had never drawn on that account while I was in Billings.

Three hours later, I stopped for gas. Filling the tank, I sensed someone standing behind me. My hands trembled as I put back the nozzle and looked over my shoulder.

"Going somewhere?" Brett asked.

"Have you been following me all the way from Billings?"

"Yes. You passed me when I was headed back to the hotel. Since you left for work before I did, I knew something was up, so I followed you. I called your cell phone. You didn't answer. Then I called the hotel and Ralph told me you had checked out. What's going on?"

"I planned on calling you later. Why were you following me?" I asked, feeling my eyes narrowing, irritated he was keeping track of me.

"There's a diner next door. We can talk inside," he suggested.

"No. I want to be farther away from Billings before it gets dark," I said tersely, and then I saw his eyes dim and the hurt look on his face. "Let's sit in my car, and I'll explain."

We got in. I drove away from the gas pumps and parked. "My picture is all over the news. Now the people that I didn't want to find me will know where I am. I can't stay in Billings any longer. I thought it would be better if I called and told you I wouldn't be coming back."

"Better for whom?"

"Better for me. I didn't want a farewell scene. I'm sorry. Eventually, you'll be leaving Billings. I thought you'd be the one leaving first. It was inevitable we'd part."

"When I get an assignment for another location it doesn't mean we'd never see each other. I care for you, Sara."

"I'm sorry, Brett. Really." I gripped his forearm and held on tight. "Just not now, maybe never, no matter how hard it is for me. I can't give any more than friendship."

"You're not even giving that since you're running away from me."

"I'm not running from you. You don't know anything about the people I'm running from. They're ruthless. You can't fight them. They'll kill you just like they'll kill me because I know too much. I don't want that to happen to you. It's better if we're not friends."

"You're not the only one with a past. You don't know any more about me than I know about you." He held my hands. "I am quite capable of defending you against anyone who shows up."

I knew Brett was strong. He'd lifted my sofa and moved it to another wall by himself, but petroleum engineers weren't fighters. "They use knives and guns," I said, feeling anxious. "You'll be in danger."

"I know how to handle guns and knives along with some other weapons. I can protect you. Also, where do you think you could hide? Your picture is on the national news. You'll be recognized wherever you go. The Billings' cops will send your picture to police departments all over the country when they find out you left in a hurry. They might believe you had a hand in the spider cases."

Convinced he was probably right, I said, "You win."

"Rex's place is about twenty minutes from Billings. It would be better if you followed me. Can I trust you to do that?"

"Yes."

A faint smile crossed Brett's lips as he got out of the car.

3

REX'S PLACE

Driving down a remote gravel lane, I saw a two-story stone house surrounded by heavy woods. Through the thick foliage, I couldn't see any neighboring houses.

Stepping over the threshold, Brett said, "Look around while I take the luggage upstairs."

It was a wonderful old house with high ceilings, crown moldings, and oak floors. The walls were all painted a soft green. To the right of the entry was a den with a large oak desk and bookcases lined two walls.

A grey and dark green striped sofa, two dark green leather chairs, a coffee table, and two end tables stood in the living room. An armoire was next to the archway leading into the dining room. From the way it was positioned, I assumed it housed a television. A landscape painting above the sofa caught my eye. In the center of it was a cave with part of the opening blocked by a huge boulder. Something about it looked inviting, but I couldn't pinpoint why. As I continued staring at it, a strong urge to go there bubbled up inside me.

"You must be hungry," Brett said, coming down the stairs.

"Is this cave located somewhere around in this area?" I pointed to the picture.

He shrugged. "Don't know. I'll ask Rex when he gets back in town. Why don't you unpack while I see what I can find for dinner?"

When I finished putting everything away, I glanced out the window that overlooked the back of the house. It appeared as if the woods continued for miles. Outside of the unlikely event that someone had followed us, the Crussetts wouldn't be able to find me here. Then suddenly, I smelled the appetizing aroma of spaghetti sauce and my stomach began growling as I hurried downstairs.

"I had no idea you knew how to cook," I said, walking into a modern, oversized kitchen with the latest appliances.

"Like I said, there's a lot of things you don't know about me. Hopefully you'll like all the things you learn and stick around awhile. And on top of my great attributes, I'll try to entice you more with a Jacuzzi out back. Wanna give it a try after dinner? I guarantee it'll help you relax."

"Sounds great. This place is really secluded. Your friend must like his privacy."

"Rex has a reputation. He needs a lot of privacy." A mischievous smile crossed his lips and he winked.

I smiled back. Rex was probably a ladies' man. That would account for the Jacuzzi.

We sat down at the table in the dining room, and Brett poured two glasses of wine from a carafe.

I lifted my glass. "What type of wine is this?"

"I'm sure you'll like it," he replied, without answering my question.

I took a sip. It sent a surge of warmth through my body. I did like it. "It tastes something like a Merlot. Is that what it is?"

"No." He grinned.

Between bites and sips, I asked, "Is it a Cabernet Sauvignon?"

He shook his head indicating my guess was wrong

I held my glass up to the light, as if I were a wine connoisseur, and tilted it. "Is it a Zinfandel?"

He shook his head again and filled my glass.

I took another swallow. "A Shiraz?"

"Nope."

"Could it be a Pinot Noir?"

"You're not even close."

I hiccupped. "Sorry about that."

"You must be enjoying the wine."

"Yes, I certainly am. Whatever the grapes, vineyard, year, or blend, this stuff is divine." Tomorrow, I would look through the recycling bin for the bottle.

After we finished eating, I went upstairs to slip on my one-piece, black swimming suit while Brett got the Jacuzzi ready.

Gradually easing into the Jacuzzi, I felt the warm, comforting water envelop my body. Springtime in Billings is a wonderful season, but soaking in the serene setting amid lush trees gave me a glorious feeling.

Brett handed me another glass of wine. "Enjoy," he said and left to change into his swimming trunks.

I leaned back, appreciating the solitude, and gazed at the stars. I listened to low soothing music and saw Brett standing above me. I sat up and stared at him. I knew he had a good build from the way he appeared in his clothes, but I had no idea. Oh, his broad shoulders, muscular arms, and pectorals took my breath away. He was gorgeous.

As he moved into the water, his deep blue eyes were mesmerizing. He put his arm around my shoulders, and his hot breath drifted over my bare skin. A burning desire for him soared through my body. I turned toward him, kissed his neck, and ached for more. What was I doing? This wasn't what I wanted. I hadn't felt like this about him before. It wasn't like me to behave like a vixen.

With a mischievous smile, he took a drink of his wine.

Had he changed his mind about me and decided to play hard to get? I stroked his arm. What was wrong with me? I should have slid away from him; instead, I moved closer. I wanted him. As soon as he put down his glass, I wrapped my arms around his neck and kissed him. I continued kissing him even when I gasped for air.

"Let's go upstairs," he whispered.

"Oh, yes," I sighed as my heartbeat raced and my breathing became more erratic. I kissed him again.

He picked up our glasses and handed me mine. "To our new relationship." He clicked my glass.

I exhaled and drank, knowing I was going to get what I wanted. A second later, we got out of the Jacuzzi and carried our glasses to my bedroom.

Brett barely closed the door before I shoved him onto the bed and climbed on top of him. My cravings for his body turned to almost animalistic urges, and I bit his lip with such roughness it surprised me. My insatiable desire for him accelerated into aggressiveness as my nails dug into his flesh. Brett reacted to my ferocious appetite with gentle yet intense responses, never missing a beat. After an hour of uninhibited love making, we stopped to catch our breath. He gasped several times, and his gorgeous chest muscles twitched from our carnal encounter as he refilled our wine glasses. I thought Conner was a great lover, yet he was no match for Brett. No one could possibly be better. And to think, I was going to leave him without ever having known this ecstasy.

"What are you thinking?" he asked.

"I'm wondering why I waited so long for this."

He smiled, put both wine glasses on the nightstand, and slowly ran his hand down my body.

Feeling someone tugging on my legs, I opened my eyes. Through foggy vision, I saw two women with solemn expressions on their faces pulling me out of bed. I felt dizzy. I tried to talk, but only gibberish came from my mouth. The woman with long black hair put a robe on me. The other one slipped shoes on my feet. I wanted to float away. They held my arms, preventing me from rising. With my feet hovering above the floor, they led me down the stairs and through the house to the backdoor. Were they angels taking me to see Mom and Dad? The black-haired woman put a blindfold over my eyes. Then I heard a door open. They continued holding my arms while I glided between them.

A crisp, cool breeze hit my face. The women remained quiet, not saying a word, as we moved along. The rustling of leaves surrounded us. I smelled pine trees. If they'd just let go of me, I could drift to the tree tops.

"Bring her here," a man yelled.

My blindfold was removed. I found myself inches from the man with the penetrating, dark eyes I had seen at the hotel. He must have followed me. I felt a convulsion of terror seize my body. I squirmed and wiggled, trying to free myself from the hands that held me firmly. He wouldn't release me. I gave up. I was trapped.

The dark-eyed man held up my trembling hand and placed a spider in my palm. I marveled at the warm, chestnut-brown color with specks of black dribbled through it. I gently touched it. Then the dark-eyed man turned over my hand and tapped it against a metal container. The spider tumbled inside, landing next to three others that looked just like it. He snapped the container lid in place and slipped it into his shirt pocket.

He led me through a cluster of cobwebs that clung to my face. He brushed them away and placed my hand on a person. I glanced down and saw spiders crawling on the stout man whose wife had been bitten in the hotel. He was lying on something that looked like a granite table. His eyes were wide open, staring straight ahead. Blood oozed from deep scrapes on his arms. His face was pale and immobile. Was I at his funeral?

The dark-eyed man guided me to a chair, sat me down, and held onto my shoulder to stop me from rising above the ground. I opened my mouth to speak. No sound escaped. My eyes darted around looking for Brett; he wasn't anywhere. He wouldn't have left me. Something must have happened to him. My heart started beating faster. The dark-eyed man ran his hand up and down my cheek. My heartbeat slowed down.

Three people blocked my vision as they moved between me and the stout man on the table. I watched as a slender blond-haired man carrying a knife walked in front of them and passed out of my sight.

The dark-eyed man lifted his hands from my shoulders. A woman put her hands there so I wouldn't drift away. He walked toward the table. I couldn't see what he was doing. I heard voices without comprehending what was being said. The dark-eyed man returned with a glass full of a deep red liquid. His face glowed and his lips eased into a smile as he held it to my mouth. I swallowed a big gulp and felt surprised it tasted good. I glanced around. Everyone was drinking, talking, and laughing.

After I took another sip, the two women who brought me here strolled out of the crowd toward me. They held my arms. I rose to my feet. I scanned the trees, wanting to float above them. The black-haired woman tugged at my arm. I looked down and saw the stout man. His eyes were gone, leaving two sunken holes. His arms hung down over the table. Blood drizzled from his wrists into containers that stood on the ground. The blond-haired man with the knife cut the skin off the stout man's stomach. My pulse raced, and I gasped for air as a wave of terror shot through my body.

The dark-eyed man gently stroked my cheek again. I no longer felt afraid. He covered my eyes with the blindfold and tied it behind my head. The women led me back to the house, slipped off the blindfold, and held onto me to keep my feet on the floor. After they removed my robe and shoes, they laid me down on the bed. I closed my eyes. My body floated to the ceiling.

4

MORE VICTIMS

The early morning sunlight streamed through the window when I awoke. I turned and saw Brett, dressed for work, sitting on the edge of the bed and gazing at me.

"Are you going to work today?" he asked and kissed my cheek.

"Where were you last night?"

"Right here, lying next to you."

My hands became clammy as I thought about the woods, the dark-eyed man, the knife, the man on the table, and feeling weightless. Was it all a dream? It seemed so real, except I knew I couldn't float away.

"You okay?" he asked.

"Yes." My skin tightened as hair raised on my body.

"I want to drive you to work in case any unwelcome visitors show up in Billings."

"Yesterday, I called the office and told them I had a family emergency, so I'd be gone for a few days. I'll tell them the emergency passed and everything was okay. If the police want to talk to me again, I'm easy to reach at my workplace. I'd never tell them to come here. I don't even know where here is."

"Just as well. Rex wants the location of his place to be kept a secret. Since I'll be driving you to work, you don't need to know the address."

"Sometimes you work late. If that should happen, I'll need the address to get back here."

"I can always bring my work home. I don't need to do it at the office."

He put his arm around me. "Don't look so worried. I'll make sure you get back and forth." He stood and headed to the door. "I need to make a few calls before we leave."

I didn't like not knowing where I was. At the same time, I certainly enjoyed his company.

On the way to work, he drove in and out of so many streets, there was no way I could memorize all of them. Some of the signs were hidden by trees and poles so I asked him for their names. Each time I did, his brows drew together in an irritated frown, and he claimed he didn't know it.

When Brett stopped for a red light, I glanced out the passenger window and saw a woman with long black hair walking along the sidewalk. Her face came into focus as she got closer. She looked like a model with her high cheek bones, ivory skin and soft brown eyes. She was the black-haired woman who had escorted me out of the house last night. How could I have dreamt about her?

"Do you know her?" I asked, tapping on the window.

The light turned green as Brett quickly glimpsed in the direction of the black-haired woman. "No," he replied, pushing on the accelerator.

When we reached the accounting office building, he wrapped his arms around my shoulders and kissed me as if we had a pleasant drive to work.

After I finished all my rush jobs, I tried to remember every detail of my dream, though I now questioned whether it was a dream at all. If it wasn't, where was Brett and why would those people want me to see something like that? If they planned on killing me, they had the opportunity last night. Maybe I could find some answers at Rex's place. For the remainder of the day, I found myself staring at the clock on the wall, unable to focus on my work.

Brett's car wasn't parked by the entrance when I walked out of the building. I called him on my cell phone.

"Hi, Sara," he answered. "I'm running late. Should be there in fifteen minutes."

"I'm standing outside the building. I'll wait for you here."

"See you soon."

A black limo pulled over to the curb. A tall man with medium-brown hair got out and turned toward me. It was Conner. My hands trembled. I saw three men staring at me from inside the limo. My eyes darted around. There was no place I could run; I was trapped. Straightening my posture, I took several deep breaths as he approached.

"Hello, Sara." A faint smile lit up his face as he stretched out his arms to embrace me.

I backed away.

"Is this how it's going to be?" His light brown eyes dimmed, and his face creased with concern. "I wanted you to be part of my life. I still do. Why did you leave?"

"What do you want, Conner?" I asked, trying to stay calm.

"I want you."

I also wanted him. I had shared my life with him. We had lived together for almost three years and even talked about getting married. He would take me to California sometimes just so I could put flowers on my parents' graves. Our relationship was great until I discovered the true nature of his family's business: drug trafficking, prostitution, pornography, and selling runaway teenagers as sex slaves. They had politicians, members of the police department, and anyone else they needed on their payroll. If any of the Crussetts got in trouble, they had ways of getting it fixed. No one in that family or their friends ever went to prison.

"Why did you leave?" he asked again, sounding hurt.

I was sure he already knew as I answered, "Because of your business." I had an urge to put my arms around him, but then it would be harder to leave him again.

"The family business has nothing to do with us."

I noticed the dark-eyed man and the black-haired woman strolling to the limo. My spine stiffened. I felt every muscle in my body tensing up.

"What's wrong?" Conner asked.

"It's that guy. He's talking to your men. I keep seeing him everywhere."

Conner looked over his shoulder. The couple was gone. "I'll ask my men what he said in a minute." He took my hand, raised it to his lips, and kissed it. I didn't stop him. I glanced at the limo again. Conner's men were no longer visible. Did the man slip them spiders? I couldn't bear to think of him dying that way.

"Come with me." I led him into the office building. The building windows were tinted. "Something is going on here in Billings. I think you're in danger."

"Danger from whom?" he asked with an amused expression on his face.

"You've heard about the spider bites?"

"Yes. That's how I was able to locate you."

"I could be wrong. I think everyone in your limo has been bitten."

Conner peered out the window, pulled his cell phone out of his pocket, and made a call. I watched him as his expression changed when he received no response.

"How?" He put away his phone.

41

"When you walked toward me, I saw three men looking out the limo windows. Then that guy said something to them. Now I don't see your men."

"You think he put spiders in the limo?"

"Yes," I responded with a quick nod while biting my lower lip. "I don't know why. I think it has something to do with me."

He yanked out his cell phone again. "I'm calling the police. Let them check out the limo. If you're in danger, you need to come with me now. My plane's at the airport." He kissed my forehead. "Don't worry, I won't hurt you."

"No. Don't call the police. I don't want anyone else bitten." I saw Brett's car pull up to the curb. "I better stay here. A friend just stopped out front to take me to where I'm staying. I don't want anything to happen to you. You need to leave Billings."

"You're not safe here."

"I've been bitten and nothing happened. I must be immune. I'm planning on leaving. I just think it's better if we each leave separately. I'll call you when I get away from Billings."

"I don't like leaving you."

"You have to, or you'll be the next victim." I saw Brett getting out of his car. "My friend is coming. With the tinted windows he can't see us, but he'll be in here soon."

"You don't want him to see me?" he asked, clenching his jaw.

"I think you'll be safer if no one knows you're here. Please go into one of the offices until I'm gone." I lightly kissed his lips. "And try to leave with a group of people."

Conner's mouth tightened as he looked at me.

"Please," I begged and squeezed his hands.

He slipped into an office connected to the foyer just as Brett entered the building.

"Why weren't you outside?" he asked.

"A limo parked out front and I felt a little nervous. I came in here to wait for you."

"Good. I'm here now, so you're safe." He took my hand and we went to his car. The limo was gone. I hoped Conner would be safe.

Driving back to Rex's place, I tried to memorize the street names again. I gave up when I realized Brett took a new route. Along the way, we stopped at a restaurant.

After our meals were served, Brett asked, "How did your day go?"

I swallowed the food in my mouth. "It was a nice, peaceful day for a change. Nothing out of the ordinary happened."

He touched my knee under the table and grinned. "That's good, because I'm not planning on you having a peaceful evening."

I felt my cheeks turn red as I sipped my wine.

"I wonder if the cops have made any progress in locating the missing couple from the hotel," he said, cutting his steak.

"I don't know." I looked at his knife sawing into meat, and thought about the stout man who lay bleeding on the table.

When we reached the house, Brett served wine. I drank slowly, savoring the flavor, and felt a rush of excitement through my body. I moved closer to him and caressed his arm.

He wrapped his arms around me and passionately kissed my lips. "Do you want to go upstairs, or should we try out the couch?" He playfully licked the side of my neck.

"Upstairs." My body oozed euphoric pleasure from his closeness.

As we moved toward the stairwell, Brett's cell phone rang. He pulled it out of his pocket and looked at the display. "Damn. I need to take this." He curled his lip downward as though offering an apology, and then headed into the den.

I went to my bedroom, undressed, climbed in bed, and waited impatiently as my skin tingled with anticipation.

Brett entered, carrying a glass of wine. "Something's come up at work." He handed me the glass. "Enjoy this while I'm gone. I should be back in a couple of hours." He gave me a kiss and left.

Putting down the glass, I opened my mouth, took deep breaths, and tried to calm my lustful desires. I thought how unnatural for me this was. In the past, I always got aroused after I had romance first: a candlelight dinner, soft music, sharing a bath, talking quietly, a bouquet of flowers, a feeling of being loved. The way Conner made me feel. Not this. It's like I wanted sex, just sex. No romance. No love.

My mind drifted to the night before as my arousal wore off. Was there any possibility it had been a dream? I wanted to remove all doubt since I hadn't seen Brett at the bizarre event. I picked up the wine glass to take a taste and found myself staring at it. Last night I felt dizzy and weightless, like I could fly, when I was led to a clearing in the woods. Had Brett drugged me? Just in case, I climbed out of bed, poured the wine down the bathroom sink, and sat the empty glass on the nightstand. This was my opportunity to check out the woods without his knowing.

5

THE CLEARING

At dusk, I got a flashlight out of my car. I headed to the back of the house where I found a path leading into the woods and followed it. The tall, leafy trees blocked out the moon and stars except for an occasional stray beam of light.

A few minutes down the path, I heard faint voices in the distance and recognized some of them from the night before. It wasn't a dream; it was real. The group had gathered again tonight. I left the path and trudged farther into the woods with my flashlight bobbing up and down. I meandered between the trees and dense foliage. The voices grew louder. I saw light ahead. I quickly covered the flashlight beam with my hand. A dim light now glowed around my fingers as I moved along.

I crept slowly, trying not to make any noise. I stopped in my tracks when I saw a silhouette of a man by a tree ahead of me. I ducked down and turned off the flashlight. Blackness surrounded me except for the haze of the light ahead. My palms became moist. My heart began hammering. I took several deep breaths in an effort to calm down. Hearing twigs snapping and rustling of leaves near me, a wave of terror shot up my spine.

"Lance, where are you going?" a woman yelled.

"I heard something," a man replied. "It must have been an animal."

It sounded like he was only a few feet away. I put my hand over my mouth for fear I'd make a noise. Bushes swayed and twigs crackled as the man, no longer searching, moved away from me. My hands trembled and the cold sweat of fear dribbled down my sides. Silently, I inched toward the light and the voices. Within minutes I saw the clearing.

Lying with my stomach against the hard ground, I looked around a bush. I was too far away to listen to everything said. I did hear, "He's the first one…two preserved…from the limo…it's gone…not him…she's alone…no…more…another…they'll be plenty…later…can I have…she drinks…"

As they milled around, I saw the granite table, their altar. A man was stretched out on it with dark specks moving on his clothing. I assumed they were spiders. I swallowed hard and felt a spasm of panic. Please, please, not Conner. Then I noticed the man was shorter and heavier. The panic dissipated. I breathed deeply. Next I saw the dark-eyed man carrying a knife. I bit my lip and covered my mouth.

He slit both of the man's wrists. Containers stood by the altar, catching the blood as it dripped down. I wanted to look away, but my eyes remained fixated. I watched him tear open the man's shirt, slice open his torso, cut off pieces of abdominal flesh, and place them on a tray. Four people went over to the altar, filled up their plates, and started eating.

I felt nauseous as fear engulfed my body. I couldn't move. I lay there staring at the mutilation of the man's body. A few people walked to the fringe of the clearing and stood in front of me. I could no longer see the horrible events occurring on the altar. I heard something that sounded like a power tool—maybe a drill or a saw.

I held my hand tighter over my mouth so a scream wouldn't escape and closed my eyes. Maybe it was only an ugly nightmare, but I knew the truth. It was too vivid and disgusting to be anything else.

Leaves drifted and rocks crunched behind me. It sounded like someone was running along the path. Remaining close to the ground, I turned and crawled away.

"She's not in the house," a woman yelled.

"Is her car there?" a man asked.

"Yes," the woman replied.

"We have to find her," a man said. "Spread out."

As I hid between the bushes, a group of people ran past me. I needed to get back in the house before they discovered what I had seen. Jumping to my feet, I flicked on my flashlight and hoped the light couldn't be seen through the heavy foliage as I leaped over a fallen tree, and sprinted. Trees and bushes had to be dodged along the way.

Finally, I saw the house. I stopped, caught my breath, and turned off the flashlight. I stayed at the edge of the woods, behind a large thicket of overgrown bushes and trees until I reached the side of the house near the Jacuzzi. I slipped off my shoes and jeans and tucked them along with the flashlight under several low tree branches. Then I ran to the Jacuzzi, slid in, and took off my T-shirt. I hoped the people from the clearing would think I'd been here while they were in the house looking for me. My breathing was erratic. I leaned back in the water and took several deep breaths.

Noise came from inside the house. I didn't look around. Instead, I moved further down in the warm water so it covered my shoulders. I gazed up at the starlit sky. I felt maybe I would be safe as long as they believed I didn't know anything. As I started to relax, the stars took form and I recognized the Big and Little Dippers. I concentrated on the other constellations and out came Leo, the lion, followed by Taurus, the bull.

"Keep looking," a man shouted, interrupting my stargazing.

Closing my eyes, I tried to relax again as I wondered why they wanted me. Since the dark-eyed man was at my parents' funeral, he must have known them. Maybe they told him I was bitten by four or five poisonous spiders when I was five and I didn't have any reaction. The doctor concluded I was immune to the venom. Did the people in the woods put the spiders in my hotel room to see if I was immune to this powerful venom? One of my parents' colleagues wanted me to be in his research study. My parents didn't want me involved.

Based on the victims' reactions to these spider bites, the venom was more lethal than what I had been exposed to in my parents' lab twenty years ago.

Footsteps pounded on the cement patio right behind me. I cringed, sucked in air, and held my breath expecting someone to grab me any second.

"What are you doing out here?" Brett asked.

I exhaled, opened my eyes, and saw him standing above me. "I felt a little edgy after you left. I thought the Jacuzzi might help." I sat up.

"The Jacuzzi isn't turned on," he said, looking at me with his eyebrow cocked and speaking in an interrogative, intense tone.

"I turned it off a little while ago. It's so relaxing lying in the water. Why don't you join me?"

His eyes narrowed. "Why didn't you put on a swimming suit?"

"I first went to the den searching for a book after you left. Then I saw the Jacuzzi when I looked out the patio door. I thought it would be more relaxing than reading. I didn't want to go back upstairs. Do you think some of the neighbors can see me?"

He gave me a boyish smile. "No. No one can see you. It's getting late, let's go to bed."

"I forgot to bring out a towel. Can you get me one?"

"Yes," he replied, and walked back into the house.

6

CLUES

Brett was on his cell phone when I opened my eyes. He smiled and strolled out of the bedroom still talking on his phone. I got ready to go to work and then headed downstairs to the kitchen. He wasn't there. After pouring myself a cup of coffee, I found him in the den holding his cell phone next to his ear. I went back to the kitchen and ate a bowl of cereal.

He stared at me as he walked toward the table. "Is there anything you forgot to tell me about yesterday?" Brett asked, frowning.

"No. Why?"

"Who was the man you were talking to outside your office before I arrived?"

"How do you know I talked to someone?" I asked, clutching my hands together under the table and forcing myself to maintain a pleasant expression.

"Are you going to tell me?" he huffed.

"Are you having me watched?"

"I'm trying to keep you safe from whoever you're running from."

"I wasn't running from that man," I said, calmly.

His brow furrowed and his posture stiffened as he took a step closer to me. "So, you're not going to tell me?"

"I'll make you a deal. You tell me the address of where we are, and I'll tell you who I talked to."

He gazed at me for a minute and then smiled. "I guess this is a draw. Are you ready to go to work?"

I needed to get my shoes, jeans and flashlight from the woods before someone discovered them. "It's such a nice morning. I'd like to sit outside and have another cup of coffee. Are you in a hurry to get to work?"

"No. We can sit outside for a few minutes."

As we sat enjoying the morning sun, Brett's cell phone rang. He went inside to talk. I ran to the woods, grabbed my things, and hid them behind a flower pot next to the patio door. I had just sat down when he returned.

"It would be nice if we could stay out here longer," he said, "but I have a meeting this morning. Can I take you to lunch?"

I skimmed my fingertips across his jaw line. "You sure can."

Again he drove on different streets, taking another route to downtown Billings. I only recognized a few intersections from the day before. I had to escape this dark cloud that surrounded me without anyone knowing, including Brett. With each new route Brett took, I knew I wouldn't be able to locate Rex's house to get my car. I had to find another way to go.

As I walked through the accounting firm's doors, the receptionist held up her hand. "Sara, I have a message for you," she said and handed it to me.

"Thanks." I read it on the way to my office. It was from Conner, asking me to return his call. To get him to leave the day before, I told him I'd give him a call when I left town. Who should I fear more—the Crussetts or the people from the clearing? Whatever his family might be responsible for, I thought Conner still loved me. Even if I had a hard time admitting it to myself, I also loved him. I dialed his number.

"Hello?" he answered.

"Hello, Conner. Did you have any problems leaving Billings?"

"Sara, I'm so glad you called. I've missed you."

"Were you able to leave without any problems?"

"I took your advice and waited to leave the office building with a group. I went with them to the local bar. I even had a couple of beers with two of the guys." He chuckled. "A guy named Lloyd Adams asked what company I worked for in the building. I told him my company was interested in possibly purchasing it, so I was there checking it out. He drove me to the airport. Do you know him?"

"No."

"The Billings' police haven't been able to locate my men; they can't even find the limo. Do you have any idea what happened to them?"

"All I know is that if they were bitten by one of the poisonous spiders, then they're probably dead." I didn't want to tell him what happened to one of them in the woods. It wasn't just because I thought he would ask more questions; it was also because I didn't want to think about it. The same fate likely befell the others in the limo.

"I need to get you away from there," he said in a determined tone. "I'll send a plane. Can you get to the airport?"

"I know I'm being watched. I think I'm safe for now. Let me put together a plan to leave."

"Sara, I can have the police help you get to the airport."

"Conner, I don't want anyone else killed. It's better if I work this out by myself, since somehow I'm immune to the spider venom. I'll call if I need you to send a plane."

"I can arrange to have one waiting at the airport all day if you think you can get there."

"No. I want a plan first."

"Okay. I'll do it your way." He paused. "Sara, I have never stopped loving you."

When I heard him say that, an overwhelming deluge of emotions I had kept sealed away broke free and brought tears to my eyes. I wanted to tell him how I felt. Then the thought of what his family had done returned to my mind. I ended up saying nothing for what seemed like a minute. "I still love you too, Conner." I should have added more to that sentence. I couldn't think of the words to express myself. "I'll call you tomorrow. Bye."

"Bye, Sara," Conner said in a voice just above a whisper and hung up.

I believed I would be safe with Conner, yet I wasn't sure about his family. I longed to be near him again. Before I could even think about it, I had to find a way to leave Billings on my own.

Using my computer, I looked up the airline schedules for the planes that landed here. It didn't matter where I went, but first, I needed money.

During morning break, I went to the bank next door to obtain a funds transfer from my San Diego account. After I completed the paperwork, the bank teller said I could pick up the money in a couple of hours. Leaving the building, I grabbed a charge card application, just in case someone saw me going in or out.

Around noon my cell phone rang. I glanced at the number. "Hello, Brett."

"Are you ready for lunch?"

"Yes. I'll meet you out front in ten minutes."

We walked to a small cozy Italian restaurant two blocks from my office. When we finished eating, I pulled the application out of my purse. "I want to buy some shoes online. I need to have a credit card so I thought I'd apply for one."

"It might take a month or so before you get the card. If you want to shop online, you can use my card."

"I wouldn't feel right about that. I guess I'll just have to be content to buy from Sherman's." The last time I shopped there sprang into my mind, and I smiled and added, "Maybe I can win another door prize."

The accounting firm's receptionist motioned to me as I returned to work. "Sara, Ralph from the hotel dropped these off for you," she said, handing me some messages.

"Thanks."

Sitting at my desk, I went through them. One was from Lieutenant Barnes, one from Sherman's, and the final one from a newspaper reporter. I called Barnes.

"Miss Jones, I tried to reach you at the Towne Hotel. Ralph Miller informed me that you had moved out. Can you give me the address where you're currently staying?"

"I'm staying at a friend's house. I don't know the exact address. You can always reach me on my cell phone or at work." I proceeded to give him my phone number.

"For our records, I need your address," he insisted.

"I'll get it tonight and give you a call tomorrow."

"If I'm not in the office, just leave the address on my voice mail."

After our conversation ended, I called Sherman's and I was transferred to an employee in customer relations.

"The prize we sent you for being our 100,000th customer was returned and stamped 'no forwarding address,'" the employee said. "Can you give me your current address?"

"I received your prize, a ring."

"Miss Jones, your prize wasn't a ring. It's a year's supply of bath oils. You'll receive a new collection every month."

"You didn't send a ring?"

"No. Can I please have your address?"

"I don't know the exact address. I'll get it and give you a call tomorrow."

"Thank you. Ask for Jane Larsen when you call."

"I will." I hung up and stared at the ring. Who sent it? Conner didn't know where I was until the spider and missing persons' story appeared on the national news. I slipped the ring off my finger to look inside the band for markings. A sharp pain shot through my right arm, all the way up to my elbow. It was most intense in my knuckles. My hand tingled. My fingers curved in like a claw. I tried to straighten them. The pain intensified into a piercing burn. I put the ring back on, my knuckles relaxed. The pain abruptly ended. I wiggled my fingers. Strange. I'd taken the ring off before and didn't have this type of reaction. Maybe I hit a nerve in my hand.

I studied the ring a few minutes. Then I reached for the phone and called John Davis, the newspaper reporter.

"Mr. Davis, this is Sara Jones, returning your call."

"Miss Jones, I'm a reporter for the *Washington Times*. Since you were with the first Billings' spider victim, Nancy Stewart, I would like an opportunity to interview you regarding your recollection of that event."

"Mr. Davis—"

He interrupted, "Please call me John."

"Okay, John. I've already told the police everything I remember about the incident. I'm sure Lieutenant Barnes could fill you in on anything you'd like to know."

"I've already made arrangements to interview Lieutenant Barnes. My readers would also like to hear from you."

"Let me think about it."

"I'm flying to Billings this evening. Can I give you a call tomorrow?"

"It's better if I call you. Can I reach you at this number?"

"Yes."

Hanging up, I thought no way would I consent to be interviewed. Since he had called the hotel, he probably didn't know where I worked. Maybe I'd be gone before he tried reaching me again. Ralph was so kind and helpful, he wouldn't hesitate telling him where he could find me.

At 3 p.m., I picked up the money. Leaving the bank, I saw the dark-eyed man and the hair on the back of my neck rose. I knew he was watching me, but why? As soon as I sat down at my desk, I placed the money in the top drawer. I thought it would be safer there than in my purse. I planned on leaving Billings after Brett dropped me off the next day. That way, I'd have an eight-hour head start before he realized I was gone. That wasn't how I wanted to leave him. We had been good friends for almost two months. Still, I suspected he was somehow involved with the people in the woods. From everything I had seen, I now believed the group was a cult. The killing and mutilation was probably their ritual. None of it made any sense to me.

I wished I could go to the police about what I knew. If I did, they'd go to the clearing to check it out and maybe run into some of the people. Then the cult would know I had seen them. Most important, the police couldn't defend themselves against the spiders. I didn't want anyone else to die because of me.

Brett was parked next to the curb when I left the building. He held my hand as we drove away. "How was the rest of your day?"

"You were right about the credit card. I went to the bank and talked to the manager. She said after I completed the application, it could take up to four weeks for approval before they issued the card."

"I told you, you can use mine."

"No. I can't lean on you whenever I need something."

"Why not?"

"I like my independence. By the way, Lieutenant Barnes called me. He knows I've moved out of the hotel, and he wants my new address."

"I'll take care of it. How did you enjoy the wine last night?"

"I don't think dinner agreed very well with me. Spicy food sometimes does that. The wine didn't stay down. I still liked it. It tasted good. I can't even guess what it was."

His features lined with concern, and he asked, "Did you feel okay today?"

"Yes. I was only sick for a short time last night. I felt fine when I went down to the den."

"I had planned on picking up a pizza on the way to Rex's place. Maybe that's not such a good idea."

"Pizza never gives me any problems. I think that's a great idea." I took a deep breath and ran my tongue across my lip as though I could already taste Italian sauce. Pizza was one of my favorite foods. I'd eat it even if I really was sick.

We drank beer with the pizza and watched football. When the game ended, we each got a book out of the den, sat on the couch, and began reading. After only a few minutes, I felt edgy as my pulse quickened and my breathing became uneven. Looking up, I met Brett's eyes and wanted him.

He gave me a sensual smile. "Should we go to bed?"

I dipped my head rapidly in overzealous agreement.

After we climbed into bed, an uncontrollable sexual craving consumed my body as I snuggled close to him. For a brief moment, I wondered how much he knew about the spider cult. Did he know what they did in the clearing? My desire for him didn't allow me to speculate long. He lightly stroked my arm as he eased above me. He made love to me and I stopped thinking about anything else. Afterwards, I laid my head on his shoulder and dozed off.

I awoke to the sound of birds chirping outside and saw Brett rummaging through my purse. He took something out and slid it under the cushion of the chair that stood in the corner. I wanted to yell at him, but I didn't want to raise any suspicion. I closed my eyes, pretended to sleep, and felt him ease under the covers. He brushed my hair away from my face and kissed my cheek.

I opened my eyes. "Good morning," I said and forced a smile.

"How did you sleep last night?"

"Great." Now I knew without a doubt he was up to something. Could he be a cult member? Last night, I thought Brett had seemed so loving and tender. I even had the urge to tell him about what I had seen. But when I opened my mouth to spit it out, a spasm in the pit of my stomach stopped me.

He went to his room to get ready for work. I took a shower and dressed. After I slipped on my shoes, I peeked under the chair cushion and saw my driver's license. I couldn't leave town without it. Yet, I didn't dare take it since he might try to get it before we left; if he discovered it was missing, I'd be watched more closely. Then, my chances of getting away would probably be nil. Feeling disappointed I wouldn't be able to leave today, I headed downstairs. At work, I would call and find out how to get a duplicate license.

Brett never went back upstairs. As we pulled out of the driveway, I wished I had taken my driver's license. We had only driven about a block when he pulled over to the side of the road.

"I forgot my notes," he said, making a U-turn.

I waited in the car while he went inside, probably to get my driver's license.

"Got it," he said, climbing back into the driver's seat. "I'll still get you to work on time." He sped out the driveway and drove a different way again. From all our trips in and out of town, I had only been able to determine that Rex's place was northeast of Billings in a sparsely populated area.

Shortly after I arrived at work, I called the Division of Motor Vehicles. I was told to go there. They'd issue a replacement license while I waited. The DMV was a mile from my office, an easy walk. I feared someone in the spider cult might follow me if they were lurking about. How could I dodge them?

While I ate lunch at my desk, Marsha, a co-worker, came into my office.

"Sara, here's the rest of the Kinsman report," she said, putting an expandable file on my desk. "I'm leaving. Bobby, my four-year-old, is sick. I have to go and pick him up at daycare."

"Oh, that's too bad. Is it anything serious?"

"Probably just a cold. He's coughing and running a temperature, so the daycare doesn't want the other children exposed. That's the rule."

I knew she had a parking spot in the garage under the building. "Marsha, I lost my driver's license. Would you mind dropping me off at the DMV on your way?"

"Not at all. I drive right past it, but we have to go now."

"I'm ready."

"Let me shut down my computer. I'll meet you by the elevator."

As Marsha drove out of the garage, I tipped over my purse. "Clumsy me. I do that all the time." I bent down and gathered up everything, making sure to remain out of view from any potential spectators.

"I spilled my purse in the car a couple of weeks ago. It took me days to find all the stuff. Every time I went around a corner, something else rolled out from under the seat."

I sat up straight. "I think I got everything. How many children do you have?"

"Three. Three boys. Bobby is the youngest. Have you found an apartment yet?"

"No."

"You aren't still staying at that hotel, are you?"

"No. I'm staying at a friend's house."

"Spiders. I just can't imagine how you could have stayed there one night after that woman was bitten in your room. After we heard about the other victims, my husband had an exterminator come to the house. He sprayed every nook and cranny. Have the police given you any updates that haven't been on the news?"

"There isn't anything new. They're still working on locating the paramedics."

She stopped in front of the DMV. "It must be awful for the victims' families not knowing anymore."

"The police are checking every lead. Thanks for the ride," I said, getting out of the car. "I hope Bobby gets well soon."

"I'm sure after the weekend he'll be fine. See you on Monday."

"Bye." I walked toward the entrance as Marsha drove away.

Within an hour, I had my duplicate license. Meandering back and forth on several streets on the way back to the office, I passed Sherman's and decided to buy a pair of shoes. That way I would be returning to work with a package. A cover story for Brett and anyone else who knew I had left the office.

7

A FRIEND ARRIVES

Entering the office building, I did a double take, thinking I saw Lindsey, a lady I met on the bus to Billings. When she boarded in Nebraska, her unusual eggplant color hair and dramatic eye makeup caused me to look up and maybe stare longer than a polite moment. My look must have been welcoming, because although several seats were vacant, she sat next to me. We began chatting and learned we were about the same age, we both enjoyed reading Agatha Christie and Lee Child novels, watching James Bond and sci-fi movies, and listening to tunes from the 1960s and 70s. By the time the bus stopped in Billings, we were good friends. Lindsey stayed on the bus to go to Oregon. We hadn't spoken or seen each other since then.

"Hello, Sara." She walked toward me with open arms, and wrapped me in a tight hug. Her former odd hair color had been changed to a light golden brown.

"Lindsey, I like your new hair style and shade, but almost didn't recognize you. Didn't you go to Portland?"

"Thanks." She pulled her hair behind one ear. "I'm going au natural with hair until the mood strikes me to change it again. I did go on to Oregon, but things just didn't work out like I'd hoped." She shuffled her feet and her voice wavered a bit. "I liked your idea of living in a small-to-medium-sized town, so I came back to Billings."

I suspected things went awry for her, but didn't want to snoop. "So, how did you find me?"

"Saw you on the national news. That's how I knew where you were staying."

Even though I was glad Lindsey had found me, I couldn't prevent a cold shiver creeping up my spine as I thought about my face splashed on television screens across the country had made it impossible for me to stay hidden from anyone.

Lindsey continued, "I had to talk the hotel clerk—I think his name is Ralph—into telling me where you worked. I told him I was your sister. I hope you don't mind."

Lindsey and I were about the same size. She had pale blue eyes and her hair color was a few shades lighter than mine. Outside that, I could understand why Ralph would believe we were sisters.

"No. I'm happy to see you," I said, thinking how nice it was to have a friend around who wasn't connected to the Crussett family or to that cult.

"I went to your office. The receptionist told me you weren't there. She thought you'd be back soon. So, I've been hanging around in the lobby."

"I'm glad you waited. Where are you staying?"

"The hotel clerk said you had checked out. I was hoping I could stay at the same hotel, motel, wherever you're staying. The clerk's keeping an eye on my luggage until I get back."

Brett strolled into the lobby. "Where have you been?" he asked, sounding irritated. "I've been trying to reach you."

"Why?"

"I wanted to make sure you were okay." He glanced at Lindsey.

"Lindsey, I'd like you to meet Brett Daborel," I said. "Brett, this is my friend, Lindsey Farrington. I met her on the bus when I was traveling to Billings."

"I'm happy to make your acquaintance, Lindsey." Brett shook Lindsey's hand. "Do you work in this building?"

"No," she answered. "I just got in town."

Brett looked at me. "Didn't you say you two met on the bus coming to Billings?"

"Yes. Lindsey was on her way to Portland and I stayed here."

"I came back to Billings," Lindsey clarified. "I'm hoping to stay longer than I did in Portland. Right now, I'm looking for a place to stay. Sara, where are you staying now?"

"At Brett's friend's place. I don't think it's safe for you to stay at the Towne Hotel. You know, there could still be some poisonous spiders there. The Cyprus Inn is down the street. I've heard it's super nice and they have weekly rates."

"Lindsey, my friend's house has five bedrooms," Brett interjected. "Why don't you stay with us for the weekend? Then you can look for another place next week."

"Oh, I couldn't impose on you like that," she replied.

"It wouldn't be an imposition. I have to go back to work tonight. You two could catch up on things."

I wasn't sure if Lindsey would be safe at Rex's place. At the same time, I couldn't warn her about the spider cult in front of Brett. Even if I did privately, she might feel compelled to tell the police. More lives would be lost and she would be in danger. "It's a long ways out. Maybe you'd rather stay in town?"

I gave her a minute to think about it, hoping she'd decide not to go.

A brief smile creased her lips. "Well, it would be nice to catch up."

I smiled back reluctantly. I didn't want her to think I didn't like being with her.

She turned toward Brett and fidgeted with her bracelet. "Are you sure your friend won't mind me staying there?"

"My friend is out of town. He's given me the complete use of his house while he's gone." He glimpsed around her. "Where's your luggage?"

"Oh, I left it at the hotel."

"It's almost five," I commented. "I need to go to my office and clear off my desk."

"I'll put this in the car," Brett said, taking my package. "Lindsey and I will go and get her luggage and be right back."

As I entered the accounting firm, the receptionist handed me three phone messages. Two were from Brett, and one was from Conner. Since it was Friday, I decided to return Conner's call. I didn't think I'd get a chance to call him over the weekend. He answered on the first ring.

"Sara, please let me come and get you."

"No. It isn't safe for you to come here."

"But Sara...."

"No! Stay away from Billings. I'm working on a plan to leave."

"Is there anything I can do?"

"Not right now. I'll let you know if I need your help."

"Can you call me tomorrow just so I know you're okay?"

"It might be difficult, but I'll try."

"Then promise me you'll call on Monday."

"I promise. I need to go."

"Be careful. I love you."

"I love you, too," I said, feeling guilty since I didn't plan on even attempting to call him again. As much as I wanted to see him, I wasn't prepared for more heartache. It was better if I stayed away from him.

After I disconnected, I took my replacement driver's license out of my purse, put it in my desk drawer, and filed away my work papers. On the way to the elevator, I ran into Brett.

"What took you so long?" He held my hand as we walked down the hall.

"I had to call a client."

Lindsey sat in the back seat of Brett's car. I climbed into the front passenger seat, and he drove out of Billings. On the way to Rex's place, he glanced over his shoulder and asked, "How did you like Portland?"

"I hated it," she said. "I only saw the sun a few times. I couldn't find a job. Have you been there?"

"Yes. I lived there for a couple of years. I think it's a great city. I'd still be there if it wasn't for the job. It rained often, I just didn't mind it. Did you tour the city and see any of the attractions—Japanese gardens, the haunted Shangai tunnels, the rivers?"

"No. I walked around downtown in the rain. That was all the sightseeing I did."

Brett pulled down the driveway, stopped next to Rex's house, and unlocked the door. "I'll get some take-out. There's a Chinese restaurant about two miles away. Are you both up for Chinese?"

"No way. Let me make dinner," Lindsey said. "Cooking is my passion and it's the least I can do to repay your hospitality."

In the kitchen, Lindsey searched through the refrigerator and cabinets; Brett and I sat at the granite counter and watched.

She pulled out various cans of food. "The selection is a little limited."

"Are you sure you don't want me to go and get take-out?" Brett asked.

"No. I've got it." She made a pie crust and filled it with a mixture of ingredients including chopped-up spam.

After she put the pie in the oven, we went and sat in the living room.

"Would you ladies like a glass of wine?" Brett asked.

"I'd never turn down an offer of vino," Lindsey said.

"Me, either." I stretched my body, already feeling relaxed.

Brett opened a bottle and poured each of us a glass. Then he went into the den to make some calls. Lindsey and I chatted and enjoyed the wine.

The timer buzzed. Lindsey hurried to the kitchen to check on her concocted pie. "Dinner's ready." She lifted it out of the oven.

"That smells wonderful," I said, setting the table.

We chitchatted about Billings and the hotel spider incidents as we ate.

Stabbing the last piece of crust on my plate, I said, "I don't know what kind of ingredients you found, but you managed to make a delicious dish."

"Indeed. I'm impressed you put such a great meal together given the shortage of supplies," Brett said as he filled our wine glasses.

"Glad you both enjoyed it." Lindsey accepted our compliments with a small curtsy.

"Did you learn to cook like that from working in restaurants?" I asked.

"I always pick up a few more tricks from other chefs."

"You're a chef?" Lindsey told me on the bus she had worked at a restaurant. Based on the matter-of-fact way she had mentioned it, I had assumed she was a waitress.

"Yes. I love to cook." She took a sip of wine. "For my first night here, I would've liked to have made something more exciting. Is there a grocery store close by?"

"The closest is five miles away," Brett said. "I'll take you shopping tomorrow."

"Great. The kitchen isn't well stocked with spices."

"Rex doesn't cook very often."

"It shows," Lindsey said. "I already know a few things I want to cook for you two. I'll put together a menu for the weekend tonight."

"You don't want to cook after the weekend?" Brett chuckled.

"No. That's not it. I'll cook as long as I'm here. I love your friend's stove with the char broiler and the double oven. What a great kitchen. It's going to be more fun to cook here than at the restaurants where I've worked."

The way she talked, I knew she wasn't anxious to leave Rex's place. After the weekend, I needed to find a way to convince her she would be better off staying in town without telling her everything.

"Lindsey, do you want the bedroom on the main floor or one upstairs?" Brett asked.

I didn't want her to stay by herself on this floor. "You'll have a better view of the mountains upstairs."

"I have a bad knee. The bedroom on the main floor will work better for me."

Brett picked up her luggage and put it into that bedroom. "I need to get back to work."

"How long do you think you'll be gone?" I asked.

"A few hours." He kissed me and whispered, "Keep the bed warm for me."

"I will," my voice tinged with an amorous purr. On top of everything I suspected about him, I still felt a little sad as he left.

"How do you do it?" Lindsey asked. "You've only been in Billings for two months. You got a job the first week. You have a boyfriend. He's gorgeous and a lot of fun. Where did you meet him?"

"At the hotel. His room was next to mine."

"How did you manage that?"

"I didn't. It just turned out that way."

"How long have you two been together?"

"Well ..." I hesitated.

"Come on, tell me everything."

"When we were living at the hotel, we went out. Nothing serious. It wasn't until after the spider situation and we came here that things changed."

"He wasn't your boyfriend while you were staying there?"

"No. We were good friends, but that was all."

She leaned closer. "He was playing hard to get?"

Not wanting to tell her the real reason, I said, "I guess he was. What happened to the guy you were going to see in Portland? Simon something."

"Simon Ellis…he didn't turn out to be what I thought he was. We went out a couple of times. Then it was over." She looked down as a sad expression crept across her face.

I stroked her arm. "Oh, I'm sorry. You were so anxious to meet him." To lighten the mood, I said, "That guy on the bus would have been more than happy to take Simon's place."

"Do you know he originally only had a ticket to someplace in Idaho? When I changed buses there, he got on my bus. He sat next to me all the way to Portland. I ended up giving him my cell number. He went back to Idaho. We talked on the phone a lot. Then he came back to Portland for a weekend and we went out. I ended it when I learned he was in the potato business, developing pesticides. The thought of being around chemicals just made my skin crawl. You know, they just don't know all the side effects."

"I couldn't agree more. My parents never allowed any pesticides around. Our house was in the middle of five acres just to make sure that pesticides wouldn't interfere with their research."

"That's right. You said your parents were arachnologists."

"Yes. They never permitted a spider to be killed, or for that matter, any insect."

Lindsey shuffled through the newspaper and pulled out the classified section. "It would be great if I could find a job in your building."

"There isn't a restaurant in my building."

"I'm going to look for an office job. I searched all over Portland for a chef position, came up empty-handed. Maybe after I start making some money, I'll check at the larger restaurants to see if they have any openings for a chef. Do you know of any jobs available in your building?"

"I know there aren't any in the accounting firm where I work. There might be something in one of the other companies." We both started looking through the want ads, circling possibilities as we finished off the bottle of wine.

It was just past 11 p.m. when we said goodnight and headed to our bedrooms.

Someone moved me around in the bed. I opened my eyes to see who it was; everything around me looked hazy. I thought I saw the dark-eyed man holding onto me. My body felt weightless and serene. I swirled my hands in the air, wanting to gracefully glide away.

A woman held tightly onto my arm, keeping me from floating out the window. She slipped a robe onto my body. I tried to see her face. She turned, leaving a muddled blur before my eyes.

The dark-eyed man carried me down the stairs and out the door. He stood me on the ground leaving me to sway back and forth, drifting from him. He grabbed my arm. My feet hovered above the ground as he took me through the woods.

My free arm swung with the breeze. I touched the wind. It felt warm and soft between my fingers. Hearing voices, I suddenly had the desire to sing. I breathlessly opened my mouth. No sound would come out.

The dark-eyed man sat me down in a chair and continued holding onto my arm. White feathers floated in the air around me; I limply reached out to catch one. The dark-eyed man tightened his grip and pulled me back into the chair. There was something in the tree in front of me. I squinted, hoping to see more clearly.

A man, surrounded by a sparkling spider web, was resting on a branch in the tree. It was beautiful. I wanted to float to him and feel the soft web. The dark-eyed man wouldn't let go of me.

A glass was put to my mouth. I looked up the slender arm holding the glass to see it was attached to the black-haired woman. I drank without putting up any resistance. It was completely flavorless. She put something in my mouth. I chewed and swallowed without knowing what it was or tasting it.

The dark-eyed man released my arm. Free from his grip, I began to drift toward the man in the tree. Before I reached him, the dark-eyed man picked me up. I tried again to speak. No sound escaped. If he wasn't holding me so tight, I could fly away.

The man carried me back to bed. He kissed my forehead. I closed my eyes and floated back to the man in the tree.

Raising my eyelids, I saw I was lying in Brett's arms.

"Did you have a nightmare last night?" he asked. "You were tossing and turning all over the bed when I got home."

"I don't know. I can't remember what I dreamt about."

"You've seemed a little edgy. It's probably because of the police investigation. I need to finish up some things over the weekend, but I won't work tonight. We can relax in the Jacuzzi."

"That sounds great." Since I was still in Billings, I might as well enjoy it and I had to admit I liked being in his arms. Also, I wasn't sure if Lindsey was safe with the spider cult possibility hanging out in the woods. I didn't want to leave town while she was staying at Rex's place. I hoped it wouldn't be for long.

Last night continued to haunt me as we ate breakfast. I couldn't get it out of my mind. I needed to find a way to explore the woods during daylight.

"What time are we going grocery shopping?" Lindsey asked.

"Let's go right after breakfast," Brett said. "I need to go to the office this afternoon."

"I think I'll stay here and get some laundry done."

Brett poured another cup of coffee. He didn't say anything about me being here alone.

I waited patiently for them to leave. They were taking their time reading the newspaper. To kill some time, I started a load of clothes in the washing machine. After they left, I planned on driving around the neighborhood to find out where I was before I went exploring.

"Are you ready to go?" Lindsey asked, putting down the newspaper.

"I just need to make a quick call first." Brett headed to the den.

Ten minutes later, they were finally set to leave. Brett kissed me goodbye. I stood by the door and watched them drive away.

8

THE NEIGHBOR

I jumped into my car, put the key into ignition, and gave it a turn. Nothing. It couldn't possibly be a dead battery since mine wasn't that old and I am almost anal about turning off interior and exterior lights. Suspicious, I slipped fingers under the latch, flipped open the hood and discovered an empty slot where the battery should have been. I lifted one of the hanging cables and noticed it wasn't damaged. Whoever had taken my battery did it carefully. Precise extraction was not typical theft perpetrated by strangers in need of car parts. I snapped the hood shut.

I put my purse back in the house and headed out to the woods. After going about fifty feet down the path, the trees and shrubbery became so thick they formed a canopy blocking out the sun. It was almost as dark as a moonless night. I heard twigs snapping and movement through the foliage in front of me. It sounded like someone was going along the trail. I slipped between the trees.

Talking came from the direction of the path. I ducked behind a shrub. The voices got louder and louder. I remained close to the ground and waited. Several minutes later, the voices began fading away as if they were leaving the woods. I stood and moved slowly toward the clearing, keeping the trail in view in case I needed to immediately retreat to the house. The sunlight broke through the trees ahead of me as I inched around some overgrown bushes. Then I spotted the clearing and fear struck my mind as the memories of what occurred there became vivid. I hid behind a large boulder and listened. Everything was still, no swaying of the trees or shrubs. I rose to my feet and crept into the open space.

Cobwebs filled the clearing. I continuously swung my hands back and forth to clear a path. My eyes swept over the area as I tried to scan the surrounding trees. With so many cobwebs, I couldn't see through them, everything looked cloudy. I stumbled on a protruding rock and fell to the ground. Leaning on my elbows, I looked around. A few feet away from me stood the altar. Next to it was a round, black container. I stayed low and inched closer. I sat up, grabbed the container and glanced inside. It was covered with a dark crust. Dry blood? I licked two fingers and ran them along the bottom of the container. The tips of my fingers were a deep red color. I held them next to my nose to smell the substance. It smelled sweet. Strange. Then I heard the rustling of leaves and voices.

I stayed close to the ground and crawled out of the clearing. At the edge, I hunkered down between some bushes with cobwebs covering my face and hair. I started pulling them off when someone gripped my hand. I froze.

"Stand up," a man ordered.

I couldn't move.

With his other hand, he took hold of my arm. "Stand up," he hissed again.

I still didn't move.

His grip tightened, pinching my fingers and sending a sharp pain through my hand. I briefly closed my eyes and pursed my lips. Then he yanked me up. The dark-eyed man stood in front of me. A furious expression covered his face. His penetrating eyes became hot with rage as he stared at me. I felt his cold breath against my face.

He clenched his jaw while his eyes inched down my body, like he was studying me. My spine stiffened and I waited motionless, wondering about his next move.

A branch cracked and my eyes drifted in that direction. I watched a short, muscular man with blond hair enter the clearing. As they both glared at me, the hair on the back of my neck rose and a chill swept through me. I controlled my breathing to keep from showing any signs of fear.

The dark-eyed man released his hold.

I stretched my fingers and rubbed them, feeling relieved that my hand was free without any permanent damage. "Do I know you?" I asked him, keeping my tone even.

"No."

"Weren't you at my parents' funeral, Martin and Samantha Jones?"

"Why would I have gone to your parents' funeral?" he asked with a solemn expression on his face.

"You look familiar, that's all." I started to move around him so I could walk back on the trail and escape.

"Where do you think you're going?" he asked.

"To finish my hike."

"You can't hike around out here."

"Why?"

"Because you are on my property and I don't allow trespassers."

"I'm sorry," I apologized. "I'm staying with a friend. Since there wasn't a fence, I thought it would be okay to explore the woods."

"It's not," he growled. "I don't allow people to go into the woods. My house isn't far from here. I'll walk with you to my place, and you can take the road to where you're staying."

"I can just follow the path back," I said, refusing to make eye contact. No way did I want to go to his house.

He grabbed my upper arm. "No. Like I said, I don't allow people in my woods. You can call someone from my house to come get you if you don't want to walk on the road. The trail isn't an option."

"Where I'm staying is close. I won't be on it long."

He tightened his hold. "That isn't an option."

I moved my hand on top of his. "You don't have to hold onto me." I tried to free my arm.

"This way I'm sure you'll get off my property."

He was too strong. I knew I couldn't break away from his grip so I stopped trying. He led me farther down the path. The shorter man followed. We all had cobwebs in our hair. It didn't seem to bother them. I could feel my hands getting moist and trembling as I wondered if he had any plans for me when we reached his house.

The path forked. I was taken down the left one. The three of us remained silent as we continued moving along. The trees in front of us thinned out. I saw a large, two-story, red brick, colonial house with a porch that wrapped around it. The house appeared to be at least 10,000 square feet. The black-haired woman and two men came out the front door. The woman walked toward us, while the men remained on the porch looking in our direction.

"Don't tell me you ran into another trespasser?" she asked.

"Yes, I did." He turned to me. "Do you want to walk on the road to where you're staying, or would you like to call someone?"

I certainly didn't want to go into his house. "I'll take the road back. I'm sorry about the trespassing."

He glared at me and released my arm. "Don't let it happen again."

"It won't," I assured him, although that wasn't my intention. Next time, I would bring something to brush away the cobwebs to better see the clearing and the surrounding trees. I pulled cobwebs out of my hair as I strolled down the driveway. I passed some people. A few I recognized from the clearing. They all looked to be in their mid-to-late twenties.

Maybe the cult, or whatever it was, only allowed members around that age.

I sensed I was being watched, even if I couldn't hear anyone behind me. I reached the road and turned around. No one was in plain sight, still, I couldn't shake the feeling that eyes were following me with every step I took. My t-shirt clung to me, drenched in perspiration. I looked for a mailbox and hoped it would have a number on it. There wasn't one. I breathed deeply, trying to calm myself. I didn't relax until I reached Rex's driveway. Just then Brett pulled in, stopped the car next to me, and got out.

"Where have you been?" he asked. "You look a mess."

"Exploring the woods. I ran into a lot of cobwebs and fell down. When I was getting the webs off me, a guy told me I was trespassing. He wouldn't even let me follow the trail back to the house."

He hugged me. "I should've warned you. The neighbor is very protective about his property. He doesn't allow trespassers."

"He stayed at the Towne Hotel. I saw him there. Why did he stay there when he owns a mansion so close to town?"

"No idea," Brett replied. "Rex told me his neighbor is a little strange."

A little strange was definitely an understatement.

Lindsey opened the car door and yelled, "We need to get the ice cream in the freezer before it melts."

Brett glanced up the long driveway. "Do you want a ride?"

"No, I'll walk."

After taking a shower to get the cobwebs out of my hair, I went to the kitchen and asked Brett, "Did you take the battery out of my car?"

"Why would I do that?" his voice was intense. "Were you going someplace?"

"I wanted to drive around the neighborhood so I could figure out where we are. I guess I'll have to check it out on foot."

"There aren't sidewalks around here. It's too dangerous to walk along the side of the road."

"I can watch for cars. That's not a problem. I just don't like not knowing where I am."

He took my hand and led me away from the kitchen. "If it's that important to you, the address here is 12940 Break View Drive. I would appreciate it if you didn't give out the address. Rex wouldn't like anyone from the police department showing up here. That could happen if you tell it to the Lieutenant."

I stroked his arm. "Thank you. I won't give anyone the address." I paused. "What about Lindsey?"

"She doesn't need to know."

"I'm still puzzled about my missing battery. Why would anyone do such a thing, especially so far from the city?"

"I'm baffled too. I didn't realize this was a crime area."

"Lunch is ready," Lindsey shouted. "Come get it while it's hot."

As soon as we were through eating, Brett left for his office. I finished my laundry and read *The Jewel Box* while Lindsey worked on her resume. I was itching to go back and skulk around the woods, but with Lindsey hanging about, any possibility of sneaking off was slim.

It was dusk when Brett walked through the door. "Does that smell good. Prime rib?" he asked Lindsey.

"Yep, with my special sauce."

We sat down at the table. Brett opened a bottle of wine.

After dinner, we got in the Jacuzzi and finished the wine. Since it was Saturday night, Lindsey went to the kitchen and brought out another bottle.

"I can't believe the neighbor wouldn't let you walk back on the path." She filled up the wine glasses. "What did he think you were going to do? Stomp on some of the weeds, kill a bush, climb a tree?"

We laughed.

"If he doesn't want trespassers, he needs to fence in his property," Brett said.

Lindsey and I agreed.

"Rex did say he was peculiar."

"Do you work with any single guys?" Lindsey asked Brett.

"Yes. Three. What kind of a guy do you like—short, tall, potbellied, skinny?"

"Someone that looks like you," she answered in a flirty tone.

Brett grinned. "Let me think." He rubbed his chin. "Maybe Rex. He's in Texas and won't be back for awhile."

Her eyes focused on Brett's face while she took another sip of wine. "There's got to be someone closer."

"The potbellied guy doesn't live far from here."

"No, he's got to have a firm body like you." She trailed a finger up his muscular arm. "Think harder."

I left for the bathroom as they joked and flirted with each other. If I had to worry about Brett and other women, then the sooner I knew the better. At the same time, I already knew he wasn't trustworthy. Whatever game he was playing, I'd pretend nothing was wrong until I could leave without raising any suspicion. Also, my body's sexual arousals didn't allow me to ignore him.

We polished off the second bottle and decided to watch a DVD. We went inside, changed out of our wet swimsuits and Lindsey put on a James Bond movie, *Casino Royale*.

Moments later, I found myself struggling to stay awake, possibly because I didn't sleep well the night before. I snuggled up to Brett on the sofa and put my head on his shoulder.

He nudged me when I was sleeping soundly. "Do you want to go to bed?"

"Sorry, I just can't seem to stay awake. Maybe I drank too much wine." I pushed down on the armrest and rose to my feet.

"I'll be up as soon as the show ends," Brett said.

Lindsey was curled up in a chair. "Goodnight."

"See you in the morning," I muttered, shuffling toward the stairs. When I reached the bedroom, I flipped off my shoes and collapsed on the bed.

"She won't need a robe," I heard a man say.

I didn't want to open my eyes as hands yanked on my arms. "I need to sleep," I mumbled.

My feet went over the edge of the bed. I was pulled to a standing position. I fell into a pair of arms and opened my eyes; I couldn't focus. Hands gripped my shoulders. I blinked several times and discovered my face was only an inch from the dark-eyed man. I slowly raised my hand up to his cheek and uttered, "Are you the neighbor?"

He placed his hand over my eyes. "Sleep," he whispered.

After I closed my eyes, he lifted me and held me in his arms. I tried to open my eyes again. My eyelids were too heavy. I listened to his beating heart while I was jarred up and down. The wind blew on my face. I opened my mouth to taste it. A hand brushed against my hair. I heard talking. The voices folded into each other.

"Will she be ready soon?" a woman asked.

"Shhh," a man said.

I was lowered onto a chair and his hands moved to my shoulders. I struggled to raise my eyelids. I managed to open only one eye. I felt dizzy as I looked at the shadowy, dark figures milling around in front of me. A gap appeared between two of them. I caught a glimpse of the altar and saw a sagging arm. A glass touched my lips.

"Drink," a man demanded.

I followed his order and took a big gulp. I gagged and coughed, spewing liquid everywhere.

The dark-eyed man wiped my face. "Drink slowly," he said, pressing the glass against my mouth.

I sipped; it tasted sweet. The glass was raised from my lips. A woman with blonde, curly hair bent down and pushed something into my mouth.

"No," the dark-eyed man said, reaching into my mouth and yanking it out. "You need to cut it smaller."

I couldn't keep my eye opened any longer; my eyelid closed. A soft hand stroked my cheek, gently opened my mouth and eased a small piece of something in. Its texture felt like meat as I chewed and swallowed. The flavor was good and juicy. More pieces went into my mouth. I ate each one slowly, savoring every bite.

"That's enough," a man said.

Warm breath covered my face as I heard a sigh. Then I felt lips against mine. Someone lifted me from the chair. I fell back to sleep.

The early morning light filled the room when I stirred to see Brett climbing into bed.

"I didn't mean to wake you," he said, slipping his arm under my neck. "Just got up to make a few phone calls." He pulled me closer. "I don't think you moved once last night."

I glanced under the covers. "I went to bed with my clothes on. Did you take them off?"

"Yes, after the movie. I didn't think you would sleep well wearing jeans. You must have been tired." He raised my head and kissed me.

Feeling his body next to mine sent a surge of excitement through me. I knew he was up to something, but I still wanted him. I wrapped both my arms around his neck. Our breath and flesh intertwined.

He brushed his lips against my cheek. "I'm glad you slept well last night."

"Breakfast is ready," Lindsey yelled.

"Doesn't she know it's Sunday?" I asked. "Sleep-in day."

"That's my fault. She was in the kitchen when I went to the den. She asked if I was ready for breakfast and I said yes. She said it would be about an hour before she had everything cooked. She was making biscuits, hash browns, bacon, and who knows what else."

"We'd better get up. We don't want to upset the chef. She's a great cook."

I had just taken my first bite when I wanted him again and stroked his thigh. He gazed at me and smiled. I laid down my fork; my appetite was gone. Tremors ran through my muscles as my desire for him escalated. My hands vibrated against the armrests. My feet twitched and I bit my lower lip. It was becoming unbearable.

"You okay?" Lindsey asked.

"Yes," I replied, gasping for air as I stood up. "I need to talk to Brett for a minute."

He gave me a puzzled look.

I took his hand, led him into the den, and kissed his neck as I unbuckled his belt.

"Can you wait until after breakfast?" he asked, holding my trembling hands.

My lips quavered. "No." I pressed up against him, and nibbled on his ear lobe.

His eyes lit up as I tugged him down to the floor. Our bodies entangled with brute force as we quickly made love.

"Lindsey is going to wonder what's taking us so long." He sat up. "We better get back to breakfast."

"Don't leave me," I pleaded. I'd never been this sexually aroused before; it became a need, not just a desire. I knew this sensation was abnormal. I had no idea how to suppress it. My fingers moved down his body.

"Okay," he said, grasping my hands. "Go upstairs, I'll be there soon. I need to say something to Lindsey before she comes looking for us."

"How long will you be?"

He kissed my cheek. "Ten minutes."

"Promise?"

He nodded.

I didn't want to wait that long, but he was right. Brett got dressed while I put on my t-shirt and panties. Then I carried the rest of my clothes upstairs.

I lay in bed, starring at the clock while my heartbeat raced and my fists tapped my thighs in burning anticipation. My teeth began to chatter. My eyes fixed on the door. What is taking him so long? He promised. Finally, he entered. He undressed and climbed in bed. Neither one of us spoke. We made love until exhaustion stopped us. He held me close as I drifted into a blissful slumber.

9

ASSIGNMENT

I awakened from a fitful sleep, reaching out for Brett. He wasn't lying next to me. My eyes moved around the room; he was nowhere in sight. I felt calm and relieved I was alone. The intense sexual hunger that encompassed all my thoughts had dissipated. I needed to sort out what was wrong with me. How could I act like a nymphomaniac?

My mind drifted to last night. Even if I couldn't recall all the details, I knew it wasn't a dream. The place existed. It might have seemed an optical illusion, but my visceral sense assured me I had been involved in a sacramental ceremony in the woods. I just couldn't understand why the cult would want me to be there and see their ritual. My thoughts tumbled to Lindsey as I wondered how I could keep her safe. As much as I worried about the consequences, she had to be warned. It wasn't fair to her that she didn't know about the danger lurking in the woods. Next time Lindsey and I were alone, I'd tell her and try to sway her not to go to the police since more lives would be lost.

I glanced at the clock and discovered I had slept all day. It was almost seven in the evening. Fulfilling my lustful desires must be taking more out of me than I realized. I needed to find a way to prevent them from controlling my very existence. But how? Confused, I dressed and headed downstairs.

Lindsey and Brett were sitting in the living room chatting when I walked in.

"Are you feeling better?" Lindsey asked as if I had been ill.

"Yes, I feel fine."

Brett strolled over to me, put his arm around my shoulders, and whispered, "I enjoyed our morning nap."

"I think I've got my hormones under control."

"Oh, that's too bad," he teased.

The corners of my mouth curved up as our eyes met. I thought about how much I liked him and wished he wasn't up to something.

"Are you hungry?" Lindsey asked. "We had lasagna about an hour ago. I can warm some for you."

"I feel starved. I can warm it up myself."

"No." Lindsey jumped up and moved toward the kitchen. "I'll take care of it. Sit down and relax. This will just take a few minutes."

Brett and I sat on the sofa. "Sorry," I said, feeling embarrassed. My behavior, throwing myself at him like a nymphomaniac, was inexcusable. "I ruined your breakfast. I don't know what came over me."

"Ruined? No. Improved." He softly kissed my lips.

I glanced at the coffee table to see the newspaper opened to the movie section. "Are you thinking about going to a movie?"

"We were talking about it. Do you want to go?"

"Yes. We haven't been to a show for a while." I picked up the newspaper. "The one that's circled, *Caesar's Revenge*, starts in a little over an hour. The girls at work talked about it. It's supposed to be a great movie."

"Okay. We've got a date. We'll leave as soon as you're finished eating."

"What about Lindsey?"

"She wants to go, too. I'll be the envy of all the guys in the theater."

I quickly ate and then went upstairs to get ready to go. While I brushed my hair, my cell phone rang. I plucked it out of my purse. "Hello," I answered.

"Is this Sara Jones?" a man asked.

"Yes."

"This is Lieutenant Barnes. A staff member from the hospital thought a mug shot we just received looked like one of the fellows who wheeled out the gurney. Could you come in tomorrow morning to look at it?"

"Of course. I'll be there around eight."

Brett walked into the bedroom and gazed at me.

"Thank you, Miss Jones. We'll see you tomorrow."

"Bye." I clicked off my phone.

"Who was that?" Brett asked with an edge to his voice.

"Lieutenant Barnes. He wants me to come in tomorrow to look at a few more mug shots. I told him I'd be there at eight."

"Do you want me to go with you?"

"No, I've gotten used to going there."

At the theater, Lindsey and I went inside; Brett got in line to buy the tickets.

"Brett sure is crazy about you. He talked about you all afternoon," Lindsey said.

"What did he say?"

"How much he loves the way your eyes twinkle when you smile, and you're a gentle spirit, soft and warm. How he likes hiking with you. Going places with you. Stuff like that. I wish I was that special to someone."

"You will be. Just give it time." I felt a cold chill and glanced toward the door. I gasped when I saw the dark-eyed man entering the lobby. A wave of terror swept down my spine. My eyes opened wider. How could he have followed me?

Lindsey touched my arm. "What's wrong?"

I swallowed hard. "The guy...the guy by the door is Rex's neighbor."

She turned. "Oh, is he good looking. Can you introduce me?"

"Are you serious?" I asked in disbelief.

"Yeah. He doesn't look like a villain. He doesn't have bulging eyes or a sinister face."

"I don't want you going out with him, and besides I don't know his name."

"Oh, come on. I'm sure he's harmless. Maybe Brett can introduce us."

"I don't want to meet him."

Brett came in carrying the tickets.

"Do you know Rex's neighbor?" Lindsey asked.

"I've met him. Why?"

"I want you to introduce us." Lindsey's eyes widened in excitement. "He's standing by the door."

Brett looked over his shoulder. "Yes, that's him. Okay, let's go over."

"I'll stay here," I flinched.

Brett took my hand. "He isn't dangerous. He's just protective about his property. You'll be safe."

Reluctantly, I went with them.

"Lance," Brett began, "I'd like you to meet Rex's house guests. This is Lindsey Farrington and Sara Jones. I believe you've already met Sara."

"Yes," he said, stretching out his hand. "I'm sorry our first meeting wasn't more pleasant."

I gave Lance a thin-lipped smile as we shook hands.

"Lindsey and Sara, this is Lance Alston," Brett said.

"I'm happy to make your acquaintance, Lindsey," Lance said, shaking her hand.

"Oh, I'm so glad to meet you." Lindsey's cheeks glowed.

She continued talking to him, and I looked away. Standing this close to him, all I could think about were my visions of the bleeding man on the altar, the woods choked with spider webs, and the knife dripping with blood used to slice open the torso.

"You're being awfully quiet," Brett whispered. "Are you feeling okay?"

"Just smelling the popcorn. Let's get some for the movie."

"Nice seeing you again, Lance," Brett said. "Sara and I are going to get some popcorn."

Lance nodded as Brett led me away. Lindsey stayed to chat.

Five minutes later, she joined us. I felt relieved since I didn't think she was safe around that guy.

About an hour and a half into the movie, my skin began tingling. My breathing became erratic as sexual desires started emerging. I wanted Brett again. Not here. Not now. What's wrong with me? I pressed my lips together and briefly closed my eyes. I couldn't stop the need running through my body. I rubbed Brett's leg.

He kissed me and placed his hand on top of mine, preventing it from moving. With my other hand, I grasped onto his arm.

"You okay?" he whispered.

"I want you," I purred into his ear.

"Can we see the rest of the show first?"

"Maybe." My fingers dug deeper into his arm. He didn't seem to notice. I no longer knew what was happening on the screen. I closed my eyes again and bit my lower lip as I anxiously waited for the movie to end.

Finally, the roll-up end credits appeared and we went to the lobby. Lindsey saw Lance and left to talk to him.

"I want to go home," I said, clinging onto Brett's arm. "Tell Lindsey we have to leave."

"I'll take care of it." He walked over to them. Within a minute he returned. "Lance is going to drive Lindsey home."

I could only think about one thing, and it wasn't Lindsey's safety. Without saying a word, I took Brett's hand, and we exited the theater.

The glow of car headlights leaving the parking lot flashed into my eyes and almost blinded me as we made our way down the sidewalk.

A guy on a bicycle snatched my purse as he rode past us. I screamed. Brett bolted after him. I had never seen anyone run that fast before.

A car screeched to a stop next to me. "Sara," the driver said. "Get in the car. Conner sent us."

"No," I objected, feeling restless to be alone with Brett. "Tell Conner I'll call him tomorrow."

"Sara," he paused, his eyes fixed on something behind me.

Brett had returned with my purse. "Is this guy bothering you?"

"No. He just wanted directions to the Stanton Hotel."

Brett moved between me and the guy in the car. "The hotel is on this street. Pull out of the parking lot and turn right. It's only a couple of blocks away."

After I watched the car drive away, I climbed into Brett's car. "Thank you for getting my purse. I'm glad you didn't get hurt in the process. You never know if thieves are carrying weapons."

"I was able to grab your purse without incident, but couldn't stop the jerk from fleeing." He slid into the driver's seat.

Wondering if I was a targeted victim, I wanted to ask questions about the purse snatcher. With my body's overwhelming need, I found it impossible to think about it now. As soon as Brett shut the door, I put my arms around his neck, kissed him, and started taking off his shirt.

"Can I move the car so we're in a more private location?"

"Hurry," I replied, clutching my hands as I wished for control over the burning desire.

He drove to the back of the parking lot. I undressed both of us. He tried to help, but he was too slow. My fingernails scratched across his flesh as we made unrestrained love in his vehicle. The urgent need subsided, and we put back on our clothes.

"I don't know what's wrong with me," I said, upset about forcing him to satisfy my sexual outbursts. "I've never been this out of control before. At breakfast and again at the theater. How am I going to go to work tomorrow? I might attack Mr. Johnson."

"Who's Mr. Johnson?"

"The office manager. He's short, bald, fat, and completely harmless."

"Good."

"He is a man. If I started attacking him, he probably wouldn't stop me because he wouldn't know how to say no. He's too nice of a guy."

He kissed me. "I'll make sure I have my cell phone on all the time. If you get that urge, give me a call. I'll be there in five minutes." He cocked his brow and his eyes shimmered. "After all, I have to protect Mr. Johnson."

The house was dark when we got there. I checked Lindsey's room, thinking she might have gone to bed. "She's not home. She should've been here by now."

"Lance probably took her out to get a drink or something. Don't look so worried. I'm sure she's safe."

We went upstairs. When I finished showering, Brett wasn't in the bedroom. I wanted to know if Lindsey was back, so I headed downstairs. On the way, I heard Brett talking in the den and assumed he was talking to Lindsey. I abruptly stopped when he said, "She has got to be the best assignment I've ever had."

Assignment? Was he talking about me? Am I his assignment? I eased closer, wanting to know whom he was chatting with. Through the openings next to the door hinges, I saw he was on his cell phone. I backed away to continue listening.

"You can't give her any more unless she needs it before the transformation."

I felt a lump in my throat. Transformation?

"That's normally what happens...She didn't go that way...Relax... She's special. I'll take good care of her...Her appetite is insatiable. I love it....I've never been with anyone before who acquired such an overwhelming sexual drive. I didn't think she'd make it through the movie." He chuckled. "I guess she takes after her dad."

He didn't know my dad...Did he?

"Her birthday is nine days away...If you need to prolong it...Only one more phase. I know she can't be ready too early...Yeah, I won't forget... He might be... Do you think that's possible?... I'll let you know .... Enjoy your evening...Tomorrow..."

He began moving around in the den, and I tiptoed upstairs. I still didn't know if Lindsey was home, but I didn't want Brett to see me. Climbing in bed, I thought about what he had said. Transformation. My hands shook. A clutching sinking sensation grew in my chest as fear gripped my mind. I couldn't remember ever telling him my birthday. Tears welled in my eyes as I realized his passion and the special way he treated me was his job. I wondered how much he got paid for being a masterful trickster.

Before I suspected he was up to something, I actually believed he could fill the hole in my heart left by Conner. Biting my lips to control the sobs, I grabbed several tissues and wiped my face. If I didn't compose myself, I might not survive to escape. I rolled on my side, breathed slowly, and envisioned a life without him. Hearing heavy footsteps on the stairs, I sat up in bed and adjusted the pillows. He had deceived me and played with my emotions. He lied to me. I decided to show him I was just as capable of deception as he was.

He walked in carrying a bottle of water. "I thought you might be thirsty." He twisted the top off and handed it to me.

I forced a smile. "Thanks."

He looked at me for a minute. "Are you okay?"

"I was just having a hard time waiting for you."

He grinned, took off his clothes, and eased under the sheets. "You don't need to wait any longer."

10

DISCOVERIES

The next morning, I heard birds singing. I felt relaxed and hoped that I could make it through the day without any erotic desires. Brett wasn't in the room. I didn't want to find myself in his arms again. The man who had trifled with my affections for money. I showered and dressed for work. My purse was lying under his jeans so I moved them. Something fell out of his pocket and rolled under the bed. I bent down to retrieve it. Picking it up, I saw it was a ring with a black stone. I held it next to mine. It was a perfect match; every detail was the same. I pondered about the ring as I slipped it back in his pocket and picked up my purse.

Brett held my hand as we drove away from Rex's place while I hid the confusion, fear, and loathing that consumed my thoughts. On top of everything, he was still responsible for my moments of happiness in Billings. He was also part of the horror that surrounded me. Gently squeezing my fingers, he gave me a warm smile. I stroked his arm and pretended nothing was wrong.

He glanced at Lindsey in the back seat. "I'll drop you off at the employment agency. Give me a call if you need a ride for job interviews."

"Thanks, I'll let you know." Lindsey pulled a few strands of hair behind her ear. "Sara, we still on for lunch?"

"Yeah." Although, I hoped to be gone by then.

Brett stopped in front of the police station, walked around the car, and opened my door. "Remember, I'll have my cell phone with me all the time in case you need me."

"I won't forget," I said, trying to hide the disgust I felt toward him.

He slightly narrowed his eyes. "Are you okay?"

I nodded and headed toward the entrance.

Barnes and Harmon were waiting in a conference room when I arrived. I was escorted in by the desk sergeant.

"Good morning," I said.

Dispensing with social niceties, Barnes got right to the point. "We had another spider incident last night."

"What happened?"

"A man displaying the same symptoms as the other victims was found lying next to a bike. An emergency room doctor confirmed he had been bitten by something. He's in a coma. The hospital lab is in the process of running tests on the man's blood to determine the type of venom.

"The way the bike was positioned beside his body, we are confident he was riding it when it occurred. A woman called 9-1-1 after she spotted him on the ground. She used a pay phone and didn't identify herself. We were able to identify the victim because he had a police record."

My purse snatcher on the bike. I suspected Brett or someone in his cannibal club was probably responsible.

"The hospital doctors aren't familiar with treating this type of reaction. They've called in a doctor from North Dakota who specializes in spider and insect bites. He should be here sometime today." He flipped through a folder, pulled out a picture, and laid it on the table. "Do you recognize this man?"

As I stared at it, fear tingled up my spine. I held my lips tightly together, attempting not to show any emotion. A cult member. The blond, muscular man whose face had been captured on the picture had been in the woods. I took a shallow breath and calmly said, "I don't think he was one of the paramedics. Have you been able to locate any of the missing spider victims?"

"No. Every lead we get ends up being a dead end." He pushed his chair away from the table and stood up. "Thank you, Miss Jones, for coming in."

"I wish I could help more." I picked up my purse.

As Harmon escorted me toward the entrance, he stopped. "Wait here, I have to get some paperwork for you."

I stayed next to the information desk, glanced around, and noticed the name Ellis under a picture on their bulletin board. I strolled over to it. Ellis was a good-looking guy with dark, brown hair, brown eyes, and a warm smile.

"Do you know him?" Harmon asked, walking toward me with a folder.

"He looks familiar," I lied. "Is Ellis his first or last name?"

"Last name." He glimpsed at the back of the picture. "His first name is Simon. He lives in Portland."

"Why is his picture on this bulletin board?" My eyes fixed on it. Lindsey went to see someone by that name. Could he be the same guy?

"He's missing. People go missing all the time. We can't post all of them on the bulletin board. One of his friends heard him mention Billings. We want his face to be familiar in case one of us sees him."

"Has he been missing for long?"

"A little over a week."

Lindsey was in Portland when he went missing.

"From what we've been told, he doesn't have any known enemies. He has a girlfriend. She's also missing. We don't have a picture of her yet. He just turned twenty-five. He probably went off with her someplace to celebrate." He paused. "Are you sure you don't know him?"

"I've never been to Portland."

"Do you think you might have seen him at the Towne Hotel?"

"Maybe." I shook my head, mesmerized by the picture. Then I turned away. "I need to get back to work."

Harmon pulled out a printed sheet from his folder. "Here," he said, handing it to me. "It's a generic list of common questions that witnesses have had during an investigation and answers. If you have any specific questions, contact Lieutenant Barnes or myself. Our phone numbers are on the bottom." He led me to the exit. "Thank you for coming in so quickly, Miss Jones."

"You're welcome." As I headed toward my office, my mind stayed focused on Simon Ellis. That wasn't a common name. He was the same age as the guy Lindsey had talked about on the bus. It had to be the same Simon. A spasm of panic struck, and my lips quivered as I recalled Brett discussing my birthday on the phone. Simon had just turned twenty-five. I was going to be twenty-five soon. Was there a connection? Lindsey didn't hesitate leaving last night with Lance Alston, even after I had told her about my encounter with him in the woods. My thoughts drifted from wondering if Lindsey was also a target or perhaps another cult member. Confused, scared, and bewildered, a tear trickled down my cheek. I wiped it away with my fingertips. I needed to leave Billings—fast!

11

ESCAPE

I sat at my desk and removed the ring. Just like the last time when I took it off, my hand ached and my fingers curved in. This time the gnawing pain traveled up to my shoulder. I slipped it back on. The pain vanished. After staring at the ring for a moment, I called Conner.

"Sara, are you okay?" he asked, and I heard the concern in his voice.

"Yes," I said, softly, as I still thought about the pain I experienced every time I removed the ring; I felt confused about it.

"Why didn't you get in the car last night?"

"How did you know I was going to be at that theater?"

"First, I want to know something," he said without answering my question.

"What?"

"What is your relationship with Brett Daborel?"

I never told him Brett's name, but I knew the Crussetts had ways of finding out what they wanted to know. "I met him when I lived at the hotel. He also lived there, and we became friends. After the spider incidents, he was going to his friend's place that had five bedrooms. He asked if I wanted to stay there. I thought it was a good idea to get away from the hotel. Now I suspect he's somehow involved with the spider problem. I need to leave."

"One of my men saw you kissing him."

"That's true. Brett wants us to be more than friends, but I can't stop thinking about you." I waited for him to say something. The phone was silent as I worried about how much he knew. I just hoped he hadn't been told how far my relationship with Brett had really gone. "Conner, are you still there?"

"Yes. When can I come and get you?"

"First, I need to know how you knew I'd be at that theater last night," I asked again.

"I have ten men in Billings. They've been there since Friday. One was bitten by a spider and taken to a hospital in a coma. We know what type of car Brett drives and his license plate number. My men tried to follow him on Friday after he picked you up. It appears he knows how to lose tails. They've been driving around searching for his car. Over the weekend I instructed them to concentrate on the theaters because I know how much you enjoy movies. We got lucky. I was disappointed to hear you didn't get in the car."

"I wanted to have a head start before Brett realized I'd left. He isn't alone. A group will be looking for me. They have a habit of using poisonous spiders to kill people. Your men wouldn't be safe. No one is when they're around."

"Finish filling me in when I see you. Have you got a plan for leaving?"

"Can you come and get me now?"

"I've been staying in Helena. I can be there in an hour. How are you going to get to the airport?"

"There's a parking garage underneath my building. You need a badge to activate the entrance gate, but not to leave. Can one of your men follow someone into the garage or find some way to get in there? Then I could take the elevator down and no one would see me."

"I'll have Mont and Sam pick you up. One of them will give you a call when they're in the garage. They can be there in about half an hour."

"Eat a lot of oysters on your way here."

He laughed. "I've missed you, too. See you in an hour."

After he hung up, I called Lindsey.

"Hi, Sara. Are you ready to go grab a bite to eat?"

"Hey, Lindsey. It took longer at the police station than expected. I need to finish a big project, so I have to work through lunch and stay late tonight."

"You still need to eat."

"There's a sandwich machine in the break room. I'll get one and eat at my desk."

"I have something special planned for dinner. You will be home for dinner, won't you?"

"I think I'll only need to stay an extra hour. What are you cooking?"

"It's a surprise. You'll have to wait and see."

"How's the job hunting going?"

"I have an interview this afternoon at Cooper Investments. They're located just a block from where you are."

"That would be great. Then we could go to lunch often," I said, enthusiastically, as I pretended I'd be staying in Billings.

"Wish me luck."

"Good luck. See you later."

"Bye." I disconnected, feeling guilty. Lindsey might not be involved with any of the horror going on. She could be completely innocent, in danger, and I didn't warn her. I couldn't leave her like that. I quickly wrote a note:

> *Dear Lindsey,*
> *You need to leave Rex's house immediately! You might be in danger. Rituals are happening in the woods behind his house. Don't go out there. They use poisonous spiders. Get out of Billings as soon as you can!*
> *Sara*

I slipped the note into an envelope, sealed it, wrote Lindsey Farrington on it, and placed it on my desk in clear sight. Then I called Brett.

"I didn't think you'd need me this soon," he teased.

"That's not why I'm calling," I said. My hands were trembling. "I have a project that has to be done today. And with going to the police station, I'm behind schedule. So I'm going to work late tonight." My bottom lip quivered, hoping he would buy it.

"How late?"

"An hour or two. I'll call you when I'm finished. Or should I plan on taking a taxi to Rex's place?"

"No. I'll pick you up. I'll stay at work until you're through."

"What about Lindsey?"

"Let me call her," he replied. "Do you think you'll want to see me before you get off work?"

His obvious hint was not lost on me, and I wanted to shout no. At the same time, I didn't want to take a chance that he might get suspicious. "Maybe. I'm hoping I can wait."

"I'm hoping you can't."

"I'll call if I need you. Bye." I found myself torn as I put down the receiver. Despite what I'd learned about Brett, some strange internal connection had me strongly attracted to him. I knew I'd miss him.

Marsha came into my office carrying a stack of folders. "Can you finish the Bradshaw report by tomorrow?" She put a folder on my desk.

"Yeah, no problem," I lied, glancing at the top page.

"Thanks." She turned and walked out of my office.

I put away my work and tried to concentrate on the requested report. Instead, I found myself staring at my phone and thinking about Conner.

I had only worked for his family's investment company in San Diego for a month when I first saw him. Almost every girl in the office was crazy about him. They had given me the lowdown on Conner from what he had in his coffee to his birthday, so I knew he was eight years older than me. He was so good-looking I didn't give his age a second thought. After we were introduced and shook hands, I remembered blushing when he didn't let go of my hand. He teasingly said he wouldn't let go unless I agreed to go to lunch with him. That was how our relationship began. He flew into town often to see me and tried to persuade me to transfer to the Houston office. Then he wanted me to quit my job and live with him. Finally, I agreed to move into his house, but not to quit my job, so I transferred to the Houston office.

The phone rang, startling me out of my reverie. I grabbed the receiver, "Hello."

"Sara Jones?" a deep, gruff male voice asked.

"Yes."

"This is Mont. We're in the garage."

"I'll be right down." Relief and fear encompassed me at the same time as I took the money and driver's license out of my drawer, slipped them into my purse, pulled out my cell phone, and placed it on top of a file cabinet. Then I walked out without clearing off my desk and hurried through the back hallway.

Mr. Johnson was waiting by the elevator.

"I just need to run to the bank for a minute," I said, as we stepped into the elevator.

He smiled and pushed the button to the first floor. I swallowed hard and held my breath. Then he pushed the button to the third floor.

When he got off, I pressed the button to the garage. I stood in the front corner of the elevator, hidden from view, and watched out of the corner of my eye as the doors opened on the first floor. My heart pounded and I took a deep breath, waiting for the doors to close. Finally, the elevator reached the garage level. Stepping out, I saw two muscular men wearing polo shirts and slacks standing next to a black sedan.

"Sara?" the taller one asked.

"Yes."

"I'm Mont. This is Sam." He opened the car door.

After I slid into the backseat, Mont closed the door. I eased down to the floor to avoid being seen leaving the building. Then I heard the engine accelerate and felt the car moving.

Fifteen minutes later, the car began jerking up and down, like we were traveling over chuck holes on an unpaved road. It didn't make sense that we'd be on this type of pavement going to the airport. A grim thought seized my mind. My hands trembled as I wondered if Conner had arranged for another destination—someplace I'd never be found.

Mont peeked over the seat at me. "Sorry about that. This road is full of potholes."

I sighed with relief.

He continued, "We're away from downtown Billings. I don't see anyone following us. You can move up to the seat."

"I'm going to stay down here until we reach the airport." That feeling started to emerge. Oh, no. Not again. I opened my mouth and breathed deeply, hoping it would pass. The muscles in my legs twitched. My heartbeat raced. I clinched my hands into fists, trying to stop it.

"Are you okay?" Mont asked.

"Yes. I guess, I'm just feeling nervous." I gasped for air. "Is Conner at the airport?"

"Let me check." Mont pulled out his cell phone and punched a number. "Has Mr. Crussett arrived? ... Yes, she's with us ... We're five minutes away..." He put his phone in his pocket. "He's there."

Oh, could I wait? My lips quivered as the erotic need intensified. Staring at the back of Mont's head, I thought he seemed like a nice guy. Oh, come on. I couldn't have sex with one of Conner's men. I got off the floor, sat on the edge of the seat, and rapidly tapped my fingertips together. Then I saw a hangar. A man stood next to it. Was that Conner? Yes, yes, it was him. My breathing became erratic as we got closer.

The car stopped. Conner opened the door. I grabbed him, yanked him inside, and unbuttoned his shirt.

"Sara, can you wait until we get in the plane?"

"No." I unfastened his belt buckle. "I've missed you so much."

"Mont, Sam, leave," Conner ordered and shut the door. We made love in the back seat.

"I've missed you," I whispered.

Conner sat up, holding onto me. "I can see that," he smiled. "I just didn't realize how much. Can we get in the plane now?"

"If we hurry," I grinned, putting on my blouse.

He pulled up his pants. "We'll hurry."

We finished dressing and got out of the car looking disheveled. His shirttails were hanging out, so was the bottom of my blouse. My hair was sticking up all over. We gazed at each other and laughed.

"Do you want to run to the plane?" he asked.

"No. I do want to walk fast."

He took my hand and we headed to the plane, passing eight of Conner's men. None of them looked familiar. I was certain they were never at his house, at least not while I was there. As we boarded the plane, the stewardess handed us each a glass of champagne.

Conner kissed me. "To us." He clicked his glass to mine, and then we drank.

I watched six of Conner's men board the plane. I had often flown with him, but never with people in the main cabin I didn't recognize. Within fifteen minutes, we were airborne. In the rear of the plane, there was a bedroom. That was where we went to catch up on time lost during our two-month separation. I loved his touch and passion as our desires were fulfilled.

"Now I know I didn't need to be worried about Brett," he surmised. I was glad he believed that.

"Have you learned anything about the people involved with the poisonous spiders?"

I wondered how much to tell him. I knew how Crussetts solved problems. Since the cult was responsible for the deaths of at least four of Conner's men, I didn't want a blood bath in Billings. Also, I didn't trust Conner. I had a strange feeling that I should be careful about what I revealed. "I know the cult does some horrible ceremonies in the woods. They're responsible for the spider-related deaths because I saw one of the missing victims at their ceremony along with a lot of spiders."

He looked at me intently. "How did you see that?"

"I stumbled on a ceremony," I said, feeling weird giving such a lame response.

"How did that happen?"

"Hiking in the woods. I was alone when I ran into it. Then I panicked and zigzagged back to the road. I tried finding the location the next day, but I couldn't."

He squeezed my hand. "Sara, you should have gone to the police."

"I know, but the police can't defend themselves against these spiders."

"Did you see that ceremony before or after you thought the spider group was after you?"

"After."

"Why do you think they wanted you?"

"Because twice at the hotel, spiders infested my room. Once, it was hundreds. And I kept seeing this one guy with dark eyes watching me along with a few others who I saw at the ceremony in the woods. I sensed I was being followed all the time." I didn't want to give him the name of the dark-eyed man or other information about him.

"Is Brett involved?"

I should have suspected that question was coming. "I know he's up to something, and all signs point to a connection with the spider cult."

"What signs?"

"I saw him sneaking my driver's license out of my purse. My car battery was taken. I'm not sure he took it. I noticed it was gone when I was staying at his friend's place."

"How does that connect him to the spider group?"

The phone call I had overheard about me being his assignment swirled around in my head, but since I didn't want Brett killed, I felt I had already said too much. "Well, I guess it doesn't. It did make it harder for me to leave."

"Do you think the reason the group was after you had anything to do with your parents?"

"I have no idea. Maybe it's something to do with me being immune to spider venom. I was bitten by several poisonous spiders when I was five. Nothing happened. Maybe somehow the spider group, cult, whatever they are, found out. The dark-eyed guy I saw in Billings was at my parents' funeral."

He hugged me. "Well, you're safe now. How are you feeling about us?"

"Isn't it obvious?"

"You can look past the family business?"

"Yes. After all, isn't your family just into investments?" That was my way of telling him I didn't want to talk about the truth.

He caressed my arm. "Yes. That's the family business." He held up my hand and kissed it. "Do you remember Bruce Carlson, our head accountant?"

"I know who he is. Why?"

"Bruce believes you took some copies of documents with you when you left. Did you?"

He already knew I did since there was a security camera by the copy machine. I gazed into his eyes. "What are you planning to do?"

He kissed my forehead. "Don't look so scared. I'm not going to hurt you. I love you. You have no idea how hard it's been without you. You left without even a note. I thought maybe you had been abducted or killed by one of my enemies." He wrapped his arms tightly around me. "Don't ever do that again."

"I'm sorry. I was just so confused. I didn't know what to do after I saw those books."

"How did you find those journals?"

"I didn't. Someone left them on my desk."

Bewildered, he asked, "Someone just left them on your desk?"

"Yes. Why would I go looking for them when I didn't know they existed?"

His eyes narrowed. "There's obviously someone working for the company who wanted you to know, maybe to break us up. Can you think of anyone?"

"No." A lopsided smile flickered on my lips. "But all the girls in the office think you're really handsome. One or more of them might have wanted to see us break up. Have you dated any of them since I've been gone?"

He looked down and held my hands. From the expression on his face, I knew he was withholding something from me.

"Where are the documents you took?" he asked with an edge to his voice as his eyes fixed on me.

I hesitated, wondering if I was safe.

"Sara, it's okay. You can tell me. You're safe."

"But what about your family?"

"I won't let them hurt you." He paused. "Don't you trust me?"

"I trust you," I said, even if I didn't. "I want us to be the way we were. Is that possible?"

"That's all I want. It might take time for my family. If you return the documents, I know our relationship can be salvaged."

Attempting to draw his attention away from the documents, I put my arms around his neck and kissed him. "I want you."

He pulled me closer just as loud static came from the speaker.

"We'll be landing in ten minutes," the pilot said over the intercom. "Please stay seated and secure your seat belt."

Conner shrugged his shoulders. "Can you believe this?" He lightly kissed me. "Bad timing."

We hurriedly dressed while the plane descended. We sat down and buckled up right before we landed.

As we were getting off the plane, the stewardess asked, "How was your flight today, sir?"

He looked at me and smiled. "That was the best flight I ever had."

Conner and I were driven straight to his home, the house I had shared with him for almost three years. I walked through the large front door and looked around at the place that was so familiar to me.

"I need to make a few calls," he said.

"I want to take a bath and relax."

"Why don't you get in the tub and I'll join you soon?" He kissed me, and then went into his den.

I headed upstairs to our bedroom. My cell phone was lying on the dresser, along with the ruby ring he had given me when I moved to Houston. I opened my jewelry box. All his gifts were still there. My clothes hung in the closet. I noticed a dress I didn't recognize. I held it up and saw it was a size larger than I wore. Also, it wasn't new.

I looked through the dresser. Everything was there, just as I left it. All I took with me was a small duffle bag. Conner thought I was going to the fitness center for a class. I only went there long enough to change my clothes and leave my cell phone and ruby ring in my locker. I wondered how long it had taken him to find them.

I strolled into the bathroom to see the large, oversized bathtub we often shared in the center of the room. I moved to the cabinet. My toothbrush was right next to his. The top drawer held my brush and combs. There was an extra hairbrush. I picked it up and examined it in the light. Whoever had used it was a blonde. Other than that, nothing had changed. I wondered how long he would have left it like this.

After turning on the bathtub faucets, I poured in bubble bath. His arms went around my waist as I took off my blouse.

He kissed my neck. "I thought you'd be in the tub by now."

"I was looking around."

"Were you looking for something?"

"No. I'm glad, just surprised, that everything is like I left it."

"That's how I wanted it so you'd feel right at home when you came back."

He probably didn't want to qualify that with an *if*. I turned and kissed him, wondering how I ever could have left him. Now, I knew there were worse evils out there. His family's business seemed mild in comparison. I got into the tub and watched him undress. He poured champagne into two glasses, handed me one, and put the bottle on the bathtub ledge as he moved into the water.

I lay between his legs with my head resting against his chest and tried not to think about anything except the way we were. This felt so good lying with him. We talked about little things and drank champagne. As soon as we got out, he dried me with a fluffy towel and carried me to the bed. I felt his warm breath as he kissed my shoulder and his hand moved gently downward.

12

RETRIBUTION

A knock on the door awoke me. Conner, already up and dressed, covered me with a blanket.

"You can come in now, Darcy," he said, sitting down at the table near the bed.

Darcy was a short, middle-aged, heavyset woman with gray-speckled brown hair. She had been Conner's housekeeper for over five years. She entered, carrying two food trays, and smiled when our eyes met. "Good morning, Miss Jones," she said, putting down a tray in front of me.

"Good morning, Darcy. How have you been?"

"Fine. We've missed you around here."

"I've missed you, too."

"Can I get anything else, Mr. Crussett?" she asked, placing the other tray on the table in front of him.

"No. That will be all."

She left, closing the door behind her.

I gazed at all the food on the tray. "Breakfast in bed."

"After yesterday, I thought you deserved it," he said between bites.

"You're the one who deserves it."

He leaned over and squeezed my hand. "I had no idea that abstinence would affect you like this. Had I known, I would have taken longer business trips." Conner traveled often on business. He was never gone for more than two nights.

Because I was happy being with him, I beamed as we ate breakfast. Then my mind drifted back to when I left him. I wondered if Lindsey had followed me all the way from Houston. On the first bus route, an elderly woman sat next to me. She convinced me that I should go to Billings. Was she somehow connected to the cult? I couldn't recall seeing Lindsey before she sat next to me on the bus in Nebraska. I instantly liked her. Did she befriend me because she was a cult member? What was Simon Ellis' connection? And what about his girlfriend? So many questions and no answers.

"What are you thinking?" Conner asked.

"Just wondering how I could have ever left you."

"Well, you're back now." He caressed my arm. "Let's try to close the hole that was left when you were gone. First, I need the documents."

My lips quivered. My eyes dropped, and I stared at the floor. I knew he'd ask about them again. I had hoped he'd wait another day.

He raised my chin and studied my face. "Sara, if you want our relationship to survive, you need to tell me the location of the documents."

"I know. They're in Nebraska."

His brows drew together in a puzzled expression. "Why Nebraska?"

I hesitated.

"Sara." He glared. "Why Nebraska?"

"The bus stop there was right next to a bank."

"So you left on a bus?"

"Yes. The bus depot was only a half a block from the fitness center."

"That was convenient for you. You didn't travel under your own name, and no one there remembered seeing you."

"I didn't want to be followed."

"What time did you get on the bus?"

"Around 9 a.m."

"You traveled under the name Ethel Martin."

I tilted my head. "How did you know?"

"I have ways of finding out things."

"What sort of things?"

"Ethel Martin's first ticket was to Rapid City, South Dakota. In Oklahoma she bought a ticket for a woman going to New York, and that woman bought a ticket to Colorado. You only used that ticket to the next bus stop. There you traded tickets. You paid women to take different routes to their destination. At one bus stop you traded tickets at least three times and paid each person five-hundred bucks."

My heart pounded in my chest as I realized I hadn't been creative enough to hide from his determined pursuit to find me. "If the spider problem in Billings hadn't caused my picture to be on the news, how long do you think it would have taken you to find me?"

"Two, maybe three more weeks."

"Would it have made any difference if I had changed my name?" I wanted to know if I had made a mistake about that.

"We weren't looking for a person using the name Sara Jones. I didn't even know you were missing until that evening." He squinted as he gazed at me. "I'm sure that's how you planned it."

I didn't respond.

He stood, put my tray on the table, and sat down next to me. "Where is this bank in Nebraska?"

"In Sidney."

"Do you have the safety deposit key with you?"

"Yes."

"Is it in your purse?"

"Yes, I'll get it." I scooted out of bed around him, took my purse from the dresser, and ripped open the inside seam. I removed the key from the lining and handed it to him.

"Thank you," he said, continuing to stare at me.

I remained quiet, slipping on my robe. The look in his eyes sent shivers up my spine.

"We're going to leave for Nebraska as soon as you're dressed." He abruptly left without saying another word.

Conner's house was located next to the homes of other family members in a gated community with security guards. Two of their top employees also owned houses here. I had been told they were executives of the investment company. I used to believe their concocted business portrayal. Their names appeared on the company stationery and they had offices in the building. When Conner was gone on business trips, I felt protected living within these walls. Now the safe haven had turned into a prison. I was trapped.

While I was in the shower, I thought about Brett. Part of me feared I'd see him again, and part of me longed for him, especially after the way Conner had questioned me. I wanted to run away from all of them. Start over again. Unfortunately, that wasn't an option. I dressed and went downstairs to meet my fate.

Conner sat at his oversized, oak desk in the den with a credenza and bookcase behind him, talking on the phone. He ended the call when he saw me. With a stern expression he rose, took my arm, and led me to the waiting limo. The chauffeur opened the door. I slid in.

Driving out of the compound, a car slowed as it passed us. A wave of terror flashed through me. The driver looked like Lance. The person in the passenger seat resembled Lindsey. Did they follow me back to Houston? If it was them, they couldn't have seen me through the limo's tinted windows.

As I attempted to figure it out, my pulse quickened. My breath came in wild gasps. My body's lustful need had returned. Not again. Conner hadn't said anything to me since he left the bedroom. The way he was acting, I didn't want him close to me. I inhaled deeply.

"Are you okay?" he asked, breaking the silence.

I squeezed my eyes shut and pressed my knees together. No matter how hard I tried, I couldn't restrain my body; the craving was too strong. "I want you so much. I can't stand it," I said, clasping onto his hand.

His expression softened and he smiled. "I just want all this business behind us." He leaned over and kissed me.

I slipped off his tie and started unbuttoning his shirt.

"Sara, this isn't a good time."

"I don't want to wait for the right time."

He kissed my neck. "Well, it is a long ride to the airport."

Conner pushed a button, sending a privacy panel across the window between us and the chauffeur. We stripped off our clothing and satisfied our passion.

Tucking in his shirt, he said, "I'm already looking forward to the plane ride."

When we arrived at the airport, we were both dressed and my hair was combed. We boarded the plane, followed by four of Conner's men. The stewardess handed us a glass of champagne, without offering anything to Conner's men. We sat down and buckled up. I glanced at the men wondering why they were going.

"We can't take off for thirty minutes," the pilot announced over the intercom.

Conner clenched his jaw, snapped off his seatbelt, and stormed into the cockpit.

About ten minutes later, he came out. His expression was hostile, furious. "Damn air traffic," he snarled as his eyes darkened. "There's an emergency, so we have to wait." He glared at the stewardess. "Get me a drink. Make it a double martini."

The stewardess jumped up and scurried to the galley. I had never seen him react like this to a delay in taking off. I had seen occasional dashes of his temper that were frightening.

Conner gulped the rest of his champagne and threw the glass against the cockpit door. It shattered, sending shards of glass across the inside of the plane. The stewardess' shoes crunched on the broken pieces as she brought him his drink. He took a swig.

"This needs more vermouth." He poured it onto the floor, splattering it on her legs.

"I'm sorry, sir," the stewardess said, reaching for the empty glass with a trembling hand. "Let me get you another one."

"Make it quick," he ordered, giving her a sharp look. "And clean up this mess."

I wanted him to calm down, but I knew it wouldn't help her if I attempted to intervene. Past experience had taught me to wait for the rage to end.

Within a minute, Conner had another drink in his hand. He tapped his fingers on the armrest while the stewardess swept up.

"Fasten your seat belts," the pilot said over the intercom. "We'll be in the air within five minutes."

Conner drained his glass and handed it to the stewardess as the plane taxied down the runway. He calmed down once we were able to go to the bedroom. I felt blood surge up into my cheeks as our bodies molded together.

After, we were lying peacefully with his arm around my shoulders and my head resting on his chest. The stern interrogator who had grilled me for information that morning was gone. I knew I'd be safe until he got the documents.

Thinking about my prior life with Conner made it hard for me to hate him, and that was what I needed to do—hate him. My heart just wouldn't let me bury those tender moments. What was wrong with me? He was dangerous. Still, I did genuinely love him. I had to somehow find a way to appease my internal struggle. Logic had to prevail and overcome my desire to be near him; otherwise, I might not survive.

Earlier I had checked my wallet to make sure nothing was missing. The money and my driver's license were right where they belonged. I thought about the bank's layout, attempting to recall how many exits it had and where they were located.

"What are you thinking?" he asked, brushing my hair from my face.

"About us. Will you ever forgive me for leaving?"

"You don't think I already have?"

"I'm not sure."

"How can I prove it to you?" he said, leaning over me.

I felt the warmth of his flesh, and our bodies became bound as we made love again.

He smiled. "Do you want more proof?"

"Let me catch my breath first," I said, returning his smile.

"Are you hungry?"

"Yes, starving."

"Do you want food brought in here or do you want to eat in the main cabin?"

Eating in the main cabin surrounded by his men wasn't anything I wanted to do. "Can we eat in here?"

"Yes." He pushed a button on the intercom. "We're ready for lunch. What's on the menu?"

"Just what you ordered: shrimp cocktails, salad, and beef stroganoff. And for dessert: chocolate cake with vanilla ice cream. Where would you like it served, sir?"

"Bring it in here."

"I'll have it right in."

We put on robes, sat at the table, and then came a knock on the door.

"Come in," Conner said.

The stewardess entered, carrying a large tray of food along with a bottle of Merlot. She placed everything on the desk, removed a tablecloth from a cabinet next to the door, and elegantly set the table before she left.

As we sipped the red wine, I wondered if maybe my arousals had something to do with the booze I had been drinking. No. I was sure it had been caused by drugs; either in the wine I drank at Rex's place, or the liquid I consumed in the woods.

"Is the wine okay?" Conner asked.

"Yes. It's good. When I was in Billings, I drank some wine that tasted like a blend of various kinds. It was almost like a mix between a Merlot and a Sauvignon Blanc. Have you ever tasted anything like that?"

"No. It sounds interesting. Did you get the name?"

"No."

We finished eating and the stewardess cleared off the table. Then we decided we needed a nap and climbed back in bed. He held me close as we dozed off.

13

RULES

"Sara." Conner awakened me, gently shaking my arm. "We have to get up. We'll be landing soon. The plane's already started to descend." I gazed at him, and he lightly kissed my lips. "Don't worry, everything will be okay."

As we put on our clothes, we had to hold onto the bed because of the turbulence. He was dressed first, sat down and buckled in, holding onto me all the time. Then he pulled me down into the chair and secured my seat belt just before we touched down.

"Boy, was that a rough landing," I said, unbuckling.

"But it was a great flight." He smiled coyly.

We disembarked and got into a waiting sedan. "Do you want me to give the driver the address?" I asked.

"No. I've got it." He leaned forward and proceeded to give the address. Sitting back on the seat, his posture stiffened as he glanced through some papers in his briefcase.

"Is everything okay?"

"Yes," he answered without looking at me.

I went to touch his arm, but he adjusted himself in the seat and placed his briefcase between us. He didn't say a word during the half an hour drive. My apprehension grew.

The car cut to the curb and he looked at me with a cold, hostile expression. When I stepped out, he grabbed my hand and held it firmly as we walked toward the bank. I wanted to cry but forced myself to remain composed while I wondered if I would be going back to Houston with him.

In the bank, my eyes darted around searching for exits. The only door available to the public was the one through which we had entered.

Outside that door was the car waiting for us with two men inside. There was no escape.

He led me over to the information desk.

"Can I help you?" a female bank clerk asked.

"Yes," Conner said. "Miss Sara Jones would like to access her safety deposit box."

The woman looked at me. "Do you have your key with you?"

"Yes," Conner answered and handed the woman the key.

She opened a cabinet, pulled out a bin of cards, flipped through them, and pulled one out. "Miss Jones, I'll need to see your driver's license."

I took my wallet out of my purse and showed her my license.

"You'll have to sign here," the clerk said, pointing to the spot, "indicating that you accessed your box today." She handed me a pen. I signed. She picked up a large key ring, and we followed her to the vault entrance. There she stopped and looked at Conner, then at me. "Would you like to go in by yourself, Miss Jones?"

Conner put his arm around my shoulders. "It's okay. Sara and I are engaged. She's getting some of my documents out of her safety deposit box."

She glanced at me, and her face creased with concern. I didn't want anyone getting hurt, so I smiled to reassure her that everything was okay. The forced effort of smiling almost brought me to tears. She unlocked the door, walked over to my deposit box, and unlocked it.

"This way," she said, leading us to a small room. She placed the box down on a table. "Let me know if you need anything." She left, closing the door.

Conner raised the box lid. On top was the note I had written. It read: "If this box is opened for non-payment, give the contents to the FBI."

He picked up the note. A muscle flinched in his jaw and his eyes narrowed as he glared at me without speaking.

My hands trembled as I held them together tightly against my chest. Looking away from him, I stared at the box. My eyes moistened as I fought back tears, fearing the love he had felt for me was gone.

He shuffled through the papers and put them in his briefcase. "Are these all the documents?"

"Yes. That's everything."

He picked up the safety deposit box and his briefcase. We walked out of the room. He put the box back in its slot, gripped my arm, and we left the vault. He handed the bank clerk my safety deposit key. "Miss Jones won't need her safety deposit box any longer," he said, and then smiled at me. "We'll be living in Texas."

"Then I'll need one more signature." She pulled out my card and I signed it. "Keep us in mind if you should move back to Nebraska. We'd be happy to take care of all your banking needs."

"Thank you," Conner said, holding firmly onto my hand. He led me back to the car.

Driving away from the bank, I looked out the window, speculating if they planned a detour on the way to the airport to get rid of me permanently. I breathed easier when we stopped at the hangar.

As I boarded the plane, the stewardess offered me a glass of champagne.

"No, thank you," I said and sat down.

She handed a glass to Conner. He sank down in the seat next to me.

I buckled up as I stared at the exit sign and wondered if he would push me out when we reached a certain altitude or have one of his men do it.

He stroked my arm. "Sara, it will all be over soon."

"That's just what I was thinking."

He chuckled. "That's not what I meant." He raised my hand and kissed it.

Conner was making me crazy. He ran hot and cold. My eyes met his and I swallowed hard. "We had a great time flying to Nebraska. Then you didn't say anything to me as we drove to and from the bank. When you opened the safety deposit box, you looked like you hated me. I can't live like this. If you're going to push me out of the plane, just do it." I lowered my head and tears trickled down my cheeks.

He wrapped his arms around me. "Relax. I'm not going to throw you out of the plane." He kissed my forehead, put his hand under my chin, and gently raised my face. "You are a shining light in my life. I found it almost unbearable when you were gone." He wiped my cheeks with his napkin. "My family has been giving me a hard time over this whole thing. After I return the documents, I'm hoping they'll ease up. I only wish you had talked to me when you saw those books. Now, it's just more difficult to work out." He softly kissed my lips. "I have never stopped loving you. I'll find a way to satisfy my family. Everything will be okay. I won't let anything happen to you." He grinned. "I've never enjoyed flying so much before. So, how about sharing the champagne?"

I gave him a half smile. "Okay."

He raised his empty glass toward the stewardess. "Miss Jones would like some champagne."

She handed a glass to me and refilled his.

It made a little more sense now why he acted distant sometimes. He was stressed. I knew how his family would like to take care of the problem. I didn't think they ever liked me. Maybe they thought I was below Conner's class since I was an employee. They were formal and polite, not warm and friendly. Then, when he read the note, he probably thought his family was right. I could never be one of them.

"Don't look so worried. I'll handle my family. In the meantime, you're going to have to follow my rules."

"Your rules? What rules?"

"I'll talk to you about them when we get home."

"What's wrong with discussing them now?"

"No. Later," he said through clenched teeth.

"Am I going to be your prisoner?"

Narrowing his eyes, he glared at me. "I said we'd discuss it when we got home."

I felt a cold chill wash over me. My lips quavered, and my breathing became labored. Then suddenly the intense sexual desire began to creep through my body. This can't be happening. Not now. My heartbeat raced as blood rushed through my veins. I gasped for air. I was on a sexual roller-coaster.

He caressed my arm. "Should we go into the bedroom?"

I attempted to control my breathing. The need churning inside me overrode my mind, and it devoured all my resistance. It dictated my every move as I stretched out my arms, pulled him closer, and kissed him.

We went into the other room, and on top of the terrible time I had in Nebraska, I couldn't stop myself from enjoying the flight as our bodies became intertwined.

Later, we were snuggled against each other in sated bliss. "Let's stay like this and shut out the rest of the world," he whispered.

"That would be nice."

"I know I'll never be able to fly again without thinking about you."

I kissed his neck. "I'm glad."

He kept his arm around my shoulders as we drove to the house. When we stopped by the gate, a couple strolled along the sidewalk. I had seen them before, in the clearing behind Rex's house. I sat up and pointed to the couple through the window. "I saw them in Billings."

Conner pushed the intercom button, "Stay put," he said to the driver. Then he looked at me. "Be right back." He got out of the limo and walked over to a security guard.

I rolled down the window.

"Find out what you can about those two," Conner said, nodding his head in the direction of the couple. "And don't let them give you anything."

"On it."

While Conner climbed in next to me, I saw the guard moving toward the couple and another guard emerging from the security building.

"Did you tell anyone in Billings you were going to Houston?" Conner asked.

"No," I replied, shaking my head. "And no one there has your address."

"If they followed you, they made a bad mistake," he said, pushing the intercom button. "You can go now."

"Yes, sir," the driver said.

As soon as we were inside the house, Conner led me into the den and shut the door. We sat on the sofa, and he held my hands.

"It's time to tell you the rules," he began. I bit my lower lip. He gently squeezed my hands. "It will be okay. First, you cannot leave the house unless it's with me." He paused. "You can go out to the swimming pool, but you can't leave the yard. Okay?"

He asked as if he was allowing me to object. I knew that wasn't an option. "Okay."

"Second, you can't make any telephone calls unless you are calling me. You can't answer the phone unless I am the one calling."

"Can I just call Paula? I want to know how she's doing. I won't talk about anything else." Paula became my best friend after I started working for the Houston investment office. We went to lunch almost every day and often talked about marrying our boyfriends. We were both waiting for a formal proposal.

"No!"

"You can even be in the room and listen when I call her," I said, trying to push a little more against his restrictions.

"No. And Paula isn't with the investment company anymore."

"Did you fire her? She didn't know I was leaving."

Conner shrugged. "I don't know why she left. I just know she's gone."

"I wonder where she went." Paula really liked her job. It didn't make sense to me she'd quit, but right now nothing seemed normal. Nothing made sense.

"Third, if someone comes here, you are to go up to our bedroom and stay there until I tell you that you can come back downstairs."

I spun my head and looked up at him. "Are you expecting company?"

"Sara," he said, sounding irritated. "Do you understand this rule?"

He must be expecting company. Who? As far as I knew he had never had business meetings here before. Things might be changing.

"Sara?"

"Yes, I'll go upstairs. What if I'm out by the swimming pool, and I don't know you have company? Will someone come and tell me?"

"If you're swimming or lying by the pool, you can stay out there. I'll have someone tell you that you can't come back in the house until I come for you. That's all the rules. Do you have any questions?"

"No. It's like I'm under house arrest. How can I go to work?" I asked, knowing that wasn't a possibility.

He rolled his eyes. "You can't." A crooked smile crossed his lips. "Besides, you don't have a job."

"I have one in Billings."

"You're not in Billings."

"Does this mean I can't have my old job back at the Investment Company?" I asked, even though I knew that would never happen.

"Correct. You will never work for my family again."

"Maybe I could just work for you."

He kissed me. "What type of work would you like to do for me?" he asked playfully.

"What type of work do you think I'm qualified for?"

"How about cleaning the pool and doing a little yard work?"

I thought he was going to mention personal services. I was glad he didn't go there. "You don't think I can handle more than that?"

"Oh, you can handle more than that." He caressed my arm. "When you moved here, I didn't want you to work. I still don't."

"We've been over this before. I don't want to be a kept woman. You already pay for almost everything. I like to work. It gives me a sense of independence. I don't want to ask you for money whenever I want to go to lunch with someone or go shopping."

"For the time being, you can't do either one of those."

I still wanted to work. I'd much rather be outside doing yard work than inside cleaning. "Okay, I'll clean the pool and do some yard work. What is the hourly rate? Will I be reporting to you or someone else?" Then I added, jokingly, "And what are the benefits? You know, medical coverage, days off, retirement?"

He gave me a puzzled look. "I thought you were joking about working for me. I don't want you working around here. This is your home. I don't want you to think of this as your place of employment."

"Most people take care of their own yards, and to be honest, I enjoy yard work. I always helped Mom and Dad. I can't just sit around and not do anything while you're at work. Then I really will feel like a prisoner."

He glanced at me and I gave him a sweet smile. "Okay, you can work for Emmanuel, but only work half a day. I don't want you worn out when I get home."

I kissed his cheek. "Thank you."

"Since you'll be outside, you have to promise you won't try to leave this yard."

"I promise."

"I don't know how much Emmanuel pays his workers. You'll have to ask him about that." He raised my hand and ran his thumb over my palm and fingers. "I hope yard work isn't too hard on your hands. Make sure you always wear gloves." After I nodded, he continued, "We've had a long day. Let's go to bed."

14

THE JOB

It had been a long time since I did any yard work. I felt a little excited about it as I put on my oldest pair of jeans, a t-shirt, and my running shoes. After I tied my hair in a ponytail, I hurried down the stairs. As I pushed an unruly strand away from my face, I heard Conner in the den say, "They'll want her…"

Assuming he was talking about me, I stealthily edged toward the door out of his line of sight.

"We need to get her on the ship tonight," he said in a harsh tone.

I swallowed hard.

"I don't care if she's only twelve."

I didn't know whether to be relieved that he wasn't talking about me or horrified for the girl.

"If she looks sixteen, it doesn't matter how old she is," he snapped.

Quietly, I turned and went to the kitchen. I poured a cup of coffee and got a bowl of cereal. The Lucky Charms were like ice cubes of sadness as I thought of the twelve-year-old girl, probably being sold. According to what I had read in their books, they used ships to transport runaway teenagers. The names of the girls were listed on some of the pages. Then, thinking back to my situation with the cult, I wondered if the Crussett family was the lesser of the two evils. The cult killed and mutilated. The victims I saw were adults. No children were on the altar. And murder, as horrible as it was, was a far cry from sex slavery.

Conner walked into the kitchen. "So, you're all dressed for work," he said, cheerfully. He was also dressed, wearing a suit. He poured a cup of coffee and sat next to me. "Emmanuel will be here within the hour to get you started. He knows you can only work in this yard." He took my hand. "I'm counting on you to keep your promise."

"I will." I knew what would happen if I was caught attempting to leave.

"I'll try to come home earlier," he said and squeezed my thigh. "Then you can show me how much you missed me again."

"Suppose I can't wait. Can you come home if I call?"

"I certainly will try," he said, standing. "Don't work too hard." He kissed me and went to the garage.

I wanted to use the computer to contact Paula. He never mentioned web browsing or emailing in his rules though I imagined he wouldn't like it. After I strolled through the house and spotted Darcy busy ironing in the laundry room, I headed to the den. His computer was password protected. Crossing my fingers, I entered the password that he used before I left, Ladyluck12: Conner's favorite dog and his age when she died. It worked. Paula's only email address I could remember was the one she used at the office, not her personal one. I searched her name, Paula Sorensen, thinking I might be able to track her that way.

A listing came up indicating a newspaper site. I knew she'd have a wedding announcement if she got married. I checked the newspaper web page. There I searched for Paula again and two entries emerged; neither was about a wedding. One was an obituary. Maybe it's a different Paula. I clicked on it and a picture of Paula, my friend, appeared. She died as a result of a car crash three days after I ran away.

Eyes watering, I sniffled and went to the other entry. It was the news article about the car crash. Her boyfriend was driving and crossed over into oncoming traffic on a small canyon road. He struck a truck head on. Paula and her boyfriend died. Miraculously, the truck driver walked away unscathed. His name was Alex Barton. Then a terrible thought crept into my mind—was her death really an accident? Grabbing a handful of tissues from the box on the desk, I dried my tears.

Emmanuel would be here soon. Not wanting anyone to know I'd been on the computer, I cleared the browsing history, turned it off, and went back to the kitchen. Tears continued streaming down my cheeks. Paula was gone. I would never see her again. I had to concentrate on calming down and think about something else. If Emmanuel thought I looked upset, he might call Conner.

A few tears still trickled down my cheeks as I drank coffee and skimmed through the newspaper to see if anything was mentioned about the spider incidents in Billings. There was one small article about the bicyclist who had been bitten. It stated that he lived in Houston and he was vacationing in Billings. I speculated that Conner or one of his employees gave the reporter the story about why the victim was there since he definitely was not on a vacation.

The doorbell rang. Going toward the door, I saw Darcy open it. I recognized the man standing there. I didn't know his name. The only worker I had ever talked to was one named Fred. He was around often, cleaning the pool.

"May I help you?" Darcy asked.

"I'm Emmanuel. I've—"

I interrupted, "Darcy, Emmanuel is here for me."

Darcy didn't walk away. Instead she stayed beside me, making me think she was curious as to why the gardener wanted to see me.

"Hello, Miss Jones," he said politely. "I understand you'll be working on my crew. What time would you like to get started?"

"Since I'll be working for you, please call me Sara."

Darcy stared at me with a perplexed expression.

"Can I ask a few questions before I begin?" I said.

"What would you like to know?"

I wanted to appear like a serious employee in case Conner talked to Emmanuel. "What are my hours and how much will I be paid?"

He tilted his brows. "Didn't Mr. Crussett discuss this with you?"

"No."

"Mr. Crussett said you could only work three or four hours a day. He wants it to be in the mornings. You'll have to ask him how much you'll be paid."

"How much do you pay a beginning person on your crew?"

He hesitated for several seconds and then said, "If they don't have any experience, I start them out at $10 per hour."

"That's what you should pay me."

He nodded. "Unless Mr. Crussett wants me to pay you more."

"I shouldn't be paid more than any other worker," I clarified. "I'm ready to get started."

"You'll be working in the backyard weeding behind the bushes. There are gloves and tools in the truck." His eyes scanned my face and his forehead creased. "Are you feeling well enough to work?"

"Yes. Why?"

"Your eyes are a little red and puffy."

"Oh, that's just from an eyelash that got in my eye. It's out now."

He seemed to believe my explanation or at least wasn't going to question it. I followed him to the truck as Darcy watched from the doorway. After trying on several pairs of gloves, I found a thick pair that fit perfectly. He handed me two trowels and a shovel; he picked up a garbage can along with a box of plastic bags. We walked around the house to the back yard.

Darcy stood by the patio door, lending credence to my suspicion that Conner told her to keep an eye on me.

Emmanuel led me behind the bushes at the back of the yard next to the chain link fence that separated it from a heavily wooded area on the other side. Darcy could no longer see me. She'd likely come out and occasionally check to make sure I was still here.

"The wires above the fence are electrified so don't touch them," he said.

Conner mentioned before that no one could climb over it. I never asked why. I looked up. "That won't be a problem. I couldn't reach those wires if I tried."

Cameron and Carina, Conner's siblings, allowed their kids to play in the woods. That was also where they walked their dogs. Beyond that, a stone wall surrounded all the Crussett property. The top of the wall was jagged to keep out intruders and surveillance cameras were situated at various locations, monitored from the security building next to the entrance gate. The security guards would know if someone tried to penetrate the wall. Once when I was lying by the pool, there was an intruder. The alarms blared and security guards rushed around everywhere. A man was captured. Conner said he had been turned over to the police. Now, I no longer thought that was his fate.

Lining this side of the chain link fence were two rows of thick, tall bushes, creating a heavy privacy barrier. Anyone in the woods was unable to see the swimming pool or any part of Conner's house except for the roof.

I had never planned on attempting to escape by climbing over the fence since I'd also have to get over the stone wall without being detected. My best option would be to find a way to hide in one of Emmanuel's trucks. I'd work on that scheme. First, I needed to gain trust so Conner wouldn't expect me to try to leave.

The space between the fence and the bushes was overgrown with weeds. The backyard always looked immaculate because this area was unseen from the house and pool. Given the size of the weeds, I was sure it had never been weeded. This was probably the only job Emmanuel could give me, since I couldn't leave the yard. It might take me all week to finish.

He put down the garbage can and plastic bags next to me. "Do you know how to weed?"

I smiled to myself. Maybe he thought I'd never done manual labor. "Yes, I do." The urge to tell him I also knew how to mow lawns, trim bushes, edge the grass, and plant trees was strong. Instead, I started weeding.

"I have to go and check on the rest of my crew. Will you be okay working by yourself?"

"Yes." Obviously Conner hadn't instructed Emmanuel to watch me all the time. With the fence being eight feet tall and an electrified wire running above it, Conner knew I couldn't leave from here.

I filled two bags and tied them. As I started putting weeds in the third bag, I heard a few branches breaking and the rustling of trees on the other side of the fence. Moving toward the fence, my eyes flitted back and forth through the woods. I didn't see anyone, and the alarm was silent. I went back to work.

Darcy peeked around the bushes. I waved to her. She smiled. "I just wanted to make sure you were okay," she said, timidly.

"I'm fine." I knelt down and pulled up a few more weeds.

"Let me know if I can get you something."

"Thanks. I will." As she retreated, I thought she probably felt nervous because she couldn't see me from the house. I suspected she had glimpsed around the bushes before without me noticing.

Emmanuel appeared while I was shoveling weeds into another bag. "It looks like you're moving right along," he said, handing me a bottle of water.

"Thanks."

"Do you need anything?"

"No."

"Then I'll get back to my crew."

When he was out of sight, I again heard twigs snapping and rustling of leaves on the other side of the fence. I stood, looked into the woods, and wondered if the kids were out there playing even if they should be in school. I didn't hear any talking, laughing, or giggling. The rustling got louder. Then I saw the silhouette of a man moving toward me. As he got closer, I backed away from the fence.

A few seconds later, I recognized the man as Brett. Cocking an eyebrow, I felt irritated that somehow he had followed me from Billings. At the same time, I saw his blue eyes brimming with concern, and my emotions began churning inside. As my heart beat briefly spiked, I was grateful that the fence separated us, and with the electric current running along the top, it wouldn't allow him to get any closer. "What are you doing here?"

"That's what I planned on asking you," he said. "You need to leave."

"How did you find me?"

"We knew where you lived before you came to Billings. Just like we know you called Conner to come and get you."

"If you knew I called Conner, why didn't you try to stop me from going with him?"

"We didn't discover you called him until after you were gone."

"Who are 'we'?"

"I'll explain later." His eyes inched up and down over my clothing. "Why are you working in the yard? Is this how you're repaying Conner for coming to get you or for leaving him?"

"No," I snapped. "I wanted to work in the yard. Conner doesn't want me to work at all. You followed me all the way from Billings. I want to know why."

"Sara, we don't have time. Right now, I need to get you away from here."

"No. Right now, I'm safe. Conner won't hurt me."

"You'll hurt him," he said, calmly.

"How can I hurt him? I don't have any weapons. If anyone hurts him, it'll be you and your spiders."

"Sara—"

"Stay away from me. I know you're a member of the cult."

"Cult?"

"The spider cult." I clenched my teeth, annoyed that he expected me to blindly leave with him. How could he believe I would even consider it? Then suddenly my pulse quickened, my breathing accelerated, and the desire surged through my body. I wanted him. "Oh, no. Not again." I gulped in air. "What did you give me? I feel like a nymphomaniac."

Staring at the ground, my thoughts, emotions, and urges collided. I couldn't understand why I wanted him since I knew what he was and how he had used me. I felt his arms wrapping around me. "How did you get on this side of the fence? And how did you get over the stone wall without being detected?"

"I'll tell you everything when you're in a safe place."

Unable to control my lust, I put my arms around his neck and kissed him. My breathing became harder. I started to unbuckle his belt. He broke off some of the lower branches on one of the bushes, creating a space for us. All I could think about was how much I needed him as we crawled in, hidden from anyone looking for me. My mind went blank when he touched me.

Afterwards, I bit my lip and inhaled deeply. "I can't keep doing this. This feeling keeps coming back. The more I try to wait, the more intense it becomes. It's impossible to have a serious conversation with anyone. I can't control it. Even when I'm mad or upset, the desire encompasses all my thoughts. Why did you do this to me? Was that part of your assignment?" Water welled in my eyes.

He held me close. "Shhh," he whispered. "You were an assignment. Now you've become so much more. You are the only one I want. What I gave you was to help you, not to hurt you. You were going through the phases too fast."

"Phases?"

"Your body is going through changes. The sexual desires emerge more often when you are emotionally charged: angry, fearful, or happy."

"I try to relax and it doesn't go away."

"The only way you can control it is if you can relax before the desire occurs. Once there, it needs to be satisfied."

"Does it ever."

"Don't worry. It will be gone soon."

"What are you talking about?" I whispered.

"I'm not saying you won't have sexual desires, but you'll be able to control them. I'll explain after I get you away from here."

"I can't leave right now. I need answers."

"Sara," Emmanuel yelled. "Where are you?"

I slipped on my jeans. Crawling out, I motioned for Brett to stay put, and then I pulled out a weed. "Just wanted to get a few weeds from under the bush," I said, loudly.

Emmanuel walked toward me. I stood and brushed myself off as I moved in his direction.

"Mr. Crussett will not like it if you're all scratched up. Don't go that far under the bushes again." His eyes dropped to my hands. "Why aren't you wearing any gloves?"

"My hands were getting sweaty, so I took them off."

He looked at my arms without touching me. "Do you have any scratches?"

Checking my exposed skin, I ran my hands over my neck and down my arms. "I've got one small one. That's all. It's right here." I pointed to the spot on my upper arm." I smiled at him. "Don't worry. I'll wear a long-sleeved top. No one will know."

"You've been out here for over three hours. I think you should quit for today. Tomorrow you can do some more weeding if you wear gloves."

"Can I leave the garbage can where it is? It can't be seen from the back yard."

"Yes. The filled plastic bags must go," he said, picking up two.

"Let me get the others." I turned and moved away from him, then stopped by a bag and glanced over my shoulder to make sure he wasn't watching me. Leaning down next to the bushes, I whispered to Brett, "You have to leave now before anyone sees you."

"I'll be back tomorrow to get you," Brett said, from the other side of the fence.

"How did you get over there?"

He left without answering.

"Sara," Emmanuel said, stepping around a bush. "Are you talking to someone?"

"No. I was just singing to myself. It feels so good to be outside." I hummed as I picked up the bag and walked toward him, grabbing another bag along the way. I glanced at the woods and saw a few branches swaying but no sign of Brett.

15

FAMILY BUSINESS

Heading toward the house, I heard the phone ringing.

"Conner Crussett's residence. May I help you?" Darcy answered. "Yes. I'll get her." She looked out the patio door. "Sara, Mr. Crussett would like to talk to you." She handed me the phone as I walked in.

"Hi."

"How is your work day going?" Conner asked.

"Surprisingly great. I forgot how much I love working outside."

"Good. I want you to quit for the day. I'll be home soon. We're having company for dinner."

"Who?"

"I'll tell you when I get there. See you in a little while." He clicked off.

I wondered why he didn't just tell me who was coming. I decided to get cleaned up so he didn't smell Brett's cologne on me. I strolled toward the stairs.

"Sara, aren't you going to have lunch?" Darcy asked.

I turned and saw her holding a plate with a sandwich and chips on it. "There's dirt and weeds in my hair. I'm going to take a quick shower and then I'll be down for lunch."

She smiled as I went up the stairs. I hurriedly showered and slipped on a clean pair of jeans and a t-shirt. When Conner said he'd be home soon, I wasn't sure what 'soon' meant.

My hands felt rough, even though I only had my gloves off when I was with Brett. Knowing Conner wouldn't let me work outside if he noticed the dry, cracking skin, I anxiously rubbed lotion into them. It didn't help. Glancing through the cabinet, searching for something that might work, I found suntan oil, poured it over my hands, and massaged it in. That helped.

As I ate my sandwich, I heard Conner's car. A few minutes later, he came into the kitchen and sat by me.

"Who's coming to dinner tonight?" I asked.

He took my hand. "Cameron."

"Is Melanie coming with him?"

"No. He's coming alone."

Fear swept through my body. Cameron was Conner's brother. He was sixteen years older. Based on what I saw in the books, he was running the family business since Conner's dad, Cedric, had a heart attack six months ago. Conner also had an older sister, Carina. For some unknown reason, Conner's dad liked 'C' names. Cameron followed the same tradition. He had three boys named Caden, Carter, and Colin. Caden was a year younger than I was and worked for the family. Carter was in college and he sometimes worked for them. Colin was only eight. I was sure the family business was also in his destiny.

Even before I knew the truth about the Crussetts, I always felt nervous around Cameron. He was tall and slender with medium brown hair, and he had a dignified appearance. His clothes were always immaculate, not a wrinkle anywhere. His face looked just as stiff; he seldom smiled. I didn't think he liked being around children, including his own. At family gatherings, Melanie had to make sure Colin didn't bother him. I couldn't imagine what type of a husband he must've been.

"Why's he coming?" I asked.

Conner held my hand tighter. "He just wants to make sure we're getting along. That's all."

My spine stiffened as I felt the muscles in my body tightening and a lump in my throat, believing Cameron had another agenda. Without warning, a rush of excitement encompassed my thoughts and my heart pounded. Not again. I clutched my thigh with my free hand, hoping the arousal would dissipate. Brett told me to try and keep my emotions under control. How could I with Cameron coming? My condition was hopeless. I stroked Conner's arm, leaned closer and kissed him. "Should we show him?"

Conner smiled. "Not that way."

Needing him, I stood up and put my arms around his neck. "Do you want to practice getting along?"

He rose to his feet. "That's why I came home. I think we're past practicing." He kissed my forehead. "You couldn't get any better."

Kissing his neck, I said, "Neither could you."

"We better get up," Conner said, moving to the edge of bed. "Cameron will be here at seven."

I wished I could just stay upstairs. Since that wasn't possible, I reluctantly climbed out of bed.

He put his arms around me. "It will be okay. Cameron mentioned he had some business to attend to after dinner. He'll only be here for a couple of hours." He kissed me.

I pondered about how to keep my emotions under control and smiled to myself. At least if I couldn't, Cameron would know we were getting along. Since one aspect of the family business involved pornography, he might want to put us in the movies. Oh, what a disgusting thought.

We got ready. I put on my black silk skirt and a white silk blouse, an outfit Conner liked. He wore a dark suit, light blue shirt, and a twill plaid tie I had given him.

"You look gorgeous," he said, walking toward me. "I want you to wear your emerald necklace." He took it out of my jewelry box, eased it around my neck, closed the clasp, and handed me the matching earrings.

As we went down the stairs, I thought we looked too nice just to be having dinner with one person. I knew Conner wanted to make a good impression on his brother. I never believed they were very close, but they were family.

The wonderful smell of prime rib and hot rolls permeated the house. I was sure Darcy had been cooking all afternoon. From the nervous way she fluttered around, I sensed she viewed Cameron the same way I did.

Conner went to the bar and opened a bottle of Merlot. He poured two glasses and carried them into the living room. We sat down and he toasted, "To us."

I took a sip and glanced at the clock. It read: 6:55 p.m. Dreading Cameron's arrival, I inhaled deeply and exhaled.

"Relax," Conner said. "It'll be okay."

I smiled, though I doubted he was right. It would have been better if Melanie were also coming. Cameron alone wasn't a good sign. Even if Conner could forgive me for taking some documents, I knew his family would be a problem.

The doorbell rang.

Swallowing hard, I stood and Conner took my hand. I heard the door open and Darcy talking in the entryway along with two male voices. Something was wrong. I grabbed Conner's arm and clung to it.

He looked at me and rubbed my hand. "Don't worry."

"Cameron isn't alone," I whispered, fear audible in my stuttering voice.

Conner's expression hardened as Cameron and a tall, muscular, bald man with a dark complexion entered the living room. My eyes met Cameron's. He glared at me with a smirk.

"Sara, go upstairs," Conner ordered.

Grateful that Conner had excused me and anxious to get away from Cameron, I hurried out of the room. Moving up the stairs, I heard Conner yell, "What's he doing here?"

After that, I didn't hear another word as I quickly went into our bedroom and pulled the door shut. I sat down in the padded chair, leaned back, and closed my eyes. I took a few deep breaths to calm down. My mind drifted back to the time before I moved into Conner's house. I smiled when I remembered one of his old girlfriends, Susan, coming to visit me unannounced at the Investment Company in San Diego. She shouted at me—calling me all kinds of names. Most of them I never heard before. I recalled feeling amused when she accused me of being a gold digger. If she only knew how much money I had.

My parents lived a frugal life. They were never flamboyant. Growing up, I knew they purchased expensive equipment. They had the latest stuff in their state of the art lab, much admired by others in their field. They never discussed money in front of me. After they died, I learned they were wealthy. Mom, an only child, had inherited a fortune from her parents. I never had to work, but I wanted to be productive like my parents and earn my own money. Still, it was nice knowing that I didn't need to worry about it. Conner knew I had an inheritance from my parents. I was certain he assumed it wasn't much since I always referred to it as a 'little inheritance.'

I couldn't believe Conner would date anyone who acted like Susan. She quit calling me names when the office manager told her she had a phone call. She trudged into his office. About fifteen minutes later, she came out and glared at me as she left the building. The next day Conner came into town. I didn't want to see him. If Susan was the type of girl he liked, I wasn't in her league, nor did I want to be. Eventually, he convinced me to go out with him again. We had three great years together. Those years I'll never regret. I wished I could change him into the man I believed he was.

Someone touched my hands and I opened my eyes. Conner stood next to the chair smiling at me.

"Let's go down and have dinner," he said.

"Do we still have company?"

"Only Cameron. He'll be leaving right after dinner."

"Who was the other guy?" After waiting and receiving no answer, I rose to my feet. "I was hoping we'd be dining alone."

He pulled me close to him and lightly kissed my lips. "Cameron still wants to make sure we're getting along."

I took his arm. "Let's show him."

We went to the living room. Cameron gave me a sinister smile as he shook my hand. I walked between him and Conner to the dining room. As soon as we were seated, Darcy came in and dished up salad.

"Melanie accepted a position on the ballet board," Cameron said, picking up his fork. "They've been after her for years to be a board member. She wanted Colin to be older before she made that type of commitment."

"How did Carter do on his finals?" Conner asked, buttering a roll.

"Well. He ended up with the 3.5 average for the semester. He's thinking about doing a semester abroad."

"Where to?"

"England. He's looking into a program at Reading and one at Oxford."

They continued talking about the family, and I relaxed thinking everything was going to be okay.

Darcy gathered up the salad plates and served the main course. When she went back to the kitchen, Cameron began, "We have another buyer for the stuff coming in from Columbia."

"Didn't Thurman want it all?" Conner asked.

"No. He wants all the pot and cocaine, but only part of the heroin."

"How much heroin is left?"

"A hundred kilos."

"My Louisiana contact will take it."

"There's a local guy that claims he'll pay top dollar. I'm meeting with him tonight. Let's see how high he'll go."

I continued eating, even though I could no longer taste my food. How could they talk business in front of me? Why would Conner allow that? Maybe they had other plans for me.

"How many are on the ship that's leaving tonight?" Cameron asked.

"Twenty-three. I saw them this morning. They all look like they're sixteen or seventeen. Most aren't that old. One's only twelve. With her boobs, she'll easily pass for sixteen."

"Good. We want to keep our customers satisfied. They especially enjoy young, well-developed, tight bodies. There are a few who don't like too much tit. They probably fantasize they're doing it with a virgin. I'd be surprised if any of the girls fit that bill." Cameron smiled. "Did you see any of the new videos that Saul's working on acquiring?"

"No," Conner replied.

"You need to see them. The guy wants more than we usually pay. I think they're worth his asking price. The star in one of them can't be more than eleven."

My eyes fixed on Conner, trying to get his attention. He never looked my way. Wondering how I could run from the room, I picked up my wine glass to take a sip and dumped it down my blouse onto my skirt.

"Oh, I'm sorry," I said, setting down the glass and standing up. "I'll be right back." I headed upstairs to change.

With shaking hands, I changed clothes. Then I sat down, cupped my hands over my mouth and breathed deeply, trying to soothe my nerves. Water welled in my eyes. Those poor girls. It was hard just knowing about the corruption. Listening to Cameron and Conner discuss it openly, like a normal business transaction, brought it all to life. I grabbed a handful of tissues from the nightstand and caught the tears before they landed on my sweater.

Closing my eyes, I slid my fingers together and attempted to quiet my mind. It was impossible as terrified faces of teenage girls appeared. Swallowing hard, my eyes flew open to escape the images.

Confused, I couldn't understand what was going on. I wasn't a member of the Crussett family or one of their employees. Why would they talk about it in front of me? Maybe Cameron hoped I'd run again. Conner should have stopped him, but he didn't. He joined in, business as usual. My thoughts flowed back to the girls. I wiped away more tears as I wondered if any of them ever had a chance to escape.

A rap on the door startled me. I stood and buttoned my slacks. "Come in."

Darcy entered. "Sara, they want you to come back downstairs."

"Thanks. I'll be right down."

Darcy left, closing the door behind her.

I felt trapped, like the girls, as I glanced at myself in the mirror, fixed my makeup, and brushed my hair. I inhaled deeply, went downstairs, and returned to my seat. Dessert was on the table.

"I'm glad you could join us again," Cameron said with a sarcastic sneer.

I said nothing as I picked up my fork and began eating. They went back to talking business which I blocked out of my head by thinking about Mom and Dad. My eyes became moist again as I thought about how much they loved me. They'd protect me from anything; they never had an ulterior motive. I wondered if Conner only pretended he still loved me to get the documents back. Was it all an act? I didn't want Cameron and Conner to know how I was feeling, so I carefully wiped my eyes with my fingertips; they were rough against my face. I laid my hands, palms up, in my lap and looked at them. They appeared dry and chapping. The suntan lotion had worn off. I should have rubbed more in when I was upstairs. Touching my fingers, they felt prickly.

"Sara," Conner said, breaking my concentration.

Looking up, I saw he was standing next to Cameron. I hadn't realized they were finished with their desserts. As I rose from the chair, Conner took my arm, and we walked Cameron to the entry hallway.

"Thank you for dinner," Cameron said, opening the door.

"You're welcome," Conner replied. "I'll look at some of the videos tomorrow."

"Let me know what you think. Goodnight."

"See you in the morning."

I stood quietly and watched Conner close the door behind Cameron. He led me back into the living room.

"Would you like a glass of wine?" he asked.

"No, thank you," I replied, sitting down on the sofa.

Conner mixed himself a drink and sat next to me. "You seemed a little withdrawn during dessert. Are you feeling okay?"

"Yes. I'm fine," I said, looking at the floor.

"What were you thinking about?"

"I lived with you for almost three years. You've never talked about business at the table before. Is this what I can expect whenever you have company for dinner?"

He put his arm around my shoulders. "Before, you didn't know about the family's business, now you do. Since I no longer have to hide it from you, I can be more relaxed when we have company."

"One of your rules was that I needed to go upstairs when you had company. I don't need to do that anymore?"

"Sometimes you'll still need to go upstairs. I'll make that decision based on the scope of what is being discussed."

"Does Cameron talk about business in front of Melanie?"

"Sometimes. He never talks about it in front of Colin."

At least Cameron recognized that Colin was still too young. "You said the family's business had nothing to do with us."

"That's right, it doesn't."

"If you're going to talk about business in front of me, then I think it does."

"No, it doesn't."

"Well, I guess we're going to disagree."

He grabbed my shoulders. "Why do you think that?"

I figured I might as well tell him what I thought. "It was hard for me knowing your family's real business. The books didn't go into details about the girls or about the content of the pornography videos. That's what you talked about at dinner."

"Where do we go from here?" He sounded irritated.

I stared at him as my lips quivered.

"Sara," he said, shaking my shoulders.

My pent-up sexual desires emerged again. I felt sickened and helpless, an unwilling slave to my body. How could I be aroused by a man who laughed at the plight of eleven and twelve-year-old girls sold as sex slaves? I couldn't even imagine how much they suffered. I tried to relax. It was impossible. The more I thought about them, the more distraught I became, and the stronger my unwanted lust overwhelmed my body. I bit my lips to hold back tears. I did not want him. I hated this feeling and myself for feeling it, but it controlled me.

"I don't know," I said, putting my arms around his neck and kissing him.

He smiled, and we went upstairs.

16

LEAVING

The sound of water running in the shower woke me. Lying in bed, I thought about what I should do. I didn't want Brett getting hurt trying to get me away from here. He talked about my body going through changes. I wondered if it was more than the overwhelming sex drive. Last night, I felt nervous and upset for a long time before I wanted Conner. Whatever I had been given in Billings must have started wearing off.

Conner came out of the bathroom and got dressed. When he was ready to leave, he sat down on the bed next to me. He took my hand and rubbed it. "I don't want you to work in the yard today. Your fingers feel rough. I don't think the gloves protected your hands enough. We'll go shopping for a better pair."

"I wasn't planning on working in the yard today. In fact, I won't be working out there anymore."

"Good. I'm sure you can find something to do inside the house."

I held his hands. "Conner, I'm leaving."

His eyebrows rose and his forehead creased. "Why?"

"As much as I love you, I can't stay knowing about your family business. I just can't. I'm sorry."

Conner's eyes darkened with rage. "Are you planning on meeting Brett?" he snapped. "Is that what this is all about?"

"No."

"Where do you plan on going?"

"I want to go home."

"This is your home."

"No. This is your home. My home is in San Diego. I never sold my parents' house. The university uses Dad and Mom's lab. The house has been empty long enough waiting for me to return. I always felt safe there." Surprisingly, now I felt calm, but extremely sad. I was doing the right thing.

"What makes you think I'm just going to let you leave?"

"I can't stay here any longer." My eyes were getting moist. "So, if you're not going to let me leave, I'd like to be buried next to my parents." Tears began flowing down my cheeks. It was hard hurting someone who loved me, even if I didn't want anything to do with him anymore. The pain I felt was insignificant compared to what he had inflicted on other people.

He put his arms around me and held me close. "I don't want you to leave."

I sniffled and said, "I thought, maybe, I could get past your family business and just think about us. After dinner last night, I can't. This is your home. You should be able to talk about whatever you want to here. Now, I know it's been a struggle for you having me live here."

"I can't let you go."

"And I can't stay."

"I want you. I won't discuss my business in front of you anymore." He gently wiped away my tears.

"Your family wouldn't like that. I think Cameron wanted to talk about it last night so I would run away again. I'm sure that's what he wants. What surprised me more was that you talked without hesitation in front of me, not taking into consideration how it would make me feel. You didn't even look at me. Then when I couldn't take any more, I found a way to go upstairs. You sent Darcy to get me to come back to the table."

His expression softened. "What will you do in San Diego?"

"I'll find a job and start over."

"Will I be able to see you?"

"I don't know. Maybe after we've been apart for awhile, I might miss you so much it'll be too hard not to see you again."

"When are you planning on leaving?"

"As soon as I get ready. Can I take my car?"

He rubbed his chin as he silently gazed at me for a minute. "I'll fly you back to San Diego. One of my men will drive your car there. Are you going to take anything with you?"

I managed a faint smile. "Well, I won't be taking any documents, if that's what you're asking."

He kissed my hand. "No, I didn't mean that. Cameron believes you didn't return all of them."

"You've got them all."

"There were a few pages torn out of a ledger. Among the documents you returned were copies of those pages. Did you take any originals?"

"No. Why would I copy them if I took the originals?"

"I didn't think you would remove any pages from a ledger." He tucked an unruly strand of my hair that was floating in front of my eyes behind my ear. "When I asked if you were going to take anything with you, I meant, your clothes, jewelry."

"I thought I'd pack a few things. Things I bought for myself. I'm not going to take any of the jewelry." A crooked smile flickered on my lips. "I don't go to fancy enough places to wear it."

"I'll make the arrangements while you get ready."

Feeling relieved that he was going to let me go, I caressed his hand. "Thank you."

He wrapped his arms around me and kissed my lips. His eyes dimmed, and I saw the pain on his face as he stood. I imagined the despair on his victims' faces. Thinking of the poor girls, I watched him walk out of the room.

My feet hurt as I trudged to the shower. I bent down and rubbed them; they felt rough, even in the arch. After showering, I started to blow dry my hair. It kept getting caught on my fingers so I gave up and left it messy. Struggling to get on my underwear, I couldn't prevent the material from sticking to my fingers. I took a pair of evening gloves out of my dresser drawer, put them on, and finished getting dressed. Then I worked on my hair again so it wasn't sticking up all over.

I packed two suitcases. There were other things I wanted to take. They were gifts from Conner, and I knew I'd think about him whenever I wore them. I slipped off the gloves and my ruby ring. I laid the ring on top of the dresser where it was when I returned. The black ring was still on my finger. Once I was home, I would work on getting it off. Picking up a suitcase and my purse, I scanned the room and reminisced about the wonderful memories created in here. Mixed emotions tumbled through my mind as I strolled out and headed down the stairs.

After leaving the suitcase in the foyer, I went to the den. Conner wasn't there. I walked through the living room, dining room, and kitchen searching for him. Then I stepped into the hallway and yelled, "Conner, I'm ready to go."

The front door opened. I saw Cameron enter, along with the man he brought to dinner last night. Panic hit, sending waves of terror through my body.

"Conner," I yelled again. No response. Had he turned me over to his family? I didn't want to believe he would do that.

Cameron crossed his arms over his chest and sneered.

"Darcy," I shouted. No response.

"No one is here, but us," Cameron said in a harsh tone. "Conner is blaming me for you leaving. We both know you had already planned on running again."

"I'm not running away. I'm going home."

Cameron smirked. "Conner had some things he needed to take care of before he could fly you home. Saul," he nodded at the man standing next to him, "is going to take you to the airport."

I wanted to ask where he was really going to take me. Instead, I turned and stepped toward the stairs. "I need to get my other suitcase."

"Wait here," Cameron ordered, taking my arm. "Saul will get it."

Silently, I watched Saul go up the stairs. The hall branched off in two directions; I didn't tell him which way to go, yet he knew. I wondered how many times he'd been here. A moment later, he came down with the suitcase, picked up the other one, and carried them out to the waiting limo. Cameron and I followed without saying a word. My feet ached, yet I held my head high and walked my normal pace. I didn't want Cameron to have the satisfaction of knowing that I was scared.

The limo driver opened the door while Saul put the luggage in the trunk. My face remained blank and emotionless as I got in the limo. Saul climbed in next to me. Conner never allowed any Crussett employees to sit by me. They always sat on the opposite side. Only Conner shared a seat with me. It didn't surprise me that Saul would plop down wherever he wanted to. This wasn't going to be a usual limo ride.

Cameron leaned in and looked at me with a smug, sadistic grin. "Have a nice trip home."

I glared at him. "Goodbye, Cameron," I said, not attempting to hide my sarcasm.

The limo drove out the gate and turned in the direction of the airport. Sensing Saul scanning my body from head to toe, I stared out the window and tried to recall everything that was in my purse. Was there anything I could use as a weapon? Maybe a fingernail file, tweezers, the tip of a comb. I snapped open my purse, stuck my hand in, and began rummaging around.

Saul grabbed it and threw it on the floor.

"We're being followed," the limo driver said over the intercom.

Saul pushed the intercom button. "Lose the tail."

A horn erupted as the limo sped into another lane. It darted in and out of traffic, weaved onto another highway and meandered through various streets, jarring Saul and me back and forth in the back seat.

"I think we've lost him," the driver said.

Saul's cold, unsettling eyes dropped to my lap. He put his hand on my knee.

"Conner won't like that," I said, pushing his hand away.

"That's not all Conner won't like."

"What else won't he like?"

A malicious smile crossed his face. "Conner says you're the best ass he's ever had. I'm going to find out if that's true."

"Conner doesn't talk that way," I said, irritated. "If you think I'm going to let you touch me, you've got another thought coming."

"Don't need your permission." He stuck his hand under my blouse.

Shoving his hand away, I yelled, "Stop that."

He snickered and pawed my breasts.

I thrust my elbow into his side. "Get away from me!"

Lifting my legs, he forced me down on the back seat.

The limo phone rang as I raised my foot to kick him. He blocked the blow and ran his hand up my slacks while I squirmed and pounded him with my fists.

"Do you want me to answer that?" the driver asked.

Saul leaned toward the intercom button and pushed it. "No."

I scooted closer to the door and sat up, firmly planting my feet on the floor.

He twisted his hand between my thighs, pushing them apart.

Punching his arm, I screamed, "Get away from me."

Saul's cell phone rang. "What now?" He yanked it out of his pocket and glanced at it. Then he put it back without answering. He clutched the waistband of my slacks and slid me toward him.

I elbowed him in the groin. He flinched as he buckled over. I smacked his head.

Grabbing my blouse, he straightened his spine and sneered. "You're not helping your situation."

"I'm going to tell Conner," I barked, shoving his arm. My fingers stuck to his blazer.

He gripped my hand and pulled it up, along with the attached threads. "What the..." he said, turning my palm over. He removed some of the threads and ran his fingers over mine. "Your hands feel like crap." He checked his blazer. "You've ruined it. I've never known anyone with such rough, scaly hands. How can Conner stand holding them?" His brows furrowed as his eyes swept over my body. "He probably doesn't need to do that to get what he wants."

He proceeded to roughly move his hand up between my legs. As he got closer to my crotch, I pushed at his hand as hard as I could. He was too strong and wrapped his fingers easily around my wrist as I tried to kick him. He smiled maliciously, and his cold eyes flared while he enjoyed the control he had over me.

His cell phone buzzed again. "I know you can hardly wait. I'll make this quick," he said, taking it out of his pocket. He gazed at the number, and then released his hold on me.

"Yes," he said into the phone. "The place...we agreed." His eyes narrowed and his brows slanted in a frown. "No... No... Not yet... That's where I'll take her." He clicked off, moved to the opposite seat, and glared at me without uttering a word. He clenched his teeth, his face tightened, and veins stood out on his neck.

I had assumed he was prepared to kill me after he had taken pleasure in my company. Something must've delayed his plans. Maybe Cameron wanted to talk to me about the missing documents—the ones that were torn out of the book. The ones I didn't have.

"We've got a tail again," the driver said.

Saul pushed the intercom button. "I'll get rid of the bastard. Take the next exit and stop wherever you can," he hissed, then shifted around on the seat. "Is this asshole following you?"

I stared at him without answering.

"Besides Conner, who else knows you're leaving?"

"No one else," I said, trying to remain calm.

"Does Brett?"

"Who told you about him?"

"Is he the tail?"

I wondered if Saul thought I was stupid enough to help him determine who it was. It probably was Brett, since he planned on taking me away today.

"Does a man by the name of Alex Barton work for the Crussett family?" I asked, thinking this was my opportunity to find out if the Crussetts played a role in my friend Paula's death.

"How do you know him? Don't tell me he's the tail."

I surmised that Alex did work for the family. "What would you do if he was?"

"We'll see about that." He jerked out his phone just as the limo stopped on a two-lane street. A horde of people moved along the sidewalk in front of shops and an office building. He pushed the intercom button. "Move farther down the street where there aren't so many people."

The limo eased back into the traffic.

Saul punched some numbers on his cell. "Hey...Where are you?...No ...Not important...I'll tell him." He hung up. "Alex is nowhere around here. Where did you meet him?"

Staring at him, I remained silent and felt the limo stop again. I looked out the window and saw a sparse number of people walking on the sidewalk.

"Stay here." Saul opened the door and climbed out. It appeared he still planned on having a confrontation, even with witnesses. I followed him and watched a sedan stop by the curb.

"Get back in the limo," Saul demanded.

"No."

His attention turned away from me when Brett stepped out of the car and walked toward us. I attempted to move around Saul. He pushed me back.

"What do you want?" Saul asked Brett.

"I want Sara," Brett replied.

A crowd started to form as people lingered to listen.

Saul grabbed my arm and jerked me in front of him. With his other hand, he drew a gun from under his blazer and aimed the barrel at my head.

A woman in the crowd gasped.

"You want this Sara," Saul snapped. "The one with the rough hands?"

"Yes."

"What makes you think I'll let her go with you?"

Brett glared at him. "If you don't, you'll die."

Saul swung the pistol toward Brett and pulled the trigger. I heard the sound of a bone cracking, flesh and soft organs being pierced as the bullet penetrated Brett's chest.

I screamed, wiggled away from Saul, and ran to Brett. Kneeling next to him as blood oozed through his shirt, I held my hands tightly over the wound, hoping to stop the bleeding. "I'm here. I'm here. Don't die," I cried.

Brett touched my cheek. "It'll be okay."

Saul gripped my arm and attempted to pull me away.

"No," I yelled. "I'm not leaving him."

Brett clutched Saul's leg.

Saul yanked me up. "Yes, you are," he ordered, pointing his weapon at my face.

Kicking him, I shouted, "Help. Someone help." No one in the crowd moved. I scratched Saul's hand, trying to loosen his hold.

Saul winced. "What have you got that's sharp?" he asked, forcing my hand up and twisting it around.

As I continued struggling with him, Brett tugged Saul's leg. Saul staggered, falling toward me. I felt something being wrapped around my waist while Saul held onto me, pulling me down with him.

Falling next to Brett, my head slammed into the sidewalk. My vision blurred. Everything around me began to spin. I caught a glimpse of Saul's eyes. They were frozen in fear. That was the last thing I saw before blackness took over.

17

A NEW PHASE

Over the course of several minutes, I awoke slowly. The gradual reactivation of my senses allowed me to smell the wonderful scent of lilacs. My eyes flashed around the stark, white room and I saw medical equipment attached to the wall. Next to the bed, a drip bag hung with a tube hooked to a hypodermic needle inserted in my arm. My hands were wrapped in bandages. I couldn't move my feet. With my bandaged hands, I managed to uncover my legs. My feet were also bandaged; the wrapping went above my ankles. I wondered how I ended up here. A large bouquet of lilacs with roses scattered throughout, probably from Conner, stood on the nightstand. I couldn't imagine anyone else could have sent them since whoever did knew lilacs were my favorite flower.

The door squeaked open. "Good morning, Miss Jones," a woman in a white uniform said, entering the room. "I thought you were awake since your heart monitor jumped."

As she came closer I saw her badge, indicating her name was Mabel, a registered nurse. "What happened?" I asked.

"You fell and hit your head." She checked the tubes attached to my arm. "Dr. Shaw's been seeing you for your head injury. He says you'll be just fine in a few days."

"What about my hands and feet?"

"You were bitten by a poisonous spider. The man who called 9-1-1 told the dispatcher that. Otherwise, we'd still be running tests to determine the cause of the condition of your hands and feet."

"What's wrong with them?"

"Dr. Alston wrapped them before I came on duty so I haven't seen them. According to the chart, they're covered with rough lesions and secreting fluids."

Thinking of pus oozing out of my hands and feet, I wrinkled my nose and pursed my lips. "I have two doctors—Dr. Shaw and Dr. Alston?"

"Yes. You're very fortunate that the son of the renowned Dr. Alston was in town lecturing."

"Renowned for what?"

"For his research and publications on spider and insect bites. He's considered the number one in his field. The young Dr. Alston is following in his father's footsteps. He decided to take you on as his patient. He checked on you earlier this morning and said he'd be back before noon."

"A man was shot right before I fell. Can you tell me his condition?"

She picked up a clipboard attached to the foot of the bed and looked through several pages. "Another man was brought in from the same location. He had also been bitten. I don't have information about a patient with a gunshot wound."

Tears filled my eyes. "Would you ... would you know if the man who was shot died?" I stammered, crying.

The nurse took some tissues and gently wiped my cheeks. "Miss Jones, I'll check on it. No one has mentioned anything about a gunshot victim. Dr. Shaw did say that you might not be able to think clearly for a few days because of your head injury. Try to stay calm while I see what I can found out."

"Could you hurry?" I sniffled.

"Yes. I'll do it right now," she said, leaving.

I brushed the tears from my face with the bandages on my hands. If Brett wasn't brought to the hospital, he must be in the morgue.

The door opened and in walked Lance, the dark-eyed man, wearing a white lab coat.

I jumped up to a sitting position as my spine stiffened and my eyebrows arched. My hands trembled, my lips quivered, and I couldn't prevent my eyes from watering as fear surged through my body. "You're ...Doctor...Dr. Alston?" I stuttered through the lump in my throat.

"Yes," he replied, approaching me. "Are you in pain?"

"No." I bit my lower lip as I tried to calm my nerves.

"Then what is the problem?" he asked, checking the tube attached to my arm.

Wondering if he really was a doctor, and beginning to feel safe since I was in a hospital with nurses and doctors coming and going all the time, I inhaled deeply, and murmured, "Brett's dead."

"Are you quite sure?"

"He was shot before I fell. He wasn't taken to the hospital, so he has to be dead."

"Brett isn't dead. I saw him last night after I checked on you. He's perfectly well and plans on seeing you tomorrow."

"That's not possible. He was shot."

"He thought there could be problems getting you away from the Crussetts, so he wore a bullet-proof vest."

The bullet struck him. I felt his blood. Maybe he wasn't injured as badly as I thought. Still, I wouldn't believe Brett was okay until I saw him with my own eyes. Lance was acting so differently from the way he was in Billings. "Why are you being nice to me?" I asked, feeling suspicious.

"Because you're my patient."

"No, that's not it. Are you sometimes nice to your victims before you kill them?" I inquired, thinking about the events in the clearing and assuming he wouldn't try anything in the hospital.

His face went still as he clutched my arm and looked at me with dark, mesmerizing eyes. "Now I know that won't be necessary."

"You were planning on killing me?"

"That was always a possibility."

"What made you change your mind?"

Just then, the door swung open. Lance's posture stiffened as he let go of my arm and backed away from me.

In came Nurse Mabel. "Miss Jones, there were no gunshot victims where you were picked up," she proclaimed. Then she glanced at Lance. "Miss Jones still has a visitor anxious to see her. When can she have visitors?"

"Let me check her hands and feet first," Lance answered. "I'll let you know after that." He started taking off the bandage on my right hand.

"Is there anything I can get you?" Mabel asked Lance.

"Can you bring in the cart in the hallway?"

"Yes," Mabel replied and left the room.

"Conner has been here since you were brought in," Lance said. "Do you want to see him?"

"Right now I want to finish our conversation before the nurse comes back. What made you change your mind about killing me?"

"It's difficult for me to discuss. Lindsey will be here later today. She'll explain."

Nurse Mabel returned with the cart and stood it next to Lance. "Do you want me to help remove the bandages from her other hand and her feet?"

"No. I'll take care of it," Lance replied.

Nurse Mabel walked out, closing the door behind her.

"Did you know Lindsey before Brett introduced her to you at the theater in Billings?"

"Yes. I've known her for a long time."

"And how long have you known Brett?"

"A long time."

"Then why all the pretending? Brett said he knew you because you were Rex's neighbor. He wasn't in Billings for a long time."

"That's right. He only arrived a few days before you."

Brett told me he had been there for a couple of months before I came. Another lie. "The elderly woman, Mildred something, who sat next to me on the bus when I left Houston, do you know her?"

"Yes, but only briefly. She was hired to convince you to go to Billings."

"What if she failed to convince me?"

"We had ten individuals lined up after her, each more persuasive than the last."

"And if they all failed?"

"We would have just kidnapped you. To be honest, I was surprised you were so easy to persuade."

"How... how did you know I'd be on that bus?"

He finished removing the bandage and turned my hand over so the palm was up. All my fingers were covered with small bumps. No pus. "I didn't know exactly what bus you'd be taking. I knew you'd be leaving soon," he said, removing the bandage from my other hand.

"How?"

My fingers on that hand were also covered with small bumps that looked like goose bumps. I had never heard of anyone having this type of reaction to a spider bite or any poisonous arthropod bite. Lance ran his fingers over mine.

"I'll answer any questions you have after Lindsey talks to you," he replied. Then his eyes narrowed and he stared at me. "Saul also wants to see you."

I flinched and pressed my lips together.

Lance continued, "I'll tell him you're well enough for visitors now."

I clenched my teeth as a surge of anger swept through me. My hands tingled. I glanced down and saw stiff hairs or something like that, sticking out of the bumps.

Lance touched them and smiled. "Good girl. Don't worry, Saul can't come and visit you."

"What's happened to my hands?" With wide open eyes, I watched the hairs retracting into the bumps.

"I wanted to see it for myself, that's all," he said. "You need to be upset for that to occur."

"My... my hands ... what happened to my hands?"

"Relax." He moved his fingers over mine. "This is completely natural for your current phase. Your hands will look fine after the transformation."

"What?"

"Lindsey will explain." He opened the bottom cart drawer and took out a pair of thick, plastic-coated gloves. "These will help if you should get angry." He carefully slid them on my hands. "We don't want any more unplanned victims."

"Victims? Unlike you, I don't have victims."

"Calm down. If I wasn't immune, I would've been your next victim."

"My next victim? What other victims have I had?"

"Only Saul, but Brett helped with him." He scanned my face. "Don't look so worried. You'll be all right after the transformation."

Saul. Remembering his empty eyes, staring at me wide-open, I believed he had been bitten. I assumed Brett had spiders. There was no way I was even partially responsible. I needed answers and could hardly wait for Lindsey to show up. Then I wondered what I would do if I didn't like the answers.

He unwrapped my feet and squeezed my toes. "Are you in pain anywhere?"

"No."

Reaching in the drawer, he pulled out a pair of heavy, plastic-coated socks, and put them on my feet. "Let's see if you can walk." He took my arm and helped me stand.

I wobbled toward the door. "My feet feel like I'm walking on loose sand."

"That's normal for your condition."

"My condition?"

"Yes," he replied without explaining. He held my arm and eased me down on the edge of the bed. Then he pulled out another cart drawer, extracted a bottle of dark red liquid, and opened it. *Venotrolia* was written on the side.

"I want you to drink this," he said, inserting a straw in it.

"Is this the same stuff I drank in Billings?"

"So you remember. Even if things were a little hazy for you, I didn't think you'd believe you were dreaming. This is almost the same. It's missing an ingredient."

"What ingredient?"

"Something that deferred your current condition."

"I don't want it."

"Now you'll be able to control your desires, if that's what you're worried about."

"I still don't want to drink it," I said, knowing I had been lied to in the past. It had taken me a long time to get it out of my system. I didn't want to find myself trying to attack some orderly.

"Sara," he said in a firm, somber tone, "You can either drink this or I'll have it fed to you intravenously. Which would you prefer?"

"Neither," I said, determined. "And you can't make me. I'm going to check myself out of the hospital."

His brows rose, creasing his forehead. "You are not well enough to leave."

I didn't feel safe. The Crussetts were outside of the hospital and the spider cult was inside. Wherever I went, they would look for me. I had the choice of running for the rest of my life or letting them get me. I wouldn't give them the pleasure of chasing me around or meddling in my life any longer. I was going home. "You can't keep me here if I want to leave." I leaned over to push the call button. He grabbed my gloved hand.

"Okay ... okay. You don't have to drink it. Your hands and feet will start to hurt in a few hours. This isn't one of the medications available here."

"Why ... why isn't it available here? It's not a medication, is it?"

"You are the only patient in the hospital that requires this formula. That's why it isn't in their stock. There is no one here who can administer it, except me. When you are in pain and change your mind, you'll have to wait until I return."

Only time would tell whether or not this was another lie. "Then I won't check myself out today."

"Good," he said, screwing on the bottle cap and putting it away. "Do you want to see Conner before you experience pain in your hands and feet?"

I didn't know if I ever wanted to see him. Yet, I couldn't avoid it forever, and I thought he deserved being told goodbye in person. "Yes," I said, exhaling in reluctance. "He did send me lilacs."

"You like lilacs?" he inquired.

"Yes, they're my favorite flower," I replied and watched the corner of Lance's lips slightly curve up. Maybe he liked lilacs, too.

"Let the nurse know as soon as your hands and feet start hurting. Don't wait until the pain is severe, because it will keep escalating. I can't give you any *venotrolia* if you've been sedated, and without it you'll wake up in excruciating pain."

"If you're trying to scare me into drinking it, it isn't working."

"Have it your way." He pushed the cart out the door.

I suspected it was my head injury that caused me to be unstable on my feet, not the spider bite. After staying here another night, I was sure

I'd be well enough to go home. Once I was there, one of my parents' former colleagues could give me something for the bumps. The door opened and in came Conner, carrying a magazine.

He smiled as he walked over to the bed, put down the magazine, and wrapped his arms around me. I pushed him away.

"Sara, I'm so sorry."

"What are you sorry about, Conner?" I hissed. "That I'm not lying dead somewhere on the outskirts of Houston or that I'm in the hospital? I'm sure you know people who can finish the job here."

"I didn't know Cameron's plan."

"After I told you I was leaving, you went to make arrangements. When I came downstairs, you weren't in the house. The only way Cameron would have known I was leaving was if you told him."

He bent down and attempted to kiss my lips. I stopped him by turning my face. He ended up kissing my cheek. Then he pulled up a chair and sat next to the bed. "Cameron called when I was on the phone with the pilot. I didn't want you to leave. I still don't. Before Cameron came to dinner, he said that it would help you feel more like you were part of the family if we discussed business when you were there. He started doing that in front of Melanie right after they were married. She likes to know what's going on. I should've known better. I still blamed him for you leaving. He said he could smooth it over if I gave him a chance to talk to you on the way to the airport."

He gripped my gloved hand. "Sara, I love you. I wanted you to stay. Since it was Cameron's fault, I thought he could help. He said he'd drive you to the airport so I could take care of some things – business things – before we left Houston. I hoped you'd let me stay with you for a few weeks in California. I didn't want our relationship to end."

"Cameron never planned on going with me to the airport. He had Saul take me. And you and I both know Saul wasn't taking me to the airport."

"Please believe me. I didn't know what Cameron had in mind. It was taking me a little longer at the office than I had anticipated, so I called him. That's when I discovered he wasn't with you. I told him if anything happened to you, I'd leave the family business. He assured me that he'd make sure you were safe."

"He was lying."

"I didn't believe him either. I called the limo phone and Saul's cell phone. No one answered. Then I sent out men to search for the limo. It has a homing device. They located it when you were being put in an ambulance. The limo driver said you had fallen and hit your head. My men followed the ambulance to the hospital. With the problems in Billings, I wanted to make sure you got there."

"The limo phone did ring, and Saul received two calls on his cell phone. He only answered the second one and seemed irritated about it. Then he moved to the seat across from me."

"Before that, was he sitting next to you?"

"Yes. He was getting real friendly." I briefly closed my eyes and crunched my face as I recalled every detail. "I'm sure he was planning on having sex with me before he killed me."

Conner's eyes narrowed and his handsome face darkened with rage. "What did he do?"

"A little foreplay—trying to get me in the mood," I said, my voice dripping with sarcasm as I cocked my head. "He rubbed the inside of my thighs, stuck his hand in my blouse, felt my breasts, pushed me down on the seat. He was quite the gentleman. I kept trying to get him to stop. He couldn't be swayed."

He clenched his jaw. "Saul is a dead man."

"Saul told me that you said I was the best piece of ass you ever had."

"Sara, I would never talk that way about you."

"I know. That's obviously how Cameron talks about me."

"I'll find a way to deal with Cameron. He won't be allowed to be anywhere near you."

"How can you prevent that?"

"Let me work on it. I can, and I will keep you safe." He held up my gloved hand and kissed my arm. "How are you feeling?"

"Okay lying in bed. I have to walk slowly. That's probably because of my head injury."

"What did Dr. Alston say about your hands and feet?"

"He said they should be cleared up in a few days."

"When can you leave the hospital?"

"Don't know. Dr. Shaw, the head injury doctor, hasn't been in to see me since I've been awake. I'm hoping I can leave tomorrow."

"Do you still want me to take you to San Diego, or will you give me another chance and let me take you to my place?"

"I want to go home," I replied.

"Can I fly you there?"

I didn't know if I'd be up for taking a commercial flight since I'd have to walk a lot. I hated Conner's business and wanted to hate him. I was in love with the human façade he wore around me. The façade that was currently talking sweetly, yet probably wanting nothing more than to imprison me in his fortress home again.

Still, when he said he loved me, it sounded genuine, and I believed him. Perhaps he wasn't a monster wearing a mask. Maybe the "facade" was the real man, and his unforgiveable criminal tendencies deep-rooted in his personality from his birth into the Crussett family. I could never look past his crimes, nor could I ignore that his feelings for me were authentic. Whether the Conner I fell in love with was the real man or just the mask he wore, I did and always would feel something for him, if only regret for what could have been. Unlike other people, he had never outright lied to me—just concealed the truth, a truth I did not want revealed to me. Our relationship was over, but he wanted to help, and part of me still trusted him.

He caressed my arm. "Sara, can I fly you to San Diego?" he asked again.

I took a deep breath. "Yes, you can take me."

"Good. Your birthday's in a few days. We've always gone away to celebrate. Right now, I'm sure you don't want to go to an exotic place with me. I would still like to spend the day with you. Is that a possibility?"

I smiled at him, remembering all the fun we had on our birthdays at romantic locations all over the world. My favorite was basking in the sun on a remote island in the South Pacific. "Let me think about it."

His eyes lit up with a warm glow. "At least you didn't say no immediately. So I must be making some progress." He stroked my cheek. "Flying with you from Billings and Nebraska. I'm ruined for wanting to fly with anyone else." He grinned.

I blushed as I returned his smile.

"I'll always want to be part of your life, even if you don't need me. Often I had a hard time not laughing when a family member mentioned that you were just a gold digger. If any of them knew just how much money you had."

"How do you know?"

"After the first time we had lunch together, I wanted to know everything about you. I had you investigated."

"Did you have all your dates investigated?" I asked, irritated.

He gently squeezed my forearm. "Only if I wanted to see them again. In your case, it wouldn't have mattered what the investigation turned up, I still planned on seeing you."

Given his family business, I understood he had to take precautions.

He continued, "When you left, I had a tab placed on your account so I'd know if and where you made a withdrawal. If everything else failed, I hoped I could find you that way." He leaned over and lightly kissed my lips.

Nurse Mabel entered. "Dr. Alston wants you to rest. He asked me to limit your visits."

"Can I have another five minutes?" Conner asked.

"Yes. No longer." She stepped out of the room, leaving the door wide open.

"I'm planning on coming back later," Conner said. "Do you want me to bring anything?"

"Some clothes and my purse. I don't know what happened to the blouse and slacks I was wearing."

"Do you want shoes?"

"No." I moved the sheet, revealing my feet. "They won't fit over them."

He touched a thick sock. "Any pain?"

"No."

"I'll pack a small suitcase." He kissed me goodbye.

Nurse Mabel brought my lunch. It was awkward eating with the gloves on. Yet, I managed.

"Dr. Shaw will be here soon to see you," she said, picking up the food tray.

Feeling tired, I closed my eyes. Just as I started drifting off, someone touched my arm. I opened my eyes and saw an elderly man in a white lab coat.

"Hello, Miss Jones. I'm Doctor Shaw. How are you feeling?"

"Fine, except when I walk to the bathroom, I feel unsteady."

"Loss of equilibrium?"

I nodded.

"Let me examine your eyes," he said, taking a small flashlight out of his pocket. He shined it in each of my eyes as he peered into them. He felt the back of my head. "Any tender spots?"

"No."

"I don't see any sign that your head injury should have caused that feeling. I'll check with Dr. Alston. It could be a result of the spider bite. If not, I'll arrange for some additional tests."

"When can I leave the hospital?"

"Before I can release you as my patient, I need to check with Dr. Alston about the equilibrium issue you're experiencing. Let me see if I can reach him now." He stepped out of the room.

Within fifteen minutes Dr. Shaw returned. "Dr. Alston confirmed that it's caused by the spider venom. I'll have my name removed as an attending physician."

"Can I leave tomorrow?"

"As far as your head injury is concerned, you can. You are still Dr. Alston's patient. I don't know when he's planning to discharge you. You'll have to ask him. If you should have any head pain, let the nurse know. I'll come and see you again."

"Okay."

"Have a nice trip back to San Diego," he said, walking to the door.

"Thank you." I wondered how he knew where I was going.

Closing my eyes again, I felt a slight stinging sensation in my hands and feet. I rolled over onto my side, thinking that another position might help. The stinging changed to itching. That might be a good sign. Maybe my hands and feet were healing. Then my hands started hurting a little. Please, don't let Lance be right. This had to be my imagination. He just planted the seed.

My hands and feet were keeping me awake. To get my mind off them, I thought about going home and sleeping in my own bed in San Diego. Then I got the urge to call an old friend. I scooted to the edge of the bed and picked up the phone just as a pain rippled through my arches. Gasping, I laid down the receiver and eased my head back down on the pillow. My feet throbbed. Maybe Mabel could give me a couple of aspirins or something to help me sleep. I pushed the call button.

A moment later, she walked through the doorway. "Do you need something?"

"I'm feeling tired. I can't seem to fall asleep. Could I have two aspirins or something that might help me relax?"

"Dr. Alston's orders were not to give you any medication without checking with him first. Would you like me to give him a call?"

"No ... No. I'll just watch some television."

"Push the call button if you change your mind," she said and closed the door.

I turned on the television and flipped through the channels. I ran across a crime show. Appropriate, given the circumstances. I propped up the pillows behind me and watched. The pain was getting worse. I found it became impossible to concentrate on the show.

The door flew open and in strolled Cameron. I stared at him as he came closer.

"How are you feeling, Sara?" he asked with a smirk on his face.

"How did you get in here?"

"No one stopped me."

"What do you want?" I knew what he really wanted was for me to be dead and buried.

"What did you do to Saul?"

"You came to see me so you could ask about Saul?" I sneered. "I should be asking you why you wanted Saul to go with me to the airport."

"He only went to protect you. I did want you to arrive there safe and sound."

"By allowing him to rape me? That's your method of protection?"

"Saul would never do that. You must've misunderstood his intentions."

"So his hands roaming all over my clothing was to make sure everything was securely in place? Is that what you're saying?"

"You sustained a head injury. You're not thinking clearly."

"Right."

He sat down in the chair. "Conner still wants you to be a member of the family. I think we need to make peace."

"I'm not planning on being a member of your family, so you can just go on hating me. You don't need to like me or even tolerate me. I'll be going home when I get out of the hospital. You'll never see me again."

Hatred shone through his icy blue eyes. "I'll make you a deal," he said. "I'll let you live in peace in San Diego, as soon as you return the other documents you took."

"Conner has all the documents."

"You gave him the copies you made. I want the originals that were removed from the one ledger."

"I didn't take any original documents."

"That's too much of a coincidence," he snarled. "Those documents go missing at the same time you copied some pages out of that ledger."

"I don't have your documents," I shrieked as an excruciating pain surged through my hands and feet. It moved up my arms and legs. Oh, no, Lance was right. My body began to writhe in agony as sweat streamed down my face.

"What the hell?" Cameron said, his eyes fixed on me.

Mabel and two nurses came running into the room. She touched my arm. The pain had spread through my whole body. I screamed again. "Don't touch me!"

Buzzers went off around me. People were yelling and shouting. I couldn't comprehend anything they said. I screamed again when someone stuck a needle in my arm.

18

RESEARCH

Opening my eyes, I saw Lance sitting in a chair next to my bed. He made a vague expression I took to be a smile as our eyes met.

"I knew I couldn't get you to take *venotrolia* until the pain became unbearable," he said. "You're just as stubborn as your mother."

So, he did know my parents. Though his perception of her being stubborn was off. She was better described as being opinionated. I noticed another IV tube attached to my arm and followed it to a bag of dark red liquid. He was feeding it to me intravenously. "I told you I didn't want it. I could've been given other medication for the pain."

"No. Only *venotrolia* can attack your pain. All other medications would just put you to sleep. Do you want to sleep the rest of your life?"

My mind felt clouded. I didn't want to believe he was right. Yet, the pain had been terrible and now it was gone. "I had a visitor when I was given a shot. Do you know if he's still here?"

"He left and he won't be back."

"You didn't—"

"No," Lance interrupted. "I've restricted your visitors. He must've upset you for the pain to escalate so quickly. It shouldn't have risen that fast."

I changed the subject. "When will Lindsey be here?"

"She was here earlier when you were sleeping. I'll call her and let her know you're awake. Are you in pain anywhere?"

"No."

He stood, carefully removed the needle from my arm, and took down the bag with the red liquid inside. "You won't need this for a while. Before I leave, is there anything you want?"

"Do you have a laptop computer I could use?"

"Wanting to verify my medical credentials?"

"Yes."

"I'll have one delivered. Next time you experience the slightest pain, will you let the nurse know?"

I nodded.

He left with the bag of red liquid.

I picked up the magazine and slowly thumbed through it as I waited for the computer. How could he be a physician and the son of a renowned doctor? He killed people. It didn't add up.

"Here's the computer you requested," Mabel said, placing it on the table in front of me. "The hospital has Wi-Fi. Just turn on the computer and click the internet browser icon."

"I don't think I can press the keys with these gloves on. Do you have a pencil or pen I could use?"

"Yes." She pulled a pencil out of her breast pocket and handed it to me.

"Thanks."

"Push your call button if you have any problems with the computer," she said as she was leaving.

Using the eraser tip on the pencil, I brought up the internet and searched for Lance Alston. Numerous pages of sites appeared. I went to the first one and saw a picture of him. It documented his research and vaccines he had developed. There were links to his clinic in North Dakota, his hospital affiliations, and his biography. I clicked on his biography. It stated he lived in North Dakota. Nowhere did it say anything about his home in Billings.

All of the educational institutions he had attended were listed. It also said that he had been mentored by his father, Lawrence Alston, who was known worldwide for his publications on cures and treatments of insect bites and exposures. There was a link to his father's site. I tapped on it. A picture of a gray-haired man with a mustache came on the screen. I saw the family resemblance: their dark eyes, nose, and the shape of their faces were identical. His father's biography mentioned he had a son, Lance. Nothing else was stated about his family—no sibling, grandparents, wife—nothing. Then I noticed that Lawrence hadn't taught or made any public appearances for over twenty years. No explanation was given. However, his father's most recent publication was only five years ago. I continued going through the site to see if he had any book signings or anything like that. Nothing.

I searched his father's name and scrolled down several pages of sites until I came across one that mentioned his wife and clicked on it. It was an article from a North Dakota newspaper. The headline read: *The Passing of Jennifer Alston is Mourned by All.* Next to it was a photo of Lawrence standing by a grave. The caption below it read: *Dr. Lawrence Alston says goodbye to his beloved Jennifer.* In that picture, he looked just like Lance. He must have been around Lance's age when his wife died.

Reading the article, I discovered they had been married for eighteen years. Jennifer was a registered nurse and worked side-by-side with her husband. The cause of her death was stated as complications resulting from childbirth. I thought how awful that must be for Lance, knowing his mother died giving him life. She died the day after my birthday, so Lance and I were exactly the same age. Given his education and experience, I had assumed he was older than that. I looked for a picture of Lance's mother and found one. It only showed her profile. Something about her seemed unsettlingly familiar.

Wanting to find a connection between Lance's research and the cult, I looked for articles about poisonous spider bites. Dr. Alston was listed on numerous site summaries. I went to the most recent one. As I started reading, the door swung open.

"Hi," Lindsey said, cheerfully, closing the door behind her. "Are you finding everything you wanted to know?"

"Almost."

"Any surprises?"

"No. However, I was wondering why Lance's father had become a recluse over the past twenty plus years. Is he ill or is it because he's still mourning his wife?"

"He isn't ill. He still mourns his wife, but that isn't why he doesn't make public appearances." She moved a chair closer to the bed and sat down. "Explaining everything was Brett's job until he got himself shot." She sounded annoyed about it.

"Lance … Lance said that he was okay." Water welled in my eyes. I'd been lied to again.

She patted my arm. "I didn't mean to upset you. Brett will be okay. He just needs to rest for a few days. That's all. He'll see you tomorrow. Lance thought you couldn't wait that long. He's concerned you might try and leave the hospital without knowing."

"How do I know Brett's okay?"

"Call him," she said without hesitation. "Even if he can't come here, he can still talk on the phone."

"Okay." I reached for the phone. "Does his cell phone number work?"

"Yes."

I punched his number. The phone rang. I waited patiently for him to answer. It got harder after each ring. Finally, after six rings, he answered.

"Hello, Sara."

"How did you know it was me?"

"The hospital showed up on my caller ID, so it had to be you since Lindsey and Lance would've used their cell phones. I planned on calling you this evening after Lindsey left."

"I've been worried about you. You should've called."

"I did. Incoming phone calls to your room are blocked. Lance is going to get it lifted this evening."

"How are you?"

"A little sore. I'll be one-hundred percent by tomorrow."

"How? You were shot."

"Has Lindsey explained anything?"

"No. She just got here."

"You'll understand when she's through. After that, if you have any questions just give me a call or wait until I call you."

"I'm glad you're okay," I said, feeling relieved.

"We'll talk later."

"Bye." I hung up, and then looked at Lindsey. "Okay, start explaining."

She pulled a notepad out of her purse and looked at the top page. "I'm sure Brett could do a better job. Here goes. You've..." She stopped abruptly when the door opened.

19

TEGENS

A nurse came in carrying a food tray. "You slept through dinner," she said. "Dr. Alston wants you on a special diet." She set the tray down on the counter, moved the computer, and then she placed the food on the table in front of me.

Looking at it, I saw he had ordered me a steak along with chocolate cake for dessert. "Thank you," I said, watching her step out of the room.

"That looks good," Lindsey said. "Go ahead, I'll explain while you're eating."

I cut into the meat.

"You've successfully completed all the phases of becoming a Tegen," she began, sounding pleased. "I'm a Tegen. All that's left is your transformation."

"Is that what you call a cult member—a Tegen?"

"We're not a cult," she said. "We're a species."

"You're a what?" I asked with my mouth full.

"Let me start from the beginning. Over a century ago, we don't know exactly when because all the documents were burned in the Chicago fire of 1871, Sir Randolph Heinrich worked on a solution to maintain the human body without aging."

"Like the fountain of youth?"

"Sort of. When he extracted a gene sequence from Hobo spiders and injected them into mouse egg cells, it yielded mice that didn't age past adulthood. Then he inserted the gene sequence into a mutagen for humans and used it on himself. It had no immediate effect, but permanently altered his DNA, allowing it to infinitely replicate. We don't know Sir Randolph's formula. We do know he stopped his own aging process."

"How old was he when he died?"

"We don't know. You see, once you're transformed into a Tegen, you never die."

"Oh, come on. You're telling me Tegens live forever?"

"Yes. And we never age."

"You expect me to believe that?"

"It's true."

I chewed the food in my mouth and swallowed. "If that's the case, then Sir Randolph can recreate his formula, showing and explaining how he did it."

"Only fire can destroy a Tegen. That Chicago fire wiped out almost all of them, including Sir Randolph. A small group escaped with a single box of spiders."

"Spiders … why do you need spiders?" I asked in a tone of disbelief as I continued eating.

"Spiders are our life blood. We need their venom to survive."

"You just said that only fire can destroy a Tegen."

"That's true. However, without the venom, a Tegen's strength deteriorates and bodily functions can't be controlled."

"Bodily functions?" My mind raced. "Overwhelming sex drive. Is that what you mean?"

"No."

"Then what?"

"Have you seen sharp little spikes appear out of the bumps on your hands or feet when you get upset?"

"Yeah."

"That's what happens. They'll cover your whole body. We refer to those spikes as needles, since they're sharp. The spider venom is secreted by our sweat glands; the needles are just regular hairs engorged with venom."

I put down my fork and raised my glove-covered hands. Bumps all over my body with spikes sticking out? No way. I returned to my food.

She continued, "We've never been without the spiders. That's why we have them thriving in various locations. There are some with us all the time. We'd rather burn ourselves than exist without the spiders."

"Are you carrying some now?"

She bobbed her head. "Yes."

"Where?"

Opening her purse, she pulled out a small, black, ovoid container covered with pin-like holes. "Do you want to see them?"

I stared at her, wondering why she would expose everyone in the hospital to those lethal spiders. "No. I don't want anyone getting hurt."

"They'll stay in their container."

"Just leave them there." I watched her put it away. "Hobo spiders, or should I say *tegenaria agrestis,* are poisonous. People bitten by them don't react the way I've seen people react to your spiders."

"Sir Randolph changed the DNA of the Hobo spider. Our spiders are no longer Hobo spiders just as we are no longer humans."

"How do you get out the venom?" I asked suspiciously. "Do you eat them?"

"No, we don't eat our spiders. We...we." She hesitated. "The spiders paralyze a person and their venom runs through the blood and organs. We consume the venom by drinking the tainted blood and eating the body. Regular blood just doesn't work," she said, matter-of-factly.

My lips quivered. I briefly closed my eyes, realizing they drugged me and made me participate. "You use the spiders for your rituals?"

"We don't have rituals, we have gatherings."

Taking a deep breath, I said, "Okay, gatherings. Go on."

She lifted an impatient brow. "The Hobo spider DNA sequence Sir Randolph inserted into the mutagen makes us biologically dependent on the venom," she said, sounding frustrated. "It's an integral component of the gene replication process that allows us to live like humans forever. Without the venom our cells deteriorate and that's the only way we can get it.

I felt a clutching, sinking sensation in my chest as I wondered how they could have such low regard for human life. "Do you think it's okay to kill people?"

"You'll feel differently after you've been transformed."

"If I have to kill people to survive as a Tegen," I said, doubting their existence, "then I don't want to be one. Why don't you find someone else who might be interested in joining your—species." Gazing at the food on the tray, my appetite was gone. I laid the napkin on top of it.

"It's not that easy. Not everyone can be a Tegen. You see, the mutagen changed Sir Randolph's DNA along with his family and his co-workers who wanted it. Since the formula was destroyed, now you have to be born with the right DNA to be a Tegen. One of your parents has to be a Tegen."

"If one of my parents was a Tegen, why did they both die in a car crash? Or are you telling me that one of them is still alive?"

"I can tell you don't believe anything I'm saying, but it's all true." She frowned and pressed her lips together. "The Joneses were not your biological parents."

"Yeah, right. They would've told me if I was adopted, and I've seen pictures of me when I was an infant minutes after I was born."

"That's only because your father gave them those pictures." She waited for me to absorb that bit of information. "Your father knew your adoptive parents. They hadn't planned on adopting a kid. He persuaded them. It turned out to be good for you and for them. They loved you."

My eyes became moist just thinking about them. "Why are you saying this about my parents? You didn't even know them."

She held my arm. "As hard as it is for you to believe this, it's all true. Your biological father wanted to help you by placing you in a home where spiders were respected." She smiled. "He loved it when he heard how much you enjoyed watching and playing with them. You had a spider colony in your bedroom. When you were in the first grade, you took a few with you to school in your little pink purse. We laughed about that and thought you were already getting used to taking spiders with you. Your teacher didn't think it was funny and you got in trouble."

"How do you know that?"

"Your father told me. The arrangement he made with the Joneses was that they could raise you without interference. They were to send him a picture of you every year along with a brief summary of what you had done. The Joneses fell in love with you the first time they saw you. They agreed to his request and formally adopted you. It was recorded. You can check it out."

"I will. If that's true, who's my biological father?"

"Lance."

"Oh, come on. I read Lawrence Alston's biography and a newspaper article about when Lance's mother died. He's the same age I am. He came to my parents' funeral, probably because they were in the same organizations since he deals with spider bites, and my parents were arachnologists. He didn't even talk to me. Every time he looked at me, he had a stern expression on his face. Then when I saw him at the hotel, he acted almost hostile toward me. That isn't how a father would behave toward his child."

She lowered her head as if she was thinking how to respond and nervously drummed her fingers on the armrest. Then she sat up straight and her eyes met mine. "Lawrence and Lance Alston are the same person."

"Your story gets more bizarre by the minute," I gasped for fresh air. Although, inside my mind something was clicking.

"This may sound bizarre, but it is resounding fact, and we can substantiate it. Lance is a Tegen. Since he's an expert in his field, he can't lecture or do anything under the guise of Lawrence because he looks too young. He's actually over a hundred years old. We constantly have to pretend we're other people since we don't age."

"If you're forced to pretend you're other people, then why don't you come forward and admit you're a Tegen? You could make billions."

"We don't have the formula for the mutagen." She shifted in her chair and clasped her hands together.

The door squeaked open, and we turned as a nurse entered. "It's time for your medication," she said, putting down a tray.

"What medication?" I asked.

"Your doctor wants you to have a shot to help relieve your pain," she replied.

Lindsey stood up. "Miss Jones' doctor has already given her medication to control the pain. Can I see the doctor's prescription?"

"Who are you?" the nurse asked, sounding annoyed.

Lindsey pulled a badge from her purse. "I'm a registered nurse and Dr. Alston's assistant," she said, showing it to the nurse.

The nurse thumbed through documents on her clipboard. "There's nothing hear about an assistant."

"Can I see the prescription?" I asked.

The nurse's eyes narrowed as she unclipped a yellow form. "Certainly," she said, handing it to me. Then she looked at Lindsey. "You'll have to leave after I give Miss Jones this shot. She needs to sleep."

"Lindsey, do you want to see it?" I asked, holding up the prescription.

"Yes." She checked the form. "This isn't Dr. Alston's signature."

The nurse took the prescription and hooked it to her board. "Of course it isn't. Dr. Frandsen signed it," she said, filling the syringe.

"My doctor is Dr. Alston," I said. "I want to talk to him before I have a shot."

"Dr. Alston isn't in the hospital. Dr. Frandsen is in charge of his patients when he isn't here."

"I have Dr. Alston's cell phone number," Lindsey said. "Let me give him a call."

The nurse put down the syringe. "Since you're his assistant, I'll finish distributing medications while you contact Dr. Alston."

Lindsey moved closer to her. "No, you'll stay right here while I call Dr. Alston."

"Miss Jones isn't the only patient that needs medication," the nurse replied, irritated.

"This will just take a minute." Lindsey stood between the nurse and the door.

The nurse clenched her teeth, but didn't attempt to leave as Lindsey placed the call, presumably to Lance, and told him the situation. After a brief pause, "Okay, that's what I'll do." Lindsey disconnected and looked at the nurse. "Dr. Alston's in the hospital. He thinks there must be some confusion regarding Miss Jones' medication. He's coming to talk to you about it."

Lindsey remained fixed by the door, blocking the nurse from leaving without a physical confrontation. Without saying a word, the nurse remained still as she glared at Lindsey.

To defuse the tension, I said, "Nurse, my call button cord keeps getting tangled in the bed railing, is there anything you can do about it?"

The nurse turned and walked to the bed. "Yes. I'll secure it in a few places." She pulled a roll of white tape out of her pocket and proceeded to attach the cord at various locations along the railing.

"Thanks," I said, giving her a smile.

Lance came into the room. "I've already given Miss Jones her evening medication," he said politely to the nurse. "Let me see what Dr. Frandsen prescribed."

The nurse handed him the clipboard. He looked at it and his mouth eased into a smile. "Dr. Frandsen has prescribed medication for a Miss Jones. It's for Sharon Jones, not Sara."

Reading the form, the nurse's eyebrows rose. "I'm so sorry, Doctor." She turned toward Lindsey. "I'm glad you checked with Dr. Alston." She walked around Lindsey. "I need to give Sharon Jones her medication."

Lance closed the door behind her. "I think she made an honest mistake. I've seen her before in the hospital. She isn't anyone we need to be concerned about."

My eyes popped wide open. "But she was going to give me a shot."

"It's good that Lindsey stopped her. However, had you received that medication, it wouldn't have hurt you. It would have put you to sleep. No lasting effect. It's unfortunate, but errors like that are made often." He looked at Lindsey. "Are you through?"

"No."

I wanted to talk to him about it; even though, I suspected Lance was in cahoots with Lindsey. He would just confirm everything she had said.

He opened the door. "I'll be in my office if you need me."

When he was gone, Lindsey asked, "Where did I leave off?"

"You had just told me that Lance was my father, and he was a Tegen."

"And you didn't believe me." She flipped through her notepad. "Let me get through this and then you can ask Lance and Brett questions."

"Okay, finish your bizarre story."

She squinted and tapped her finger tips together. "Just wait and see. You'll know I'm telling the truth."

"Go on." What an elaborate tale to explain why they mutilate people. Still, I couldn't shake the feeling that it wasn't all lies.

"Lance didn't want you to know he was your father until you completed all the phases, because if you didn't, he couldn't allow you to survive."

I rolled my eyes. "So if I don't want to join your group, he'll kill me?"

"That's not exactly how it works. You had to be born with the correct genes to become a Tegen. Sometimes, we know a Tegen's child doesn't have the right DNA when they're very young because they hate spiders. A potential Tegen will have a biological affinity to spiders and be immune to their venom. The Tegen ring has to be accepted by their body and—"

I interrupted, "What does that mean?"

"The stone in the black ring you received is actually a tightly spun spider web from the Tegen Cave that has become petrified. The web has also been embedded into the band. When a potential Tegen puts on the ring, their body chemistry and the ring complement each other. If that occurs, they can't take off the ring without having their hand, or at least a few fingers, feel numb and painful. They'll stay numb until the ring is put back on, so potential Tegens don't take it off. No one wants to be in pain."

"There was a time I could take the ring off without any problems."

"That was before you were bitten," she clarified. "A potential Tegen doesn't become sealed to it until venom runs in their veins."

"No. I took it off after I was bitten the first time."

"I know. Brett saw it off your finger. Your father thought you didn't receive enough venom, so spiders visited your room again."

"The ones that were all over my legs?"

"Yes. He wanted to make sure you got enough venom. Brett confirmed you had been bitten numerous times."

She had an explanation for everything. My eyes dropped to Lindsey's hand, and I saw a ring on her finger that looked like mine. Attempting to hide the uneasy sensation running through my body, I swallowed hard and took a deep breath. "Do I have to wear it forever?"

"You'll want to wear it all the time. Once you've gone through the transformation, you can take it off. Brett and I didn't wear our rings in front of you."

I ran my trembling left hand over my right fingers and felt the ring through the glove.

"Sometime after a potential Tegen has been bitten," she went on, "their nails turn a reddish-purple. Normally, that doesn't occur until a few days before the potential Tegen's twenty-fifth birthday. With you it happened too early."

"Your cult ... I mean species, put the spiders in my room. It wouldn't have happened if you hadn't done that."

"You're just not normal, that's all."

"I'm the one that's not normal?"

"Can you just let me finish?"

I nodded.

"Your nails changing color that early worried Lance because you have to be able to walk into the cave."

"I'm not going into any cave." Looking at her pale blue eyes, I felt a little sorry for her. She had been sent to deliver an absurd tale. Even if most of it was unbelievable, there were a few pieces of truth woven in. "Go on."

"A day or two after you were bitten, you should've been sick for a week to ten days with flu like symptoms: headache, sore throat, nausea, things like that. In your case, it only lasted for a few hours. The plan was Brett would take you to Rex's place and take care of you there."

Recalling the intimate moments I shared with Brett, I said, "He took care of me alright."

Lindsey lightly shook her head as she cocked her brow. "That's not what I'm talking about. He was going to act like your nurse; make sure you drank plenty of liquids, feed you soup, wipe sweat off your face and body, stuff like that. Since Brett never got to play nursemaid, Lance was really concerned.

"I guess I can't join your species because I wasn't sick long enough."

"I've never heard of anyone before that didn't get sick for at least a week. No … no … once I heard a guy was only sick for five days. Not two or three hours. Your father was worried you were moving through the phases too fast. You can't go to the Tegen Cave before your birthday, so he wanted to prolong your next phase."

"What happens if I go through the phases too early?"

"I'll get to that later." She brushed her hair away from her face. "Your next phase was heightened emotions. That should have happened before the reddish-purple nails. Lance tried to lengthen it by giving you some *venotrolia* with a special drug in it."

"What drug?"

"Something to prolong that phase."

"Like a date rape drug?"

"In your case, it was something like that, but you were the aggressor. Every Tegen undergoes a unique emotional reaction. The handler is usually there to keep them from going on a killing spree, or harming themselves. Brett just happened to get lucky that he was assigned to a woman whose reaction was sexual desires instead of depression, anger, or temper tantrums. Rarely are they happy emotions."

"You're telling me that Lance is my father, and he gave me a drug so I'd want to have sex with everyone? I've never heard of a drug that could cause that. I think the *venotrolia*, or whatever you want to call it, was responsible for my sexual desires. You know, I couldn't even control myself. I could be in the middle of a serious discussion and all of a sudden attack the person. I just can't believe a father would want a daughter to act that way."

"Lance didn't know that would be your heightened emotion. He wasn't any happier about that than you were. He still needed to prolong that phase. He didn't want you to have sex with everyone. That's why Brett was with you. All potential Tegens have a handler that helps them through that phase."

"Brett was my handler?"

"Yes. A handler gains the trust of the potential Tegen and stays close to that person through the phases. The handler reports back to the parent regarding the progress. The parent is the one who is responsible for their offspring. A child will never know their Tegen parent unless they complete the phases."

"Then I would never have been told that Lance was my father?"

"Right. It's only after the child completes the phases that their handler tells them about Tegens. Since Brett couldn't do it today, Lance thought about telling you. He decided against it since he suspected you didn't trust him. He asked me to do it because we were friends."

He was right. I didn't trust him. After the way she deceived me in Billings, I didn't trust her either.

Lindsey continued, "The phase you're in now, the problems with your hands and feet can be very dangerous and painful. Lance didn't want you to suffer long. That was another reason he wanted you to stay in the heightened emotional phase until you were closer to your birthday."

"What do you mean when you say 'dangerous'?"

A sad expression crept across her face. "You can accidentally kill someone just by getting mad."

"How?"

"When you get upset, the needles appear, and you could scratch someone who isn't a Tegen. Poison will be injected into that person through the needles. You'll poison them the same way as one of our spiders. Your hands and feet are covered so you won't hurt anyone."

Lance did mention something about how Saul was my victim. "If you can poison someone, why do you need the spiders?"

"The venom we produce is slightly different from the spiders. I don't know the technical words to describe it. I just know that if we poison someone, they still have to be bitten by a spider if we're going to drink their blood. I guess our venom isn't powerful enough."

She glanced at her notepad and fumbled through a few pages. "Let me get back to your biological parents. I never knew Jennifer, your mother. I've only been a Tegen for twenty-three years. Hattie, a Tegen, knew her and worked with her at your dad's clinic in North Dakota. Jennifer was twenty-one years old and a registered nurse when she met Lawrence. Hattie said he fell in love the first time he saw her. Six months later, he married her. Most Tegens never marry because we don't age and humans do.

"Tegen men can impregnate a human. The fetus secretes a chemical which the mother becomes addicted to and needs to survive. Once the infant is born, the chemical is no longer produced, and the mother dies. Lance and Jennifer didn't plan on having any children."

"She knew about Tegens?" I asked.

"Yes. Lance told her everything." Lindsey leaned her elbow on an armrest. "Hattie also loved your mother. She says that Lawrence always looked adoringly at her. I've been crazy about Lance since I first met him. I'd be satisfied with even a fraction of the love he felt toward Jennifer."

"You and Lance are a couple?"

"Yes, but not like he was with your mother. He kept trying to duplicate Sir Randolph's research. He wanted her to be with him always. Jennifer was growing older, and she knew he never would. When she turned thirty-nine, she decided to have a child and got pregnant without talking to Lawrence about it. He didn't even know she was pregnant until she was three months along. He was heartbroken. Even an abortion wouldn't have helped. The outcome would have been the same. She kept telling him she wanted to give him something to remember her by. Also, Jennifer couldn't bear to have him see her age. I'm sure Hattie wants to talk to you about your mother."

"Is Hattie in Texas?"

"No. She was in Billings. Now she's back in North Dakota. Lawrence was able to keep your mom alive for almost a day after you were born. He promised her he'd take good care of you."

"Then how could he kill me?"

"A Tegen is responsible for his or her offspring. If the child cannot become a Tegen, that child is terminated."

"Tegens kill their own children?" I asked, feeling shocked that anyone could do that.

"Yes," she said, sadly. "The genes of a Tegen are still part of that child. That child can't live a normal adult life."

"Why?"

"You've seen your hands and feet. Even if a Tegen's offspring can't become a Tegen, that eventually will happen to them. And daughters of Tegens can only give birth to one normal looking baby. Sons of Tegens can't father a child unless they become a Tegen. Before that, they can impregnate a girl, causing her to miscarry and die. If a son cannot be a Tegen, it's better if he's eliminated when he turns twenty-five, if not sooner."

"Why twenty-five?"

"That was the age set by Sir Randolph since he believed it was the pinnacle of adulthood before a person begins to decline athletically."

"You started the process by having the offspring bitten by a spider," I said. "That didn't just happen. Maybe some people needed to be older."

"No. The Tegens who escaped the Chicago fire tried that hypothesis and waited for an offspring to show signs. It turned out to be a disaster."

"How?"

"Have you ever heard of the World's Columbian Exposition of 1893?"

"Yes."

"Hundreds of people ended up going missing."

I cocked my brows. "Tegens' children were responsible?"

"Yeah." She tapped her fingertips together. "They were older than twenty-five and went on a killing rampage. With other potential Tegens, everything happened at once. The offspring had heightened emotions at the same time the bumps appeared. They poisoned almost everyone around them. Besides being able to walk into the cave you also need to wear the ring. It has to be the right size. It was impossible to get it on their finger over the bumps. They were in excruciating pain when they died. After those problems, Tegens followed the twenty-fifth birthday protocol. Even if that meant starting the process by having the potential Tegen bitten by one of our spiders."

"How about younger than twenty-five?"

"No one has ever started the phases by themselves too early. Unfortunately, there have been some situations where we have had the potential Tegen bitten too early. Like in your case if the heightened emotions hadn't been extended by Lance. You can't go to the cave until your birthday."

"You said some children were eliminated before their twenty-fifth birthday—why?"

"As I said, the potential Tegen child has to like spiders. If they don't, we know then they can never join us."

"You kill children?"

She fidgeted with her hands. "They can't have a normal life. Their mutated DNA causes severe birth defects which will manifest before twenty-five."

"Like what?"

"They lack morals. They become self-centered killers. Some have even killed their adoptive parents." She cast her eyes down. "None of us want to kill our children if it isn't necessary."

Cringing, I sat quietly staring at her, thinking how hard it would be to have to kill your own child, let alone at a young age.

Lindsey continued, "Daughters of Tegens who have the ability to transform can't bear children after the transformation is complete."

"You said daughters could only have one normal looking child. What would the second one look like?"

"I've only seen a picture. The baby didn't look human."

"What happens to the first child that a Tegen's daughter has given birth to if she gives that child up for adoption?"

Lindsey gave me a cocked smile. "You're talking about yourself, aren't you?"

"How did you know?"

"Lance knows you had a son when you were seventeen. We're keeping track of him. The doctor who delivered him is a Tegen."

"I didn't know the baby was a boy. I wanted to see him. Mother thought it would be too difficult on me since I wasn't keeping the baby." Over the past eight years, I've often wondered what my child looked like and hoped he was happy. "Does he like spiders?"

Lindsey nodded.

"If Lance is my father," I asked suspiciously, "how could he keep the promise he made to my biological mother to keep me safe if I couldn't become a Tegen?"

"That promise has plagued him ever since you were born. Several of us," she said, her eyes boring into mine, "have told him we'd help out if it came to that."

"You told him you'd kill me if I couldn't become a Tegen?"

"Yes," she said without batting an eye. "I knew it would be hard on him if he had to do it. Lance said it was his responsibility. It's difficult for any Tegen to kill his child. Most Tegen men only spend a few years with the mother; Lance was with your mother for over eighteen years. In the end, he would have done what was required, regardless of how he felt about it."

"Lindsey, have you had any children?"

Her lips quivered. "I was married and had a son when I was told about Tegens. I accidentally killed my husband and left my child. I didn't know about the needles until it was too late."

"You didn't have a handler?"

"I did. It was difficult because I was married. My handler rented a house around the corner from where I lived. We became the best of friends, but he couldn't be with me all the time."

"Was your son's name Simon?"

"Yes. How did you know?"

"Just a guess. A picture of Simon Ellis was hanging in the Billings police station. I saw it when I was there on Monday. Simon was missing and he lived in Portland. That's when I suspected you might be a member of the spider cult."

"It's not a cult. Now I know why you left me a note instead of warning me in person to be aware of the woods and not confiding in me that you were leaving."

"What happened to Simon?"

"I was with Simon the first two years of his life, and it was difficult." Lindsey sucked in air. "At least I never have to do it again."

"He didn't become a Tegen?"

"No."

"How about his girlfriend?"

"Was her picture also hanging up?"

"No. Sergeant Harmon told me that Simon's girlfriend was also missing. He asked if maybe I had seen him at the hotel."

"His girlfriend was pregnant. I knew she'd never come to full term. She'd die when she miscarried. I thought it would be nicer if they went together."

"How far along did Simon get in the phases?"

"He liked spiders. He was immune to the venom. Unlike you, he was sick for over a week when it was introduced into his system. He didn't like wearing the ring. That's when we first suspected there could be a problem. We still remained hopeful because there have been some incidences where the bonding to the ring occurred after the heightened emotions."

"Who's we?"

"The handler and me. I gave Simon some *venotrolia*, thinking that would help. He started beating up his girlfriend. The handler had to rescue her twice. She kept going back to him. The handler couldn't understand it. The poor girl was black and blue all over."

"That was his heightened emotions?" I asked, opening my eyes wider.

"That's what we thought, but he continued rejecting the ring. One night he almost killed his best friend. The handler couldn't let him out of her sight. Simon even got a stack of books on making bombs."

"Do all Tegens have to be a handler sometime?"

"No. The parent of the child requests a friend to be the handler. It shows trust in that person. Most of us are honored to be asked. Since sometimes the handler has to get very close to the subject, the parent won't ask you if you're in a relationship. We wouldn't want our partner to take on that type of assignment."

"Tegens get jealous?"

"Oh, yes. We have all the same emotions we had before we went through the transformation, except we learn to look differently at killing."

"Getting back to Simon. What happened?"

"He told his handler he hated the ring; it made him feel nervous and eerie whenever he put it on."

Wearing the ring never bothered me. It was only a problem when I tried to take it off. "If he liked his ring, he would have been okay?"

"Maybe. We still watched for bumps to appear. Had that happened, the handler would've told him about Tegens. He might've decided to wear the ring regardless how he felt about it."

"Did he turn twenty-five?"

Her eyes became cloudy. "Yes. We waited for signs until there was no hope left. His violent behavior continued to accelerate. The handler tried to keep a close watch over him so he wouldn't hurt anyone else. One evening he got away from her. He ended up throwing an elderly couple down a steep flight of stairs. The woman died, the man was hospitalized, and Simon laughed. No one knew he was responsible. He bought five rifles and three pistols. We have no idea what he had planned." She paused and tapped her fingers together. "Anything else?"

"Why all the lies? You pretended you were meeting a boyfriend, unemployed, and you didn't know Lance or Brett?"

"Each of us had a role to play. You would have suspected something wasn't right if we all knew each other. You might have thought we were connected to the Crussett family. You never would have learned the truth about any of us if you hadn't progressed through the phases."

Gazing at her face, I knew she had no other choice than to lie in order to gain my friendship. "Since you have the ability to poison someone, do Tegens ever abuse that?"

"There have been some problems. We're only to use that ability if we need to feed, or if we're in danger, or protecting someone. You're the first potential Tegen I've ever heard about that needed to be protected." She shuffled through her notepad again. "That pretty well covers it."

"What happens during the transformation?"

She hesitated. "I think you should ask your father about that."

Mulling over everything she had told me, I asked, "If I decide I don't want to be a Tegen, do you know how long it will take my hands and feet to clear up?"

She glared at me. "They won't. There's no easy way to say this. If you don't go through the transformation, you'll die."

"I don't have a choice?"

"You don't have a choice if you want to live. If it is too hard for you to think about killing anyone to survive, you can choose to die. You can be given drugs to help speed up the process when the pain becomes unbearable."

"Am I hearing you right? Either I join your cult and become a killer, or I die?"

"Yes. And it's not a cult." She sounded exasperated.

"Right, it's a species," I groaned, feeling as frustrated as her regarding semantics.

"To stay a healthy Tegen, you have to drink *venotrolia* at least twice a week. Most of us drink it every day. You only have to attend a gathering bi-monthly. That's where we eat a spider victim. You can go to more gatherings if you want to. Also, once every three to five years, we spend some time in the Tegen Cave. It helps rejuvenate our bodies and minds."

"Tell me about this Tegen Cave."

"Besides going there for transformations and to be rejuvenated, it's a place where Tegens find comfort. After your mother died, and your father had made arrangements for you, he went to the cave for a month. Hattie stayed with your adoptive parents until they had the routine down of caring for a newborn. Then she joined him."

"How long do I have to decide if I want to join or die?" I asked, even if I didn't believe those were my only two options.

"If you're going to become a Tegen, you'll want to do it on your birthday. The pain in your hands and feet will soar, and the *venotrolia* will stop helping. You have to be able to walk by yourself into the cave. No one can help you."

"Why?"

"I don't know. That's how it's always been done. Maybe it's to show that you're doing it out of your own free will. No one is forcing you."

If she was telling the truth, then it wasn't my free will. I was being forced. So walking into the cave must be symbolic.

She continued, "That's why your father was so worried you were going through the phases too fast. If you can't walk into the cave, you can't join us. Last year a Tegen daughter was lost because her pain became so excruciating. Her father knew she wouldn't be able to walk on her birthday, so he took her to the cave before she turned twenty-five."

"She died?"

"Yes."

The door opened and a nurse entered. "Miss Jones needs her sleep," she said to Lindsey. "It's after ten."

"I'll leave now," Lindsey said. Then she looked at me. "Give Brett a call if you have any questions."

"I will."

"See you tomorrow." She hugged me before walking out of the room.

20

VERIFICATION

When Lindsey was out of sight, I used the pencil to punch in Conner's number on the phone.

"Hello, Sara," he answered. "I tried to come and see you. Dr. Alston has restricted your visitors again and your room phone is blocked. I left your suitcase with a nurse named Mabel. She mentioned you had to be sedated yesterday. How are you feeling?"

"Better. I'm going to have to stay in the hospital a few more days."

"Will you be out in time for your birthday?"

"Don't know. Did Cameron tell you he came to visit me?"

"No," Conner replied, sounding irritated. "Why was he there?"

"He believes I still have some documents."

"I've already told him you don't. I'll talk to him tomorrow morning. Did he upset you?"

"I'm not sure. My hands and feet started hurting when he was here. Dr. Alston believes it happened because I was upset."

"Sara, I'm so sorry," he said in a slow, heavy voice. "I'll check with Dr. Alston and see if he can prevent Cameron from seeing you when you can have visitors again. Is there anything you need that I can get you?"

"Yesterday, you said you had me investigated when we started dating."

He hesitated. "Yes."

"Did the investigation indicate I was adopted?"

"What's this all about?"

"Due to my reaction to the spider bite, I gave the hospital permission to complete a family history," I lied. I didn't want him to know any more than necessary. "They received my parents' records today electronically.

After that, they asked me if I was adopted, so blood types or something must not match."

"I thought you knew. You were only a few days old when you were adopted."

I wondered what other parts of Lindsey's story were true. "Did it say who my birth parents were?"

"The report is down in the den. Do you want to hold on while I find it or should I call you back tomorrow?"

"All these years, and I never knew."

"Sara, I don't want you getting upset. From everything you've told me about your parents, I know they loved you."

"Don't worry about that. I know they did. I'm just surprised they never told me. Maybe that was part of the adoption agreement. I'll hold on while you look for the report."

"I'm going down the stairs right now. I'll put on the speakerphone in case you get tired of waiting."

I stayed patiently on the line and heard file drawers opening and closing.

"Okay, I've got it," Conner said, and I heard the shuffling of papers.

"How big is the file?"

"It's not all that big since you only lived in San Diego. That's also where you went to college. Here it is." He paused. "Records concerning your biological parents were sealed. There is a note stating that all the adoption papers were signed by your biological father. Your biological mother might be dead."

"If a record has been sealed, is there any way you can find the information?"

"Is this that important to you?" he asked in a serious and quiet tone.

I couldn't tell him why I wanted to know. "I'm just curious since my parents never told me I was adopted. That's all."

"Let me see what I can find out tomorrow morning. Do you think Dr. Alston will allow you to have visitors in the afternoon?"

I didn't feel up to seeing him again. At the same time, I wanted to know more about the adoption. "I can't have any more visitors because of Cameron. I'll still try to convince Dr. Alston to let me see you."

"Your phone might still be blocked. Can you give me a call if you're successful?"

"Yes."

"It's late. I want you to get to sleep. I'll wait for your call before I come tomorrow."

"Thanks for the information."

"I love you, Sara."

"I love you, too. Goodnight."

I pushed the call button.

"Is there something you need?" the nurse asked, standing in the doorway.

"I'm tired. I don't want the phone to ring. Is there anything you can do about it?"

"After ten o'clock, all phone calls in this wing are blocked. You don't need to worry about it waking you up."

"Thank you," I said, feeling relieved. Before I talked to Brett, I wanted more information. I was sure Lindsey had told him and Lance that I doubted her story. Closing my eyes, I felt an overwhelming sadness that everything I had been brought up to believe about my childhood was a lie. Someone should have told me sooner that I was adopted. My heart began pounding in my chest and chills surged through my body as I feared my future. My emotions were colliding, leaving me with an empty sensation. Tears streamed down my cheeks and I sobbed, afraid there was no way I could escape this nightmare. I wished I were a child again so I could climb on a parent's lap and feel comforting arms around me.

The clanging sound of carts being pushed along the hallway woke me. A nurse came into my room carrying a food tray. It wasn't Mabel. I liked her gentle touch. She seemed so motherly.

"Good morning, Miss Jones," the nurse said, putting down the tray on a table. She pushed it in front of me.

"Good morning. I haven't seen Nurse Mabel for a while. Am I still one of her patients?"

"Yes. She'll be in later this morning. We can all help you if you need anything."

"I know. I just wanted to know about Nurse Mabel."

Lance walked in as I was eating. He closed the door and sat in the chair next to the bed. "I understand from Lindsey that you questioned everything she said. Now that you've had a chance to think about it, do you believe anything at all?"

I wasn't prepared to talk to him about it yet. I first wanted to know if Conner could get the adoption record. "If you needed to, how were you planning to kill me?" I said, calmly between bites.

He stared at me with raised brows and didn't immediately respond. "Since that won't be necessary, I don't think that's anything we need to discuss."

"How have you killed your other children? Given how old Lindsey said you were, I'm sure you've had to eliminate some along the way."

His eyes became glossy. "Was that all you heard Lindsey say? Or was that the only part you want to remember?"

Maybe he was my father. He had been kind to me since I came to the hospital. "Sorry," I said. "I've always thought the Joneses were my biological parents, and now I don't know what to believe."

He scanned my face. "I know. Your whole world has changed over the past few months. Now you know the truth about the Crussett family, and you've been told the truth about yourself. I can understand why you want to cling to what you've been raised to believe. It's hard letting go."

"How do you know about the Crussett family?" I asked as I felt my jaw tighten.

"When you moved to Houston, I attempted to have Conner Crussett investigated."

Was everyone having everyone investigated?

He continued, "When the first investigator I hired was found dead in his Houston office, I thought he must have been investigating the wrong people. I didn't suspect it was the Crussetts. When the second investigator was also found dead, I knew it couldn't be a coincidence. There had to be more to the Crussett family than owners of an investment company. I didn't know their business until I engaged a man to work for them."

"Someone on the Crussett payroll is actually your employee?"

"Yes."

"Do I know him?"

"Yes. It's Fred, the guy who cleans the swimming pool. He works for Emmanuel."

"I worked for Emmanuel for three hours."

"I heard," he said with an amazed expression on his face.

"Is Fred part of the group that Lindsey told me about?"

"No. He was hired to keep track of you. He's skilled in using weapons and knows how to find out information. He also knows how to blend in. I had him stay on with the Crussetts even after you left in case they found you. After your picture appeared on the national news, I knew Conner was on his way to Billings before he arrived."

"I saw you at his limo in front of my office building. Why didn't you do anything when you saw me talking to him?"

"Because I knew you cared about him." He glanced at his watch. "I'm giving a lecture to some of the hospital interns this morning. Brett should be here with Lindsey soon. Maybe he can help convince you that Lindsey told you the truth."

"Brett's well enough to see me?"

"Yes. He's anxious."

"I can have visitors now?"

"I'm still restricting them. Brett and Lindsey are on the approved list."

"Can Conner visit me this afternoon?"

"Do you want to see him?"

"Yes. I guess."

"Are you planning on having him check to see if you're adopted?"

"Yes," I smiled.

"Okay. I'll put him on the list."

"Thank you."

He stood. "I'll see you this afternoon."

I dialed Conner's number and told him he could visit me.

"I've got someone checking on your adoption," he said. "The information should be on my desk sometime this morning. I stepped out of a meeting when you called. I need to get back."

"What time do you think you'll be here?"

"Between one and two."

"See you then."

"Bye, Sara," he said and hung up.

21

THE DOCUMENTS

A tall nurse with short, curly, auburn hair entered my room followed by two muscular men dressed in blue hospital scrubs who were pushing a gurney. One man had a groomed goatee and a tattoo on his lower arm. The other man was shorter and had a broad face with a thick head of unruly hair.

"How are you feeling today, Miss Jones?" the nurse asked, giving me a warm smile.

"Fine," I replied, suspicious of her intentions. "Why?"

"Dr. Alston wants your feet x-rayed," she said, glancing at the clipboard in her hand. "The lab is ready for you now."

"Dr. Alston never mentioned anything about an x-ray."

"Here's his order." The nurse held up the clipboard. "Would you like to see it?" she asked with a cheerful, pleasant smile.

"Yes, I would."

She handed it to me. The top sheet was a hospital form with my name on it. Underneath that it stated my feet were to be x-rayed and gave the various angles along with a comment specifying that my feet were to be kept elevated. It was signed. I couldn't make out the name. Even if I could, I wasn't familiar with Lance's signature.

"Would you like me to explain any of the symbols to you?" she asked.

"No. That won't be necessary." I handed back the clipboard.

"Any other questions?"

I shook my head, leery as I wondered about the tattoo. I had never seen one on any hospital employees before. "Will this take very long?"

"No. We'll have you back within the hour."

Since I wouldn't be gone very long, Lance knew I'd be back in my room before Brett and Lindsey arrived. I still felt uneasy as they moved me to the gurney.

"Make sure she's strapped in securely," the tattooed man said, as he tightened down a cord. "Yesterday, we had a patient fall off a gurney."

A strap was being moved over my shoulders, forcing my elbows next to my body. "I don't think my arms need to be fastened in."

"This is so your arms won't accidentally get bumped," the short man responded. "We'll remove it as soon as we reach the lab."

Lying flat on my back, I was wheeled down the hall and into the elevator. Besides the nurse who was with us, two other nurses stepped in. One had bright red hair. Her eyes dropped to the tattooed arm and remained there until she got off on the second floor. I wondered if she was admiring the design or if there was another reason she was checking it out.

When we reached the first floor, the nurse with the short, curly hair raised her arm and pointed. "Take her that way. I'll meet you in the lab," she said, and then walked the opposite direction.

The tattooed man pulled the gurney and the short man pushed as we went down a narrow hall with offices on each side. The hallway became wider. I noticed a sign stating X-Ray Lab with a red arrow underneath indicating the direction. That wasn't the way we were going.

"Isn't the x-ray lab the other way?" I asked.

The gurney stopped. The tattooed man moved so he was between me and anyone who might walk down the hallway. "Sara," he said, softly. "You're not going to the lab. Mr. Crussett wants to see you. He hasn't been allowed to visit since your theatrical performance when he was here."

I shuddered. "Cameron Crussett?"

"Yes. We're taking you to him." He raised the top part of his uniform, revealing a gun attached to his belt. "You can lie there and let us do our job, or you can make a fuss and some innocent people will get hurt. How do you want to handle this?"

"Does Conner know?" I asked, gasping for air.

"You're going to make this difficult," he said through clenched teeth.

I swallowed hard. "I don't want anyone getting hurt." So much for Conner being able to control his brother. A dreadful anguish rolled over me, knowing it was my fault I was in this predicament. I should have followed my instinct and not left the room without insisting on talking to Dr. Alston first. I licked my dry lips as my hospital gown became damp from perspiration. I heard my heart hammering and the chattering of people. I couldn't yell for help or escape without having innocent bystanders harmed. I wondered how Cameron planned to explain my disappearance to Conner. Maybe he'd blame it on the spider people.

"Alex, someone is coming," the short man said.

Could this guy be Alex Barton, the truck driver responsible for Paula's death?

"Are you going to cooperate?" Alex asked.

"Yes," I replied. "Is your last name Barton?"

"Why?" he asked, tilting his brows.

He was the killer. I wanted to see him squirm. "Saul mentioned your name when he was taking me to the airport."

"What did he say?"

"He was on his cell phone, so I don't know what it was about."

His jaw tensed, and he lowered his eyes to the floor. Without saying another word, he moved to the front of the gurney. Even with my pulse racing and hair standing up on the back of my neck, I still managed to smile.

Going further down the hallway, the voices kept getting louder. Three men wearing white lab coats and four people dressed in street clothes walked passed us. A sign on the wall read: "Information" with an arrow underneath, pointing the direction we were headed. More people hurried down the hall. No one looked my way. We went around a corner, and the hall opened up to a foyer. I assumed Alex and his buddy were taking me toward the hospital entrance. Then Lindsey walked by us.

"This strap is pinching my arm," I said loudly, hoping to get her attention.

The gurney came to an abrupt halt. Alex walked to my side. "You don't need to shout," he said through gritted teeth. "Which arm is bothering you?"

"My left."

He ran his hand under the strap. "I don't feel anything squeezing. Does it still hurt?"

"No. It feels better now."

His eyes narrowed as he stared at me. "I don't want to hear another peep out of you," he snapped, whispering, and then continued pulling me along.

Another gurney escorted by a police officer squeaked by us. The officer was chatting with the patient lying on top. He was oblivious to the crime happening right next to him. There was no way I could get his attention without putting everyone around us in danger.

A moment later, I was pushed through a double set of sliding doors and across a sidewalk.

A heavyset man with bulging eyes approached. "Any problems?" he asked as he helped Alex and the short man lift the gurney into the back of an ambulance.

"No," Alex replied.

"Where's Darlene?"

"Mr. Crussett wanted her to pick up something. She'll meet us at the place."

I needed to stay calm. If poisonous venom could be secreted from my fingers when the needles appeared, I didn't want that to happen until I had an opportunity to use it. Wouldn't that surprise Cameron? I worried that my hands might be tied and I wouldn't be able to take off the gloves.

Alex closed the ambulance door and sat close to me. "How are you doing?" he smirked.

"Couldn't be better," I replied, giving him a wide, fake smile.

The throbbing sound of ambulance came from off in the distance along with a police car siren. I felt a vibration as the engine accelerated and we moved. The siren became louder while I was jerked back and forth, like the vehicle was making sharp turns.

Alex jumped to his feet and pushed the intercom button. "John, is that cruiser after us?"

"No," John replied.

"Then why are we in the parking garage?" Alex asked, glancing out the window.

"A car with the hood opened was in the closest exit and another car blocked us from going the other direction. I'd already been asked to move from the entrance a few times. I told the security guy I was waiting for a patient. A cruiser was parked right next to me, and the cop heard everything I said. Also, it sounds like an emergency. More cops are headed to the hospital. Several ambulances are parked on the first floor of the garage. We won't draw any attention in here. We'll get on the road soon."

Alex sat down as the sirens faded away.

"We've got company," John said over the intercom. "The car that blocked us from leaving is coming up the ramp. Let's see if they're after us."

"How many?" Alex asked.

"I only see two in the car. This level is almost deserted, just a few cars." The ambulance jolted to a stop. "Not a coincidence. The car's right next to us."

Alex swung open the back door and jumped out. "What do you want?" he shouted as car doors slammed shut.

Voices rang out, "Her...get back...no...stop there...which one... him...no..."

Wanting to see and hear more, I pushed my right hand tight against my body and slid it out from under the strap. I heard a loud thud and the ambulance shook like something had hit it. A gunshot echoed through the parking structure as I undid the other straps. Easing my feet to the floor, I stood and listened. I only heard movement outside. Then I made my way to the door.

Standing by the open door, I saw Cameron's men were lying face down, motionless, on the cement floor. Brett and Lindsey were wrapping the one furthest away in some kind of threadlike material. Was it spider webs? Alex was ten feet away from me.

Gripping the ambulance door handle, I slipped out, staggered toward him, raised my sock covered foot, and kicked Alex as hard as I could. "Ouch," I yelled as I felt the pain, but it was worth it. I kicked him again, "Ouch," and again, "Ouch."

Brett looked at me. "What are you doing?" he asked with a puzzled expression on his face.

"I hate him. He killed my friend." My voice shot up several octaves.

"He won't hurt anyone else. Your foot is going to throb if you kick him anymore."

"I'm through."

"You okay?"

I nodded. With a sore foot, I stumbled to the ambulance, sat down on the back bumper, and watched Brett and Lindsey wrap the other two men. Lindsey raised the trunk lid of their car. Brett piled Cameron's men inside.

"What's going to happen to them?" I asked, hoping Alex would end up on an altar someplace.

"We don't waste food," Brett replied, straight-faced as he walked toward me. He put his arms around me and pulled me close with my feet hovering a foot above the floor. "I've missed you." He smothered my lips with a kiss.

"I was so worried about you. I didn't think you had survived the gunshot wound."

"When I was lying on the sidewalk, I told you everything would be okay." He lowered me down, backed away, and his eyes moved down my hospital gown. "You're too exposed for climbing."

"I'm not planning on climbing."

Brett smiled without saying a word. He climbed into the ambulance, opened several drawers, and pulled out a hospital gown. He put it on me backwards over the other gown so it tied in the front.

"How do your feet feel?" he asked.

"Tingly."

"You shouldn't be standing," he said, lifting me into his arms.

Lindsey came toward us, carrying a can with a nozzle, and sprayed everything inside the ambulance.

"Why is she doing that?" I asked Brett.

"To remove fingerprints. We don't need to wipe it down."

"Cameron tried to kidnap me. You're destroying the evidence."

"We don't like cops involved," he explained. "All they'll find is an abandoned ambulance. I doubt it's registered to any of the Crussetts' businesses."

Lindsey stepped from the ambulance, closed the doors, and sprayed them. Then she went to the front cab, sprayed inside and the outside along with the bumpers, a dent near the rear, and dispersed the remainder in the can everywhere else. "All done," she said with a pleased expression.

"Move the car to the parking lot," Brett said to her. "I'll get Sara back to her room by taking her to the top of the hospital and down the stairs or elevator."

"Why can't we ride with Lindsey and go through the entrance?" I asked.

"We don't know if Cameron has stationed any of his men there."

"You've got a point," I said.

Lindsey got a rope out of the car, handed it to Brett, and then climbed into the driver's seat. "I'll see you in a few minutes."

We watched her drive away. "How are you planning on getting me to the hospital roof?" I asked.

Brett grinned. "You'll see. I want you on my back." He swung me onto his back. I wrapped my legs around his waist and my arms around to his neck. Brett secured us together with the rope, took off his shoes and socks, and tied them to his belt. He climbed on the parking garage ledge.

"Is this safe?" I asked, feeling uneasy, even if he appeared to know what he was doing.

"Yes. Don't worry. This isn't my first time," he said as he rubbed the end of the rope, making it glisten. He flung it toward the hospital. The shiny end attached to the side of the building.

"Hang on," he said, gripping the rope with his hands. He swung over to the hospital and scaled up the side, using his hands and feet.

I should have been terrified. Instead, I found being on his back invigorating as he moved through the air high above the ground and up the building. We were on the roof within a few minutes.

"How did you do that?" I asked.

"You'll be able to do that once you've gone through the transformation," he replied, cutting the rope that held us together.

I lowered my feet. "But how?"

"Because part of our DNA comes from our spiders," he answered, putting on his socks and shoes.

I felt my eyes opening wider, my brows rising, and my forehead creasing.

"Don't look so shocked," he said. "We'll talk about it when we get to your room. And don't worry if we were seen by spectators. From a distance we probably would have looked like window washers, and we'll be out of here soon enough that any one closer won't have time to check it out. On top of that, I doubt if we were spotted." He picked me up and carried me down the first two flights of stairs without us passing or hearing anyone.

"What time are you getting off today?" a female voice asked. It sounded like she was a flight of stairs below us.

"We can't stay in here any longer," Brett whispered, opening a door. He moved into the hallway and sat me down on a chair. "I'm going to find a wheelchair."

Several nurses and doctors walked past me. No one stopped to say anything. Five minutes later, Brett came back with a wheelchair. He lifted me into it and pushed it to the elevator.

When we reached my room, Lindsey was there and so was Nurse Mabel.

"Where have you been?" Mabel asked as she helped me get back in bed.

"I got tired of staying in my room," I said. "Brett got a wheelchair and pushed me around the halls."

"That needed to be cleared by the nurse on duty. Dr. Alston left specific instructions you were to rest and sleep as much as possible."

"I'm sorry. I didn't realize I had to ask for permission. I won't do it again."

"I'll have to put that in your chart," she said, sounding irritated. "Since you need to rest, your visitors can't stay long." She stepped into the hallway and left the door wide open.

"I guess no one told her that I had been taken for an x-ray," I said.

"Is that the excuse they used?" Brett asked, shutting the door.

"Yes. I even saw the request. I couldn't read the physician's signature." I looked at Lindsey. "I should've checked with Lance like you did yesterday, especially after I saw the one guy's tattooed arm."

"Yes, you should've called him regardless of that," Lindsey said, firmly. "I don't know if this hospital has a tattoo policy. They do in Bismarck. Lance doesn't allow any of his employees at his clinic to have one exposed."

"The form looked official, and the nurse seemed so professional."

"How many were there?" Brett asked.

"Three."

"A nurse and two guys?"

I nodded.

"What happened to her?" Lindsey asked.

"When we got off the elevator on the first floor, she excused herself and went in the opposite direction. Shortly after that, I knew something was wrong when I was pushed down a hall away from the x-ray lab. The man pulling the gurney said that Cameron wanted to see me, and he couldn't come to my room. The man also said if I didn't cooperate people would be hurt. I stayed quiet as I was pushed along before I saw Lindsey walk past me."

"That's when I heard you say something about your strap being too tight," Lindsey said. "We didn't know there was a problem until then."

"I'm glad you heard me."

"I think everyone in the foyer heard you," she snickered.

"The nurse who came with the two guys, have you ever seen her before?" Brett asked.

"No."

"Can you remember what she looked like?" Lindsey asked.

"She's tall, probably around five-ten, and has short, curly, auburn hair."

"Slender, heavy?" Lindsey asked.

"Average size. I'm pretty sure her name is Darlene."

"How do you know that?" Brett asked.

"The ambulance driver asked about her. She was supposed to go with us, but Cameron sent her on an errand. Probably the first life he ever saved."

"And he'll never know it," Lindsey commented.

"If a nurse comes in here that you don't recognize, push your call button," Brett said. "Don't eat or drink anything she gives you. I'm going to be hanging around the hospital. If anything happens, call me on my cell phone. Something needs to be done about Cameron."

"Before your nurse kicks us out, are you starting to believe anything I told you yesterday?" Lindsey asked.

"Well, I know you have abilities that normal humans don't have." I looked at Brett "What was that all about when you said I was part spider?"

"Didn't Lindsey tell you about Sir Randolph's experiments?"

"Yes, I told her," Lindsey confirmed.

"He changed his and our ancestors' DNA," Brett said. "That's why you can secrete poisonous venom from your fingers. After you've gone through the transformation, you'll be able to move like a spider when you want to. You can project small clusters of hairs on your hands and feet that act like climbing claws."

"I never told her about that," Lindsey confessed. "Do you believe you were adopted?"

"I'm having that checked. Like you said, there'll be a record."

"Good," Brett said. "Is there anything I can tell you that might help convince you that Lindsey told the truth?"

"Come here," I said to Brett. I watched him walking toward me. "Unbutton your shirt. I want to see your chest."

He grinned as he undid his shirt. "Lindsey can stand guard outside the door. I don't want your nurse interrupting us."

"That's not what this is all about," I clarified and saw the disappointed look on his face. "I want to see where you were shot." I ran my glove-covered hand over his chest. "I can't even feel you."

"You can take your glove off. I'm immune to your poison." Brett helped free my hand.

I ran my fingers over his chest. "Nothing seems different. Where were you shot?"

"Right here," he said, pointing to a spot that appeared to be close to his heart.

"I can't see anything," I said. "Were you shot in the heart?"

"Yes," he replied. "I should have been more cautious. That's why it's taken me several days to heal. Had I just been shot in the arm, I would have been back to normal within a couple of hours."

"Do all Tegens heal so easily?"

"Yes, as long as they feed," he said, buttoning his shirt.

The door swung open. "Miss Jones needs her rest," Mabel said, walking into the room. "You can come back later today and visit her."

Brett started to help me put my glove back on.

"Did you take off her glove?" Mabel asked, sounding annoyed.

"I just wanted to see her fingers," Brett replied.

"Dr. Alston has left specific instructions that Miss Jones is to wear her gloves all the time. No one is to take them off. I'm going to have to tell Dr. Alston about this."

"I'm sorry," Brett said. "I didn't know."

Mabel gave him a disapproving glance and stood by the door, waiting for him and Lindsey to leave. Brett delicately kissed my lips.

"See you later," they both said as they left.

"Let me get your lunch," Mabel said. Within a few minutes, she was back with a tray.

My hands and feet started throbbing a little while I ate. I didn't want a repeat of Friday. I quickly finished eating, and then pushed the call button.

Mabel appeared in the doorway. "Do you need something?"

"My hands and feet hurt a little."

"I'll call Dr. Alston and see what I can give you."

The pain increased. I closed my eyes and attempted to recall everything Lindsey had said. Could it all be true? I saw Brett bleeding. He shouldn't have healed that fast, if at all, with a bullet in his heart. Should I tell Conner that Cameron tried to kidnap me? Since I didn't want to explain how I was rescued and what happened to Cameron's men, I decided not to say anything about it. Also, I wanted to get as far from the Crussetts as possible. The less Conner knew the better. I felt a hand on my shoulder and raised my eyelids.

"Will you drink *venotrolia* now?" Lance asked, holding a container with a straw protruding from it. "Or would you rather wait until the pain becomes unbearable again?"

"I'll drink it now," I replied. I slowly sipped the red liquid from the straw. Even knowing what it was, it still tasted good.

"I understand you had an unpleasant morning," he said. "We're going to have to do something about Cameron. He isn't going to let you go until he gets the documents."

"He already has them," I said. "How do you know about the documents?"

"Earlier I mentioned I had an employee working for the Crussetts," he replied.

"Yes. I remember."

"I thought you might leave after you knew about their family business. Fred kept track of you. One night when you stayed late at the office, he watched you copying some pages out of a journal. The next day you left Houston."

"I didn't see him."

"Of course you didn't. He's good."

"Then he knows I didn't tear out any pages."

"Yes. Given the reason he knows that, he can't tell Cameron. The Crussetts have enemies. It appears that at least one of their other employees actually works for someone else. When that employee heard you had left, it gave him the perfect opportunity to take some documents, assuming you'd be blamed." He paused. I saw a malicious twinkle in his dark eyes as they met mine. "What do you think we should do about Cameron?"

"Whatever you want. It doesn't matter to me. He isn't one of my favorite people."

"I'm going to let the spiders take care of him. We just need to find a time and place." He took my right hand, pulled off the glove, and felt inside it. "Just like I thought—your glove is moist. You must have secreted some venom this morning. Had you stayed calm, you wouldn't have needed any *venotrolia* until late tonight or tomorrow morning. You're going to need more than *venotrolia* soon. I can't provide you with anything else in the hospital." He slipped the glove back on my hand. "I'd like to take you to Bismarck. Would you be willing to go there?"

"Can I take what else I'll need to my home in San Diego?"

"No. It's only available in North Dakota."

"Why Bismarck?"

"The Tegen Cave is there."

"But I haven't decided yet."

"I know. However you decide I can make you more comfortable at my clinic. When the *venotrolia* doesn't work anymore, I have equipment I can use on your hands and feet that will eliminate the pain. There aren't any apparatuses like that here or in San Diego." He paused and gazed at me. "Is there anything I can say or any questions I can answer that might help you decide?"

As I looked at his face, all I felt was indifference toward him. My father, the one who loved and took care of me all my life, died four years ago. Genetics or not, this man sitting next to me was a stranger—a stranger who would have willing killed me if the needles hadn't appeared on my hands and feet. "Let me see what I find out about being adopted. Maybe I'll have some questions then."

He stroked my arm. "No matter what you decide, I'd like to take you to my clinic. It'll be the best place for you since you can't avoid the pain, regardless of your decision. I'll be back later." He stood. I didn't say anything as he headed out the door.

Leaning on my pillow, I raised my gloved hands and stared at them as I thought about the pain I had experienced since I arrived in this hospital bed. Suddenly, the door squeaked open, and I dropped my hands to my lap.

"I've been here waiting for Dr. Alston to leave," Conner said, entering the room. "Has he told you when you can go home?" He sat down in the chair next to the bed and held my arm.

"No. He wants me to go to his clinic in North Dakota, since they don't have the right equipment here to treat my hands and feet."

"He can't just give you medicine to take care of it?"

"No. He told me that after the treatment, my hands and feet will completely clear up and look the same way they did before I had a reaction to the venom. There won't be any lasting problems."

"That's good," Conner said, smiling as his fingers drifting down my bare arm. "How long does he think you have to stay at his clinic?"

I shrugged my shoulders. "He didn't say. I'm still trying to decide if I want to go."

Conner squinted. "Do you have an alternative?"

"Not according to him. I was really looking forward to going home."

"You can go home after your feet and hands have been cured. You shouldn't put it off. No matter how long you have to stay at his clinic, the sooner you go, the sooner you can go home." His fingers wrapped around my forearm right above the glove. "Can I fly you to North Dakota?"

"I don't think so. He'll probably want me to go with him in case I have any pain along the way."

"When you're better, can I take you home to San Diego?"

Looking at his handsome face and his sad, soft brown eyes, as much as I tried to suppress my feelings, part of me still loved him. "Yes," I said, though I wasn't sure if I would ever be leaving Bismarck.

His eyes lit up. "How are you feeling right now?"

"Earlier I had some pain. Now I feel okay."

He leaned over and kissed me.

"Did you find out anything about my biological parents?" I asked, hoping to redirect the conversation.

"Not much. I did discover you weren't born in California. Your biological mother died from childbirth complications. That's all. Your adoption record is well sealed. I can't even get any kind of a court order to obtain the information." He touched my cheek. "I'm sorry. It appears your biological father doesn't want you to be able to locate him."

"Thanks for trying." Nothing he had said contradicted what Lindsey had already told me.

"I met with Cameron this morning. He still believes you have some documents, but he promised he'd leave you alone."

So much for Cameron's promises. "I don't have any." I had the urge to tell him what happened this morning. I kept quiet about it, believing the consequences could be too great.

"That's what I told him. We have enemies. An employee might not be loyal to us. It wouldn't be the first time. Whoever took them didn't plan on turning them over to the authorities, or we would've already heard something. The documents were probably taken as a bargaining chip for something. They just don't realize we don't bargain. I'm surprised nothing has surfaced since they took them over two months ago." He kissed my arm. "You don't need to be concerned about that. Just concentrate on getting well. Is there anything you want me to bring you?"

"I might need some clothes. I'm not sure yet if I can wear my own clothes at the clinic."

"Let me know after you talk to Dr. Alston. We'll have to celebrate your birthday later." He gently brushed my hair away from my face. "I'd like to take you to a secluded island. How does that sound?"

"Let me think about it." I needed to get him out of my life completely. Spending more time with him would only make it harder. I wondered how I would feel if I agreed to be transformed. On the other hand, if I didn't take that path and what Lindsey said was the truth, then I wouldn't be celebrating anymore.

He kissed my cheek. "Don't look so worried. You don't need to decide right now. You can think about it when you're at the clinic."

"I will," I said, uncertain. Maybe I should go with him. Regardless of how Conner felt about Cameron, he would mourn his death, and that time was coming soon.

"I better go, since your visitations are restricted. Your nurse told me I couldn't stay very long. I don't want to be crossed off your approved visitor list." His lips touched mine. "I will always love you," he whispered. As he stood up, he smiled. "I'll be back tomorrow morning. Bye, Sara."

"Bye," I said as he left.

22

THE MORGUE

As I finished breakfast, Nurse Mabel stepped into my room. "Dr. Alston wants you to have a CAT scan," she said. "He'll meet you there."

"Are you going to be the one taking me to him?" I asked, wondering if this was another Cameron attempt.

"Yes. You received a phone call early this morning. The nurse on duty forgot to give you this message." She handed me a blue slip of paper.

The message was from Conner. It read: "Sara, something has come up. I have to go to Dallas. I should be back this evening. I'll call you then."

"Let's get you in the wheelchair." Mabel held onto my arm as I got out of bed and moved into the seat. She wheeled me to the elevator.

Brett and Lindsey were sitting on a bench next to it talking. Lindsey saw me and stood up. "I was on my way to see you," she said, going into the elevator with us.

"I'm getting a CAT scan," I said and turned to Mabel. "Is there anywhere close to the lab my friend can wait?"

"Yes, there's a waiting room."

"That's where I'll stay," Lindsey said.

The elevator stopped on the third floor. Mabel pushed me down the hall with Lindsey right behind us. As we turned into another hallway, I saw Lance standing by the lab entrance.

"Dr. Alston, would you like me to wait for Miss Jones?" Mabel asked.

"No. That won't be necessary. I'll call when she's finished."

Mabel nodded and walked away. Lance pushed my wheelchair into the office next to the lab, and Lindsey followed.

She closed the door and looked at me. "A Tegen who's been watching the hospital from the parking lot spotted Cameron entering with five people: two women dressed like nurses, one man in a white lab coat, like a doctor, and two men had on blue hospital scrubs."

"Who is this Tegen?"

"Her name is Janice," Lindsey said. "You've never met her."

I wondered if Conner mentioned to Cameron that I'd be going to North Dakota soon.

"I wanted you out of your room for a while," Lance said. "You're not going to have a CAT scan. I am curious about Cameron's current plan. By now he knows his first plan wasn't successful. He's probably trying to figure out what went wrong."

"I'm going to help Brett," Lindsey interjected. "I'll be back when it's over."

"When what's over?" I asked.

"You better get back upstairs," Lance said to Lindsey as he avoided my question.

Lindsey hurried out of the room and shut the door behind her.

"Cameron won't stop going after you until you're dead. Our only option is to kill him first," Lance said.

"Wasn't that already your plan?"

"Yes, but not in the hospital."

"But that's where Cameron and his men are. Are you going to deal with them in the hospital now?"

"Yes. It'll be handled discreetly."

"Discreetly? How? There are so many people here."

"Cameron will be told you're in the lab on the second floor having some tests done. The lab on that floor is being renovated. No one works there on weekends."

"How will you get their bodies out of the hospital?"

"Brett and Lindsey will wear hospital scrubs and take them on gurneys to the morgue in the basement. It won't be a problem getting them out from there." He paused and gazed at me for a minute. "Did Conner verify you were adopted?"

"Yes. He wasn't able to find very much about my biological parents."

"Did he find something?" Lance asked with squinted eyes.

"Just that I wasn't born in California, and my mother died from childbirth complications."

"I'm surprised he was able to obtain that much information. Those records were sealed." He picked up his medical bag, took out an envelope, and handed it to me. "Your mother wanted me to give you this letter right before your twenty-fifth birthday."

The envelope was addressed to *My Daughter*. As I opened it, the smell of lilacs filled the room. I pulled out the letter, written on fancy stationery.

Centered at the top were their names – Dr. Lawrence and Mrs. Jennifer Alston. Under that was an address in Bismarck, North Dakota. Deeply inhaling the lilac fragrance, I began to read.

> *My dearest daughter,*
>
> *The first time I looked at your sweet little face, I knew you could be a Tegen. When you were born, your little fingertips were all rough. Your father said that was a good sign. Within a few hours, your fingertips were baby soft. I would have loved to have seen you grow up. Tegens don't raise their own children, so I knew you'd be placed in a loving home. I'm sure their lives have centered on you. It's going to be hard for you, someday, when you won't be able to see them anymore.*
>
> *I had lived with your father for a year when he told me he was a Tegen. It was the most bizarre tale I had ever heard. I thought he was trying to break up with me. But after he told me about himself, he asked me to marry him. I thought he might have been having a hallucination problem. I still loved him, so I agreed to marry him. In fact, I fell in love with him the first time he smiled at me. It took some time, but he was finally able to prove he was a Tegen.*
>
> *I knew if I bore him a child, I would not survive. I saw myself getting older and Lawrence looked just like the man I married. He was still twenty-five. He kept trying to duplicate the formula that Sir Randolph had discovered. He wanted us to be together forever. I would have done anything to become a Tegen, but it wasn't possible.*
>
> *My sweet girl, you can be with your father forever. All kinds of opportunities can unfold for you. If you want to change your career, it's easy. Time is on your side. Most Tegens change what they do, along with their names, about every twenty years.*
>
> *I've been in love with your father for almost nineteen years. He's taken me all over the world. I've worked by his side. My life could not have been more perfect. Since I could not be a Tegen, I wanted to leave part of our love behind. You, my sweet girl, have been loved by your father since you were born. As long as you live, part of me will also survive. Don't be afraid of the transformation. Your father will stay by your side. Remember he loves you and so do I.*
>
> *Love Always,*
> *Mother*

I had a hard time holding back tears as I looked up and saw Lance staring at me. "How did you prove to Jennifer that you were a Tegen?"

"You can refer to me however you want," he said in an angry tone with narrowed eyes. "When you talk about Jennifer, you will call her 'Mother'."

Tears ran down my cheeks. "I didn't mean any disrespect," I sniffled. "I just found out I was adopted. I had a mother who raised me. It's going to take time for me to understand this."

He patted my shoulder. "Your mother would be mad if she knew I snapped at you." He handed me a tissue. "When I told her I was a Tegen and what that meant, she thought I needed some psychological help. To prove it to her, I cut my arm. She watched as it healed. I climbed up the side of my house without a ladder. Then she knew I was different, but that didn't convince her I was a Tegen and over one hundred years old. I showed her pictures of the man I referred to as my father. I put on the wig, mustache, and eyebrows I wore when it was taken. She still doubted it. It took time for her to see the truth, but eventually, she came to believe it."

"I can understand the way she felt. It isn't an easy concept to absorb. It goes against everything we've been taught about life expectancy."

"You look just like your mother," he said, getting his wallet out of his pocket. He opened it and gave it to me, showing me her picture.

The woman in the photo had hair a little lighter than mine and blue eyes. Other than that, I did look like her. She had a warm smile. I could feel my eyes getting moist again as I gazed at the picture. She died so I could live, and now, I didn't know what to do. Could I kill people to survive?

"Do you have any questions I can answer?" he asked, putting away his wallet.

"Yes," I said. "I just don't know where to begin."

He pulled a locket out of his breast pocket. "This was your mother's. She wanted you to have it." He opened it. "That's your mother holding you," he said, pointing to one side of the locket.

A few tears trickled down my cheeks as I stared at it. She looked so happy. I recognized myself from a picture that hung in my San Diego home. On the other side was a picture of Lance and Jennifer. He put the locket around my neck. "Why did you have the adoption papers sealed?" I asked.

"I'm sure you now understand why we don't raise our own children. Because of that, we have the adoption papers sealed and direct the adoptive parents never to tell their children that they are not their own offspring. If they knew, they might come looking for their biological parents. We can't have that."

"I still haven't made my decision, but I will go with you to Bismarck. I've already told Conner I need to go there, since you have special equipment that will help my hands and feet heal."

He gave me a half smile. "I'm glad you've made that decision. We'll leave tomorrow morning."

"If I do decide to become a Tegen, how long will it take?"

"The transformation will take somewhere between twenty-four and forty-eight hours. It all depends on the subject."

I wanted to know what happened during the process. Before I could ask another question, the door flew open, interrupting us. Brett and Lindsey walked in.

"They never went to Sara's room," Brett said. "We've been searching the hospital for them." A crooked smile briefly crossed his face. "I even had your nurse keeping an eye out while we looked on the other floors. I told her you were expecting a visitor and asked her if she could tell the person you'd be back soon. On our way here we checked with her. No one has stopped by your room."

"I should have headed to the foyer after Janice called about Cameron and his people," Lindsey said. "I just assumed they'd go to Sara's room."

"So did I," Lance said. "Have you checked with Janice in case they left?"

"Yes," Brett said. "They're still in the hospital."

"We'll get Sara back to her room and maybe they'll surface," Lance said. "One of them could have walked past her room and noticed she wasn't there. They might be waiting someplace for her to return. We need to take care of Cameron before we leave for North Dakota. I don't want him following us there."

Brett looked at me. "You've agreed to go to Bismarck?"

"Yes, but that's all I've decided."

"Let's go," Lance said as he stood. He pushed my wheelchair out into the hallway.

When we reached the elevator, a man dressed in blue hospital scrubs got off. "Dr. Alston, I've been looking for you," the man said. "Saul Fazio has come out of the coma. We've been paging you."

Brett and Lindsey gave each other a puzzled look.

Lance looked straight at the man in blue. "I'll be right there after I return Miss Jones to her room," he replied, pushing me into the elevator. Brett and Lindsey followed along with the man.

On the sixth floor as Lance was pushing me toward my room, he stopped and turned toward the man. "Tell the staff attending to Mr. Fazio that I'll be there in fifteen minutes. If he's hungry, order him a liquid dinner. I don't want him to eat anything solid." The man nodded, and Lance didn't move until the man stepped back into the elevator.

"What floor is Saul on?" I asked.

"The fifth," Lance replied, continuing down the hallway.

As soon as we were in my room, Mabel rushed in. "Dr. Alston, a medical technician has been looking for you. They need you in room 512."

"The technician found me," Lance replied. "Before I leave, I want to check Miss Jones' hands."

"Would you like me to do that?" Mabel asked, helping me get back in bed.

"No. I'll handle it."

After Nurse Mabel left, I said, "I didn't know Saul was still alive."

"He's been in a coma," Lance said.

"Sara," Lindsey said. "We can't feed on him if he's been dead for more than an hour unless we've preserved him; like we did the men in the parking garage."

"The ambulances that picked you up and Saul on Thursday got there before Saul could be taken care of," Brett clarified. "He's technically already dead. Lance has been keeping his body alive since we weren't able to preserve him. It isn't possible for him to regain consciousness." His eyes moved to Lance. "What do you think this is all about?"

"Maybe they're trying to make sure I can't be reached while they attempt to get Sara out of here."

"Do you want one of us to go with you to see Saul?" Brett asked.

"You stay with Sara," Lance instructed. "Lindsey, take the stairs to the fifth floor and remain in the stairwell. I'll join you after I check on Saul. If I'm not there in fifteen minutes, then head to room 512."

She nodded in agreement. "Okay."

"We'll be back as soon as I figure out what this is all about," Lance said, as he left with Lindsey.

Brett leaned over the top of the bed and took something off it. It was a small object about the size of the tip of my little finger. I couldn't make out what it was. "I want you to wear this," he said, putting it under my sock.

"What is it?"

"A bug. A listening device. I want to hear everything that's said to you."

"How long has my room been bugged?" I asked, irritated.

"I only put it there after you left with your nurse. I planned on sitting by the elevator so I wanted to make sure no one came in here from another direction. People getting on and off the elevator block my vision to your room."

I felt relieved that he hadn't heard my conversation with Conner.

"I don't think we'll flush them out in the open while I'm here," Brett said. "I'm going to go and sit in the waiting area. If someone should come to get you with some kind of excuse, go with them. It's better if we can take care of Cameron and his people outside, we don't want any spectators. To use the bug effectively, all you need to do is talk about where they're taking you. I'll be close by." He bent down, kissed me, and then left the room.

Mabel came in with a food tray. "Your dinner came up a little early," she said, putting it down in front of me.

Wondering why my dinner would come up earlier than anyone else's, I didn't dare eat it. "I don't feel hungry right now. Could I get something later?"

"I'm sure Dr. Alston would like you to eat it now. It says it's a special order."

"He had mentioned he just wanted me to have a liquid diet today, so he could run some more tests. Can you call him and make sure I should be eating this?"

"I will. We don't want you to eat anything he didn't order."

Five minutes later, Mabel returned with a slender woman wearing a nurse's uniform. "You were right," she said. "I wasn't able to reach Dr. Alston. He sent Ann to get you for additional tests."

Ann was attractive, five-foot-seven with shoulder-length blonde hair. Believing she was one of Cameron's people, I moved to the edge of the bed. Mabel held my arm as I slid down into the wheelchair.

"I'm glad I don't need to go on a gurney. I like the wheelchair better," I said, knowing Brett was listening.

Ann wheeled me down the hall. There were five people, dressed in street clothes, on the elevator when she rolled me in and pushed 'B', the button to the basement floor.

"I didn't know there were labs in the basement."

"It's temporary since two are in the process of being remodeled," she replied.

The elevator stopped on the second floor. Two men wearing scrubs stepped in. I noticed Ann gave them a half smile. Everyone got off on the main floor except for the two men and us. They rode down to the basement and walked out of the elevator behind Ann.

The basement looked like the rest of the hospital. I had expected it to look more like a basement with gray cement walls. It appeared deserted; I didn't see or hear anyone in front of me as Ann wheeled me along, followed by the two men.

"Is it always this quiet down here?" I asked.

"No. It's only like this on Sundays since most of the offices are closed." She turned and went down another corridor. On the wall was a sign stating "Morgue" and an arrow pointing in the direction we were going. I wondered if that was where Cameron planned on meeting us.

She stopped next to a large double-door with "Morgue" written on it.

"Am I going to have a lab test in the morgue?" I asked.

She didn't respond. One of the men opened the door. She wheeled me in. In the far corner of the room, I saw Lindsey, tied up with tape over her mouth. Next to her was Darlene in a nurse's uniform.

"Lindsey, are you okay?" I asked even if she couldn't answer me. I wanted Brett to know she was here. Lindsey blinked. I knew they wouldn't have been able to capture her unless she didn't put up any resistance. She probably wanted to be captured so she'd be taken to Cameron.

"And how are you, Darlene?" I asked, wanting Brett to know she was also here.

"How do you know my name?" she hissed.

"One of the guys mentioned it yesterday when they dropped me off at the x-ray lab."

She squinted. "They dropped you off?"

I nodded. "Yeah."

"Did they wait for you?"

"No."

Ann wheeled me to the center of the room. She took a small object out of her pocket and held it to her mouth. "We've got her."

"Is that a walkie-talkie?" I asked.

Her face hardened as she glared at me.

A man's voice came over the walkie-talkie, "We'll be right there." It didn't sound like Cameron.

I was certain that Brett was close by, waiting for Cameron to show up. Four of the people Cameron had entered the hospital with were in this room. Only the one wearing a white lab coat was missing. I smiled to myself as I thought Cameron had no idea what laid ahead for all of them.

The door swung open. Cameron marched in, and his eyes darted between Lindsey and me. A second later, a man dressed like a doctor stepped into the room. A guy in hospital scrubs locked the door behind them.

"How are you doing, Sara?" Cameron asked, sarcastically.

"I was doing better before I was brought down here," I replied, feeling my body tense.

"I bet you were." He glanced at the man in the white lab coat. "This is Gerard. He's going to help me find out where you put the missing documents. I'm not concerned about the authorities. I just don't want them to fall into the hands of anyone else."

Gerard gave me a sinister smile as he unlatched a metal box that stood next to the door. He raised the lid, pulled out a small folding table, and positioned it next to me as the legs dropped to the floor.

"Is Gerard a doctor?" I asked.

"He's the type of doctor I need right now," Cameron replied with a stern face.

Gerard took a folded towel out of the box and placed it on the table. Spreading out the towel, he exposed two syringes along with several small bottles.

"What do you think Conner will say about this?" I asked.

"Conner won't know." Cameron's eyes fixed on me as he walked closer. He leaned down and held onto my locket. "Did Conner give you this?"

I didn't respond.

"Does it have a picture of Conner in it?"

As my mouth tightened, I stared at him.

He yanked the locket off my neck and opened it. "This is great," he snickered. "You and Dr. Alston. And a baby. This I'll have to show to Conner. No wonder the Doc just happened to be in Houston when you had your accident. And you're going with him to Bismarck. How interesting. You must have had the baby before you moved to Houston. Conner always thought you were sensitive and gentle, but you abandoned a baby? Is the baby in Bismarck?"

I remained silent.

"Drew, go and get the Doc. Tell him we have his girlfriend."

One of the men dressed in blue scrubs left.

"I had planned on you being in a car crash on the way to the airport. Now I just need to tell Conner that you ran off with the Doc," he said, slipping the locket in his pocket.

"Is that what happened to Paula—you staged a car crash?"

"I didn't believe her when she said she knew nothing about your disappearance. I don't tolerate anyone lying to me."

"Do you want me to get started now?" Gerard asked.

"No. Let's wait for the Doc. We'll try another form of persuasion first." He strolled over to Lindsey. "It's too bad you befriended Sara. Her close friends don't survive. Is Brett still in the hospital?" Cameron yanked the tape off her mouth.

She moistened her lips with her tongue. "I don't know."

"Yes, you do," Cameron growled and then slapped her.

Lindsey's eyes darkened with rage as she glared at him.

"Are you going to tell me or should I have Gerard start with you?"

"He's somewhere in the hospital. I don't know where."

"Good. I like cooperation," Cameron said.

Under Lindsey's seat, I saw a piece of rope drop to the floor. My eyes flashed over Cameron's people for signs that one of them noticed. From the expressions on their faces, I gathered they didn't. Lindsey's hands were still behind her back. I was sure they were no longer bound.

The door opened. Drew pushed Lance in, pointing a pistol at his back.

Lance stumbled to regain his balance. Then he looked at Lindsey and me. "Are you both okay?" he asked as Drew locked the door behind them.

Lindsey and I nodded.

"Dr. Alston," Cameron said. "You don't need to play coy with us." He took the locket out of his pocket. "I know about you and Sara. Is the baby in North Dakota?"

"No. The baby is in Houston," Lance replied. "Why do you ask?"

"Since you and Sara are going to be running off together, I can't imagine you'd leave your child behind."

Unless Conner looked closely at the pictures in the locket, Cameron might've been able to convince him it was true. I knew he wouldn't get that chance.

Cameron nodded to Drew. Drew raised his gun to Lance's head. Cameron turned and faced me. "Now, will you tell me what you did with the documents, or do you want to see how far your boyfriend's brains can be splashed across the room?"

"I'll tell you," I said as I started to take off my gloves. "First I need to get these gloves off. They're pinching my fingers."

Cameron moved closer. "Is this another stall?"

"No."

He stretched out his hand and yanked off one of the gloves.

"The place where the documents are hidden is…," I began. Then the ceiling exploded with the sounds of crashing and banging of metal. Everyone in the room looked up just as the heating vent cracked open.

Darlene, standing next to Lindsey, swung her gun toward the vent. Lindsey grabbed Darlene's wrist as a bullet discharged, striking the wall next to the sink. Lindsey scratched the woman's forearm. Blood oozed from the slashes. Darlene attempted to raise her pistol again, but Lindsey moved too quick and knocked it out of her hand. The weapon landed on the tile floor with a clank.

Drew pointed his gun at Lindsey and aimed the barrel with intent. Lance reached out and wrapped his hand around the weapon before Drew could fire. Taking advantage of the surprised look on Drew's face, Lance snatched the gun out of his hand and threw it against the wall as Drew turned to attack. Lance deftly stepped to the side and flipped Drew onto his back. In the same movement, Lance ran his hand down Drew's arm below his sleeve. Blood flowed from the deep lacerations left behind.

Brett jumped down from the heating vent as gunfire erupted.

I pulled off my other glove, gripped Cameron's arm, and scratched his neck. Cameron hit me on the side of my head, striking my ear. Staggering to my feet, I continued digging into his flesh. He slugged my shoulder, but he couldn't stop me as I ripped off his shirt. With my sharp needles, I tore into his chest. He tried to grab my hands as we struggled.

A loud thump echoed through the room as I fought with Cameron. Suddenly, he collapsed with wide open eyes. The shooting ended. The morgue became quiet. I glanced around and saw Cameron's people spread out on the floor, completely still.

Staring at Cameron, my mind became consumed with the innocent people he had killed or injured. Without any remorse, he destroyed the lives of the girls he sold. He had killed Paula just because she was my friend. Rage boiled inside me as I thought about her. I sprang on him, tore slivers of skin from his chest and ate a piece.

Lance pulled me off Cameron. He dropped several spiders on him. "You have to wait," he said.

I squirmed, trying to free myself from Lance's hold. My body trembled. Anger and revenge surged through me as all I could think about was Cameron, the despicable man who lacked humanity. I needed to stop him and make sure there was no way he could hurt anyone else. As I continued twisting and wiggling, I managed to get away from Lance. I leapt on Cameron and dug my teeth into his forearm, but I was only able to slightly pierce his skin. I bent down and sucked up the blood.

"Sara, you have to wait," Lance snapped, pulling me off Cameron again with Brett's help. My body shook as I wriggled and kicked.

"Why do I have to wait?" I yelled.

"Cameron has to stay alive while the spider's venom circulates through his body." Lance gently stroked my face as Brett held onto me. "Relax. You can eat as much of him as you want in a few minutes."

My heartbeat slowed down. My body no longer shook. "Why did you allow yourself to be captured?" I asked Lance.

"I wanted to know where they had taken you. I was more than happy to be a captive. When he told me they had my girlfriend, I wasn't sure if he was talking about you or Lindsey." Lance knelt down, pulled the locket out of Cameron's pocket, and checked it over. "I'll get the chain fixed. Now you know how much you look like your mother," he said, sounding pleased. "Cameron thought it was you." Lance slipped the locket into his pocket.

"You told him the truth." My lips curved into a big smile. "The baby is in Houston."

Lance wiped Cameron's arm, and then he sucked out some fresh blood. "You can drink and eat as much as you want now," he said, rising to his feet.

"Use this," Brett said, handing me a pocket knife.

Lying down on Cameron, I made a deep slash in his arm with the knife. I sucked out his blood. Next I cut off a large chunk of meat. While I chewed, I looked up and watched Lance, Brett, and Lindsey wrapping the others. Then I noticed blood on my hands, arms, and all over my gown. What have I done? A wave of horror shot through me and tears streamed down my cheeks. Gasping for air, I dropped the knife on the floor and glared at Cameron's slaughtered body as water continued flowing from my eyes.

"What's wrong?" Lance said, hurrying toward me.

"Look … look … what I've done," I sniffled. "I killed Conner's brother."

"Shhh. It's okay," he said, moving me to the wheelchair.

"What am I going to tell Conner?"

"Nothing. Cameron planned on killing you. You did this in self-defense." He brushed my blood soaked hair away from my face. "Conner doesn't need to know Cameron tried to kill you and how it ended."

I buried my face in my hands and sobbed.

Lance stroked my hair. "Sara, if things were reversed, you'd be lying there. He would've left without feeling an ounce of guilt."

I lowered my hands and sat up straight. "Cameron was an evil person. I'm glad he's dead. I just know Conner will still miss him."

Lindsey handed me a towel.

Wiping my face, I saw Lance, Brett, and Lindsey, all wearing rubber aprons, looking at me. It appeared they were waiting for my permission to finish off Cameron. "Go ahead."

They bent down next to him. I couldn't watch the horrid scene of Cameron being devoured a few feet from me so my eyes darted to the sink attached to the wall in front of me. When I heard bones cracking and the distinctive sound of chewing, I cringed, pressed my lips tightly together, and covered my ears with my fingers.

Ten or fifteen minutes later, Lance washed his hands and arms. He made a towel damp, came back to me, and cleaned the blood off my face.

"Why aren't you covered with blood?" I asked.

"I've learned to eat slowly and carefully. We do need to be able to walk through the hospital without being noticed."

Lindsey and Brett stood up and went over to the sink. I saw them wiping their faces and washing their hands. They also looked clean as they walked away from the sink. Brett searched through some cabinets, pulled out a body bag, and put the remains of Cameron in it.

"What are you going to do with him?" I asked.

"There's a small abandoned warehouse outside of town that will burn along with some refuse sometime this evening," Brett replied.

"Did you rent a warehouse?" I asked.

"No," Lance replied. "Since we can only take two or three bodies back to Bismarck with us, we've been checking out the warehouse district. We don't want anyone to know how Cameron and his men actually died. Burning them is the best solution. Conner will believe that Cameron was involved in a drug deal that went bad." He helped Lindsey lift the wrapped bodies onto gurneys.

"I doubt Conner will believe that," I said, thinking Cameron would be prepared for that type of contingency. He met with shady people all the time.

"Regardless, he'll have no way of finding out what really happened."

Brett got a bucket, filled it, and mopped the floor where Cameron had lain.

"Lindsey," Lance said, "try to find a couple of hospital gowns and a roll of white gauze."

"Okay," she replied, leaving.

Lance put Gerard's medical supplies back in the metal box along with the folded table. "Brett, can you take this outside and spray it inside and out? Then throw it in the dumpster."

Brett nodded as he picked up the metal box and left.

"What happened with Saul?" I asked.

"He didn't regain consciousness. I had already told his family that he no longer had any brain activity. They wanted a second opinion. When they got it, they had him unhooked from the life support systems. They wanted to donate his body to my clinic for scientific research. I thanked them and said I wouldn't be able to preserve the body to get it back to North Dakota. One of Saul's relatives is a mortician. They called him to pick up the body. I completed the paperwork."

Lindsey entered, carrying the gowns and gauze.

"Let's get everything off Sara," Lance said to Lindsey.

"No. I can do that," I said, pulling off my socks. I rose to my feet, removed the bloody gown. Feeling a little embarrassed, I stood naked, wiping myself off with wet towels. Lindsey handed me a dry one. I quickly rubbed it over my skin and draped it around my body.

"What about your hair?" Lindsey asked.

"Get me another towel."

Lance gave me another one. I bent down and put it around my hair like I just got out of the shower. Lindsey tucked in all the straggling ends. She cleaned the wheelchair while I slipped on a hospital gown. After I sat down, Lance wrapped my hands and feet with the gauze.

"The medical supplies are gone," Brett said, walking into the morgue. "I've moved an ambulance to the back of the hospital. I'm sure it won't be missed for a few hours since there are half a dozen available."

"You're right," Lance agreed. "They don't have very many people working on Sunday evening. No one will check on it. How many cars did Cameron and his people drive to the hospital?"

"Two," Lindsey said, holding up a handful of key rings. "The keys have got to be among these."

"Is Janice close by?" Lance asked, putting on his white lab coat.

"Yes. She's still in the parking lot," Lindsey said.

"I had her stay there just in case Conner showed up while we were dealing with Cameron," Brett said.

"Have Janice drive one of the cars," Lance said. "Lindsey, you take the other one. Leave them in a conspicuous place by the warehouse—fingerprint free."

Lindsey nodded, "Okay."

"Brett and Lindsey, put on the gray shirts and pants hanging on the rod next to the door," Lance instructed. "Then get the bodies out of here. You shouldn't be stopped. In case you are, tell them you're taking the bodies to Fazio's mortuary. If you have any problems after that, call me in Sara's room."

"We're on it," Brett said, slipping on a gray outfit.

"How long do you think it'll take them to identify Cameron's body?" I asked.

"With the cars there, the police might suspect. Since he'll be badly burned along with his employees and the warehouse, they won't have a positive identification until we're on our way to Bismarck," Lance said.

I felt relieved. I didn't want Conner coming to the hospital to tell me about Cameron. I wouldn't know how to comfort him.

Lance pushed the wheelchair out of the morgue. Brett and Lindsey followed, pulling gurneys. We went toward the central elevators. They went the opposite direction.

As soon as we reached my room, Mabel came in. "What happened to your hair?" she asked.

"Some gel from the ultrasound accidentally got in Miss Jones' hair," Lance replied.

"Do you want me to help you get that washed out?" Mabel asked.

"I thought I'd take a shower," I said.

Mabel looked at Lance. "You said she should stay off her feet. Is it okay if she takes a shower?"

"As long as it's a quick one," he said, removing the gauze from my hands.

"I'll order your dinner," Mabel said. "It should be up here when you get out of the shower."

"I don't feel hungry," I said.

"Is it okay if she doesn't eat any dinner?" Mabel asked Lance.

"Why don't you just get her some dessert?" Lance said. "I want her to have a large breakfast tomorrow. I'll be taking her to my clinic in Bismarck for the treatment she needs. I'd like to have her ready to leave here at nine."

"She'll be ready," Mabel said, leaving the room.

Lance scanned my face. "Are you still upset about Cameron?"

"Not about Cameron, just about Conner."

When the gauze had been removed from my hands and feet, I stood up and went into the bathroom. The warm water running over me felt so good. Scrubbing my body and hair, I saw a stream of red suds going down the drain. I stepped out of the shower stall, dried myself off, and put on a fresh hospital gown. I wrapped a clean towel around my head and looked in the mirror. Staring back at me was the reflection of a killer. Yet I no longer felt any remorse. How was that possible? With downcast eyes, I inhaled deeply as I worried about my apathy toward the crime I had just committed.

As I walked toward the bed, I sensed Lance studying me.

"Are you okay?" he asked.

"Yes," I replied, easing down on the side of the bed. My feet dangled over the edge.

"I'll be right back," he said, going into the bathroom. He came out, carrying a bundle of rolled up towels with a small piece of a hospital gown sticking out one side. "I don't want anyone running into a towel with blood all over it. I'm going to get you another pair of gloves and socks. Make sure no one touches your hands or feet."

"I will," I said as he left.

A moment later, my body trembled as I thought about Cameron again and mourned for his family. I was responsible for the loss of a husband and father. What's wrong with me? One minute I didn't feel any grief at all for my actions and the next I felt sad. I had probably saved a lot of lives by getting rid of Cameron. I should be proud of what I had done. At the same time, I was having a hard time coming to the realization that I was now capable of killing a person. Maybe if I decided to become a Tegen, I could find a way to put my new ability to good use. Help people.

Mabel sat a food tray down on the table. "You look like you're freezing. Let me get you under the covers."

"No," I said, emphatically. "Not until Dr. Alston brings back some more gloves and socks."

"I'll get you a warm blanket," she said, going into the hall. Within a minute, she was back carrying two. She put one on my lap and bent down to tuck in my feet.

"I can do that," I said, slipping my hands under hers to block her from touching the needles.

Lance walked in. "Is everything okay?" he asked.

"I just wanted to wrap up Miss Jones' feet. She's shaking."

"These socks will keep her feet warm," he said, approaching me.

"Let me help," Mabel said, reaching for a sock.

"I'll take care of it," I said, grabbing a sock. I tucked my foot into it.

"Is there anything you would like me to do?" Mabel asked Lance.

"No," he said.

As Mabel left, I thought both Lance and I had been too curt with her. On the other hand, I didn't want her accidently getting hurt.

"How does that feel?" he asked when he slipped on the last glove.

"Good. Now I just need to dry my hair."

"I'll get your nurse to bring in a hairdryer." He stepped out of the room.

Mabel came in. She insisted that it would be easier if she blow dried my hair. I allowed her to do it without putting up a fuss. "Are you feeling warmer now?" she asked.

"Yes. Thank you."

She pushed the table with the food tray on it in front of me. "I'm afraid the ice cream has melted."

"It still looks good," I said, eyeing the chocolate cake.

"Just buzz when you're finished," she said, leaving.

I had just dug into the cake when the phone rang. I picked up the receiver. "Hello?"

"How are you doing?" Conner asked.

"Good," I said, feeling grateful that Conner didn't know about his brother yet.

"Did you get the message I left this morning?"

"Yes."

"I had hoped I'd be back in time to see you today. It didn't work out."

"No problem," I said as I thought Cameron had probably sent him on an errand to make sure he wouldn't show up here at the wrong time.

"What did Dr. Alston say about going to his clinic?"

"He's made plans for me to leave tomorrow morning on a medical plane. The treatment will start on Tuesday."

"On your birthday?" Conner asked in a bewildered tone.

"Yes. He thought it would only take a few days for my hands and feet to heal."

"That sounds great. So can I pick you up next weekend?"

"Providing everything goes as planned," I said, wondering if I'd still be alive then.

"Do you have the phone number to his clinic?"

"I'll call you tomorrow night and give you the number."

"Should I pack another suitcase for you?"

"No. I won't need any more clothes as I'll be wearing hospital gowns and sleeping most of the time during the treatment. I don't know if they'll let calls through."

"Just as long as you're getting well, that's all that counts. Then you can show me how much you missed me when we're flying to San Diego," he teased.

"I'll plan on it," I said, wondering how I could use the knowledge I had acquired regarding the Crussett family business.

"I want you to get some sleep so you're rested for tomorrow. Remember I love you," he said, his voice filled with warmth.

"I love you, too. Talk to you tomorrow night."

"Goodnight, Sara." He clicked off.

23

BISMARCK

At quarter to nine the next morning, I was dressed in a pair of dark grey slacks and a white silk blouse. After enduring scratchy hospital gowns for four days, the soft fabric felt so good against my skin. While I straightened the collar, Brett walked through the doorway.

"Did everything go okay last night?" I asked.

"Just as planned."

A nurse, not Mabel, came in pushing a wheelchair. "I guess you're going to be leaving us today," she said, sounding cheerful. She held onto my arm as I sat down in the wheelchair. "Dr. Alston will meet us at the entrance. You'll be going to the airport in an ambulance." The nurse pushed the wheelchair out of the room. Brett followed with my suitcase.

When we reached the entrance, Lance and Lindsey were there waiting. "I'll take her from here," Lance said, as he moved behind the wheelchair.

The nurse touched my shoulder. "Have a good trip to North Dakota."

"Thank you. Could you say bye to Nurse Mabel for me?"

"I will," the nurse said, and then headed toward the elevator.

Lance wheeled me through the sliding entry doors to the ambulance. Brett put my suitcase in the trunk of a car that was parked behind it. Then he climbed into the front passenger seat of the ambulance. It drove away.

"I thought I was going in the ambulance," I said to Lindsey.

"No. We needed an ambulance to transport some bodies—the three guys who tried to kidnap you."

I scooted into the back seat of the car. Lindsey slid in on the other side. Lance and a man, whom I had never seen before, got into the front seat. The stranger sat behind the steering wheel.

"Sara Jones, this is Jacob Tillman," Lance said, referring to the driver. "He's a medical student. He'll be driving us to the airport and then returning the car."

Lance finished the introductions as the car pulled out of the parking lot. Then he chatted with Jacob about his clinic and the research they were working on.

"I'm looking forward to my internship there," Jacob said. "When would you like me to start?"

"Sometime in the middle of June," Lance said. "I have another intern starting on June 16th. Millie, my receptionist, will make arrangements for your housing. She'll be contacting you."

"Great. Will I have an opportunity to meet your father when I'm there or will he still be in Africa?"

Lindsey looked at me and smiled.

"I'm not sure what his schedule is. Last year he dropped in to see how the research was going."

Lindsey coughed to disguise a laugh and held her hand over her mouth. I raised an eyebrow.

Lance turned around. "Are you okay?" he asked, with a stern expression on his face.

She nodded.

"Dr. Alston, during your lecture you mentioned the vaccine your research team was working on for bee allergies; the one that only had to be administered once every five years. Can you fill me in on the status?"

"Of course," Lance said. He briefed Jacob about the vaccine while Lindsey and I sat quietly in the back seat. It was so technical that I couldn't understand what he was saying, so my mind began to wander to the looming decision that I had to make soon.

We drove into a small, private airport. Jacob stopped the car next to an airplane. Brett and the ambulance driver were carrying a filled body bag toward the plane's storage compartment.

"What are those?" Jacob asked, casting a suspicious sideways glance.

"Fortunately, while I was here I received three donated bodies for my research," Lance said to Jacob, opening the door.

Jacob's expression relaxed. "Can I help you load them?"

"I'd appreciate that."

Lindsey stepped out of the car and opened the trunk. I watched the bodies being moved from the ambulance to the plane and Lindsey dealing with the luggage.

When they were through, Lance opened my car door. "Are you ready to go?"

"Yes." I swung my legs to the outside of the car and stood up.

"Thank you, Jacob," Lance said. "I'm looking forward to having you on my research team this summer."

"So am I," Jacob said. "Do you need any help getting anything else on the plane?"

"No, thanks. I can manage things from here. See you next month."

"Have a good flight." Jacob waved as he got back into the car.

After Jacob drove away, Lance led me up the stairs to the plane's entrance.

My eyes scanned the interior. Behind the cockpit was a galley. Next to it were seats against both sides of the plane. At the rear stood a bed secured to the floor and surrounded by medical equipment attached to the walls. It certainly didn't look anything like the inside of Conner's plane. There was nothing luxurious about it. Also, it hadn't been purchased with dirty money.

I lowered myself into a chair and buckled up. Lance took the next seat. Brett and Lindsey sat across from us.

When we reached cruising altitude, Lance said, "I want you to lie down and sleep."

"I'm not tired."

"It'll be good for your hands and feet."

I unhooked my seatbelt. He followed me to the bed. After I was under the covers, I started strapping myself in. I couldn't get one to snap shut. Lance helped.

"You don't need to wear the gloves until we reach Bismarck," he said.

I took them off and freely wiggled my fingers. "This feels so good not having my hands inhibited." I looked at my palms. The small bumps had spread, covering every inch. I rubbed my hands together.

"Do your hands hurt?"

"No. They feel strange, but not painful."

"Take these," he said, handing me two pills along with a bottle of water.

"Why?"

"They'll help you relax."

I plopped the pills in my mouth and drank a large gulp of water.

"Try to get some sleep," he said.

I smiled, closing my eyes.

I stirred when I heard the sound of loud banging and heavy footsteps. The airplane door stood wide open. I leaned over, looked out a window, and saw people unloading the storage compartment. I didn't recognize two of them.

"You're awake," Lindsey said, peeking around the door.

"Can you help me with these straps?" I asked her, as I snapped one off.

She walked over and undid the straps that bound my legs to the bed. "You must have been more tired than you said you were. You slept all the way here." She handed me my gloves. I slipped them back on.

"On the way to the airport, what was so funny that made you laugh?"

"When Lance mentioned that Lawrence came to the research lab last year. You'd laugh too if you saw him in the ridiculous wig he wears when he's pretending to be his father. I have to keep my lips together so a snort doesn't accidently escape in front of a student."

"Need any help getting into the car?" Brett asked me, entering the cabin.

"No. I'm fine." I sat up and felt the plane spinning.

Brett gripped my arm. "Are you okay?"

"Is the plane moving?"

"No."

"It feels like it's going in circles," I said, gasping for air.

"Lance thought you might be a little dizzy when you woke up. The pills he gave you were powerful. He said it should wear off in fifteen or twenty minutes."

"He's got to stop giving me poison. Where is he, by the way?" I held onto the railing of the bed as I stood and regained my equilibrium.

"He's outside, giving instructions," Brett answered

Brett tried to hold onto my arm as I headed to the door. I pushed his hand away. "I am quite capable of getting out of here by myself."

"Your feet don't hurt?"

"Not now," I said, moving down the airplane stairs in my sock-covered feet.

Brett opened the back door of a black limo. "Crussetts aren't the only ones who have limos," he said, smiling as he closed the door behind me.

Lance got in on the other side and motioned to the driver to leave.

"Aren't Brett and Lindsey coming with us?" I asked.

"No. They're going to the clinic in the ambulance to help unload."

"I've had enough hospital food and their antiseptic ambience. Just drop me off at a hotel. I'll call and let you know if I decide to become a Tegen."

Lance's eyes flitted across my face. "Wouldn't you rather stay at my house instead?"

"That's an option?" I asked, feeling surprised.

"I hadn't planned on taking you to the clinic."

"Okay," I said as my curiosity piqued about his house, and I wondered if it was the same place he lived with my biological mother. "Your house will be acceptable."

"Hattie has everything set up for you. She's a Tegen, so you can talk freely around her. Most of the people who work at the clinic aren't. My driver is not a Tegen."

After what Lindsey told me about Hattie, I was anxious to meet her since she had known my mother. "Is there any way Tegens can identify each other?"

"Yes. Tegens' arms contain special glands. By stroking each others' arms, pheromones are secreted that we use to recognize each other."

My eyes popped wide open. "Is it poisonous?"

"No, and the pheromones are only secreted if the arm is touched by another Tegen's hand."

Gazing at Lance, I asked, "What would you like me to call you?"

"Do you believe now that Jennifer and I are your parents?"

"Yes."

"Then I'd like you to call me 'Father' or 'Dad'. If that makes you uncomfortable, you can just continue to call me Lance."

Could I call this stranger father? "I don't know. Let me think about it."

"Do whatever you want."

The limo stopped in front of a large metal gate. It opened for us. We drove in and through a heavy wooded area. The trees began to thin out. They still lined both sides of the driveway. We went around two curves and stopped in front of a stunning mansion that looked like something out of *Gone with the Wind*. Not what I expected in the woods near Bismarck. The exterior of the gorgeous southern colonial was white stone with a deep portico and round columns. The large windows were flanked with deep green shutters. I continued staring at the house until the driver opened the door.

Lance got out first. "Take the luggage upstairs. Hattie will tell you where to put Sara's." He made it sound like I had more than one small suitcase. A woman with long black hair stood next to the front door as I entered the house.

"You should try to stay off your feet," she said, motioning me to sit on the cushioned bench in the foyer. I recognized the woman from Billings. She was the one who looked like a model. She had escorted me into the woods.

"Put Miss Jones' luggage in the corner bedroom overlooking the backyard," she said to the limo driver. She walked closer and embraced me in her arms, taking me by surprise.

"Sara, this is Hattie," Lance said.

"I'm so glad you've come," Hattie said, smiling as she stroked my arm.

"So am I," I said, smiling back.

"I knew your mother," she said with trembling lips. "You look just like her." Her eyes glistened.

Lance glanced at her for a minute, then turned and looked at me with a solemn expression on his face. "Are you hungry?"

"Yes."

"Marie has everything set up out on the terrace," Hattie said. "Marie is Lance's housekeeper."

Lance led me through a tastefully decorated and elegant living room filled with what appeared to be priceless antiques. I wanted to stop and admire the furnishings, but I continued at his pace. We walked across the dining room floor to the terrace. I smelled lilacs when we went outside. The terrace was bursting with flowers framed by a lilac bush on each side. More lilac bushes surrounded the outer edge of the lawn; a cluster was on a small hill. The table had been set with a bowl of sliced fruit, lunch meats, cheeses, and breads. Lance pulled out a chair for me.

"It's beautiful out here," I said, feeling amazed.

"Thank you, but I can't take credit for it," Lance said. "Your mother decided what she wanted. The gardener planted everything according to her specifications. Every gardener has kept the yard looking exactly the same."

"I love the smell of lilacs," I said, putting fruit on my plate.

"Lilacs were your mother's favorite flower," Hattie said.

Lance looked at Hattie. "They're also Sara's favorite."

She smiled at me. "I guess it isn't just your mother's looks you've inherited."

After lunch, Lance rose to his feet. "I need to check on some patients at the clinic. I'll be back in a few hours."

"This will give me a chance to show Sara the house," Hattie said.

"She needs to rest, so make it quick," Lance said.

Hattie nodded as he left.

"Do you want anything else to eat or drink before we get started?" Hattie asked.

"No. I couldn't eat another bite."

I walked by her side into the kitchen. It had a breakfast nook that looked out into the garden. Marie, a middle-aged, dark skinned, stocky woman, was loading the dishwasher. She immediately stopped when she saw us.

"Sara, I'd like you to meet Marie," Hattie said.

"I'm happy to make your acquaintance, Marie," I said, smiling at her.

"Marie, this is Sara Jones, Dr. Alston's house guest."

"Miss Jones, let me know if there is anything I can do to make your visit here more comfortable," Marie said.

"Thank you. I appreciate your kind offer."

"The door over there," Hattie pointed to one in the corner of the kitchen, "leads to Marie's apartment."

We left the kitchen and went into a game room; in the middle stood a pool table. Cherry wood covered the bottom half of all the walls. At one end of the room was a large fireplace.

"How long has Marie been working for him?" I asked, wondering how he handled the no-aging issue.

"She's been here for five or six years. Lance can't keep any employees longer than ten years. He tries not to get very close to any of them. He sometimes has to come up with some pretty elaborate excuses why their services are no longer needed.

"That's a problem all Tegens have to face. We can't work and be friends with someone who isn't a Tegen for more than ten or fifteen years at the most. We can't tell them why we don't age. It's been an extra difficult problem for your father since he's renowned in his field, and he loves what he does. I love it too, but I'm not in the same visible position that he is. Sometimes I've had to leave the clinic for a few years and work in a hospital. I try not to be very friendly with anyone who isn't a Tegen."

Her eyes moved to the pool table. "Do you know how to play pool?"

"Yes. I'm not very good."

"I'm sure your father will teach you all his tricks. He's good."

"He seems to be good at everything except conversation."

Hattie didn't comment as she led me into the den. It also had cherry wood on all the walls, including the two with bookcases that reached the ceiling. The desk had carvings that ran along the edge and down the legs. On one side of the room was a grand fireplace. Above it hung a painting of my biological mother. My eyes welled up with tears as I thought about her letter and saw her warm smile. She seemed so happy.

Hattie put her arm around my shoulders. I didn't say anything as I stared at the painting and breathed deeply, trying to calm down. "Do you live here?" I asked.

"No. I have a house close to the clinic, but I'll be staying here for a while. Your father doesn't want you left alone."

I wanted to tell her I could take care of myself. Right now, because of the pain I had experienced in my hands and feet, I wasn't sure if I could. "I'm surprised that a house like this exists in Bismarck."

"Lawrence Alston had it built over a hundred years ago. Your father is the original owner." She took my arm and we walked into the living room.

The fireplace covered almost an entire wall. Above the mantel was a painting of Lance and my mother. They were holding hands and smiling. It was strange to see Lance so happy. "I've never seen Lance smile before," I said.

"He seldom does anymore. He used to smile all the time. Sometimes that painting is put in temporary storage and replaced with a landscape for obvious reasons. Marie and her helpers have commented about how much Lance looks like his father. They've never suspected they are the same person. In the upstairs hallway is a fake picture of Lawrence looking like he's in his sixties."

"Where do they believe Lawrence is living?"

"If anyone asks, we say he lives in Montana. We also tell them that he wants his privacy. We don't give an exact address."

We moved into the dining room. Ten chairs stood around the ornate table with additional chairs against a wall. There were two large buffets on two of the walls. In this room, a mirror hung above the fireplace.

"All of the furniture was purchased by your father right after the house was built," Hattie said. "Now everyone would call them antiques. They weren't back then. Let me show you the upstairs."

We strolled into the large foyer. Hattie held gently onto my arm as we slowly went up a large, ornate, curved stairwell. Upstairs, we strolled along a massive hallway toward oak double doors at the end.

She stopped before she reached those doors and opened one on the right side of the hallway. "This is a guest bedroom," she said. The décor blended with the rest of the house, and against the far wall stood a canopy bed. "All of the bedrooms have a bathroom attached." She opened the bathroom door. Next to the sink was a small table that had some personal toiletries on it along with a comb and brush.

"Is this the bedroom you're staying in?"

"No," she said, reluctantly. "Has Lindsey told you anything about her relationship with your father?"

"Yes."

"She sometimes stays in this room. That's her stuff."

"According to what Lindsey said, I thought they were more than friends."

"They are, but," she hesitated, "your father would never sleep with another woman in the bed he shared with your mother. Lindsey knows that."

Wanting to know more about Hattie, I asked. "Do you have a boyfriend or someone special in your life?"

"Yes," she said, beaming. "Rex. He owns the house you stayed in when you were in Billings."

"Is he a petroleum engineer?"

"Yes. He was my handler. That was when he was a doctor. Tegens often change their profession. We have opportunities to go back to school."

We left that room, and she opened the double doors. "This is the master bedroom." In the center of the right wall was a giant, rosewood, 4-poster bed with carvings on all of the posts and the headboard. A large picture of my mother hung above the fireplace. On the nightstand was also a picture of her. French doors opened up to a balcony.

I walked outside and saw it overlooked the backyard. "This is a great view," I said, looking at the lilacs. "Is there something past the bushes on the hill?"

"Just the woods." She fidgeted with her fingers. "Why?"

"The lilac bushes look wonderful. They just don't seem to line up with the others."

She laid her hand on my shoulder. "That's where your mother is buried. Your father always wanted her to be close to him."

A dreadful grief rolled over me. I suddenly felt a lump in my throat. My mother. The woman that gave me life. The woman I didn't even know existed until a few days ago. Tears were trickling down my cheeks when I heard Hattie sniffling.

"Lance won't like it if he comes back and we're both crying," she said as she wiped my cheeks with her hand. Hattie went into the bathroom and came back with a handful of tissues. We dried our faces. She flushed the used tissues down the toilet.

"Let me show you the other bedrooms." We stepped out into the hallway and she opened the next door. It was a nursery, ready for a baby.

"Your mother wanted everything to appear to be normal." She walked over and opened another door. "It connects to a room where a nanny would stay." Hattie stood quietly and looked around the room. "The women at work gave her a baby shower. She glowed just like any expectant mother. She was happy."

I noticed the unused baby toys, the rocking chair that was never used to rock a baby to sleep, unwrinkled linens and blankets lined the bottom of the cradle, and infant shoes stood on top of a dresser. Next to them I saw a picture and went closer. It must have been taken right after I was born; Mother was holding me. She did look happy. On the table by the cradle was a picture of Lance, Mother, and me. They were smiling.

"Your father was able to keep your mother alive for almost a day after you were born," she said in a solemn tone. "We always have spiders with us. Your father worried that your mother could accidentally be bitten. He invented a vaccine just for her. I'm sure that helped keep her alive. He also had her hooked up to equipment. She wanted to see you."

"Who took the pictures?"

"I did."

I wondered if Lance was keeping all the baby things as a shrine to my mother's memory. "Will this room always remain a nursery?"

"Maybe now your father will think about changing it back. I don't think it's good for him to have that constant reminder."

She was right. He should change it back. There will never be a baby in this house.

"You need to get off your feet." She then showed me to my room.

It was a corner room with a canopy bed. The balcony overlooked the backyard. The windows on the other wall faced the woods. I opened the door to the bathroom. My toiletries were lying on the table next to the sink. "Did someone unpack my suitcase?"

"Yes. Lance had Marie unpack it. He wanted you to be able to relax." She looked at me. "You're not upset about that, are you?"

"No. I didn't have anything in it that she shouldn't see. I never packed my suitcase. I only found out what was in it when I got dressed this morning."

"Who packed it for you?" she asked with a puzzled expression.

"Conner," I replied, certain she knew who he was. I opened the closet door. There were nightgowns hanging in it. "Who do these belong to?"

"All but one was your mother's. Your father didn't want you to wear hospital gowns while you were here."

"Which one wasn't?"

"The black one."

I held it up. The fabric was soft. It was nicely tailored with long sleeves. "Did my father buy me a black nightgown?"

"Yes."

How strange. "I am getting tired."

"Why don't you put on one of the nightgowns and take a nap?"

"I'll wear the black gown."

"No," she replied in a firm tone.

"Why not?"

"Well." She paused. "I'll explain after you're in bed."

I took off my clothes, slipped on a light blue nightgown, and climbed under the covers. "Okay, I'm ready."

Hattie pulled up a chair and sat next to the bed. "The black gown is to be worn to the Tegen Cave, if you decide to join us."

"Does everyone wear black when they go there?"

"Yes. Tegens can see in the dark. Black doesn't stand out. It's more of a relaxing color. That's also the color our spiders like."

"How do you know that?"

"I don't have any proof that's what they like. It's part of the information passed down over the years. Lindsey did tell you about Sir Randolph, didn't she?"

"Yes."

"Then you know all of his documents were destroyed in the Chicago fire of 1871. Tegens just know about the color black through word of mouth. None of us want to take a chance of being unwelcome when we go to the cave, so we wear black." She rose to her feet. "Now it's time for you to sleep."

"No. Please stay. I'd like to ask you some questions about my mother."

She smiled as she sat back down. "Okay, just for a few minutes. What do you want to know?"

"What was she like? How did she meet my father?"

"She was warm, kind, loving, and as pretty as can be. I think your father fell in love with her the first time he saw her. He was looking for a registered nurse. Your mom had just graduated. She applied for the job along with twenty others. You see, Lawrence is very famous in his field. His clinic is known all over the world. Everyone who applied wanted to work for Lawrence Alston. Your mother just wanted a job. The other applicants had years of experience. All your mom had was a degree, but she had completed an internship at the local hospital. She was so nervous, looking at the floor. Lawrence raised her chin and asked her name. She only gave him her first name, Jennifer. He asked her if she had a last name. She blushed and said yes. Then he waited for her to say it. After a noticeable pause, he asked her, 'What is your last name'?" Hattie smiled. "You should have seen the way he looked at her—absolutely adoringly."

"What was she like to work with?"

"All the patients in the clinic loved her. She was always cheerful and fun to be around. It can be very difficult for someone to leave their family to come to the clinic for treatment. She knew how to comfort them when they were troubled and in pain. Your mother was my dear friend for over eighteen years. I still miss her," Hattie said, as her voice cracked. She touched my cheek. "I need to let you get some sleep."

"One more question?"

She nodded.

"What happens during the transformation?" I asked.

She hesitated. "Why don't you ask your father about that?"

Lindsey didn't want to tell me and now Hattie. It must be awful.

Hattie continued, "It was hard when I had to cut ties with everyone I knew before I became a Tegen. That's the hardest part for all new Tegens. Yet, I've never regretted being transformed." She stood. "I better let you get some sleep before your father comes home." She kissed my forehead. "I hope you decide to join us."

24

THE NURSERY

The room was dark when I raised my eyelids. I turned on the nightstand lamp and glanced at the clock: 7:20 p.m. My body felt stiff as I eased out of bed. I slipped on the robe that hung in the closet and opened the door. Making my way to the stairs, I heard voices and saw Lance approaching me.

"How did you sleep?" he asked.

"Good."

"We were just about to sit down for dinner. Would you like to join us?"

"Yes," I replied, as my stomach growled. "I'll put on some regular clothes."

"No. Your nightgown will do. You should go back to bed as soon as you're through eating." He held onto my arm as we went down the stairs.

Brett, Lindsey, and Hattie were sitting in the living room drinking wine. Or was it wine? We greeted each other. Feeling like I could hardly move, I sank down on the sofa. Brett's eyes fixed on me. He slightly smiled. It didn't hide the worried look I saw on his face.

"Are you feeling well?" Lance asked me in a clinical, apathetic voice.

"I'm not in pain. I just feel stiff all over."

"Maybe a glass of wine will help," he said, walking to a buffet. He poured a glass of red liquid from a carafe and carried it to me.

"Is this really wine?" I asked as he handed me the glass.

"No."

I took a small sip. Every time I drank *venotrolia*, I felt better. I loved the taste.

"We're all anxious to know if you've made your decision yet," Lindsey asked.

Lance glared at her. I could tell from his expression he wasn't pleased that she had asked. "Sara," he said. "Tomorrow is your birthday. If you haven't decided by then, you still have a few days. Your birthday is the first day you can go to the cave. It isn't the last."

"What day would be the last day?" I asked.

"Saturday," Lance answered without hesitation.

"How do you know that?"

"I've studied every Tegen and compiled statistics on the phases of their natural progression before transformation. There are observable, repeating patterns. Yours is uncommon, but not without precedent." He paused and looked at me with raised brows. "Tomorrow could be a long day. Let's proceed to the dining room."

Holding onto the armrest with my gloved hand, I slowly rose to my feet. Lance took my arm. Brett held onto the other one as they escorted me into the dining room.

Marie served salad and fresh baked rolls. Next, she brought out a standing rib roast along with all the trimmings. Lance had her slice and serve it. Occasionally, Brett stroked my arm and gave me a reassuring smile, like everything was going to be okay. He also gently rubbed my thigh whenever he had the opportunity. I wasn't disturbed by his gestures because I sensed he just wanted to touch me, nothing more. Hattie and Lindsey glanced at me between bites. They smiled whenever our eyes met.

During dinner, we talked about the weather and the new restaurant that was opening in town. Lindsey planned on applying for a job there. Most of the time, everyone ate in silence under a cloud of tension and anticipation. I could tell everyone was thinking about the same thing. After crème brulee was served, a pain shot through my feet. It was intense and unrelenting, but I didn't want to spoil dessert for anyone.

"Are you okay?" Brett asked.

"Yes. I'm fine," I said, trying to bear the pain.

Brett turned and stared at me. "Sara, are you okay?" he asked again, suspiciously.

"I already told you I'm fine."

Lance laid down his spoon. He looked at Brett. "Why do you think Sara isn't feeling well?"

"Her thigh muscle tightened up."

"Sara?" Lance questioned.

"My feet hurt a little. That's all."

"No, that's not all," Lance said, standing. "I've already told you that once the pain starts it escalates. You're going upstairs."

"I'll carry her," Brett said.

"No. I'll walk." I pushed my chair away from the table and headed out of the dining room. My feet ached more with every step I took. Reaching the stairs, I relented and wrapped my arms around Brett's neck. He carried me up to my bedroom with everyone following. I didn't like that much attention. I didn't want them to see me in pain.

When Brett laid me down on the bed, the throbbing pain was almost unbearable. I bit my lower lip, determined not to tell anyone. I couldn't prevent water from welling in my eyes.

Lance looked down at me with a frown. "I wish you would tell me when you're in pain and not be so stubborn."

Tears clouded my vision as they ran down my cheeks.

"Hattie, take off her gloves and socks," Lance said. "I need to get some things."

"Can I help with something?" Lindsey asked, going out the door after him.

Hattie and Brett removed my socks and gloves. Lance and Lindsey came back into the room. He was carrying something that looked like a set of deep purple flood lights. On the side of the stand was the name "Purdrollins." Tubes were attached to them. Lance also had his medical bag. Lindsey held a box of medical supplies.

Lance plugged in the lights and shined them on my feet. Whatever radiated from them didn't feel warm; in fact, it felt cool. It immediately helped. He pulled a syringe out of his bag and promptly filled it. Without hesitation, he pushed up my sleeve of my gown and gave me a shot. It only stung for a second.

"Are you feeling better?" Lance asked.

"Yes, much better."

He ran his hands over my feet and up my calves. "Sara, it's spreading. The bumps are now on the top of your feet." He paused as his face lined with sadness. "I'll only be able to help control the pain for a few days. I don't think you'll be capable of walking into the cave after Thursday; the pain will be so severe."

"So I only have until Thursday to make my decision?"

"Yes," he said. "You have to be able to walk into the cave to join us."

"I know," I said, peering into his eyes. Scanning the room, I saw everyone staring at me. Hattie's eyes were glossy. Her lips quivered as she blinked several times and swallowed hard. The sorrow on her face made my heart ache. I wanted to embrace her and tell her everything was going to be okay. I couldn't since I wasn't sure if it would be.

My eyes moved to Brett. His face was pinched with worry. I sensed the pain he felt. Even though we had only known each other a couple of months, we had shared intimate moments. I was certain he cared deeply for me.

I looked at Lindsey and saw the blank expression on her face. She wasn't outwardly displaying any emotion. I believed she liked me. Maybe not enough.

Lance set up another piece of equipment with a plastic bottle hanging from it. "I'm just getting this ready in case you need it later," he said. "As long as the lamps and the shot I gave you are working, you won't need this. Are you comfortable?"

"Yes. My feet have stopped hurting. I'd like to be alone so I can make a phone call." Brett glanced at me with bleak eyes as he walked out the door, followed by Lindsey. I suspected he knew who I planned to call.

Hattie handed me a phone. "What's the number of the clinic?" I asked.

"Are you going to call the clinic?" she asked, perplexed.

A smile flickered on my face. "No. I told Conner I'd give him the number. I don't want to give him this number. If he should call the clinic, can you have someone tell him that I'm not able to take phone calls?"

"Yes," she answered. "I'll make sure the receptionist knows."

"The clinic number is on the card," Lance said, giving me a business card.

"Can I have the letter Mother wrote me?" I asked.

"Certainly," he said, taking it out of his medical bag. "It's yours."

Hattie stared at him as he handed me the letter. From her expression, I knew she didn't know anything about it.

Lance looked at her. "Let's leave Sara alone." When he reached the door with Hattie by his side, he turned toward me. "There's a bell on your nightstand. Ring it if you need anything or if you feel even the slightest amount of pain."

"I will," I promised.

I didn't want to call Conner. Yet, I couldn't avoid it and the anticipation of Conner finding out about his brother was weighing heavy on me. I needed to find out what he knew. Did he suspect I was involved? I dialed his number and waited as his phone rang five times.

"Hello," he answered.

"Hi, Conner."

"Is this the number where I can reach you?" he asked, his voice dragging.

"No. I'm using one of the office phones," I said, and then began giving him the clinic number.

"Sara," he interrupted. "I'm at Carina's house. There's a family problem. Can you call Darcy and give her the number?" He sounded tense and nervous. "I need to get back. I'll call you tomorrow."

"I don't know if they'll let me have calls once the treatment starts."

"I remember you telling me that. I'll still try to reach you. Call me if you can. Bye, Sara," he said, anxious to end the call.

"Bye." I put the phone back in the cradle.

The family must have been told about Cameron dying in a warehouse fire. I wondered who they thought could be responsible. Conner did say they had enemies. Originally, he suspected one of them was responsible for my disappearance. Conner would never know that Cameron tried to kidnap me and wanted me dead. All of Cameron's men who had been involved were dead, and I'd never tell him. On top of all of Cameron's faults, he still was Conner's brother. Who would run the family business now: Carina or Conner? Or would his father become active again?

I called Conner's house. Darcy immediately answered, "Mr. Crussett's residence. May I help you?"

"Hello, Darcy. It's Sara."

"Oh, Sara. I'm so glad you called, but Conner isn't here right now."

"I know. I just called his cell phone. He wants me to give you the number of the clinic here."

"Yes. Yes. The clinic. Did Mr. Crussett say anything else to you?" she asked, hesitantly.

"No." As much as I didn't want to know any details, I still asked, "Why?"

"Oh...oh...oh nothing."

"Darcy, are you okay?"

"Yes...yes...I'm not the one in the clinic. How are you feeling?"

"Fine."

"Good. Can you give me your number for Mr. Crussett?"

I read her the number on the card.

"Sara, I hope you can come home soon. We miss you. I need to go and get things ready for Mr. Crussett's company that will be arriving later this evening."

"Who?"

"I don't know. He wants all the guest rooms ready."

"I better let you go. It's been nice talking to you, Darcy. Bye."

"Bye, Sara." She disconnected.

Darcy probably didn't want to tell me about the family tragedy since I wasn't well. She'd never know I was responsible. I wondered who would be staying at Conner's house. Probably some of his top men. The compound must have been crawling with guys, patrolling the outer wall.

At a time like this, cameras and the current security system wouldn't be enough.

I picked up Mother's letter and read it again. It brought tears to my eyes. She would have done anything to be a Tegen. I didn't know if I could. Could I kill to survive? I didn't have any problem with Cameron, but he was a monster. The people in Billings who were consumed by Tegens were actually killed by the spiders. The spiders were planted and, according to Lindsey, the victims had been selected, not random. Would it be fair if I fed, yet never participated in the kill? I didn't know. Would I lose my humanity if I became a Tegen? Lance helped people. He had invented dozens of vaccines to offset the impact of various spider and insect bites. He had saved lives. His clinic was devoted to research and curing people.

Lindsey said I'd feel the same way about things as I did now, except I'd view killing differently. I knew I only had two options—either become a Tegen or die. Mother gave her life for me. I closed my eyes. My mind spun spirals trying to figure it out.

I felt edgy as I opened my eyes. Feeling pain free, I got out of bed. The fluorescent hands on the nightstand clock said: 12:30 p.m. I wanted to see the pictures in the nursery again. I stepped out of the bedroom into a dark hallway. The beam of light coming from my room was enough for me to make my way to the nursery. It seemed strange walking on my bare feet, but not painful.

Entering the nursery, I turned on the lamp standing on the dresser near the door. Then I picked up the family picture of Mother, Lance, and me. It was still hard for me to call Lance Father. I quietly closed the door. I sat down in the rocking chair and studied the photo. They looked so happy. Tears blurred my vision when I thought about the moment it was taken; they both knew their life together was ending.

Lance opened the door, wearing a robe. "Sara, what are you doing in here?" he asked, walking toward me.

"Looking for answers. I have so many questions."

"What do you want to know?"

I held up the picture and pointed at his image. "You used to be so happy."

"Yes, I was. All that changed when your mother died. You remind me so much of her."

"You seem so cold. Did all your emotions die with her?" Trying to stay calm, I took a deep breath. "You don't love me, your own daughter. I'm just another research subject."

Lance stroked my face. "I love you more than you can imagine. I've watched you your entire life from a distance. I'm not used to consistently and directly interfering with your life until recently. I hope I can overcome my emotional difficulties and gain your trust, and someday we can have a relationship that circumstances have denied us till now."

"I hope so too." My eyes dropped to the picture again. I felt his pain about Mother's death. Emotions overcame me, and I sobbed.

He stroked my hair. "Sara, what have I done?"

I was crying so hard I couldn't talk. I just held up the picture. He took it from my hand and looked at it. "She ... she died because of me," I stuttered.

He knelt down and put his arms around me. "No, Sara," he said, tenderly. "She died because of me. She didn't want me to see her age. I never noticed she was getting older. She looked the same to me as the first time we met. She was so excited when she found out she was expecting you. We both knew what that meant. She never regretted it for a minute. She was beaming all the time, even when she went into labor. You are her legacy. I'm grateful that she was able to spend some time with you before...," his voice cracked and he swallowed hard.

He brushed the hair away from my face and continued, "She rejoiced when she found out you were a baby girl. She couldn't have been happier. I only wish I could have duplicated Sir Randolph's formula. That, I will always regret." He held up my chin. "Sara, never blame yourself for your mother's passing. She wanted you. You are her lasting joy...and mine." He got a tissue and wiped away my tears. "Are you ready to go back to bed now?"

I still felt like an emotional wreck and unsure of myself, but I knew he loved me. "Will you stay with me?" I asked.

His eyebrows rose. I thought my request took him by surprise. "Of course," he said without hesitation.

He held onto my arm as we walked out of the room. Instead of turning toward my room, he led me into his. The room he had shared with my mother. We got in bed and he put his arm around me. I laid my head on his shoulder and thought about the times I'd slept with my parents, the Joneses, after I had seen a scary movie. They made me feel safe. Now, Lance—*Father*—also made me feel safe.

"Do you feel better now?" he asked, tenderly.

"Yes."

"Good." He lightly stroked my cheek.

I closed my eyes, and all my worries disappeared into sleep.

25

THE BIRTHDAY

Sunlight streamed through the windows when I woke up alone in his bed. The medical equipment from my room had been moved in here. The bathroom door opened and out came Lance, dressed in a pair of slacks and a long-sleeved shirt.

"How did you sleep?"

"Great," I replied. "I hope I didn't keep you up too late."

He sat down on the bed. "No, you didn't keep me up. I fell right to sleep. Would you like to stay in here?"

Glancing around the room, I sensed the love my parents had shared. "Yes."

"Marie will bring you up breakfast. When you're through eating, I want to set up the lamp on your feet. You're not in pain, are you?"

"No. Will either you or Hattie be here today?"

"I'm going to work in the den this morning. Hattie's already gone to work." He picked up a gift-wrapped box that was on the nightstand. "Happy birthday," he said, handing it to me.

I smiled as I removed the wrapping paper. Inside the box was a photo album.

"Your mother put this together for you," he said. "She wanted you to have it on your twenty-fifth birthday."

I raised the cover. On the first page was a picture of Mother wearing a nurse's outfit and Lance wearing a doctor's white lab coat. They were shaking hands. Under it, she had written: "Our life together begins."

"You can look through it while I go down and tell Marie you're ready for breakfast," he said as he started to stand. "I'll be right back."

"Can I ask you one question first?"

He eased back down. "Yes."

"Do you have other children?"

"Yes. I have six sons. The house you stayed at in Billings is owned by one of them, Rex. He's also Hattie's boyfriend. You're my only daughter. That's another reason your mother was so excited when she found out she had given birth to a girl."

"Do your sons call you Father?"

"No. I've never given them that option." He paused. "Your mother is the only woman I've ever married. I liked their mothers. Those relationships were different than the one I had with her. I was only with their mothers for a few years. I knew where my sons were as they were growing up. I didn't constantly keep track of them like I have with you." He stood. "I need to make some phone calls. I'll be back later. Ring the bell if you feel even the slightest pain."

I bobbed my head. Then he left and I began looking through the photo album. On the following pages, Mother had put in pictures of places they had been. Under each one, she wrote where and when the picture had been taken. They always looked happy. There were pictures of them playing in a pool. In one, Lawrence was holding onto her. Under it she had written: "Here I'm teaching your father to swim." Another one showed them rock climbing with numerous ropes tying them together. Mother was dangling incompetently below him. She wrote: "Here I'm teaching your father to rock climb." I smiled at her warm sense of humor.

There were a lot of pictures of them on beaches. In one, she was lying on top of him. She had written: "Here I'm protecting your father from the sun." I wished I had known her.

Marie came in, carrying a food tray. I put the album on the nightstand. She placed the tray in front of me without saying a word.

"Good morning," I said.

"Good morning," she said, looking around the room. She seemed irritated, like she was upset that I was in Lance's room.

I wanted tell her that it was okay since I was Lance's daughter. I knew she wouldn't believe me. Hattie had said that Lance didn't sleep with any women in here. Maybe Marie was trying to figure out our relationship.

"Will you be needing anything else, Miss?" she asked, almost curt.

My eyes dropped down to the tray. There were eggs, potatoes, and bacon on one plate, toast on another, and a cup of coffee. "No. Everything looks great."

She glanced at me and left.

Boy, did she have an attitude problem. I was eating the last piece of toast when Lance walked through the doorway.

"How is everything?" he asked.

"Good." I paused. "Is Marie upset because I'm in your room?"

"Yes. She told Hattie you looked just like Jennifer. She thinks we're related. She's right. Although, how we're related, she's got it all wrong."

"So she believes you slept with your cousin or something?"

"Yes. She doesn't approve. I'm going to tell her we switched rooms since it was easier to hook up the equipment in here. She's a good cook; I don't want to replace her yet."

I took another sip of coffee. "I'm through. That was a big breakfast."

"You need your strength," he said, picking up the tray and moving it to the floor. He sat next to me. "I want to talk to you about something."

Seeing the solemn expression on his face, I wondered what it was about. "Okay."

"I know you are concerned about killing people. Tegens have rules that we all live by. We only kill in self-defense or to eliminate the most depraved criminals: murderers, drug czars, and those who have committed other heinous offenses against people. We never kill anyone who doesn't deserve it. We do not eliminate someone just because we do not like that person. There have been Tegens who have sought revenge against people they knew before they became a Tegen. We do not tolerate that."

"How do you enforce that?"

"Our organization has established procedures to punish Tegens who abuse their power."

"An internal Tegen police force?"

"Close enough." He rubbed his chin with his knuckles "There are Tegens who can't bring themselves to poison anyone, not even to survive. We do not force them to participate in that process. They still need to feed. They go to our gatherings, like you saw in Billings, and feed."

"Are there very many Tegens who can't kill?"

"No. But there are some. Often it takes new Tegens years before they are involved in the poisoning. One Tegen cannot consume one body, so we share. At a gathering, only a few are involved in obtaining our food."

"If I become a Tegen, I won't need to kill anyone?"

"Yes, but you will need to feed."

"Is that fair if I always have someone else doing the killing?"

He stroked my hand. "Yes, it's fair. After someone becomes a Tegen, he or she begins to look at killing differently. You will too eventually, sooner than you might think. And we don't do it personally. We just have to set free one of our spiders. We can use our own poison to subdue the person. We still need a spider to release venom in the body in order for us to obtain nourishment from it. That's why you had to wait when we were in the morgue."

"What happens to the spiders after you've let them go?"

"Are you worried about them?"

I nodded.

"Brett told me how carefully you gathered them up when they were all over your legs. He was expecting to charge in there and rescue you from the spiders. I was impressed how well you handled it since you haven't been transformed." He tapped his fingers together. "You don't need to worry about the spiders. We call them and put them back in a safe place."

"Spiders can't be trained. They barely have brains," I said, adamantly.

"These are mutant spiders. They are genetically conditioned to go toward a sound when we call them."

"What sound?"

He stood and took a small object out of the top dresser drawer. "We use this," he said as he handed it to me.

The device was a two inch round disk about a half an inch thick. One side was black, the other white. There was a button in the middle of each side. "Can I push the button?" I asked, referring to the one on the black side.

"Go ahead."

I pushed it and heard a soft, deep, resonant sound, almost like the stroke of a piano key. "The spiders can hear that?"

"They feel it, even with other noise in the area. If you were trying to retrieve one, you would continue to hold down the button until it came. The spiders have to be within thirty feet when you send out the signal. They're too far away in the house; they didn't sense it."

"Where are the spiders here?"

"Some are in the basement and in the den, secured so that Marie and her staff don't accidentally run into them."

I pointed to the button on the white side. "Does this one also retrieve them?"

"No. The devise is also a GPS. You push that button if you are in trouble. It is programmed to other Tegens' cell phones."

"Whose?"

"Friends, family. We try to limit it to five. Those Tegens will contact others if the need should arise."

I decided this was my opportunity to ask the difficult question. "What happens during the transformation?"

"You become changed into a Tegen, just like me," he said, giving an ambiguous answer.

"That's not what I meant."

He lifted an eyebrow. "I know. The description of the process can be frightening. I think it would be better if you didn't know the specifics. You won't have any problems going through it since you have always enjoyed being close to spiders. All potential Tegens like spiders, but most have not cared for them the same way you did."

I wanted to know more, even though it wouldn't help me make my decision. "Have you read the remarks Mother wrote in the album?"

"Yes," he said as his eyes lit up. "I guess your mother taught me how to do everything." He reached over and picked up the album. "Did you see the last page?"

"No. I'm not there yet."

He opened it and showed me the last picture. It was of Mother, pregnant, standing and holding a bouquet of lilacs. She had drawn an arrow to her stomach. The caption read: "This is you. I'm going to teach you to love lilacs."

I stared at the picture. "She taught me well."

"I'm going to set up the purdrollins. I don't want your feet hurting."

"Is that what the lights are called?"

"Yes."

I uncovered my feet and allowed him to put the purdrollins right above them.

He flipped the switch. "How does that feel?"

"Good."

"I'll be working in the den. Remember if you're in pain, ring the bell. If you want anything to eat or drink, push the call button." He motioned toward a small protruding round circle against the wall next to the bed. "It buzzes in the kitchen. Marie will come up and see what you need."

I went back to looking through the album, enjoying every picture until someone knocked on the door. "Come in," I said, knowing it wasn't Lance because he would just walk in.

In came Hattie, carrying a vase containing a bouquet of lilacs with roses scattered throughout. "Happy Birthday! This was delivered to the clinic this morning." She put down the vase on the nightstand, pulled off the attached envelope, and handed it to me.

I already knew they were from Conner before I read the note. It said: "Happy Birthday, Sara. Get well soon. I can't wait to fly with you again! Love, Conner."

Hattie sat on the edge of the bed. "Conner called right after I told the receptionist that you couldn't take any calls. She seemed confused, since you aren't listed as a patient at the clinic; she does what she's told." She took my hand. "How are you feeling?"

"Fine. I'm not having any pains."

"I'm glad Lance moved you into this room. It's bigger and brighter than the other one."

"Marie doesn't like me being in here."

"Lance has taken care of that."

"Does Lindsey know I slept in here?"

"No. She didn't stay here last night." Hattie looked around the room. "You've slept in here before. I'm sure you can't remember that."

"That must have been when Mother was still alive."

"Yes. You also stayed in here with your father the night before we left for San Diego." She stood up. "I need to talk to Lance about one of our patients. Is there anything I can get you before I leave?"

"No. I have everything I need."

I looked at the flowers and the card briefly. My eyebrows furrowed in confusion. Thoughts of all the terrible crimes Conner had committed swirled around in my head. Still, I couldn't allow myself to dwell about him now. I went back to the album.

When I finished looking through it, I came to a resolution. I picked up the bell and swung it back and forth, sending a jingling sound through the house.

Within a minute, Father hurried in. "Where do you hurt?" he asked anxiously.

I smiled at him. "I don't hurt anywhere. I've decided I want to go to the cave today."

His face glowed. He grinned from ear to ear and walked toward me. "Hattie had planned a birthday party for you tonight. I know she won't be disappointed when I tell her it will have to wait." He kissed my cheek, went to his medical bag, and filled a syringe. "This will help with the pain," he said, raising my sleeve.

"I'm not in pain."

"That's how I want you to stay. This should help so you don't experience any on the way to the cave." He gently stuck the needle in my arm. "Hattie will get you ready and take you there. I'll be inside waiting for you."

His eyes were brilliant with excitement as he left. I'd never seen him that happy before.

Hattie came running into the room and hugged me. "I'm so happy," she said, sounding ecstatic. "We were all anxious for you to make a decision. You'll see that life as a Tegen is good." She took my hand. "Let's go in your room and get you ready there."

She held onto my arm as we walked down the hall to the other bedroom. "You have to shower and wash your hair. You can't wear any deodorant, lotion, perfumes, colognes or any makeup. All of your clothing has to be black, including your underwear. The only piece of jewelry you can wear is your black ring," she said as she touched it, "and you must wear it."

"Why?"

"First, it's bonded to your body. And second, it draws the spiders to you."

"Leaving it on my finger won't be a problem. I can't take it off without having a stabbing pain running through my hand."

"Can you stand long enough to shower by yourself, or do you want me to be with you?"

"I did it by myself in the hospital. I should be fine."

"Okay. I'm going to my room to get cleaned up. I'll be back in a few minutes."

After I showered, I slipped on the black nightgown that hung in the closet over my black underwear. I was sitting down at the vanity, blow drying my hair when Hattie returned. She wore a black blouse, black slacks, black shoes, and her hair was tied back with a black ribbon.

"I don't know if I can get my shoes on my feet," I said.

"You'll be going into the cave barefooted. That will make it easier for you to walk."

I didn't want to tread over any terrain with bare feet. "Can I wear black socks?"

"Don't worry. You can wear socks until you get there. You'll be fine without anything on your feet in the cave. The dirt there won't hurt them. Do you want me to finish blow drying your hair?"

"No. I'm almost done."

As soon as I finished, Hattie tied my hair back with a black ribbon, just like hers. Then she picked up my gloves and socks. "You need to wear these until you get to the cave," she said, putting them on me. She took my arm. "You look great. Are you ready to go?"

I stood. "Yes." Then we headed to her car. I bit my lower lip and felt my hands shaking through the gloves as we drove away from the house and out the opened metal gate.

She patted my leg. "Try to relax. You'll be one of us soon."

I stared out the window and saw the sun streaming through an opening in the heavy, wooded, foliage. I heard the sound of water cascading over boulders as we passed a swift moving river strewn with rocks and fallen trees along its edges.

Forty-five minutes later, Hattie turned up a dirt road surrounded by rocky and barren land. After we had driven on it for a several miles, I noticed a wooded area of evergreens and aspens with a row of cars parked along the side. Hattie pulled in front of them and stopped.

She got out and walked around the vehicle as a man, dressed in black, approached from behind the car. Hattie opened my door. "This is Daniel. He'll be carrying you up to the cave."

Daniel was tall with dark curly hair, a nice square jaw, broad shoulders, and had a muscular build. After we greeted each other, Hattie told me to remove my gloves and socks. I followed her instructions and dropped them on the floor.

From under the seat, Hattie pulled out a thermos and unscrewed the lid. "Drink some of this. It will help prevent your hands and foot from hurting while we go up to the cave."

I took a sip. It was *venotrolia*. After another gulp, I handed it back.

"Do you want any?" she asked Daniel.

He nodded and raised the thermos to his mouth.

Hattie swigged a little, replaced the lid, and pushed the container under the seat.

Daniel picked me up and carried me along a dirt trail with Hattie right behind us. We had been on the path for a long time when he sat me down on a make-shift bench made of a piece of wood supported by a tree stump and a stack of rocks.

While he stretched, I gazed up the path looking for something that resembled a cave. I didn't see any opening in the side of the mountain. Since Hattie or Daniel hadn't said a word during our trek, I decided not to ask.

Daniel lifted me into his arms again. After we went for about another fifteen or twenty minutes, he stopped by a row of bushes. Hattie stepped in front of us, bent down, and touched something in a cluster of bushes. The center bush moved, making an opening. Daniel walked through it. Hattie followed and put her hand in a crevice next to a rock. The bush moved back into place.

"It won't be too long now," she said as we continued along.

Everything I had been through to make this journey suddenly flashed in front of me: running from Conner, meeting Brett, the poisonous spiders, the victims, being hospitalized, and Cameron's hatred. The life I had known would soon be ending. My body would be changed forever. A sense of dread came over me, yet I knew I had made the right decision.

The woods became denser until we reached some large boulders, blocking us from going any further. Hattie ran her hand over one of the rocks. It slid to the side, and a cave appeared. Daniel eased me down to the ground.

"Daniel and I go in first," Hattie said. "Wait a minute and then enter. Just walk toward the light."

Hattie kissed my cheek and went in with Daniel, leaving me standing alone by the entrance. My mouth became dry as I counted slowly to sixty. I licked my dry lips, inhaled deeply, and walked into the cave. Everything was dark inside, except for the flickering of a light a long distance ahead of me.

After I had taken a few steps, I heard noise behind me. I turned and watched the boulder moving back into place, covering the opening. My body trembled as I walked along in the still darkness. The dirt under my bare feet felt soothing—not at all what I had expected. I squinted as I looked around, hoping somehow I could see Father. Someone breathed close to me. It sent a chill through my body. I would have felt better with a reassuring arm to cling to while I moved along. However, I knew that wasn't the Tegen way.

As I got closer to the light, I could see people standing on both sides. I recognized Lindsey. Passing her, I saw Brett. His face was immobile. Then he winked at me. I smiled. Finally, I saw Father next to the light. He was all dressed in black, like everyone else.

When I reached him, it looked like I was at the end of the cave. I hadn't felt one spider or a cobweb. Father held onto my arm. With his other hand he touched something behind him. A section of the cave wall moved, revealing a cavern. He led me in, and then released my arm. The opening disappeared. It was pitch black. I couldn't see anything. A surge of fear ran through my body. Searching for Father, I swung out my hands and touched his arm. I grasped onto him tight as we walked through the darkness.

He stopped and gently stroked my cheek. "Remove your nightgown and lie down on the surface behind you," he whispered.

With trembling fingers, I began unbuttoning it. I found the task difficult since I was shaking so hard. Finally, I managed to get the nightgown to drop to my feet. I stepped out of it. Still unable to see anything, I cautiously lowered myself onto a surface that bounced like a hammock. It felt silky and soft against my bare skin.

Father kissed my forehead. Next, I sensed him backing away from me.

I smelled a sweet aroma and felt movement in my hair. A prickly sensation began to tickle my hands and feet and crept up my limbs. Millions of tiny arthropod feet swarmed over me until my entire body was enveloped. They began to enter my ears, nose, and mouth. I attempted to raise my arm to stop them. It wouldn't budge from the surface, as if glued down. I unsuccessfully tried to lift a leg. Then I realized I was paralyzed motionless in a spider's web. My heart pounded against my ribs. I tightened my closed eyes, but it didn't prevent the spiders from squeezing under my eyelids and scuttling over my eyeballs. I opened my mouth to scream. No sound escaped. My throat became parched. My lungs burned. I felt an unimaginable pain in every cell.

After what seemed like hours, I relaxed. I could smell the sweet aroma once again. The pain dissipated as spiders still moved through my torso.

26

THE AFTERMATH

"I'll see you in a week," I said, pulling Father's door shut as I stepped out into the reception area of his clinic.

"Ready to go?" Conner asked, standing by the entrance.

"Yes."

As soon as the plane reached cruising altitude, Conner and I went into the bedroom. This time it was because I wanted to be with him in order to put my plan into motion, not because of an overwhelming need. He quickly undressed. I stripped off my clothing slowly, enjoying him watching me.

"I was starting to wonder if you were ever going to be allowed to leave that clinic," he said, wrapping his arms around my waist.

"I probably could have left a little earlier. I just thought you needed time to be with your family."

He pulled me down onto the bed. "It has been a struggle. Melanie is still in shock. Caden has stepped in like a trooper. He's been helping me organize Cameron's papers, question employees, and follow-up on leads. He called while I was waiting at the clinic and said that Viltro has some valuable information. Viltro's an employee. He didn't want to discuss it on the phone. I'm anxious to hear what he has to say when we get home."

"Conner, remember I can only stay for a week then I have to go back to the clinic for additional treatments," I lied. A week was the length of time I had given myself to carry out my scheme. Also, Father wanted me to be close to him so he could monitor my diet. During a Tegen's first year an excessive amount of *venotrolia* and flesh must be consumed to replenish strength drained from the transformation.

"Let's talk later," he said, and then he smothered my lips with his as his hand moved up my thigh.

When the pilot announced it was time to prepare for landing, Conner and I were lying with our legs intertwined and my head resting on his shoulder.

"Time to deal with problems again," Conner said. A muscle tightened in his jaw.

We hurriedly dressed and buckled up before the plane rapidly descended. He held my hand. I looked at his handsome face, the face of the man I would have a hard time forgetting. I had begun to feel differently about Conner before the transformation. Now I no longer was infatuated with his intangible charms. I planned on permanently destroying any semblance of a relationship, and with it, as much of the Crussett business as I could before returning to North Dakota.

I had thought Carina might be the one running the business, or maybe Cedric would be active again. Since Conner was going through Cameron's papers, it must have fallen on his shoulders. "How are your parents handling Cameron's death?"

"Better than I would have expected. Father's been busy making inquiries. He might decide to return to the workforce. Mother thinks it would do him good. She's probably tired of having him around the house all day. Cameron always kept him informed. I suspect this isn't anything you want to hear about."

"No ... no. I asked the question. I know this is a hard time for you. I want you to feel free to discuss it with me."

"I'm glad you feel that way. With everyone reporting to me right now, it would be difficult to keep things from you."

Conner's eyes drooped and a sad expression crept across his face.

"How are you doing?" I asked.

"I had no idea how much I would miss Cameron. You only knew him as my stern, older brother. I remember all the great times we had together. He always played with me when I was growing up. He took me to ball games, fishing, and camping. I don't think he's ever done that with his kids."

The loving brother certainly wasn't a quality I had ever seen in Cameron. As far as his boys were concerned, I thought he merely tolerated them.

As we exited the plane, the limo driver opened the door. While we slid in, I caught a glimpse of several black sedans parked next to the hangar.

"Until we locate the culprits responsible for Cameron, we've increased our security," Conner said as one of the black sedans pulled ahead of us. "You'll be completely safe. An investigative team has been researching the Billings' murders. I received their report yesterday."

"Can I see it?"

"We'll go over it together so we can plan our strategy."

"And what is that?"

"I hoped you would want to be involved. If not, I'll handle it since they managed to terminate six of my men."

"How's the guy in the Billings hospital doing?"

"He died. The police, the same Lieutenant Barnes and Sergeant Harmon you talked to, are still working on locating victims. There haven't been any additional disappearances since you left. They want to ask you a few questions."

"Can't you take care of that?" I asked, knowing his family's influence. I immediately regretted it when I realized I might have been misinterpreted as asking him to have someone killed.

"Occasionally, we run into a cop that wants to be a hero: follow his oath, protect the people."

"That's not a bad thing."

He frowned, looked down, and tapped his fingertips on his thighs. "They're difficult to deal with."

I took a deep breath so as not to betray my disgust. "How did they know I was staying at your place?"

"Your hospital stay, the spider bite. That's how they tracked you down." He took my hand. "Don't worry. They'll only be allowed to question you once. After that, I'll find a way to handle them so they won't be bothering or pestering you again."

Driving through the gate to the Crussett compound, I saw half a dozen guards glancing into the limo along with three who were walking along the outside parameter. Conner pushed the window button. It slid down, "Any visitors?"

"Four are at Mr. Cedric Crussett's house. They were expected. Dr. Thomas is checking on Mrs. Melanie Crussett. Two youngsters are visiting Colin."

Conner motioned for the driver to continue.

An armed guard stood by Conner's front door. Looking around, I saw two more approaching from the backyard. Conner nodded at the first guard as we stepped over the threshold. The limo driver took my small suitcase, filled with cash, *venotrolia*, and equipment, and brought it upstairs.

Conner led me to the den. "I need to return some calls," he said, handing me the report. "You can read it in here or the living room."

"I'll stay here." I sat down in a cushioned chair. "If you don't mind."

"No problem. The telephone calls might make you feel uncomfortable."

"If that happens, I'll go to the living room," I smiled, hoping to obtain information.

As he dialed a number, I opened the report folder. The first page was devoted to the couple I pointed out to Conner at the compound gate when I returned from Billings. It started with their pictures and home address. They lived in Houston. Next to that appeared a red asterisk and a comment: "Recently returned from Billings. Phones tapped. No suspicious calls. Successfully tailed. Subjects reported to work at 8:30 a.m., left at 4:30 p.m. All associates investigated. Nothing out of the ordinary."

At the top of the following page it stated: "Portions of this information were provided in our prior report on the disappearance of Sara Jones. This report will focus on the individuals that are believed to be members or associates of the Billings, Montana 'spider cult' who came in contact with Jones. It includes those hired to influence or obtain information from Jones. Report is laid out in the order Jones was contacted."

Below that was a picture of Mildred Belkin, the elderly woman who sat next to me when I left Houston on the bus. "Belkin had been hired by a white, unidentified man, approximately 6'1", 190 pounds with gray hair, unshaved face, and thick prescription glasses. Her job was to convince Jones to go to Billings, Montana. Belkin arrived at the bus station at 7 a.m. and waited for Jones to show. She purchased a ticket for the same bus Jones took and sat next to her. The unidentified man appeared at the second bus stop and paid Belkin the remainder of the agreement. No contact with him after that."

I turned the page and saw Lindsey Farrington's name and her picture. My attention drifted to Conner's conversation when he said in a raised voice, "It sails tomorrow night."

My eyes remained fixed on the report as I listened.

"I need one more…she's too heavy…get rid of her…no…we've been over this before…two more…late afternoon…twenty, no less!" He slammed down the receiver.

"Is everything okay?" I asked, innocently.

Clenching his teeth and shaking his head, "Nothing you have to worry about." He leaned back in his chair and regained his composure. "Have you got to the interesting part yet?"

"It's all interesting. I'm only on the third page. How did you manage to track down the first woman who sat with me on the bus?"

"By hiring experienced investigators who know their stuff," he grinned. "You'll know when you get to the part I find interesting."

"Did you get a hold of Caden?" I asked since I had been concentrating on the report instead of listening closely to his calls.

"No. I left a message." He picked up a notepad. His eyes narrowed as he gazed at it.

"What's wrong?"

"Gerard. He's a mystery."

I knew he was talking about Dr. Gerard, the guy Cameron brought to the morgue who wasn't really a doctor. Still, I asked, "Who's Gerard?"

"Dr. Gerard. He died in the fire along with Cameron. It doesn't make sense."

"Why?"

"Gerard was used to obtain information. He wasn't muscle. He wouldn't have been with Cameron to make a deal. Why was he there?"

I shrugged my shoulders.

"I didn't expect an answer. I'm just thinking out loud." He lifted the receiver. "One more call."

My eyes dropped to the report, but my ears concentrated on his call.

"No, not there ... Empire ... the new place." I heard Conner open a drawer and flip through some papers. "5730 ... don't send them that way ... Get Sam to help." He hung up just as the doorbell rang.

I recalled seeing Empire Street on a document. Was that where they stored their porn DVDs or something worse? I looked up and met his eyes.

"I wanted to spend time with you," he said. "It's not going to be easy."

I gave him a fake smile. "I understand."

Someone knocked on the door.

"Come in," Conner said.

Darcy peeked in. "Mr. Caden Crussett would like to see you."

"Tell him to wait in the living room," he said, standing up. He came to me, leaned down, and lightly kissed my lips. "This shouldn't take long." He walked out, closing the door behind him.

After making sure he was out of earshot, I went to his desk, looked at the notepad, and saw scribbled notes: "Why Gerard? Had Cameron planned on interrogating someone? Missing documents. What price does he want? Buy, then kill."

Hearing movement in the hall, I hurried back to my seat and picked up the report. A second later, the doorknob turned.

"Would you like something to drink?" Darcy asked.

"Iced tea."

"I'll make it just the way you like it," she smiled and eased the door shut.

Thinking about the missing documents, I wondered if the thief was anyone I knew. Then I flipped to the third page of the report and began reading again. "Farrington sat next to Jones on the bus from Nebraska to Billings, Montana." It went on to say, "Farrington had arranged to be on the same buses as Jones. Based on numerous interviews and telephone conversations, Farrington was thought to be a member of the spider cult. That was just a cover. Her job was to befriend Jones in order to obtain documents Jones had in her possession regarding the Crussett family business. She was working with two individuals identified as Brett Daborel and Fred Shoeman."

Fear gripped me. My body tensed as I stared with horror at the page. They know about Brett, too. I sucked in air, leaned back in the chair, and the tension dissipated, realizing they didn't know the truth. Then I wondered who Fred Shoeman was. My eyes moved to the report again. "Since Farrington was not able to obtain the documents while on the bus with Jones, it became Daborel's job." I drummed my fingers on the armrest.

The report continued, "Farrington left Jones in Billings and went on to Portland, Oregon to see a man named Simon Ellis. Investigators were unable to interview Ellis since he disappeared around the same time Farrington left Portland. She returned to Billings to assist Daborel in obtaining the information. She stayed with Jones and Daborel at a home owned by Rex Larsen, a petroleum engineer who works for the company used by Daborel for his cover. When Jones was hospitalized in Houston, Farrington visited her on two occasions.

"Investigators were not able to determine Daborel, Farrington, or Shoeman's employer(s)."

The following page was devoted to Brett. Below his picture it began, "Daborel was instrumental in having Jones placed in the room adjacent to his at the Towne Hotel. He had paid the hotel clerk, Ralph Miller, to make that happen. While Jones was there, Daborel befriended her as per the plan. He was unable to obtain the information.

"His cell phone logged a call each day reporting his status regarding their relationship. The calls were traced to another cell phone purchased by an unidentified person using the name Karl Mathews. That person also checked into the Towne Hotel and specifically requested room 839, the room next to Jones. Daborel's room was on one side of hers and the unidentified man on the other. In a phone conversation, Daborel was informed that Crussetts were close to locating her. After that, he released captured spiders as a scare tactic to get Jones to move out of the hotel. Innocent people were bitten. That appears to be how the spider cult scenario began. The origin of these spiders, and their exact species, are still undetermined. In order to heighten the scare tactic, the disappearance of Nancy Stewart and Phil and Shelley Kessler on the way to the hospital from the hotel was orchestrated.

"Two Billings police department officers have questioned Daborel regarding the spider incidents. He's not a suspect. The officers have not been able to locate the man using the believed fictitious name, Karl Matthews.

Several tapped and recorded telephone calls revealed that Daborel intended to appear as a member of the spider cult in case Jones became suspicious about his behavior." I squinted, wondering how that wouldn't make me suspicious. Then it clicked and I understand: it wouldn't make me suspicious about his intent according to the report—obtaining the documents. I read on. "Daborel continued pursuing Jones for the documents in Houston. He tried to snatch her when Saul Fazio was taking her to the airport. The only weapon Daborel carried was poisonous spiders, which resulted in both Fazio and Jones being bitten. Fazio died from the venom. Jones required hospitalization and treatment, thus confirming there was no collaboration on Jones' behalf. During the kidnapping attempt, Daborel was shot and believed dead. He recently resurfaced in Billings."

That concluded the report. I wondered who had influenced the investigators since most of the "report" was contradictory, suppositions, or bogus. At the same time, I was relieved that my actual relationship with Brett wasn't mentioned and puzzled that they either failed to gather or omitted any data about Father. Also, there was nothing stated after I was hospitalized, except Lindsey visiting twice.

Conner entered, slamming the door behind him, baring his teeth. I jumped. "Viltro doesn't want to talk to anyone but 'the man' and he wants to get paid for whatever he's got regarding Cameron's death," he said. "He's our employee. He doesn't get extra compensation for doing his job. Who does he think he is?"

"Who's 'the man'?"

"I am. He insists on talking to my father. According to Caden, Viltro almost inferred I had something to do with Cameron's death."

"Can't you have Viltro brought to you?"

"It's not that easy. Viltro has been interrogated before. He has scars to show for it. We wouldn't get anything out of him that way. He claims his information will tell us who's responsible for Cameron's death. It'll be destroyed if he's taken by force. I can't have that after his insinuation."

"What are you going to do?" I asked, wondering what information he could possibly have since Cameron and his men all perished in the morgue.

"Call Cedric," Conner said, sitting down at his desk. That was the first time I had ever heard Conner refer to his father by his first name.

"Rosanne, can I speak to my father?" Conner said into the receiver. A moment later, "An employee, Viltro Fazio...yes, Saul's brother...he claims he has information that will disclose Cameron's assassin...no...he won't...only to you...there's more, he wants to get paid for it...this will be the first." He chuckled. "Agreed...when...I don't know what he was waiting for...maybe he just got it...yes...sounds good." He hung up.

"Is he going to see him?"

"Yes, the day after tomorrow. He's curious, although he doesn't believe it will lead us to the responsible party, maybe to a hired thug. That's more than we've got now."

"Is Viltro still working for you?"

"He was a bodyguard assigned to Carina until yesterday. That was probably when he got the information. After that, Viltro requested to be kept in a secure location until he talked to my father. He doesn't want me to know where he's being held. Strange."

"Do you think he cooked up some kind of evidence to incriminate you? Saul wouldn't have died if he hadn't been with me."

"Cedric would never fall for that. The information will be carefully scrutinized. If that's what Viltro has done, he'll be leaving my parents' house in a body bag." He pointed toward the report on my lap. "What did you think?"

"I had no idea Brett and Lindsey were after the documents. How did they know I had them?"

"Fred Shoeman."

"Who's that?"

"The guy who cleaned the pool. He worked for Emmanuel until he tried to sell the missing documents to a friend who Shoeman thought was a family enemy. He was wrong. That's when we questioned him. I suspect he was the one who put the other set of books on your desk."

"Didn't you ask him about that?"

"He collapsed. Somehow he escaped while we were waiting for him to recuperate."

"Lindsey did visit me a few times in the hospital. She never mentioned anything about documents. I haven't seen Brett since he was lying on the sidewalk. I thought he was dead."

"So did I until I got the report from the investigator. Daborel needs to be taken care of."

"I wish we could forget about everything that happened in Billings. It was a nightmare, and now it's over."

"I lost men. This Lieutenant Barnes thinks I had something to do with the spider incidents."

"What are you talking about?"

"Phil and Shelley Kessler. The missing couple from the hotel. They were drug dealers."

Squinting my eyes, I knew they had been targeted. Lindsey had said Tegens didn't go after innocent people, like Nancy. She hadn't mentioned that couple.

He continued, "The guy who was bitten as he rode a bike works for my family. Then you, a witness in the spider-related investigation deaths, came and stayed with me in Houston. Barnes thinks there's a connection."

"That's absurd."

"We'll handle Barnes and his sidekick, Sergeant Harmon." He winked at me and smiled. "It is strange to have someone after me for that type of crime. Spiders would never be my choice for weapons."

"I know." My lips curved into a lopsided smile. "You got squeamish when one decided to join us in bed."

"I'll try to put the Billings problem on hold until Cameron's killer is located."

"Then what?"

"Daborel and Farrington will be handled swiftly. You won't have to worry about them again."

Hiding my concern, I asked, "How are you going to do that?"

"Fire."

I felt a lump in my throat, but kept my face from showing any emotion. "Why?"

"We can't shoot or stab spiders. That's the only way we can guarantee any 'weapons' they're carrying are destroyed."

"That's so gruesome."

"We do what we have to do. If I had to burn a thousand people alive to protect you, I'd do it without hesitation."

I forced myself to rise, go over to him, and wrap my arms around his neck. "Do you think we can have a nice evening and enjoy a warm, soothing bath?"

He kissed my arm. "I need to make one more phone call. Why don't you head upstairs?"

"I'll get the bath ready," I said, moving toward the door. I eased out into the hallway and leaned against the wall, out of his sight, to listen.

"Caden, tell Viltro that Cedric will see him the day after tomorrow at 2 p.m." He clicked down the receiver.

Quickly turning toward the stairs, I stumbled. As I caught my footing, I picked up a magazine from the side table just as Conner entered the hall.

"Why aren't you upstairs?"

"I thought I'd grab a magazine," I said, holding it up.

"Do you think you'll have time to read?" he asked with a raised brow.

I smiled, laying it down. "Silly me. I noticed them here and took one without thinking."

"You can read tomorrow. I'll get a bottle of champagne and tell Darcy we'll be eating upstairs since guards will be periodically checking the first floor. The alarms on the windows and balcony doors have been set. Don't open any of them."

"See you in a minute," I said, heading to the stairs.

The sun glared through the window. Conner's arms were wrapped around me so tightly I couldn't move. Attempting to wake him, I kissed his neck and chest.

He stirred and his eyes dropped down to mine. "Good morning."

"Do you have to go to work today?"

"Yes, and it's going to be a long night. I have a dinner meeting with my father at eight. I tried to leave my evenings free while you were here; it's not working out. What have you decided about a trip to your favorite island in the South Pacific after you've finished your treatments?"

"I haven't decided yet," I lied. I had no intention of going with him.

He kissed me. "Take your time." He gazed into my eyes, pulled me closer, and gave me a slow, passionate kiss. "You have no idea how much I enjoy waking up with you. You look a little pale. Why don't you lie by the pool today?" He climbed out of bed.

"I thought I'd go shopping instead."

"Shopping?" He sat down next to me. "I'd rather you stay here and get some sun."

"No. You promised on the phone I could do whatever I wanted. Today, I want to go shopping."

He scanned my face. "I'm going to have Mont follow you to make sure you're safe. We don't know why Cameron was killed. Until we do, we have to take precautions. Every member of the family has been assigned one or two bodyguards."

"I'm not a member of your family." I paused after hearing what I said. "Yet," I added, remembering my pretense.

"Sara, please."

"Okay. Does he have to go with me into the dressing room?" I asked with a crooked smile.

He grinned. "No. I'll even have him stay in his car while you shop. I want you to wear a beeper." He stood, picked up a bracelet from the top of the dresser, and put it around my wrist. "We give something like this to everyone in the family. See this button?" He pointed to a greenish-blue circle that looked like a stone. "Push this if you are approached by anyone unfamiliar. It has a GPS. Mont will come to your aid." He stroked my face and kissed me. "I don't want anything to happen to you."

"Do you want me to wear it all the time?"

"Yes. Will you do that for me?"

"Is it okay if it gets wet?"

"Yes. It works in water."

After Conner left for the office, I spent the morning in his den copying documents and writing down information that I thought might be useful in the future. I searched for the name of the ship to no avail. I put the documents and my notes into a nine-by-twelve envelope, addressed it to S. Alston in Bismarck, North Dakota, and slipped it into my purse.

27

FREEDOM

At 1:30 p.m., I drove out of the compound with Mont following in a black sedan right behind me. I headed straight to the mall. Mont parked in the next stall, facing the south mall entrance.

"Remember to use the button if you need me," he said as I got out of my car.

"I will."

Inside the mall, I continuously kept looking over my shoulder, fearful Mont might not have stayed in his car. My first stop was at a self-service post office where I stamped and mailed the envelope. From there, I went to a craft store and purchased a thick, white, permanent magic marker. As I stepped out into the hallway, a large, athletic-looking woman with short, black, spiked hair plowed into me. She stared at me without apologizing. Given her appearance, I wondered if she was a Crussett employee. Had Conner sent another person to keep track of me?

Moving toward the payphones, my head swung between them and the craft store where she entered. She hadn't emerged from the store when I reached the phones. I decided it would be safer if I used one down another corridor. I continued moving along at a swift pace. Stopping at that bank of phones, I scanned the area, searching for her. She was nowhere in sight. I picked up the receiver and dialed Brett's number.

"Hello," he answered.

"Hi," I whispered, paranoid that someone might be listening. My eyes were fixed in the direction of the craft store.

"Are you ready to return to Bismarck?"

"No. Conner had an investigative team check into you and Lindsey." I filled him in on what the report said and what Conner planned after Cameron's murder had been resolved.

"Then I have nothing to worry about." Brett chuckled. "They'll never figure it out."

"One of their employees claims he has information about the killers. Is it possible there was another person we didn't see?"

"I doubt it. When will Conner get the information?"

"This is the strange part. The guy won't talk to him about it. He'll only give it to Cedric, Conner's dad. They're meeting tomorrow."

"What explanation did he give?"

"From what Conner told me, the guy inferred Conner played a role in Cameron's death."

"Whatever this guy has fabricated, if Conner's in trouble it might spill over on you."

"It could be even worse than that. He might have something that indicates our responsibility."

"Where are you now?" Brett asked, sounding worried.

"At a mall. No one can hear me."

"Why don't you make up some excuse and return to North Dakota?"

"There's something I have to take care of first."

"Can't it wait?"

"No," I barked at him.

"I'm leaving for Houston tonight."

"Brett, no. It's too dangerous. And I want to say good-bye to Conner on my own terms."

"I won't contact you after I arrive. I just want to be close if you should need me."

I wanted to tell him I didn't need his help, but I knew I couldn't sway him to stay put. "Promise me you won't mention any of this to my father."

"I think he should know."

"Promise, or I won't contact you if I'm in trouble." The phone went silent as I waited for his response.

A minute later, "I promise," he sighed, reluctantly. "And always have the GPS button with you."

"I never go anywhere without it. I need to go before I'm missed. Be careful."

"I will. Bye, Sara."

I cautiously went to a car rental office that stood at the other end of the mall. I used a phony driver's license I acquired in North Dakota. The agent wanted a credit card. I convinced her to allow me to put down a $5,000 deposit in lieu of that. The $200 tip helped.

Making my way to the west entrance, I stopped and bought a cup of coffee. My eyes darted around looking for the woman with the spiked hair again. I didn't spot her anywhere. I exited the mall, hurried to the road, and walked along the outside perimeter of the parking lot until I reached Mont's row. I inched toward his car, keeping my head low to avoid being seen. Loud music blared from a jeep parked three spaces from him, drowning out the sound of my approach and anyone walking by.

When I reached his car, I saw his head buried in a newspaper. I stayed low and used the white magic marker on the trunk, the passenger side, front fender, the side of the hood outside his line of vision. Then I crept around and applied it on the passenger door behind the driver. Hunkering close to the ground, I zigzagged around the vehicles and then stood at the end of the row, next to the mall entrance. I turned and walked back to Mont's car, admiring my handiwork.

He looked out the opened driver's window. "You're the first woman I've ever known to go shopping without buying anything."

"I'm not through. I thought you might like some coffee," I said, handing it to him. "Leaving the mall, I ran into a friend and chatted so it might not be hot."

"It feels warm. Thanks."

"I'll probably be a while."

"Not a problem."

I entered the mall again. I placed a call to the police department on a payphone.

"May I help you," a woman asked over the line.

"I'm so upset," I said, talking in a high-pitched tone.

"What's the problem, Miss?"

"I just pulled into the south parking lot of South Pointe Mall. Oh, it's so disrespectful. It's awful."

"What's awful?"

"There's a black car parked on the row leading to the entrance. You can't help walking right past it. All over the back and sides in white paint is written Cops Suck and other terrible obscenities about our police force. It's awful. The police in this city do such a great job. How could anyone put that on their car? I just don't understand it. Is there anything you can do about it?"

"The car's on the south side?" she asked.

"Yes."

"There's probably nothing we can do about it, but we'll check it out."

"Thank you."

As I hung up, the spiked-haired woman walked passed me. It appeared she was going to the exit. I stayed put, watched her go out the doors, and disappear in the parking lot. I went into a department store and purchased a blouse and skirt without trying them on. Then I headed to a cell phone store and bought three phones, paying cash and displaying my fake ID. While the phone batteries were being charged, I went to a computer store and tried out the latest model by searching for the quickest route from the store to Pier 29, the departure location for the Crussetts' ship.

Leaving the mall through the south entrance, I sighed when I saw Mont's car was gone. I put my package in my trunk along with the bracelet and took out my duffle bag.

At 3:45 p.m. I parked the rental car on the street next to Pier 29. I snuck around the rusty, drab metal buildings until I could see the moored ships along the waterfront. There I waited, hidden in the shadows.

Twenty-five minutes later, a limo pulled up next to a ship and Conner emerged. He moved up the gangplank with two men. I saw the name *Freedom* on the side of the vessel and shook my head, thinking about its cargo.

Knowing the ship's name, I turned to leave and bumped into something. I looked up and found myself staring into the chest of a muscular, tall man with an unshaved face and an acerbic reeking body odor like dead fish mixed with liquor that forced me to hold my breath.

"Whatcha want?" he blurted out, his voice low and raspy.

"I was just looking at the water."

His eyes moved up and down my body, studying me closely. "Turn around."

"Why?"

"Do it," he snapped.

I followed his instruction since I wasn't sure if he worked for the Crussetts and I didn't want to draw any suspicion. I sensed him looking me over suspiciously; he didn't try to touch me.

"Get outa here."

I hurried back to the rental car, resisting the urge to look over my shoulder, and then drove away.

Driving around the area close to the mall, I decided to leave the car at the Sunlight Hotel, a block away, and rent a room under my false name.

I stepped into the mall from the north parking lot and made a couple of quick purchases just for an alibi. I left through the south entrance and saw Mont standing by my car.

"I'm through," I said, unlocking my trunk. I dropped the bags in it and carefully eased the bracelet back on my wrist.

"Any problems?" Mont asked.

"No." I glanced at his prior parking spot. "Where's your car?"

"Some punks were playing loud music. I complained and in return they wrote all over it. Someone was offended by the words and called the cops. I left and came back with the car over there." He pointed to a dark blue Buick. "Mr. Crussett tried to reach you. Is your cell phone on?"

I pulled it out of my purse. "I must have forgotten to turn it on earlier." I climbed into my car and called him. Voice mail came on. I left a message to humor him.

Around six I pulled into Conner's garage.

"How did shopping go?" Conner asked, meeting me in the hallway.

"Good." I held up my packages. "I ran into a friend from college. She's here on business and will be leaving in the morning."

He carried my packages as we went up the stairs.

I continued, "She wants to meet later for dinner and drinks. Since you're going off to a meeting, I didn't think it would be a problem. I told her I'd give her a call."

"Right now, it's too dangerous for you to be driving around in the dark."

"She's staying at the Sunlight Hotel. That's where we tentatively planned on eating. Mont could drop me off."

"Sara?"

"Conner, I won't be a prisoner," I hissed.

He dropped the packages on a chair and wrapped his arms around me. "I just want you to be safe. Mont can drive you."

"I'll be fine," I said, gazing into his eyes. I saw a genuine but controlling love I couldn't reciprocate.

Kissing my neck, he unbuttoned my blouse.

"Just a minute, let me give her a call." I pretended to make a call as Conner undressed. Then he removed my clothes, lifted me into his arms, and gently laid me on the bed. Looking at him, a torrent of emotions flooded through me. I still cared deeply for him, and feared I always would. With a pang of regret, I knew I had to continue deceiving him in order to accomplish my goal.

He leaned over me, and I felt his hot breath on my bare skin. My heartbeat spiked as he trailed kisses down my chest. I raked my fingers through his hair and my desire for him consumed my thoughts.

An hour later, we showered and dressed. Conner looked immaculately groomed in his dark gray suit. I wore a short, sleeveless, rose-colored dress that was easy to slip off.

"What time do you think you'll be home?" he asked.

"She has an early flight, so I can't imagine I'd be later than eleven. How long do you think your meeting will last?"

"No idea," he said, shaking his head. "I'll be looking forward to climbing in bed next to you."

I gave him my best fake smile.

After I entered the hotel, I looked around for someone, any woman whose name I could memorize. I got in the elevator along with a middle-aged woman wearing a business suit. Around her neck a badge with the name Mary Gregor inscribed on it hung from a chain. On the fifth floor I went to room 501, the room I had rented earlier. I wrote Mary's name on a piece of paper and slipped it into my purse. Then I changed into my black jogging outfit, grabbed my backpack, left the hotel through the rear exit, and drove to Pier 29.

In the darkness, I crept between metal and brick buildings along the pier until I was within a hundred feet of the *Freedom* slip. No light illuminated my location. After the transformation, I had no problem seeing in the pitch blackness. Looking around a shipping container, I sensed someone breathing behind me.

"Raise your hands," a man with a deep, Slavic accent ordered as an object poked into my shoulder.

I had never played Jason Bourne before, so I suspected I might be caught. I had hoped it wouldn't happen this soon. However, I was prepared with my new Tegen strength and some karate moves I had seen on television. Also, Brett had taught me a little aikido right after my transformation.

"I'm not doing anything," I replied, raising my arms.

He started to move his hands down my jogging suit. "Stop that!" I turned and met his gaze. He was a short, burly man, wearing a pair of slacks, dress shirt, and a tie. He wasn't a dock worker.

He held a pistol inches from my chest. "This way," he nodded toward the ship.

With a quick chop from the side of my hand, I knocked the gun to the ground at the same time as I scratched his face with my other hand.

He snatched the gun from the ground and clutched my arm. "What do you want here?"

My knee slammed into his groin while he raised the barrel. He moaned, buckled over in pain, and released my arm. I grabbed his pistol from his hand and swung it against his head. He tumbled to the ground and landed on his face. I nudged him with my foot and saw his eyes were wide open with a blank stare.

With all my strength, I yanked him between two large, metal crates and kicked the gun underneath one of them. I returned to the edge of the shipping container, scanned the area, and put a ski mask that I purchased at the mall over my head. I approached the ship, keeping myself concealed behind containers, crates, and dock equipment. I slowly made my way to the first rope securing the ship to the dock. I gripped it in my hands.

"Ivan's not answering. Do you want me to look for him?" I heard a man say as I scurried up the rope without looking in the direction of the sound.

"We don't sail for an hour. Give him a few minutes," another man said.

I hurried across the deck and leaned against the cabin, then exhaled to relax just as the door flew open.

A man slightly under six-feet tall with a mustache stepped out. He turned toward me. In a panic, I ran the needles protruding from my hand down his arm.

He drew his pistol, aimed the barrel at me, and yanked off my ski mask. "Another passenger," he said with a smirk. "You look the right size, but I'm afraid you're too old." His breathing became heavy and labored.

My movements were forced and concise as I struggled to grab the gun from his hand. A tall, thin man ran in my direction and snatched the pistol out of my grip. A bullet discharged into the fiberglass wall. He lunged on top of me. I squirmed and kicked. Yet, I was no match until the venom took effect. He crumpled to the side. I stood and picked up the weapon.

In the blink of an eye, a brawny man as tall as a basketball shooting guard charged out the door and pulled a rifle from the holster secured to his back. My hand trembled as I aimed the pistol and pulled the trigger. The slug completely missed him. He lowered his rifle toward me. He didn't get a shot off before I fired again. The bullet penetrated his chest. Blood splattered onto the deck and the bodies in his path as he sprawled on top of them.

I stayed next to the wall, slipped back on the ski mask, and waited in terror, knowing reinforcements would arrive. A man peeked out the door. I scraped his bald head before he retreated back inside. I moved stealthily around the deck, peering in windows without seeing anyone. Quietly, I stepped inside, made my way down the stairs, and heard pounding on a door at the other end. My eyes swept back and forth as I eased closer to the door.

Unhooking the latch, I heard a blast and felt a searing pain in my arm. Blood oozed from the wound as a short man with a sturdy chin and recessed hairline yanked me around.

"Who are you?" he snarled.

Touching his bare forearm, my heart pounded rapidly and I said, "Nobody."

His eyes narrowed and his face tightened. "Who do you work for?"

"Myself."

"Huh?" he mumbled, dropping his weapon as he stumbled toward me. His hands shook, his bottom lip quivered, and his eyes opened wider. He fell to my feet and attempted to hold onto my legs, but his strength was gone.

I raised a foot and stepped away from him. A strange, unfamiliar sensation surged through my body, like a rush of adrenaline. I sensed additional strength being unleashed inside me as I unlatched the door. It sprung open. I saw those imprisoned on the *Freedom* with tears running down their faces. They all talked and shouted at the same time. Their voices melded together.

A petite girl with long, flowing, blonde hair brought her arms around me and held on tightly. "Please, help me," she sniffled.

"I will," I said, patting her back. "Everyone be quiet." I counted them. I came up with less than twenty. "How many are you?"

"Sixteen," a tall, thin girl with short, flaming red hair said. "Why is your face covered?"

"So I won't be recognized. Do you know if there are other girls on the ship?"

"Yes," the girl answered, sobbing. "My friend, Susie, is here. I don't know where."

"Don't worry, I'll find her, but first I'm going to get all of you off this ship." I noticed two girls lying in a bed with their eyes fixed toward the door. "Is something wrong with them?" I asked, pointing.

"Drugs," the tall girl answered.

"Can they walk?"

The tall girl nodded.

"I'm going to take five of you out of here at a time."

"Me first," they all yelled.

"Okay, we'll all leave together." Looking at the tall girl, I asked. "What is your name?"

"Melanie."

I thought how ironic—Cameron's wife's name. "Everyone hold hands." They followed my instruction. I led them into the hallway with the petite blonde clinging onto my waist. "Stay here while I get the two on the bed."

The blonde wouldn't let go. She went with me into the room and stayed attached. I lifted the two girls from the bed, pulled them into an upright position, and held each one by a hand. We stepped over the threshold and moved to the front of the line.

"Melanie, can you hold onto these two while I make sure everything is clear?"

"Don't leave us," several girls cried.

"I'll be right back," I said, prying the blonde's arms from my waist. I stroked her wet cheek. "I won't leave you."

The girls were crying, moaning, and whimpering as I went up the stairs thinking none of their captors could be alive. Otherwise, the noise would have drawn their attention.

Going out the door, I scanned the deck. I spotted shining eyes between a tarp and a box. I rushed in that direction and yanked off the tarp, revealing the hidden man. He pounced and plunged his arm forward with a shimmering flash of metal in his hand. A piercing pain arose in my ribs. Blood poured down my side. When I attempted to breathe, the pain in my lungs made my body convulse. Warm liquid soared through my torso. I looked down and saw his hand gripping the handle of the knife protruding above my waist in a shining wet blotch staining my clothes. I grabbed his arm where I could see skin and squeezed hard. He yanked his arm away with the knife secured in his fist and raised it for another strike.

I leapt out of its path. The knife plunged into the deck. Wearing a stunned expression because I was still standing, he reached for the knife. I slammed my foot on his hand. He flung out his other hand, knocking me down, and grabbed his knife. Raising it above his shoulder, he froze. His eyes opened wide. His body hit the deck with a thump.

I ran my hand over my wounded side and didn't feel any blood flowing from it. I gazed down. Carefully, I slid a finger through the hole in my jogging suit where the knife had penetrated. I touched the lesion. The spot no longer was painful or bleeding. I felt amazed, but I didn't have time to dwell on it.

Propping the door open, I yelled, "Melanie, come up now."

She appeared, holding onto the hands of the two drugged girls.

"Go down the gangplank and over to those buildings," I said, motioning as the blonde wrapped her arms around me again.

I counted as the girls marched off the ship, some of them holding hands, others huddled together. I followed with the blonde. She was number sixteen. Watching for any sign of danger, I led them close to the road and moved as quickly as possible.

I took the backpack off, unzipped it, and pulled out two cell phones. "Melanie, call 911. Tell them you and a group of girls were held prisoner, and you just escaped. You're at the entrance to Pier 29." I gave her a cell phone.

"Share these phones and call your parents, whoever you want. Make it brief," I said, handing the other cell phone to a girl who appeared to be a little older than the rest.

"I want to go home," several girls cried.

Then I reached into my backpack and came out with a wad of $100 bills. I handed five to each girl. "Use this money to get home. Have the police help you get away from here as fast as possible. This is all I can do for you. I need to get the other girls." I extracted the blonde's arms from me. "You'll be okay."

Running up the gangplank, I heard a low buzzing sound and hoped it wasn't some kind of alarm. I hurried inside, down the stairs, and opened each door along the corridor. No girls. I ran back up the stairs and searched the bridge. Behind it was a locked door. I kicked it. It didn't budge.

"Please, not again," a girl yelled from inside.

"I won't hurt you," I shouted. Searching around for a tool, I noticed a key ring lying on top of an instrument panel. The third key I tried worked.

Pushing the door open, I saw four girls huddled in the corner, looking bruised and emaciated in their underwear. The room was barren except for two beds without any sheets or blankets, and a toilet, standing against the far wall.

"I'm getting you out of here. Follow me," I said. The girls didn't budge. "Melanie told me you were here, Susie."

The girl with an ivory complexion, long auburn hair, and green eyes began to cry. She had a natural beauty under the tarnish of abuse. "Is Melanie okay?"

"Yes. Come. Hurry," I said, taking her hand. "Hold hands. Don't let yourselves get separated." I picked up some tarps by the gangplank as I took the girls off the ship.

When we reached the first building, I handed the girls tarps and discovered I only had three. "I'll get another one." I turned and saw a black sedan stop next to the ship. Four men jumped out, carrying rifles, and headed to the gangplank. "No time," I whispered, wrapping a tarp around two girls. I moved toward the street with the girls in tow.

As we got closer to the road, blue and red lights throbbed ahead of us. I removed my backpack, pulled out money, and handed $500 to each girl. "Go," I said, pushing the girls in the direction of the police cars.

I stayed hidden around the corner of a building and watched the girls being secured and comforted by the officers.

At the rented car, I took a plastic bag with a wet towel inside out of the backpack and wiped the blood from my outfit. It didn't clean-up well, but I thought it no longer looked like blood, just dark stains that might pass for coffee or motor oil.

I drove three miles, stopped at a payphone next to a convenience store, slipped on rubber gloves, and called the police.

"Houston police department. May I help you?" a man asked.

Trying to mimic a deep, raspy voice, I said, "My son saw boxes and boxes of child pornography at 5730 Empire."

"What is your name?" the man asked. I hung up.

Within thirty minutes, I was back in my hotel room and checking my wounds. It appeared the one in my shoulder had just grazed the skin since it was almost healed. I couldn't see any sign of a bullet. The knife wound was also healing nicely. At the rate my body was mending, I thought both would be invisible within an hour. I showered and changed back into my dress. To dissolve fingerprints, I sprayed the room, my jogging outfit, and the inside of the duffle bag. Wearing plastic gloves, I stuffed the black outfit in the bag. Next, I slipped the plastic gloves, the spray can, and the money into an oversized purse I had purchased at the mall.

Carrying the duffle bag and the oversized purse, I went to the rental car. I put on the gloves again and sprayed the vehicle along with the outside of the duffle bag. I threw the bag into a dumpster, and then I headed to the hotel bar and had a glass of wine. The clock on the wall said 11:46 p.m. when I stood and left the hotel.

Outside I was greeted by Mont who looked nervous and preoccupied. "I was just coming to look for you," he said.

"Why?"

"Mr. Crussett couldn't reach you again."

"I turned off my cell phone. I didn't think he'd be home yet." I climbed into Mont's front passenger seat.

"He's not," Mont said as he started the engine.

I awoke with a start as loud voices echoed through the house. Conner wasn't lying next to me. His side of the bed was untouched. I assumed he never made it home last night.

The voices continued in the background as I showered, put on a pair of jeans, a short-sleeved cotton sweater, and sandals. I hurried down the stairs, hoping to hear their reaction to last night's event.

Conner stood talking in the living room and wearing the same clothes he wore to the meeting last night. Art, Carina's husband, and another man were sitting on the couch. Jack Shelton, who also lived in the compound two doors from Conner, sat in an armchair. The three men wore suits with their ties hanging loosely around their necks. They turned as I approached. Art gave me a smile.

"Sara." Conner took my hand. "Excuse me," he said to the men as he led me into the kitchen.

"Why are they here?" I asked, trying to sound innocent.

"Nothing you need to worry about," he said, his jaw muscles tense with frustration. As he gazed into my eyes, I saw love and sadness in his. "There was a problem last night. Why don't you have breakfast and enjoy the pool while I deal with this. Later this morning, Barnes and his sidekick will be here to talk to you about the Billings investigation."

His eyes drooped and his face was pale. Knowing I was responsible, I felt a tinge of sorrow, no guilt. I touched his cheek. "Have you been up all night?"

He moved his head up and down.

"Maybe I should go to San Diego for the rest of the week so you can deal with your work. The police can talk to me there."

He embraced me. "No. No. I want you here." He raised my chin and smiled. "So I can wake up to those gorgeous brown eyes." He bent down and kissed me. "I need to get back."

Darcy was rinsing a stack of plates and loading the dishwasher. It appeared a large group had eaten here.

"Darcy, do you know what happened?" I asked, pouring coffee.

"Not much. It has something to do with a ship, enemy attack, DVDs, police, and lost cargo."

"Police ... Have they been here?"

"No, but I think someone might have been arrested."

"Anyone in Conner's family?"

"No."

Now I suspected the Crussetts didn't own the ship or the building on Empire Street. I had assumed they did. I should have known they'd be too smart for that. Sadly, I sat down thinking everyone in the compound would probably go unscathed. At least the girls escaped and were free. I smiled to myself.

Voices occasionally rang out. I was only able to catch a few words as I ate. Not enough to know their plans. There was no place I could go to listen without being seen. I needed to know everything they had discovered. An idea flashed into my mind. I changed into a two-piece, pink bikini and headed to the swimming pool.

Outside, I inched a lounge chair closer to the dining room patio door. I went in through that door, got a bottle of water, and returned to the pool, leaving the door ajar.

Reclining on my back, I closed my eyes and listened.

"There's got … someone," I heard Conner say.

"Sharpshooters, yes … that, no one," Art said.

"Let's move on," Jack Shelton said.

"What do you want the boys to do?" the unidentified man said with a low-pitched, tenor voice.

"Track down the caller…wait," Conner said. "…the fingerprints turn up."

Holding my breath, I raised my hands. Fingerprints. They're all over the ship. I inhaled deeply since I had never been fingerprinted. No one has them. I mulled over all my moves last night, hoping I hadn't left anything besides my fingerprints behind that would lead them to me.

Shuffling of feet drowned out the voices. "Later," Conner said as I heard a door closing.

I scooted the lounge chair away from the patio door. I stretched out on it again and closed my eyes.

"You look relaxed," Conner said. I raised my eyelids. "I'd like to join you, but Barnes will be here soon."

"I better get dressed," I said, standing up. "Is he going to talk to both of us?"

"Probably just you."

28

INCRIMINATION

Darcy showed Barnes and Harmon into the den where Conner and I were waiting. We greeted each other and briefly discussed my treatment.

Barnes' eyes became fixed on Conner. "We'd like to talk to Miss Jones alone," he said.

Conner stood and gently squeezed my arm. "I'll be in the living room if you need me."

I nodded as he walked out.

"Miss Jones, we're here to ask you some questions about the spider-related deaths," Barnes said, pulling a tape recorder out of his briefcase. "We had planned on discussing this with you at the local police station, but they were limited on space." He moved his hand towards the recorder button. "Do you mind?"

I shook my head. "Have you located the paramedics?"

"No." He curled the ends of his handlebar mustache. "Based on some of the victims' affiliations, we're examining other angles."

"Conner mentioned that the bicycle victim worked for his family's business, the missing husband and wife were drug dealers, and somehow you thought he was involved."

Barnes' continued to fiddle with his mustache as his forehead creased and he looked at Harmon. "That isn't what we told Mr. Crussett." He scribbled on a notepad. "Potential evidence was found in Mr. and Mrs. Kessler's room that suggested they might have a connection with Mr. Braydon, the bicycle victim. That evidence was not disclosed."

"Maybe he read it somewhere."

Barnes drummed his fingers on the arm of his chair. "There haven't been any additional spider victims in Billings since you left with Mr. Crussett. You and Saul Fazio were bitten in Houston. We're working with the Houston police force to determine if there's a connection. Currently, the common link appears to be Conner Crussett. What is your relationship with him?"

"I'm his girlfriend. We've been together for almost three years."

"Were you working for him while you were in Billings?"

"No. I was working for the accounting firm. You know that."

"As a key witness in our investigation, you abruptly left with Mr. Crussett without giving notice at your place of employment or contacting us. Explain."

"I was afraid. I just wanted to get away."

"Why were you afraid?"

"Spiders. I found them in my room at the hotel twice after Nancy was bitten. Three times in my car. It was awful." Trying to appear convincing, I fidgeted with my hands and my lips quivered. "You couldn't protect me. I had to leave."

"Do you think someone was targeting you?"

I bobbed my head, raised my index finger to my lips, walked over, and flipped off the recorder. "Is it possible we could finish this interview in your police car?" I whispered.

Barnes gave me a puzzled look while he stroked his mustache. "Of course. We came in a police van, equipped for discussions."

"Conner will ask why."

"I can handle that," Barnes said, heading toward the door. He opened it and stepped aside. I walked out of the room first. Barnes and Harmon followed me to the front door.

Conner came into the hallway. "Already finished?"

"The recorder is broken," Barnes said. "There's a recording system hooked up in the van. We'll finish the interview there."

"Can't you finish the interview another day?" Conner asked.

"We're already here," Barnes said. "This shouldn't take too long."

Barnes, Harmon, and I went to the police van while Conner stood on the porch next to a security guard and watched. Harmon opened the vehicle's sliding door. We climbed in.

The back of the van had a short couch, three swivel chairs, and surveillance equipment along the two outer walls. The only window was the one in the back door. Barnes motioned for me to sit on the couch. He and Harmon sat down on chairs. Barnes pulled down a panel, releasing a table, and lowered it between them and me.

"Let's go on," Barnes said, turning on the tape recorder. "Do you think someone was trying to injure you with the spiders?"

"Please," I said, flipping off the recorder.

Barnes ran a finger over his mustache as he took out his notepad.

I began, "I thought it was Cameron, Conner's brother. Now I don't know." I shook my head and bit my bottom lip. I pulled a small, black, ovoid-shaped container covered with pin-like holes out of my pocket. "I found this in Conner's glove compartment."

Barnes reached for it while Harmon was busy writing.

"It has spiders inside," I said, giving it to him.

"When you opened it up, how did you prevent them from escaping?"

"Because of the holes, I suspected it might hold spiders. I captured three flies. Carefully, I lifted the lid and shoved them inside after I saw the spiders. There are at least four in the container. Don't let them die or you won't be able to verify they're the same type of spiders responsible for the deaths."

"How do you know that?" Barnes asked, suspiciously.

"Her parents were arachnologists," Harmon explained.

"Right," Barnes said, gingerly putting the container in a compartment in his briefcase. "You suspect Conner Crussett wants to harm you?"

I lowered my head and cradled my face in the palms of my hands. "I'm so confused. If he wanted me dead, he's had opportunities. No. He'd never hurt me. His nephew, Caden, Cameron's son, sometimes drives his car. Maybe he put them there."

"Earlier you said, you thought Cameron Crussett was after you. Why?"

"Do you know anything about the Crussetts' real business?" I asked.

"Some things."

"They're corrupt. Cameron thought I had information about the business that I was going to expose."

Barnes began curling the ends of his mustache again. "Did you?"

"No," I said, shaking my head. "Taking that kind of stuff would be a death wish. Cameron just hated me. I don't know why. Saul Fazio, his employee, was taking me to the airport when I was bitten. He probably hadn't planned on Saul being a victim, but spiders can't be controlled. Cameron was responsible for the death of my friend, Paula Sorensen."

"How did she die?"

When I finished telling them everything I knew about Paula's death, I said, "I confronted Cameron about it when he came to see me in the hospital. He confirmed my suspicion and my body went into shock. Every inched throbbed with pain. You can check that out with the hospital staff. After that, he was no longer allowed to visit."

"Why didn't you report it to the police?"

"I planned on doing that after I was well. Now it's too late."

"Does Conner Crussett know his brother tried to kill you?"

"I told him everything I'm telling you. He thinks I'm paranoid or something. He doesn't believe his brother would go after me."

"Why do you stay with Mr. Crussett?"

"I love Conner. He needs me, especially after the loss of his brother." I watched Barnes and Harmon glance at each other. Barnes' forehead creased. Harmon's eyebrows bounced and he lightly shook his head. I kept a solemn expression on my face.

"Miss Jones, I think you should come with us for your protection," Barnes said.

"No. I'm staying with Conner until I go back to North Dakota for treatments.

"When is that?"

"In four days."

Barnes put his notepad and the recorder in his briefcase. "We'll want to talk to you again after we check on a few things. During your treatment, can you have visitors?"

"Yes."

Barnes handed me a business card. "Call if you need anything or would like us to pick you up."

I nodded, slipping it in my pocket.

Harmon opened the van sliding door. We all stepped out.

"Thank you for your cooperation," Barnes said, shaking my hand.

After I shook Harmon's hand, I headed toward the house, feeling good.

"How did it go?" Conner asked, leading me to the couch.

"Okay. They just asked questions about why I left Billings in a hurry and my relationship with you. That was all."

"What did you say?"

"I said I left because I was afraid of the spiders and the police couldn't protect me against them. And I was your girlfriend. Stuff like that."

"Good. I feel beat. I'm going to lie down until my father calls."

"For another meeting?"

"Yes. After he's talked to Viltro." Then he smiled. "Do you want to take a nap with me?"

"Will you get any sleep that way?"

"Probably not. I'll make up for it when you're gone." He pulled me closer, kissed the tip of my nose, and held my hand as we went upstairs.

When Conner finally dozed off, I slowly climbed out of bed, dressed, and headed for the den. I opened his top desk drawer and took out a folder he had hurriedly slipped in it right before Barnes and Harmon entered. I also picked up the spider cult investigator's report and sat down. Skimming through the folder, I read that a dock worker saw a woman with long hair wearing a black jogging suit put on a ski mask and go over to the ship. He didn't see her go up the gangplank. The man wasn't sure about her hair color since it was dark. He doubted it was blonde. I wondered where he was when he spotted me. One of the buildings had two floors. Maybe he was on the second floor, looking out a window. I felt a spasm of panic, thinking the man might be able to identify me. I briefly closed my eyes, breathed deeply, and sensed my pulse slowing down.

I turned the page and learned the ship was owned by a company, Ellsworth and Son. George Ellsworth had been arrested. Next to his name were five dollar signs. Below that was a round punctured hole that went through the pad. It appeared it was caused by a sharp object being thrust down, maybe a pen.

A loud thud came from the direction of the hallway. I leapt to my feet, put the folder back in the desk drawer, and eased the door open while I held the investigation report. Darcy rushed past me toward the entrance door. "What was that?"

"Someone at the door," she said, opening it.

Peeking out, I saw Tyler, a muscular brut with a square jaw, wide flat nose, and deep hard eyes, encompassed in an almost freakishly tall frame I guessed to be at least seven-foot. Another of Cedric's ogre size employees, necessary to handle ferocious tasks.

"Mr. Crussett wants to see Conner, now," Tyler growled.

I threw the report down on the chair and ran up the stairs. "Conner," I said, shaking his shoulder. "Your dad sent Tyler to get you. Something's wrong. Whatever Viltro told him, he must have believed it." My hands trembled as I worried if they had discovered anything about what happened in the morgue. Would Conner protect me?

Sitting up, he held onto my arms. "Relax. I had nothing to do with Cameron's death. I'm not guilty of anything."

Only through his twisted, entitled sense of logic could that sentence be accurate. "But Tyler..."

"Don't worry. I'll take care of it," he said, slipping on his clothes. He smiled. "Was he carrying a noose?"

"No," I said, shaking my head.

"See? I'm not going to be strung up without a hearing." He sat down and put on his shoes. "I need to go." He gently kissed me, and then he hurried down the stairs.

Wanting to read more about the problems the night before, I headed back to the den. On page three in the folder were notes about the girls.

None of them had suffered any serious physical injuries. Some would need psychiatric care. The girls' description of their rescuer: a woman wearing lightweight sweats and a ski mask over her head, five-foot-seven, eight or nine, slender, a sweet voice. She fought all of the men single handedly. She was a skilled marksman, a knife thrower, and could beat the crap out of anyone. I smiled, thinking I didn't have a gun, knife, or the skills to use them, and my fighting ability was limited. At the same time I didn't need to worry about self-preservation. One girl said I was just like Lara Croft in *Tomb Raider*.

On the following page Conner's handwriting became so sloppy I couldn't make out some of his comments. There were a few names I was able to decipher: Lewis, Genaro, Zeth, and Thurman, with a question mark next to each. Those names I recognized from documents I had copied the day before. I wondered if they were under suspicion. At the bottom of the page "FINGERPRINTS!" were scribbled four times. Nothing else was written in the notepad. I then realized that my own fingerprints were all over the page. I grabbed a handful of tissues and began wiping the sheets. A wave of fear shot through me when I noticed I was smearing the ink. I threw the folder back in the drawer, closed it, and hoped Conner would believe he was responsible for the smudges.

Inhaling deeply, I sat quietly trying to think of all the different scenarios I could use to take care of the Crussett business. I couldn't get past the "What if?" question as I worried what was going on at Cedric's house—Viltro's information. Were they talking about me? And worse, did they suspect Brett, Lindsey, and Father were involved?

At 8 p.m., Darcy peered in. "Aren't you going to have any dinner?"

"I didn't realize it was that late. I was waiting for Conner."

"From all the commotion that's been going on, he could be awhile. He might have already eaten at his father's house."

"I know. Are guards still going in and out of the house?"

"No. Two have been taking turns walking around the outside."

I thought food might help calm me down. "Thanks, Darcy. I'll eat in the kitchen," I said, rising from the chair.

After dinner, I got a book and went upstairs. I sat in the corner armchair with my feet tucked beneath me and attempted to read. I couldn't concentrate and gave up.

I took my time getting ready for bed, anxious about what Viltro had to say. Just after eleven, I climbed in bed, alone. Unable to relax, I tossed and turned searching for a comfortable position.

About an hour later, I heard the door open. I knew it was Conner when the bathroom water faucet turned on. I lay in bed, pretending to sleep. I didn't want Conner to think I was concerned about what Viltro might have offered.

He slipped under the covers, raised my hair, and kissed the back of my neck. I felt his warm breath on my cheek and turned toward him. He pulled me tight against his body. My worries vanished, and I believed I was safe.

29

THE WAREHOUSE

Lying in bed, I watched a bird on the window ledge as Conner showered. I sensed something was wrong. The night before we had made love. His touch felt slightly different, a certain tenderness was missing. Yet, he held me closer. In the darkness I glanced into his eyes. They were cloudy, not glowing, like they had always been previously. Was my imagination working overtime, or had Viltro stumbled upon the truth?

"I've made arrangements for us to spend the whole day together," Conner said, getting dressed in a polo shirt and casual slacks. "I'm going to check on a few things while you get ready."

"Are we going someplace?"

"Yes. I've kept you cooped up here long enough. You'll like where we're going."

"And where is that?"

"It's a surprise." He tied his shoes. "See you downstairs."

Knowing I was in trouble when Conner didn't try to kiss me before he left, I felt a clutching, sinking sensation in my chest. I had the urge to call Father, but I didn't want him in harm's way. Fire destroys. The Crussett family was my responsibility. I needed to deal with it.

With trembling hands, I forced myself to get out of bed. I showered, put on a pair of white linen slacks, a sleeveless blue silk blouse, and sandals. Fixing my hair, I decided I would try to refrain from using my newly acquired abilities until I discovered everything they knew. Also, I needed to be careful. I'd rather have Conner and his men suspect spiders than to learn what I had become. If they did, all Tegens would be in danger.

Just in case the Crussetts already knew too much, I had to be prepared to call Father. I opened my purse to move my cell phone to my pocket. It was gone. My heart beat frantically. I reached for my small suitcase, fearful it would be empty. I unlocked it and stared at the contents—nothing was missing. I took out the container of *venotrolia* and gulped down the liquid.

Outside the den, I said, "I'm ready." Peeking in, I saw Conner sitting at his desk, wearing a black top that covered his arms and hung snuggly against his body. "Are we going scuba diving?"

"Yes," he replied, approaching me.

"Let me get my suit," I said and turned towards the stairs.

He gripped my arm. "I got you a new one. It's on the boat."

I swallowed hard, realizing I was trapped. "Maybe I should put on shorts?" I asked, thinking I might be able to escape through the upstairs balcony door.

"Everything's on the boat. You don't need anything."

"Breakfast?"

"We'll eat there."

My pulse raced as I walked by his side with his arm around my shoulders to an awaiting limo.

"Why aren't we going in your car?"

"Security."

The driver opened the door. Fear swept through my body when I saw a blowtorch leaning against the seat on the far side.

"What's that for?" I asked, climbing in.

"Brett Daborel left Billings two days ago. He might be in town. I'm prepared in case we cross him, and he intercedes with his weapon of choice."

"Spiders? Why would he do that?"

"Just a precaution."

The limo stopped at the gate. A man, wearing a black bodysuit with a holster hanging from his shoulder, got into the front passenger seat.

As we drove onto the road, I quickly scanned the nearby cars without seeing anyone I recognized. Conner sat quietly by my side. I noticed his clenched jaw. My eyes dropped to the bodysuit. The material wasn't rubber. It appeared thicker and looked like a blend of canvas and plastic. It definitely was not a scuba suit. "We haven't been scuba diving since we went to the South Pacific last year," I said, pretending everything was okay.

"No, we haven't," he said in a stern tone without looking at me.

I laid my hand on his leg. "Is something wrong?"

He put his hand on top of mine. "We're getting closer to discovering what happened to Cameron."

Staring at the blowtorch, I asked, "Did you get some good information from Viltro?"

"Yes." He lifted my wrist and touched my bracelet. "When the button is activated, in addition to letting someone know you're in trouble it also becomes a mike. Cameron pushed his button. Viltro had a recording."

Turning my face toward the window, I bit my lower lip. Before I attempted to do anything, I needed to know what was on the recording. Was Father in danger? I took a deep breath, slid closer to Conner, and held his hand. "Why was Viltro concerned about giving it to you?"

"He had a reason," Conner said, gazing at my face with a sad, remorseful expression.

"Can we have a good time today, or are you going to worry about it?"

He lightly rubbed my hand. "I'm still planning on spending the rest of the day with you."

The limo stopped next to an old brick warehouse with boarded up windows and surrounded by similar structures. Four two-foot blowtorches stood against the building along with a dozen men. They all wore bodysuits and were heavily armed. Each had a knife strapped to their thigh and a holster under their arms or on their back with either a pistol protruding or the handle of a rifle rising above their heads.

"We're here," Conner said, stepping out. He stuck a black pair of gloves along with a ski mask in his belt.

As my muscles tensed, I eased toward the car door. "This isn't a boat."

"It's on the other side." He clutched my arm as I got out.

"I don't want to get my white pants dirty. I think I'll walk around the building."

"There are fences on the sides," he said, leading me toward large, wooden, double doors.

Going into the structure, I knew I should have left when I had the chance. I just hoped no one else would suffer.

Five men followed us inside. The smell of moist, rotting wood lingered in the air. Dark stains and shallow puddles of murky water were scattered on the floor. In front of me stood a cluster of chairs, a stand with a bag dangling from it—like used for an intravenous feeding, and a table covered with electronic equipment. Next to it sat a heavyset, middle-aged man with gray speckled hair and a shaggy beard. He also wore a black bodysuit. As we got closer, I saw the chair by the table had leather straps attached to the arms and legs. I stopped. Conner tightened his grip on my arm, cutting off my circulation, and forced me to move forward.

My eyes swept around the large open space. Several huge electric fans were placed sporadically throughout the structure. Large wooden containers lined one wall with blowtorches spread out in front of them, approximately one every ten feet. On the opposite side were rows of crates, stacked almost to the ceiling. Three men stood by them with blowtorches adjacent to their feet. Two caldrons with flames rising above the rims abutted the double door at the rear. Two man clad in a black bodysuits stood next to them.

"Sara, sit down," Conner said, gesturing toward the chair with the leather straps.

"But we're not at the boat."

"Sit," he snapped.

"You lied to me," I said, trying not to show any emotion.

Conner nodded toward two large, armed men. They each took one of my arms and forced me down into the chair.

"It wasn't the first time," he said, looking in my direction, yet avoiding eye contact.

"I know. You lied to me for three years: where you were going, what you did, and about your family. Yet, when you said you loved me, I believed you. Was that also a lie?" I asked, quivering my lower lip.

"This isn't about us. It's about the role you played in my brother's death."

I squinted and wrinkled my nose. "What did I do?"

Conner turned toward the bearded man. "Play it."

The flip of a switched turned on the recorder. I anxiously waited as the bearded man adjusted knobs. It began with static, then came: "Sara, you have to wait," a man said. I knew it was Father. "Why do I have to wait…Cameron has to stay alive while the venom circulates…you can eat …small abandoned warehouse will burn…don't want anyone to know how Cameron and his men died."

The tape recorder shut itself off with a loud, resonant click. The room was heavy with silence as Conner stared at me with eyes full of rage and sadness.

My body trembled. "That recording has been faked." Even though I knew he wouldn't believe me, all I could do was to spout blatant lies in desperation.

"I insisted it was to my father and the rest of my family. Then it was tested by a forensic analyst and found to be accurate."

A brawny man with a scared cheek approached Conner. "Mr. Crussett, your father has arrived."

Conner's attention turned toward the door. Cedric, wearing a navy blue tailored suit with a dress shirt and tie, stepped into the building. He was a tall, slender man with thinning gray hair and a narrow face. He strolled up to the table.

"It's nice to see you again, Sara," Cedric said, glaring at me. Then he looked at Conner. "How's it going?"

"We just got started," Conner answered.

Cedric pointed to a spot thirty feet from me. "There," he said. The brawny man moved a chair to that location. Cedric sat down.

Conner continued, "Who is the man on the tape?"

"Someone who came to help me since you didn't," I hissed.

"And what's that supposed to mean?"

"Cameron tried to kill me three times. You kept saying you'd keep him away from me, but you couldn't. He wouldn't listen to you." I wanted him to know his brother's lies.

"Three times?"

"Yes. You already know about Cameron having Saul take me to airport. That wasn't where we were going. Saul tried to rape me. If it weren't for Brett, I'd be dead. Where were you? Then twice in the hospital he tried to kidnap me. Twice. The first time, he had his men, dressed like hospital employees, pretend they were taking me to the lab. They pointed a gun at me and claimed if I didn't cooperate they'd start shooting innocent people. They put me in an ambulance. Brett came to my rescue again. Where were you?"

"Why didn't you tell me?"

"Because you couldn't do anything. Cameron called all the shots. The last time, he used different people. They also were dressed like medical staff. I was taken to the morgue. Brett helped me get out alive. Where were you?" I shouted. "That recording has been sanitized. The beginning is missing. If it were there you'd know what really happened. He was going to have Gerard inject me with who knows what. He still believed I had the missing documents. I didn't."

I felt adrenaline pumping through my veins. I didn't want to stop. "He killed my friend, Paula, because he didn't believe she didn't know where I was when I left. I didn't tell anyone. She was innocent. Now she's dead. Go on; tell me you didn't know about it!" My heartbeat raced and tears trickled down my cheeks. I gasped for air, trying to calm down.

Conner stood silently, staring at me.

"Conner," Cedric said, loudly.

I caught a glimpse of Cedric's hostile eyes glaring at me as Conner went over to him. They talked quietly for a few minutes. Then Conner returned.

"Sara," he began, "Let's move on."

"Why? Is the truth about your brother that unpleasant?" I snapped, rising to my feet.

"Strap her down," he ordered in a loud, authoritative tone.

"No," I protested, swinging my arms as two men forced me back in the seat. One held firmly onto my forearms while the other one secured the straps. I kicked my legs until they were bound tightly against the chair with my feet hovering just above the floor.

"What is your relationship with Fred Shoeman?"

"The guy who took the missing documents and was mentioned in the investigation report?"

"Yes. That's him."

"I talked to him sometimes when he was cleaning the pool."

"Was he involved with Cameron's death?"

"No."

"Someone else was besides Brett. Who was it?" His jaw clenched.

"Brett's strong. He didn't need help."

"Did Lindsey help him?"

"No. No one helped him."

"I'm going to ask you nicely one more time. Who helped him?" he asked in a tone that sent a shiver up my spine.

"No one." My eyes darted around the spectators. I wondered what was going to happen next.

Conner stepped towards me and flung his hand across my face.

My cheek burned. My lips trembled. "Conner."

He pulled up a chair in front of me. He sat, raised his right ankle onto his left knee, and folded his arms across his chest. "Why are you forcing me to do this to you, Sara?"

Conner's face was covered with signs of stress and grief caused by my betrayal. "No one helped Brett. Honest."

He cast his eyes downward. "Sara." He lifted his head and looked at the bearded man. "Give her a little persuasion."

The bearded man attached square pads to my upper arms and above my ankles. Each pad had a wire leading to the steel box on the table. He leaned back in his chair and moved a lever on the box.

I screamed as the electrical current ran through my body. My head flung back and forth, my feet jerked violently, flinging my sandals off. My arms wiggled, causing the chair to bounce up and down. Feeling the hair stiffen on my hands and feet, I crunched my eyes tightly closed as I screamed again.

It stopped. My chin dropped to my chest. Perspiration streamed down my face. My blouse clung to my damp body. I felt numb and tried to focus my eyes. All I could see was a dark haze in front of me.

"I have an appointment," I heard Cedric say. "Keep up the good work." Heavy footsteps pounded against the concrete floor. It sounded like several men were leaving.

"Sara, are you ready to talk now?" Conner asked in a strained voice.

Images began to take form and I squinted, trying to see my hands. The microscopic Tegen hairs were relaxing. An odd, unfamiliar sensation crept through my body, like every one of my organs was tingling. The pain subsided. If I was to pretend to die from being electrocuted, it would be drawn-out and horrifying. I needed to find a way to free myself from being bound so I could be shot, attempting to escape. Could I pull at Conner's heartstrings?

"Sara," he said again, raising my chin. "Are you ready to talk?"

I looked at my tormentor, the man who had held me in his arms the night before. The man I once thought I would love forever. "I've told you the truth," I sniffled softly. "I hurt all over. I can hardly hold my head up." I swayed it back and forth.

He stretched out a hand and placed it on my cheek. I saw his sad, drooping eyes and the pain on his face.

"Don't...don't touch me," I whimpered. "You said you'd protect me."

His eyes became cloudy. "I'm not the only one who lied." Conner turned to one of his men. "Wipe her face," he said, stiffening his spine. He tapped his fingertips on the arm of his chair.

A man dabbed my face with a towel.

"Sara, you need to answer my questions."

"Can I please have something to drink?" I asked in a voice just above a whisper. I bit my bottom lip. "Please."

"Water," Conner said, glancing over his shoulders.

The brawny man brought Conner a bottle of water. Conner removed the cap and held it against my lips.

I leaned my head back, took a sip, and allowed the water to run down chin. "It's hard to drink like this. Can you untie my arms?" I looked down at my hand. "Never mind, I can't raise my fingers."

Conner's eyes moved to the bearded man and then darted to the other men standing nearby. "Take a break."

The man rose and walked to the entrance with the others.

Conner untied my arms and rubbed them with his hands. "Can you feel that?"

"A little." I raised my arm slightly and dropped it in my lap.

Shaking his head, he took my hand. "The feeling will come back."

Attempting to look forlorn with a solemn expression on my face, I slightly lowered my eyelids. "I know you're going to kill me. My body hurts. Please do it now." Tears flowed down my cheeks.

He picked up the towel on the table and dried my face. "You're not going to die. You'll feel better later." He lifted my hand and kissed it. "I need you to answer some questions. Can you do that for me?"

I nodded. "Your father wants me dead."

"We have an agreement," he said, looking down and stroking my hands.

His eyes never met mine. I knew he was lying, but so was I.

"Are you ready?" he asked with tenderness in his tone.

"Yes."

He released my hands and turned around. "Don."

"Are you going to shock me again?" I asked, quavering my lips.

"Just answer the questions. You'll be fine." He patted my knee.

The bearded man returned to his seat behind the desk.

"Did Lindsey or Fred help Brett kill Cameron and his men?"

"No. In the morgue Brett threw spiders at them. They were all bitten."

"It happened in the hospital morgue?"

I bobbed my head up and down.

"On the recording, why did Brett tell you to wait?"

"Because Cameron killed Paula I wanted to kick him. He was moving around too much so Brett wanted me to wait until Cameron was lying still."

"What was the statement on the recording, 'you can eat' all about?"

"Brett was bringing me a box of chocolates when he got detoured to the morgue. He told me I could eat them while I waited for Cameron. I couldn't as I watched Cameron and his men suffering."

"He needed help moving the cars to the warehouse. Who helped him?" he asked with an edge to his voice.

"If someone helped him, I never saw them. He took me back to my room before the bodies were moved. Can't you ask Lindsey or Fred if they helped him?"

"We'd ask them if we could find them. Do you know where they are?"

I shook my head.

"Two days ago you went shopping at the South Pointe mall."

"Yes. You already know that."

"At the same time you were there a woman was seen at the pier who matches your description. Was that you?"

I shook my head as I gripped the chair arms, preventing my hands from shaking. "No. Mont would have known if I left the mall."

Conner reached over and laid his hand on mine. "A woman, matching your description, rented a car that day. She put down a cash deposit instead of providing a credit card. Was that you?"

"No."

"What was the name of your friend who you had dinner with at the Sunlight Hotel?"

"Mary Gregor."

Conner turned toward a short, auburn-haired man. "Check it."

I swallowed hard and pressed my lips together, realizing I might have put Mary Gregor in danger—a complete stranger I just bumped into in the elevator.

"Why are you lying?" he asked, his eyes boring into me.

From his expression, I knew he had evidence. "I'm not," I insisted.

"Yes, you are. Both the dock workman and the woman at the rental agency have identified you from your picture. Do you need enticement to tell the truth?" He released my hand and leaned back in his chair.

"Wait...wait. Please. It was me."

He put his hands on my knees. "Why?"

"I wanted to save the girls," I said, knowing if I didn't confess he'd go after someone innocent. Also, I knew Sara Jones would die before the day ended.

His eyes narrowed. "You were involved with the incident that occurred with our shipment?"

"Uh-huh."

"Who did you give the information to?"

"What?" I asked, perplexed.

"What group, person, did you tell about the shipment?"

"No one."

"A woman who was approximately your height and build was seen on the ship. Are you telling me that was you?" he asked, cocking his eyebrows.

"Yes."

"Sara, you don't even know how to shoot a gun or use a knife. That wasn't you. Who was it? Lindsey? Did she help you carry-out your plan? Some of the crewmembers showed signs identical to the spider victims. Did you recruit Brett? Is that why he left Billings?"

I stroked his arm. "No, Conner, I did it alone."

"Okay, let's say you did it by yourself," he said in a tone of utter disbelief. "How did you accomplish that task?"

"I used spiders."

The bearded man jumped out of his seat and backed away.

"Do you have any spiders with you?" Conner asked.

"No. I used them all on the ship. I only had a dozen. They die after they've bitten someone."

"Don," Conner said, looking at the bearded man. "Relax. If she had spiders with her she would have already used them." His eyes moved to me. "Go on. Where did you get these spiders?"

"At the mall."

Conner shook his head. "They don't sell them there."

"I didn't buy them. I met a guy that gave them to me."

"A stranger?"

"No. I had made arrangements with Brett to get me some spiders. He had the guy deliver them to me."

"What's the name of this guy?"

I shrugged me shoulders. "Don't know."

"How were you able to identify him?"

"He wore a baseball cap with *Yankees* on it and large sunglasses."

"Describe him."

"Short, maybe five-foot-two, chunky with a belly that hung over his pants, and he walked with a cane."

Conner put his elbow on the armrest, bent his arm, and rested his forehead on his fingertips. "How did you manage not to get shot during your rescuing efforts?"

"Several of the men were bitten before they saw me. They attempted to use their guns, so I had to fight with them until the venom took effect."

Conner's eyes opened wider. "You fought with some men?"

I nodded.

He stroked my cheek. "Sara, you're going to have to do better than that."

A banging sound, loud talking, and commotion by the door caused me to look up to see what was going on. Conner also turned his attention that direction.

30

REVENGE

Caden, a tall handsome man with tawny brown hair, walked toward us and was flanked by two large, muscular men. He resembled his father, Cameron. Caden wore a dark, pinstriped suit. The men accompanying him also wore suits. They weren't prepared for spiders.

"I knew you'd have a hard time interrogating her," he said, his eyes were hot, and his jaw was rigid.

Conner rose to his feet. "I'm getting answers."

"Why is she untied?"

"Caden," Conner moved away from me, nodded his head to the side, and motioned for Caden to follow. They stepped fifteen feet away.

My eyes fixed on them as I tried to listen.

"...don't need to wear one," Caden huffed.

"...spiders...rescue," Conner said and briefly glanced at me. Then he led Caden toward the rear entrance.

Occasionally their voices became loud. I couldn't make out anything they were saying. My eyes flitted back and forth between Conner's men as I wondered which one had tipped off Caden that my arms were no longer bound.

As much as I didn't want to contact Brett, I knew it was time and this might be my only opportunity. I carefully began to pull my disk with the GPS button out of my pocket when I saw Caden rushing toward me. Before I had a chance to push it, he snatched it from my hand.

He looked it over. "What the hell is this?"

Conner came over to us. He didn't look at me. Still, I could tell from his expression he was irritated. He took the gadget from Caden. "I noticed it earlier in her purse. It's just a harmless noise maker." He clicked the buttons several times on both sides, and then he smashed it on the floor.

"Is she carrying anything else?" Caden asked.

"No."

"I'm going to make sure." Caden began to feel my blouse.

"I'll handle this." Conner ran his hands down over my clothing. "She doesn't have anything." He stared at Caden. "Remember the agreement," he said, sounding firm. Then he headed toward the entrance.

Agreement, maybe Conner didn't lie about that.

Caden glared at me with an implacable hatred that sent chills through my body. "Tie her up."

After my arms were secured to the chair, he began, "It's time for the truth."

"I've told the truth."

"It's your fault my father is dead. You bitch!" He slapped me across my face.

Closing my eyes, I clamped my teeth together in a determined effort not to scream. I didn't want to give him that satisfaction.

"You're going to wish you were dead before I'm through," he growled, digging his fingers into my shoulders and squeezing. "Open those fucking eyes."

I kept them tightly closed and felt his next blow, slamming the side of my head hard with his fist, thrusting my body. The chair tilted. Someone grabbed it and pushed it back into an upright position. Slowly, I raised my eyelids, feeling dizzy as my ears rang, my temples pounded, and tears streamed down my face. I still refused to utter a sound.

I watched his lips moving without hearing a word. He removed his suit coat, revealing a holster strapped around his shirt with the handle of an automatic sticking out just below his left armpit. He loosened his tie and rolled up his sleeves while the ringing in my ears continued. He shook me as his lips flapped up and down.

"What?" I mumbled. I felt a twitching in my head, like blood rushing through my veins. Voices gradually came into focus. I heard men speculating about my ability to hear.

"She's faking it," Caden said. He leaned closer to me, his face only six inches away, wearing a look of complete contempt. "Besides Brett, who else helped you kill my father?"

"No one."

With a smirk on his face, he sat back in his chair. "She needs persuasion," he said to Don.

The equipment made a sizzling sound as Don pressed the lever.

The pain shot through my body again. I couldn't prevent a scream from leaving my throat. My hands swung wildly out of control. My feet pounded against the chair as it jerked around. My head flopped back and forth. My tongue swelled.

When it finally stopped, I was incapable of holding my head up; it tipped to the side. My eyesight was blurry. I knew the hair on my hands was stiff again, prepared to inflict venom in anyone that touched them. My wet hair draped down in front of my face. I closed my eyes, hoping the nightmare would end. Someone pulled my hair away from my face.

As my sight returned I saw Caden smiling.

"Why are you making this so hard on yourself?" he asked sarcastically.

I briefly looked down while that strange sensation encompassed my body. I felt my strength being rejuvenated.

"Sara?" he hissed, his cold voice cut through the air.

"Wha," I murmured, squinting, pretending not to understand as the hair on my hands subsided.

"Who helped you?" he asked through gritted teeth.

"Please…kill me now. I…I can't feel my body anymore," I said, softly, attempting to sound pathetic.

"If that was only an option." His eyes darkened with rage as they bore into mine. "I'd like nothing more than to see you retching in pain and blood oozing from a bullet hole in your chest. Or, drenching you with gasoline, sticking a match, and watching you squirm while the flames engulfed every inch of your body. Only charred remains would be left just like my father. Conner wouldn't even be able to recognize his whore." His upper lip twisted in a sneer. "But first, I'd still need answers."

Gunfire erupted outside the building. Caden bolted to his feet and drew his pistol.

"Mr. Crussett," a man yelled as a black van crashed through the double doors and sent shattered wood and debris through the building. I caught a glimpse of the men around me slipping on ski masks and gloves while Caden headed toward the stacked crates.

The van stopped twenty feet from me. The doors flew open. Out sprang three people, two men and one woman, wearing black bodysuits with their faces hidden behind ski masks, carrying weapons. I knew Brett was one of the men.

The sound of gunfire echoed through the structure. Instinctively, I tried to duck down. It was impossible with the restraints holding me in place.

I found it hard to determine who was who since almost everyone wore a black bodysuit and their faces were covered. I studied the attire of three people from the van closely and concluded their suits were made of heavier material. They were darker than those worn by Conner and his men. Also, their hands were uncovered.

"Sara, you'll be okay," Brett said as he ran past me shooting.

Then I recognized Father when I saw him climbing up the wall and Lindsey with her long, light-brown hair sticking out below her ski mask.

I watched as a dozen of Conner's men came charging from all directions. Lindsey shot a man carrying an unlit blowtorch. He stumbled, dropping it. She grabbed it and swung it into his hip. He moaned. She struck him again. I heard a cracking sound as he landed on the floor, motionless. She moved swiftly to the side and clambered up the wall.

Looking toward the entrance, I noticed Conner dodging around the men as he rushed toward me. He was fifteen feet away when he buckled over with blood squirting from his leg. A tall, lanky man with his face hidden behind a mask hurried to Conner's side and helped him stand.

"Get Sara out of here," Conner yelled.

The lanky man sprinted to me, cut the leather straps around my arms and legs, and yanked me up. A bullet struck him in the arm. He gasped. Another slug hit him below his neck. Blood poured from his wounds as he collapsed to the floor. My eyes moved to the rows of crates, the direction of the attack. I saw Caden holding a pistol with the barrel aimed at me. I dropped to my knees. The bullet ripped through one of the table legs, splitting it in half. The metal box containing the electrical equipment crashed to the floor, sending sparks flying around it.

A loud blast came from the back of the room. I turned to see a caldron lying on its side, flames engulfing the wall, and a large shattered container surrounded by shrapnel. Thick smoke rose to the ceiling as my eyes searched for Father. Next to the entrance, I spotted a man shooting from the rafters and assumed it was him.

I grabbed the gun lying next to the dead, lanky man, and turned back to the crates. I couldn't see Caden anywhere. Staying low, I scanned the room looking for him. Then I saw a man, carrying a blowtorch with the flame projecting ten feet, approaching Lindsey.

"Behind you," I shouted, raising the pistol and pointing it toward him.

She leapt to the side as I pulled the trigger. The bullet missed him. Lindsey turned and shot the man in his head. His body smacked against the floor along with the lit blowtorch. The flame consumed him within seconds.

Someone knocked the gun out of my hand. It clanked onto the concrete. I turned and saw Caden with a smirk on his face.

"Conner's going to be disappointed you didn't survive this battle," he said with his pistol against my chest. "So much for his agreement."

With the needles protruding, I grabbed Caden's neck as I felt the searing pain of the bullet penetrating my body. My knees folded under me. I fell, holding onto his neck.

Caden freed himself from my grip while I caught a glimpse of Father charging toward me. With blood drizzling from Caden's neck, he sprinted away, heading to the crates.

"It won't hurt long," Father said, bending down. He threw his arms around me.

"I'll take care of him," Brett said from behind Father.

"No need. He's been poisoned," I said, but Brett was out of earshot, running toward Caden.

"We're almost through," Father said and went to the van.

Lying on the floor, I watched Brett tackle his prey, knocking the gun out of Caden's hand. Caden crawled toward his weapon. Brett grabbed his legs and yanked him back while Caden struggled to free himself. Brett released his hold and Caden jumped up only to be met with a fierce blow to his face. Brett flipped him to the floor. Caden staggered to his feet then crumpled in a heap. Brett grabbed the pistol, turned, and shot a man sneaking up behind him.

Brett hurried back to me. "Are you doing okay?"

I nodded.

"Pretend you're dead."

"That's my plan. I just wanted to watch a little longer," I whispered.

"Just don't move when they check you."

"I won't," I replied, knowing a pulse wouldn't be detected. Father had explained the healing process. He told me that would happen if I lost a lot of blood, and my breathing would become soft and shallow. They would think I was dead.

I got a quick look at the automatic rifle behind Brett. A gunshot rang out. I saw blood on his black bodysuit. "Play dead now," he whispered as his head hit the floor with a thump.

Bursts of gunfire continued resounding throughout the building. Someone landed on my legs. I didn't move as I heard shouting, banging, heavy footsteps, and smelled thick, nauseous smoke with the odor of burning garbage. Fingers touched my neck, lightly pushed down, and then they were gone.

Five minutes later, silence descended over the room except for the crackling of burning wood and debris striking the floor.

"We got all of them," a man shouted.

I sensed a person kneel next to me. Arms pulled me up. Hands brushed my hair away from my face, "Nooooo," Conner screamed, holding me against his chest.

I listened to his sobs and felt his tears as I heard his heart beating while mine was breaking. He sniffled as his lips touched mine. My arms dangled at my side. It took all my willpower not to raise them and wrap them around Conner's neck.

"It's Brett and Lindsey," a man with a husky voice said. "You two, carry Caden out of here."

"Mr. Crussett, she's gone," another man said.

Conner held my head tighter against his chest as his tears streamed down my hair and onto my face. I sensed someone tugging at him.

"Mr. Crussett, we have to go," the man said.

Conner gently laid me down, put his hand on my cheek, and kissed my forehead. I knew it was his way of saying goodbye.

"Mr. Crussett, your father's on the phone," a man yelled.

Conner stroked my arm as he rose. I listened as he limped away along with other footsteps pounding on the concrete floor.

A moment later, "Shut the door," a man shouted.

I opened my damp eyes and saw black heavy smoke and flames spiraling up the walls.

Brett gripped my arm. "Not yet."

Believing there was an escape plan, I waited, motionless.

"Now," Father said.

Brett and Lindsey leapt to their feet. Father took my hand, helped me stand, and embraced me. "I'm sorry, Sara," he said as my eyes water. "You need to get in the van."

"Wait," I said, slipping off the bracelet and letting it drop into a pool of blood.

With his arm around my shoulder Father led me to the vehicle. "Climb in and sit against the far wall," he said, yanking out a body with a badly damaged faced, dressed in a black bodysuit.

Feeling my lungs burning from the heavy smoke, I asked, "Where did you get the bodies?"

"A morgue. Ready for closed-coffin funerals."

Holding onto the door, I stepped inside and eased down next the wall. My chest throbbed from the gunshot wound. My eyes drifted over the two bloodless bodies with torn, distorted faces lying in the van. I watched Father pull another one out.

I heard a loud crash outside. Smoke billowed through the van. Gripping my chest, I rose to my feet and peeked out. The roof was collapsing around Lindsey with flames rising above her head.

I opened my mouth to yell, and then brought my lips together, knowing they might be able to hear us outside the structure. My bottom lip quivered as Lindsey struggled, trying to push large, burning timbers with a gloved hand. I needed to help her and began to move out of the van.

Brett grabbed my arm. "Lance will help her," he said.

My eyes darted around. All I could see was thick black smoke and flames shooting up everywhere. Suddenly, through the haze, I saw a silhouette running. When he came closer, I saw it was Father. He was carrying a fire extinguisher. He opened the valve and sprayed it toward Lindsey. The flames around her subsided. She leapt over the fallen timbers. He brushed sparks off her, threw the extinguisher, and sprinted with her to the van as the heat from the fire intensified.

Brett laid a severely damaged woman's body with brown hair sticking out around a scraped skull, down by the shattered table and hurried after Father. He slammed the door shut behind him just as a heavy object plowed into vehicle roof, causing the van to violently vibrate.

"Over here," Father said, standing next to the front seat and motioning.

I followed Lindsey to Father. Brett lifted up the floor, revealing a hidden compartment that ran the width and length of the van up to the front seats. One by one we quickly slid into the space. A large, burning, timber landed on the windshield, sending shards of glass everywhere.

"Hurry," I yelled to Father.

Stepping into the compartment, Father grabbed a backpack. He opened it and handed each of us a canister with a straw attached. He stretched out on the floor between Lindsey and me.

Brett, lying on my other side, raised his hand, and pushed a lever. Steel beams moved into place above us. He turned a switch. I heard a humming sound and felt a soft breeze surrounding us.

"Drink," Father said, opening his canister.

Removing the cap, I knew it was *venotrolia*. I inserted the straw and struggled sipping it in the confined space.

"This isn't easy," Lindsey commented.

"Try to get at least some of it down," Father said.

"Did Brett call you after I talked to him?" I asked Father.

"No," Brett said. "Lance already knew."

"How?" I asked, suspiciously.

"Before you left Bismarck, you saw a lawyer and had a will drawn bequeathing all Sara Jones' assets to my clinic," Father said. "I assumed there could be a problem. Two days later, I received your spider container from a Billings' police officer. He wanted verification the spiders enclosed were the same type that had bitten you and Saul. After that, I flew to Houston. At the same time I had fireproof suits and this van delivered from Billings.

"How did you know you'd need them if Brett didn't tell you?"

"I called him before I left," Lance said.

"But Lance was already on his way," Brett justified.

Banging, crashing, shattering continued outside when a loud explosion wildly shook the van, causing it to jump at least three feet and jerking it around. I thought it was going to tip over. It stopped, slightly tilting at our feet.

"Relax, we're safe here," Father said, squeezing my hand.

Just then I heard the throbbing sound of a fire engine approaching.

"I thought it would take them longer to get here," Brett said as the sound became louder.

"What happens now?" I asked.

"We wait without saying a word until the floor above us opens," Father said.

I turned my face toward Brett. He stretched his neck and gently kissed my lips. "Try to sleep. It'll help your body heal."

I wrapped my fingers around his thumb and closed my eyes.

After listening to pounding, yelling, and the screeching sound of the van tottering back and forth for what seemed like hours, I dozed off.

Flying back to North Dakota, I felt good I had freed those girls and caused a ripple in the corrupt Crussett family business. I wanted to find ways to continue to use my powers to help others like the kidnapped girls. I was glad my relationship with Conner was over. The man I had fallen in love with didn't exist. Maybe part of me would always love some aspects of Conner. The wonderful memories of the good times we had spent together couldn't be wiped away. Although, they were beginning to fade as thoughts of more ways I could destroy the corruption that surrounded him swept through my mind. With the exception of his injured leg, Conner's family would believe he walked away from the fire unscathed. I knew that wasn't the truth. The woman he had loved was gone—Sara Jones was dead.

An article appeared in *The Texas Daily News* entitled: "Caden Crussett Indicted for Murder." An excerpt read: "Mr. Crussett started a fire in a warehouse to cover up his crime. A few innocent bystanders had been injured trying to get everyone out the building before it became engulfed in flames. During the episode Caden Crussett was bitten by a poisonous spider. He is currently in a coma at St. Mark's Hospital. After he recovers, he will be arrested for the murder of Sara Jones."

ABOUT THE AUTHOR

Inge-Lise Goss was born in Denmark, raised in Utah, and graduated from the University of Utah, magna cum laude. She is a certified public accountant and has audited oil and gas companies for more than twenty years.

Goss lives in the foothills of Red Rock Canyon with her husband and their dog, Bran. She spends most of her time in her den writing stories. There, with her muse by her side, her imagination has no boundaries, and her dreams come alive. When she's not pounding away on the keyboard, she can be found reading, rowing, or trying to perfect her golf game, which she fears is a lost cause.

To find out more about the author visit her website at
www.Inge-LiseGoss.com

www.ingramcontent.com/pod-product-compliance
Lightning Source LLC
Chambersburg PA
CBHW071124170626
46809CB00002B/492